EMBER

A NOVEL

BROCK
ADAMS

HUB CITY PRESS
SPARTANBURG, SC

Cover and book design: Meg Reid
Proofreader: Beverly Knight
Copy editor: Kalee Lineberger
Cover:
"Green Northern Lights in Black Sky" © Forrest Cavale
"Trees and House Under a Starry Sky" © Martin Sattler

Library of Congress Cataloging-in-Publication Data

Names: Adams, Brock, 1982-
Title: Ember / Brock Adams.
Description: Spartanburg, SC : Hub City Press, 2017.
Identifiers: LCCN 2017014154 (print) | LCCN 2017027706 (ebook) | ISBN
    9781938235337 (ebook) | ISBN 9781938235320 (softcover)
Subjects: LCSH: Regression (Civilization)—Fiction. | Survival—Fiction. |
    GSAFD: Science fiction. | Dystopias.
Classification: LCC PS3601.D3685 (ebook) | LCC PS3601.D3685 E45 2017 (print)
    | DDC 813/.6—dc23
LC record available at https://lccn.loc.gov/2017014154

HUB CITY PRESS
186 West Main St.
Spartanburg, SC 29306
1.864.577.9349
www.hubcity.org
www.twitter.com/hubcitypress

for Jill

EMBER

GUY

MOUNTAINTOP

THE MISSILES ARE TO HIT JUST BEFORE EMBERSET, and the people have come to watch.

Guy closes his eyes and shivers as the ember slips toward the horizon. His wife, Lisa, huddles against him, and they listen to the hushed voices of the others who've gathered on the mountaintop in the northernmost corner of South Carolina. They watch as the orange egg yolk that used to be the sun wobbles its way down the blue-black wall of the world.

"When?" Lisa says. She has both arms wrapped through the crook of Guy's elbow.

"Soon."

Guy watches his breath hang in the late-July air as the ember creeps lower. The warmth that bathed the planet before the sun began to die feels like an impossible dream. It could never have existed on this cold earth.

They said there wouldn't be much to see when the missiles hit the ember. It might pulse, might shimmer momentarily before returning to normal. Guy wants to see it anyway. He wants some sign that the ember is growing stronger, that the slow slide into darkness is ending.

He's not alone. A hundred people stand on the mountain.

They watch, even though Guy knows the scene will never match the one that started it all, when two-and-a-half years ago every nuclear missile in America soared into the sky at once. They burst like fiery worms from the silos in Wyoming and Nebraska, in Colorado and South Dakota. They came from everywhere they'd been expected, and nearly everywhere else too: they geisered up from hidden silos beneath the Everglades, roared from abandoned buildings in the heart of New York City, and streaked skyward from the foothills north of Guy's home.

They cocooned the earth in tendrils of smoke. They blocked out the failing sun.

Guy had felt the futility of it all sit like a cold stone in his gut. He'd heard the critics, the scientists who balked at the plan, challenged the very physics of it. He watched the missiles take to the air anyway, and it was beautiful—god, it was beautiful to see, the flames disappearing into the sky, the hope of the world riding away into the vastness of space. They shuddered forth from every corner of the globe, seventeen thousand rockets all told, minus the one that malfunctioned over Bangladesh, flattening Dhaka and vaporizing fifteen million people in an instant.

They called their plan the Big Bang, and they said it would work. Go on with your lives. All will be well.

The missiles have been traveling for thirty months, and now they are there, straining impossibly against the ember's gravity.

Guy and Lisa watch. The ember burns a faint red-orange and spreads its silken light across the Piedmont that spreads out before them. Around them is silence. The onlookers stand in clusters, and Guy imagines he can hear the moisture in their breath crystalizing and tinkling against the cold stone. He knows it's not that cold, but the year-round persistence of the chill makes everything seem frigid. It's midsummer in the Deep South and the evening temperature is in the thirties.

The ember touches the horizon. Nothing happens; the star shines on, dull and unwavering. Shadow sweeps over the mountain-top as it dips below the edge of the earth. A woman begins to cry.

The crowd disperses. No one speaks. Guy and Lisa stay on the mountaintop and watch as the sky fades from orange to purple and into black. The stars come out and shine cold and hard in the distance. Guy wonders if those stars are dying too. They are light years away, so he's seeing them as they were thousands, millions of years ago. They may already be as lifeless and frozen as the rest of space.

They're alone on the mountain. The dark is complete and a cold wind blows in from the north. The matchstick pines bend and their needles rustle against each other.

"It didn't work," Lisa whispers.

"We don't know that." The lie feels silly as it dangles in the air between them.

"Yes we do."

He moves behind her, wraps his arms around her, pulls her to him. He speaks quietly, his mouth close to her ear. "You never thought it would anyway."

"And you did?"

Guy looks into the sky, where the stars are bright, spilling from one horizon to another. He tries to pick out a constellation, but the stars seem foreign, nameless. "I hoped."

"Lot of good it did you."

Guy takes his wife by the hand and leads her back to the car. Inside, they turn the heater on full blast. Lisa warms her hands in front of the vents. "They're going to reinstate the Twerps," she says.

Guy nods. "Probably."

"We should get more supplies."

"We've got plenty, Lisa." They already have a small stockpile of food and water and emergency supplies at home. It takes up most of the space in the office closet. Guy shakes his head. "We're not Bunker Boys."

"Did it ever occur to you that the Bunker Boys might be right?"

"We won't be Bunker Boys."

Lisa tucks her hands into her pockets and looks out the window. "I can't take another winter."

"Yes you can."

"I can't. No one can." She's looking at him now, piercing him with her gray-green eyes. "The bottom half of the planet is freezing over. It's going to happen to us too. It's going to be worse than last winter."

Guy tries to think of something optimistic to say to her. He's glass-half-full, and Lisa is glass-half-empty. She's less than that. There's never any water in her glass. Problem is, more often than not she's right. She's right about this too. Guy shrugs. "The scientists will think of something else."

Lisa shakes her head.

She doesn't need to talk. Guy knows what she's thinking. She's thinking, *You can't really believe that.* She's thinking, *Don't bullshit me.* She's thinking, *We're fucked.*

Guy looks over at her as he puts the car into gear. Her cheeks are flushed pink. The tip of her nose is bright red. Still, she's beautiful, perfect. He thinks to himself, *Why isn't she enough?*

FIREWORKS

IT'S FIFTY-FIVE DEGREES IN THE CONDO. MOST OF the Twerps—the government's Temporary Winter Reserve Protocols—were lifted when the snow melted, but not that one. The regulations state that thermostats can be set no higher than fifty-five. Even in the summer, the heater has run every night. In bed, Guy and Lisa lie beneath a sheet and two blankets. Their dog, Jemi—a four-year-old boxer—pulls herself into a tight ball on the floor at the foot of the bed. Outside, a sliver of a moon drips blue light onto the treetops. Guy can see Lisa's face in the glow; she's lit like she's underwater, like she's behind a sheet of ice. Her eyes are open.

"It's going to be colder tomorrow," she says.

"Summer's not over."

Lisa is silent. She turns away from him and scooches her body close to his. "I'm cold," she says. "Hold me."

He turns to her and wraps an arm around her middle. They lie nestled like two stacked spoons.

She presses against him, and then she turns, kisses his chest, his neck. She climbs on top of him, pulls him inside of her. Her hair is light on his face and her breasts brush against his chest as she moves. Lisa is older than Guy—forty-one to his thirty-nine—and in the last year or so, her desire has kicked into overdrive. Sure, she liked sex when they were young and acrobatic, but this is the first time in their fifteen years together that her sex drive has been stronger than his. It makes her feel warm, she says. Many mornings she wakes him up this way.

A few minutes later, they're done and covered in sweat. She's breathing heavily. "Now it's hot," she says.

"Mmm."

She pulls the covers back and the cold air descends on them like a wave. Guy can barely make her out in the dark, long pale legs and small breasts, her arms thrown above her head. Her face dissolves in and out of focus—her wavy hair splayed out on the pillow, her mouth in a loose smile of contentment. The sweat on his body chills, and Guy shivers. He pulls the blankets back up to his chest. Lisa is breathing deeply now, her arm draped across her face. Guy closes his eyes.

Jemi wakes Guy up. She's beside him, breathing her hot breath on him and wagging her tail. She touches his arm with her nose, wet and cold. "Okay," Guy says. "Okay, I see you." He gets up and dresses—jeans, shirt, jacket, beanie—and puts the collar on the dog. He opens the door and lets her out.

Their condo is part of a string of two-bedrooms running along a creek at the edge of the woods. The front door opens to a wooden walkway that leads to the parking lot, and stairs lead to the units above and below them. Jemi trots down the boardwalk to the lawn. Guy follows, the splintering planks rough and cold under bare feet. The ember is rising, burning with a hazy light that falls softly through the trees. It can't seem to chase away the morning chill.

Jemi finds a spot in the grass and squats to pee. She holds her tail at a weird angle, curving up over her back.

Guy remembers the first time he saw Jemi, the day after she was born. The mother dog lay on a pink blanket and looked up at Guy and Lisa with exhausted eyes. The puppies looked more like guinea pigs than dogs, tiny and squirming with their eyes squinted nearly shut and their ears pressed back on their heads. They suckled at the sagging teats of the mother, who lay on her side, breathing slowly, seemingly oblivious to the writhing mass of life feeding from her.

Lisa knelt beside the mother and put her hand on the dog's head. Then she touched each of the puppies, running a finger over the smooth short hair on their backs. She stopped on one, a female, with fur the color of maple syrup and a white spot on her chest. Lisa pulled her from the teat like she was plucking an apple from the tree. The dog kicked its legs and chomped its little jaws. Lisa held it in her palm, and then she cradled it like a baby and looked up at Guy and smiled, her cheeks pink, her teeth so white and straight, her face alight with a glow that he hadn't seen on her in months. "Look at her!" she said.

Guy looked at the dog. It was like a slick, blind rodent. "She's cute," he said.

Lisa squeezed the tail between two fingers. "Oh, I love her little tail. Do we have to get rid of it?"

"Normally you dock them with boxers," the breeder said. "I suppose we don't have to, if you don't want to."

"I love her little tail."

So they hadn't docked the tail, and they hadn't cropped the ears, and now they had this syrup-colored dog named Jemima with big floppy ears and a long tail that curved over her when she peed. And they loved her.

Jemi finishes peeing and Guy kneels to pet her, but she trots past him to the condo. Guy follows her in and feeds her. He sits on the couch, opens his laptop.

It's on all the news websites: The president had made a speech late last night, several hours after the Big Bang was supposed to have happened, hours after they went to sleep. Guy watches the speech as Jemi curls up in a patch of the pale yellow emberlight that slips between the curtains and stretches across the carpet.

Guy calls to Lisa, who shuffles into the living room, her face still scrunched with sleep. Jemi gets up to greet her, her tail going like mad, her eyes squinted in happiness as Lisa scratches her behind the ears. Guy watches the two of them. He and Jemi like each other just fine, but this is Lisa's dog.

Lisa sits on the couch beside Guy. "Watch," Guy says. He starts the video again.

The president looks haggard. Her hair refuses to stay where her stylists put it, and stray strands keep falling across her forehead. Her eyes are red and her lids heavy. Yet she smiles. The video opens with five solid seconds of her beaming at the camera before she begins to speak. "Good evening, my fellow Americans," she says. Her smile broadens. "It worked."

Lisa sits up straight. She looks at Guy in disbelief.

"Early reports from the Geophysical Institute indicate that the Big Bang was a success. The missile impact appears to have created a reaction on the surface of the sun."

It feels strange to hear it called the sun. The name *ember* started as a joke on a late night talk show, and it stuck. The word *sun* seems like something from another era. Normally, saying it feels forced. This time, though, Guy finds it reassuring. Maybe it's not the ember anymore. Maybe it really is the sun again.

The president continues. "A major solar event has been detected, and we have every reason to believe that it is indicative of the reinvigoration of the sun's fusion process. We will feel the effects of the event in three days, when the coronal mass ejection reaches Earth. We expect fantastic auroras across our great nation."

The auroras became commonplace when the sun became the ember. The first aurora knocked out the power, as it would do a dozen more times, and Guy and Lisa watched from the blacked-out parking lot as the great sheets of green stretched and spread across the sky above them.

The president pauses and looks at someone off camera. Her lips twitch, and then she smiles, faces the audience. "Every July, our nation celebrates its independence by lighting up the sky. The sky will be bright this year, as well. Celebrate, America. As the aurora lights the sky, look to it fondly, for it is a messenger of the warmth that's still to come."

She continues for a while, outlining the way the planet will change: the winter will be cold, she says, but only slightly more than usual. By next summer, the sun will be back up to full strength, and weather will return to normal. She winks at the camera. "In the meantime, you can lose the jackets. The fifty-five degree limit is hereby lifted. Stay warm, America. God bless you, and God bless this great nation of ours."

Guy gets up and turns the thermostat up to eighty. The heat clicks on and warm air begins to flood the condo. He grins at Lisa. Her eyes are huge and her face is flushed. She squeals and jumps from the couch and into his arms. He holds her off the ground with her legs wrapped around him, and they turn slowly and kiss with their eyes closed. He feels Jemi's tongue on his hand, and he looks down to where she's standing, tail flapping wildly, and he sets Lisa down and scratches the dog on the head.

"I can't believe it!" Lisa says. She goes to the window and frowns up at the ember. "Why didn't we see the Big Bang?"

"Maybe it was too far away. The ember is huge." He still finds himself calling it *ember*. *Sun* just doesn't feel right—not yet. "The explosion was just too small to see. Or maybe they timed it wrong and it happened after sunset." He stands next to her at the window. The emberlight shines on his skin. It feels warm, but maybe that's just the heater filling up the condo. "It looks brighter, I think," he says, looking up to where the ember hangs in the sky like a frozen lemon. "It definitely looks brighter."

Lisa looks at it and nods. "It does. I think it does."

They open a case of beer and drink the day away, the house warm with electricity-fueled air, the news channels alive with the rush of victory.

On the night of the solar storm, they drive to the high school where Guy teaches and sit in the center of the football field. The school is shut down for the summer; the lights are off and the darkness rests over them like a black bowl. The grass is yellow and withered, struggling to find nourishment from the dim ember in this cold summer.

Guy and Lisa lie on their backs and stare into the sky as the aurora plays overhead. It's stronger than they've ever seen it: the bands in all shades of green and pink drift in from the north and quiver and bend their way across the entire sky before disappearing over the southern horizon. It turns the sky into a piece of modern art—paint in the verdant shades of energy spread across the black canvas of the universe. The colors change as they arc and stretch. One minute a wave is the grayish green of the moss on the underside of a stone in some hidden forest, the next, it's an avocado dangling from a tree in California. The pinks are the lost memories of an orchid.

Guy turns to Lisa. Her face is an otherworldly shade of green that shifts and melds with the silver of the moonlight. She looks like she's floating a few inches below the water of a lily-pad-strewn pond. "You look like a ghost," Guy says.

"What?" She's only half listening as she gazes at the sky.

"It's a good thing."

He pulls her to him. They hold each other close in the cold as the colors of the ember's breath swirl around them, the lights of a mobile dangling above the crib of the world.

OUTAGE

THE POWER GOES OUT SHORTLY AFTER DAWN. HE knows because the heater clicks off and the silence sits dense around him. The room is full of the blue morning dark.

Jemi is beside him, smiling her dog smile. Guy takes her outside.

The aurora is still there. The ember is rising in the east; it's beginning to peek above the trees, and the entire eastern horizon is lit like the pale petals of a daffodil stuck in a vase for too long. The aurora charges in from the north. The bands are miles across, glowing with fury, phantoms streaking across the heavens. Their power fills the air; they imbue the morning with a sort of electricity.

Guy realizes that he's crouching. The aurora is so close, so strong. It's going to crush him, burn him; it's going to sweep across him and he'll combust like a vampire who strayed into sunlight.

The morning is silent—no birds, no insects, no barking dogs. The world is smashed flat and cowers before the onslaught.

A great band the color of absinthe seems to reach down from the sky. The air crackles, and as if on cue, every car alarm in the parking lot goes off. The noise is piercing in the quiet dawn. Jemi turns her jaws skyward and yowls.

Sleepy neighbors stumble from their condos. They shut off the car alarms and drift back inside.

Guy pulls on Jemi's leash. She's glued to the ground as she stares up at the sky. "Let's go," Guy says. She whimpers and follows him, her tail between her legs.

In the condo, the cold is already beginning to creep back in. He looks at the thermostat. They'd set it on seventy-two when they went to bed, and it's already down to sixty-nine. He looks out the window at the aurora. It feels like he's watching a dangerous predator from afar; it's a lion on the other side of the bars of a cage, a shark behind the glass wall of the aquarium. He feels safe inside, but the light growls with its terrible potential.

Guy feels like he ought to be doing something, but he doesn't know what that something is. He climbs back into bed and goes to sleep.

Beneath his sleep, there's a part of Guy that is waiting for the power to come back on. At some point, he tells himself, the thermostat will spark and the heater will rumble back to life. The refrigerator will start humming and cooling down its insides. The clock beside the bed will blink red digital numbers and the ice machine will knock around and turn out half-moon-shaped ice cubes.

But there's also some part of him that knows this isn't going to happen.

Lisa wakes up when the ember is high and shining with the luster of dull metal. She puts her head on his chest and drapes a leg over him. Her head is almost completely under the covers.

Guy wraps his arm around her. He loves this. He could lie like this forever.

"The power's out again?" she says. Her breath is warm on his chest.

"Yeah."

"I'm so sick of it going out in the aurora. It's been happening for three years. You'd think they'd have figured out how to keep the power on."

Guy can feel her eyelashes on his skin.

"They usually have it on by now, right?"

"Depends," he says. "That first time it was out for a while. And remember that time a year ago? It was out until dark." He feels her nodding.

"Maybe this is the last time. That was the last aurora, so they'll turn the power back on and it will just be normal again." She smiles at him. "It's really over!"

He kisses her and her mouth is warm and soft. She snuggles against his chest, and in a moment, she's asleep. Jemi groans and stretches on the floor beside them. Guy pulls Lisa close and trails his fingertips across her back. He feels peaceful, content at home with his small family, the only family he'll ever have.

Lisa hadn't cried on the way home from the doctor. She sat beside Guy in the car, staring out the window. It was winter—a normal winter, one of the last ones—and the sun was nearly down, the cold coming on fast with the night. She fooled with the radio, found a Bob Marley song that sounded strange, the tropical sounds out of place in the winter night.

They'd started a year earlier. That was what they had decided—when she was thirty-five, they'd start trying. And they had tried. They were doing it every day, all the time, until it felt like a chore—Guy screwing her in whatever position she had read was most conducive to pregnancy. Screwing her when the calendar said she was ovulating, screwing her when she said her temperature was just right. And month after month, she'd get up one morning, blood on her panties, and she'd sigh and go into the bathroom and come out a few minutes later; she'd get in bed and cuddle up close to Guy, her head on his chest, and he'd say, "We'll get it next time."

After a year they went to the doctor. Guy sat in the waiting area as the doctor examined Lisa, and then he held her when she walked dazed from the examination room. He squeezed her hands in his as she relayed what the doctor had said: how he'd sighed and frowned, gave her medical jargon, percentages. It was all a haze that slipped into Guy's ears and lodged itself somewhere in his middle, a great painful knot.

The doctor told her that it gets harder to conceive as a woman gets older. Thirty-five is not too old for most women, but it varies from person to person. Things dry up in there, hormone levels change, the ground becomes unfertile.

Basically, he told Lisa she'd missed her chance.

But she didn't cry in the car, and she didn't cry when they went inside and sat on the couch in silence, drinking beer. She held the neck of the beer bottle with two fingers and drank quickly. She drank four beers without talking. Then she said, "I feel like I'm a murderer."

She looked stoic, her mouth straight, her eyes focused somewhere past the walls of the house. "What are you talking about?" Guy said.

"We might have had a baby," she said, "but we won't."

"That doesn't make us murderers."

"We could have had him, and we don't. Because we wanted it all for ourselves." She got up and went to the fridge and got another beer. She sat down on the couch and took three big swigs, then rested the bottle on her knee. "Murder is taking a life, right? And there might have been a life if we hadn't been so selfish."

"You can't look at it that way. You can't murder somebody that doesn't exist."

"But the only reason he didn't exist is because we decided he shouldn't exist. We could have decided at any time to have a kid, any time over all these years, and we didn't. We didn't, because we wanted time for ourselves. And we wanted to go to stupid fucking Africa. And we didn't have the money. All that bullshit and now it's too late."

"We don't even know what would have happened. If you could have ever gotten pregnant."

"I told you what he said." She took another pull from the beer. "He might as well have said, 'Whoops, you blew it.'" Her voice was wobbly by now. "I don't know. I just feel like there's so many other ways we could have done things, and all these other worlds are out there where we did things differently, and in a bunch of those worlds we've got a child. Some little boy or girl, and that child's not here in this world because I just fucked up."

Guy put his arms around her, tried to pull her close, but she was stiff, distant. "You can't blame yourself for this," he said.

"Then we're both to blame."

They sat there for a long time, drinking their beers. Outside, the wild wind came down out of the mountains and froze the water along the edge of the creek, chilled and hardened the forest ground.

"I think it's part of us that's dead too," Lisa said.

"We're fine," Guy said. "We still have each other. We can do so much together."

"That's not what I mean. We can be fine for now, but we'll die. We'll die one day, and then there's nothing left. With a kid, I don't know, it's like he's a part of us left on Earth when we're gone. But now there's nothing. We'll just be dead and that's it."

That night, in bed, she cried. She cried with her whole body, her legs and arms wrapped around Guy, her breath coming in heaving gasps. Her tears were hot on his chest, her face scrunched so that it was nearly unrecognizable. Her eyes, those beautiful eyes, gray like smooth marble, were raw and red-rimmed from the tears. Everything about her was salty and warm, and he tried to kiss her, but she turned from him; she shuddered on the other side of the bed until she fell asleep.

She never said so, but Guy felt that Lisa blamed him for the child they never had. When they first met, it felt like they had all the time in the world. He was twenty-five and teaching middle school in Florida; she was the school's assistant librarian. It was too easy— too easy to flirt when his class came to do research, too easy to fall in love in the teacher's lounge and the noisy school cafeteria. They were married and lived together in relative luxury. The pay wasn't much, but they didn't need much, and they socked away money for their big plans. They were comfortable, and it would have been so easy to have children then; it was the next natural step. But Guy and Lisa talked of children as something they'd do later. They joked: once they had kids, their lives would be over.

So they lived with wild abandon. When Lisa suggested quitting their jobs and joining the Peace Corps, Guy jumped on the bandwagon, researched it, and pushed it forward until they were interviewing and going through medical examinations and finally getting sent off to darkest Africa, off to Malawi, where Guy would teach advanced English in a high school and Lisa would lead an adult literacy program. She was thirty-two by then, and they were to be abroad for two years. Leaving a year when they got back for her to get pregnant before the seemingly-arbitrary deadline of thirty-five that she'd placed on herself.

And they were madly in love over there, living in a tin-roofed shack in the middle of the village, that huge African sky so blue and wide above them. Lisa loved the work. It was a side of her Guy had never seen: she ran her program with such confidence, and the way those people looked up to her, the way they'd follow her—it left Guy in awe of his wife.

They came home from Malawi and struggled to find jobs. They got work at last, up on the edge of the mountains in South Carolina, but money was tight. At last, they'd saved enough, and Guy tried to get Lisa pregnant, and it was too late. So their hope for children had died. It died a quiet death amid heat lightning and the dry summer winds of that village in Malawi, somewhere out there in the craggy green hills of eastern Africa.

Guy could see it in Lisa's eyes sometimes, the blame—not that she hadn't wanted to go to Africa too, but he knew somewhere in her head was the notion that it was all his fault, and that if only she'd been with someone else, she'd be a mother by now. She'd be driving a minivan and lounging by a pool, getting tan while her kids splashed and yelled. The blame sat like a bell jar over their life, stifling them, filling everything with tightness and heat. It caused so many of the problems they'd had over the last five years.

Guy thought it might be what drove him toward Heather.

It's definitely what drove them up into the mountains to get their dog. The dog with the tail she shouldn't have and ears the wrong shape. Jemi, something small and alive.

Guy gets out of bed, his skin prickling with goose bumps. He goes into the kitchen and gets the orange juice and milk out of the fridge.

The refrigerator is dark and quiet; it's colder in there than it is in the house, but not by much.

The thermostat reads sixty-one.

Guy pours himself some cereal and sits down on the couch to eat it. He looks out the window, up at the sky and the ember. He's feeling antsy, like there's something he ought to be doing. Every summer is like this; months on end with school out of session and nothing to do. The power outage only makes it worse.

At least he can leave the house in the summer. Last winter was agony: In the coldest months, the Twerps restricted all business— including school—to a three-day-a-week schedule. On those forced days off, he imagined he was locked up in a gulag somewhere in the vast northern stretches of Siberia.

Back when Siberia was still habitable. During that long winter, huge expanses of the northernmost parts of the globe became iced-over wastelands. Thousands froze to death.

Snow sat two feet deep across the South. It piled against the sliding glass doors of Guy and Lisa's home and made the condo feel closed in. Even if Guy wanted to leave, the Twerps forbid using the car, and even if he could have used the car, there was nowhere to go. Everything else in town was closed down too. Torture.

Now the sky is an arcing blue over the treetops, and it looks as warm out there as it's going to get. Guy finishes his cereal and gets his running shoes from the closet.

He tells people that he runs to stay in shape, and this is true, in part. He's five ten, only a few pounds heavier than he'd like to be; he's kept himself looking better than most men his age, and that's enough for him. His hair is graying; he wears it short because the gray's less noticeable that way. Still, Guy is proud of how he looks. He can, without dishonesty, claim to be an athlete. When he runs, he runs fast. And that's the real reason he runs: he likes to feel fast. He likes to push himself to the breaking point. He likes the pain.

Outside, the air is crisp and cold, but the ember beats gently on his shoulders, and he warms up as he turns onto Main Street. The city passes him by, strangely quiet. The downtown shops are closed and sleeping in the Sunday afternoon. His footsteps echo on the empty streets.

He cuts through a neighborhood, and the houses are dark and shuttered. Up ahead, a couple carries bags from their house and puts them into the back of an SUV. Farther down the road, he sees another loaded car, the trunk held shut with bungee cords, stuff sticking out at odd angles from the back windows. A woman and an old yellow Lab stand next to the car. She's trying to convince the dog to get in the front seat. The dog ignores her, watches Guy as he runs by. Guy waves and then turns back onto Main Street and accelerates homeward.

Back in the condo, Lisa is awake. She's sitting on the couch with a book propped up on her knees, a blanket wrapped tight around her. "Good run?" she says.

Guy leans down and kisses her. "It's beautiful out there. Almost like a real summer."

"Are you about to shower?" Lisa says, closing her book. "Because the water's not working very well."

"What do you mean?"

"It's not very strong. It comes out when you turn it on, but the water pressure sucks."

Guy tries the faucet. The water sputters, then a weak stream trickles onto the dishes, pings against the bottom of the sink. "I guess all the utilities are screwed up this time."

"Why don't you call the utilities people?"

"They know what's going on. They've done it a hundred times."

"Still might as well try them," she says. "The more people bitch, the more likely they are to do something about it."

Guy gets his cell phone from the drawer and turns it on. Most of the time he keeps the phone off; he doesn't want anyone calling when he's not prepared to deal with them. More importantly, he doesn't want his phone ringing when he's not certain he'll be the one to answer it. "No signal," he says. "Try yours."

She finds her phone. "Same here," she says, frowning. "Why are they out? They don't normally go out in the aurora."

"Ours haven't, but some of them go out every time. The aurora screws up the satellites. This one just hit ours."

"So what do we do about the power?" She's absently scratching Jemi on the head. The dog is sitting on Lisa's feet, staring up at her and wagging her tail.

"Wait," Guy says. "Like we have before."

Lisa settles down on the couch and picks up her book. She doesn't get antsy; she's perfectly content with a static life, with staying indoors. She'll stay like this all day.

Guy takes his clothes off and gets in the shower, turns the water on, and yelps as it hits his skin. It's dark in the shower—no power, no lights—and it's like he's standing in an Alaskan waterfall in the middle of the night. He grits his teeth and bathes under the sputtering flow, the pressure getting weaker all the time.

MOONLIGHT

AT NIGHT, THE CONDO IS AS COLD AS THE AIR outside, and with the power out, there is nothing to see and nothing to do inside. Guy lights a candle and they step onto the porch in their jackets and hats. The condo is built onto a steep hill that leads down to the creek, so though they enter their home at ground level, the porch hangs twenty-five feet in the air. They stand at the railing and look out at the woods. The wind is blowing somewhere high above them, and broad cloudbanks scud by overhead, covering the moon and blanketing everything in a heavy darkness. The underside of the clouds is a sheet of black, occasionally wisping open and revealing stars, a planet. With no city lights to reflect, the clouds don't have their usual gray-orange hue.

They sit down on the porch swing. Guy has brought the acoustic guitar outside with him, and he plucks a couple of strings aimlessly.

His fingers feel numbed by the cold. He clinches his fists, and then he stumbles through "Blackbird," one of the only songs he mastered when he took guitar lessons years ago. Lisa sings bits and pieces of it, pausing occasionally to eat cashews from a tin. Her voice is ghostly in the quiet night.

Guy finishes the song and that heavy silence settles in again. The air is still. Huddled together on the swing, with Lisa's warmth seeping into him and his flowing right back to her, it's pleasant; it's like they're camping, like they've chosen to distance themselves from the heat and the light. Jemi sleeps on the wood-planked floor of the porch. She's making faint yelping sounds, twitching her feet as she chases dream squirrels.

"Have you heard the train today?" Lisa says.

"I don't remember," Guy says. Two train tracks run through the woods behind the condo, a couple of hundred yards away from the porch. All day and all night, randomly but frequently, trains rumble by. Tonight, the woods are quiet in every direction. "I don't think I've heard it today."

"I started listening this afternoon. I've been waiting for it, and I haven't heard it."

The trains are loud, but Guy likes them. They're an affirmation in the middle of the night, a reminder that the world is alive and well on the other side of their window. Maybe he had noticed that they were gone. Maybe he had felt it somewhere inside him, some uneasiness at the absence of the ordinary.

Lisa picks at the last crumbs of the cashews until there's nothing but dust left. She tosses the tin to Jemi, who wakes up and buries her snout in it. "You know what would be crazy?" Lisa says.

Guy is plucking another nameless tune on the guitar, the notes disappearing hollowly into the cold.

"If the power stays off," she says. "If it's off for good."

"It's not going to be off for good. They're probably fixing it right now."

"But what if it is, though? The aurora last night was stronger than any of the other ones. What if it knocked the power out all over? Maybe it fried all the satellites and the power plants. The power could be out across the whole country, maybe the whole world."

"The world's too big for that. It can't—"

She cuts him off. "What if last night was the last night of an era, the Electric Age, or whatever you want to call it? And we're in the new Dark Ages?"

"You're right," Guy says. "That would be crazy. But I'm saying it can't happen." He imagines a blacked-out globe spinning through space. It's unsettling, and he wants to push the thought away. "The world's too big and there's too many independent sources of power out there. And they've done this a dozen times before. The power's on somewhere, probably almost everywhere, and they're working to get ours back on."

The clouds part and the moon shines with a phantasmal glow. It's like light shining through the fabric of a bridal dress that's been locked in an attic for fifty years. The moon itself is a sickle that hangs above them like a frown. Guy tries to remember what it looked like years ago. Is it dimmer now? Is its glow tarnished by emberlight? Has it lost the luster that it stole from the sun? As he watches, the clouds slide back in and swallow up the moonlight.

Jemi has finished licking the tin and is now tearing it apart with her teeth, ripping it to shreds. Lisa watches her. "You think I have to go to work tomorrow?" she says.

"I don't see why not."

"If the power's out, we can't run the library."

"You should at least go check." Guy leans the guitar against the railing of the porch. He sits back and puts his arm around his wife. "If it's still out when we get up, I'm going down to the power company and complaining. I'm getting tired of this."

From the other side of the creek, right at the edge of the woods, there's a small, scraping sound, like branches brushing together, and then there's an enormous crashing, something big running away. The sound fills the night. Jemi leaps to her feet and sticks her head between the slats of the porch railing and *bow-wows* at the woods. It's a bark that's deeper and more menacing than her normal bark; it's what Lisa calls her "big-girl bark." Jemi does it when someone knocks at the door, or when a raccoon skitters along a tree outside—it's the bark she does when she's protecting her property, protecting the house and Guy and Lisa. She barks and the crashing fades away into the woods.

"Okay," Guy says. "You scared it off."

24

"You think it was a deer?" Lisa says.

"Probably." Guy stands up and leans his elbows on the railing. He looks out across the water. In the daytime, it's easy to see the other side of the creek, the deep woods that stretch to the railroad and beyond. Tonight, the night is so close around them that it's hard to make anything out.

Jemi stands tense. The short fur on her back bristles. She growls; it's a low and throaty growl, a sound Guy has never heard her make before.

Lisa strokes the dog. "What's the matter, pup?"

Jemi keeps growling. Her eyes are black and focused, staring across the creek.

"What's she looking at?" Lisa says.

"I don't know," Guy says. He looks across the creek, squints, strains to see the woods in the dark. He sees the outline of the trees against the sky, the thin line where the creek meets the rocky edge of the land. His vision blurs and shifts as his eyes try to adjust to the dark and the distance. Things seem to move in the woods, shapes that drift into existence fleetingly before disappearing again.

Jemi snarls, shows her teeth.

"I don't—" Guy says, and then the clouds slide back for an instant and the sickle-moon pokes through and spills its faint white light across the woods. The creek reflects it like a silver snake. Guy's eyes adjust and he sees him—a man stands on the far side of the creek, right at the edge of the trees. Jemi barks again, an explosive bark that makes the muscles in Guy's back tense up. The man takes a step back. The moon is white on his head, on the top of his smooth, bald head. He's watching them, his eyes black points in the disk of his face. He takes another step back and the moon goes behind the clouds and then he's gone, and there's nothing but nighttime where he stood.

Jemi whimpers. She lies down in front of Lisa, and Lisa scratches her behind the ears.

Guy stares into the woods. He listens but hears nothing. It's impossible to tell whether he even saw anything to begin with. The woods look too dark and dense to hold anything, as if beyond the creek there's nothing but a tangled mass of black limbs.

"What'd you see out there, sweetie?" Lisa says to Jemi. "You're a good girl. You're keeping us safe. Good girl." Jemi's tail thumps timidly on the wood. Lisa looks at Guy. "What was she barking at?"

She didn't see him. Guy looks into the woods again. "I don't know. Probably nothing." He picks up the guitar and gathers up the shreds of the cashew container. Jemi snatches one away from him. It dangles from the corner of her mouth. "Let's go in," Guy says. They go inside and Guy pulls the door shut behind him and locks it.

"It's already gotten so cold in here," Lisa says. She picks up the blanket from the couch and wraps it around her, and it makes her look like she belongs in a Nepalese village high up in the Annapurna Range. "I'm going to get a shower." She feels her way into the bathroom.

Guy looks at the thermostat; it's down to fifty-six. He takes off his clothes and climbs beneath the bedcovers. He stares at the ceiling, at the faint shadows that appear and vanish as the clouds slide around in the sky. He listens to Lisa in the bathroom. She's fumbling around in the cabinet, feeling for whatever beauty products she's got in there. Guy opens the drawer to the bedside table and pulls out a small plastic flashlight. "Hey," he says. "Use this." Lisa takes it and turns it on. She sets the light on the counter and turns the knob for the hot water in the shower; there's a groaning noise from the pipes, the spatter of a few drips in the tub, and then nothing else. She tries the cold water and nothing happens.

"Damn it," she says.

"It was getting weaker all day," Guy says.

"It better be working tomorrow. I'm going to be disgusting. I haven't showered since yesterday. I can't go to work like this."

"You don't stink too bad."

"Dick." She climbs into bed beside him. He's nearly asleep before Lisa speaks again. "Guy."

"Hmm?" She has rolled over and now clings to him, her nails digging slightly into his skin.

"Things feel weird," she says.

"It's going to be fine."

"You keep saying that."

"It will."

They are quiet again. They listen to Jemi's heavy breathing. Lisa is holding him tight. She says, "I feel like there's something going on and we're missing it."

Guy is nearly asleep. "What do you want to do about it?"

"I don't know. I don't know what we can do."

THUNDER

GUY WAKES UP TO THE SOUND OF LISA CURSING IN the bathroom. "The water's still not working," she says. She's sitting on the closed lid of the toilet, naked, her arms folded tightly across her chest. "What am I supposed to do?"

"Go to the library all stank, I guess," Guy says.

"I'm probably going to be late anyway."

"What? What time is it?"

"Almost one-thirty." She goes into the closet and there's the sound of hangers sliding around.

"Why did we sleep so late?" Guy says. He gets up and finds his jeans. Jemi is sitting by the door, looking impatient. He takes her leash out of the cabinet and slips the collar around her neck. "How late did we stay up?" he says.

"I don't know." Lisa comes storming into the living room in

slim-fitting brown pants and a baby-blue turtleneck. She sits on the couch and slips on her shoes, then throws a jacket on and buttons it up. "If the power's still out, we're going to have to set some other sort of alarm. I can't be late to work." She gathers her stuff and Guy opens the door for her. She kisses Guy quickly. "I'll see you later." Then she's gone.

Guy takes Jemi outside and stands in the grass looking up at the ember. It looks the same as the day before: watery yellow and far away, dusting the blue sky around it with a leaden light. It feels colder today than it did yesterday. It's like someone began to heat the oven but changed his mind, and now whatever heat was generated is slipping away.

They go back inside and Guy gathers up his keys and his wallet and puts on his watch. He gives Jemi some food and looks at her water bowl. Empty. He turns on the faucet in the kitchen and nothing comes out. He does a quick inventory of the available water in the house. There are a few bottles and a big half-gallon pitcher in the fridge. There are also Cokes and orange juice and four beers.

And then there are the emergency supplies. There are a few cases of water stacked in the office closet along with the food and flashlights and whatever else. They stocked the closet together last fall, before the hard cold of winter swept in. It was enough to last them a week or more—enough to make it through any winter power outage. It wasn't enough for Lisa, though. She kept coming home with more stuff—jackets, blankets, a propane stove—until Guy put a stop to it. She was hoarding. She was turning into a Bunker Boy.

Guy hates the Bunker Boys, those nutjobs who began stockpiling canned goods and building bomb shelters in their backyards the minute the sun began to die. They never believed in the Big Bang. They screamed and railed about it to anyone who would listen. To Guy and most of the world, they were just the crazies, the rednecks, the gun-toting survivalists. As the winters got colder, though, their numbers swelled. Guy and Lisa watched on TV as they marched on DC. They gathered in the mall, ten thousand of them in tri-corner hats waving signs that said things like *Prepare or Die* and *Tell the Truth Madam President* and *The Founders Would Know What to Do.*

And all at once, a year ago, the Bunker Boys went silent. Good riddance, Guy figured.

That water in the closet is supposed to be for emergencies. Guy wonders at what point the emergency officially begins.

He goes into the guest bathroom and fills the dog bowl with water from the toilet. He puts the bowl down and Jemi drinks. "Pace yourself," Guy says, and Jemi looks at him, the water dripping from the corners of her mouth.

He heads outside to his car, a small blue Toyota. He cranks the engine and adjusts the heater, pointing every vent in the car straight at his face, and then he pulls out of the parking lot and heads up the hill to Main Street, turns toward downtown.

He reaches to turn on the radio and realizes that it's already on. He turns the volume up and still he hears nothing, just a faint hiss coming from the speakers. He flips through the preset stations. Two classic rock stations, one alternative, one pop and one talk radio station all whisper back to him with dead air. Guy switches to the AM frequency and puts the radio on scan. The AM stations are the same as the FM—the washed-out hush of empty air waves. One station, high on the AM scale, has a sound. The scanner moves past it and Guy mashes the button to turn it back. It's a harsh beeping sound, like the croak of a robot frog. It's the emergency broadcast warning. It beeps six times, and then a computerized voice says, "This is the emergency broadcast system of Davidson County, Tennessee." The broadcast is coming all the way from Nashville. Guy turns the volume up. It goes on: "Please stay tuned for an important announcement." The beeps return, six beeps, then the same message again.

It plays over and over, but the important announcement never comes. Guy listens to it as he drives downtown, past the stores, all of them still empty even though it's normal business hours. He turns down a side street and into the parking lot of the power company, a squat, cube-shaped brick building with hardly any windows. The parking lot is deserted. There's a sign taped to the doors, and Guy pulls close enough that he can read the hand-written letters: WE'RE WORKING ON IT. Guy idles in the parking lot, staring at the sign.

Clouds are building above the western horizon. There haven't been as many bad storms since the weather got colder; sometimes a steely drizzle comes down with thunder rumbling in the distance, but the torrential stuff was generated by the endless heat of those old summer days. These clouds are different. They're tall, heavy, and purple, full of tension and promise. They stretch up into the blue sky like the tentacles of a bloated octopus.

The wind picks up and Guy puts the car in gear. He drives toward the police station as the clouds sweep in along the edge of the mountains. The leaves quake as the trees bend.

The parking lot at the police station is full and cars line the block out front. Guy drives down and finds a spot near the corner. He gets out and walks along the sidewalk. The wind from the storm is blustery and cold; he pulls a beanie from his jacket pocket and covers his head.

About a hundred people have gathered in front of the police station. Guy does a quick scan of the crowd and can't spot anybody that he recognizes. This is typical. Though they've lived there for years, Guy and Lisa know few people in town other than their coworkers. They aren't exactly antisocial, but they've always preferred each other's company to that of friends. They stay in on the weekends, eating and watching movies, or they travel into the mountains to hike the winding trails with Jemi, alone in the vastness of the wild. Throughout the early years of their marriage, all they needed was each other. Guy wonders if they'll ever feel that again.

The crowd moves about, pressing itself closer to the doors of the station. The bodies are close together and in motion, but there is little sound. People mumble to each other and feet scrape along the asphalt. Leaves skitter across the ground as the wind gusts. At the front of the police station, a few stairs lead up to the double glass doors that lead inside. Yellow crime scene tape stretches across the bottom of the stairs and the crowd pushes right up against it, stretching it. More bodies jam the wheelchair ramp that crawls up the side of the building. Everyone struggles to see those blind and empty glass doors.

Far in the distance, the first peal of thunder mutters and washes in with the wind.

Three men sit in the grass near the edge of the parking lot. Two are younger—twenty-five, maybe—and the third is older than Guy. Their heads are shaved, completely smooth and white, the bald tops of high rounded mountains. The sight of those men makes Guy's stomach twist in on itself. He thinks of the shape in the woods on the other side of the creek, that moonlit figure that came into view for a second and disappeared: a bald man in the woods, watching him and Lisa. These men sit in silence, eyes on the doors of the station. Guy moves to the other side of the parking lot.

Guy reaches the back of the crowd and stands beside an old woman with an enormous purse. She turns to him. "They've been doing them on the hour," she says.

Guy nods, stares straight ahead. Maybe if he ignores her, she'll pick someone else to talk to.

"Making announcements. Same speech every time, though," she continues. "I'm tired of hearing it, but it's better than sitting at home in the dark."

"Mm-hmm," Guy says. He looks at his watch. It's a few minutes to four. The crowd squirms and grumbles. The clouds stretch out overhead and then the ember is gone, blocked out behind the deep purple. The temperature drops several degrees instantly.

At exactly four o'clock, the door to the police station opens and a huge officer steps out carrying a clipboard. The man waddles; he must weigh three hundred and fifty pounds. He's got close-cropped black hair and a heavy black mustache and dark wraparound sunglasses that he keeps on, even though it's as dark as early evening under the fast-moving clouds.

The crowd is noisy when he comes out. He stands patiently, and after a while, the shouting and questions die down. There's no sound except for the wind in the trees and the far-off thunder.

The officer clears his throat. "Please let me have your attention," he says. "I'm Officer McCloy. I'm going to give a statement now, and I'll continue to update you each hour, on the hour, until eight o'clock. At that point, we will be giving updates every four hours— one at midnight and one at four tomorrow morning—then we'll resume hourly updates at eight. The police department will do its best to provide you with all the information that is currently available to us."

He pushes his sunglasses up into his face and looks down at the clipboard, and then he begins to read. "At approximately two o'clock in the morning on Sunday, power went out citywide. This has been common during the auroral events of the past few years and was not considered a risk to government services. It was in fact anticipated due to the unprecedented strength of Sunday's solar storm."

The old woman leans over to Guy. "Same old story," she says. "They need some new news."

McCloy goes on. "The hospital immediately began running on its emergency generators and was briefly able to make contact with the University Medical Center in Greenville. Greenville reported a power outage as well. The hospitals then lost contact with each other.

"We have reason to believe that this is a major outage that is affecting the entire upstate area of South Carolina, and it could perhaps extend even further. Local efforts to restore power have been unsuccessful. Additionally, communication is currently impossible by cellular phone, landline phones, computers, or any other electronic devices. We have had limited success within the department in communication through battery-powered radios; all contact we have made, however, reports the same problems: power outages and lack of communication."

The crowd grumbles. The thunder speaks again, closer and louder. McCloy flips through the papers on the clipboard. "Local authorities are working around the clock to remedy the situation and to keep the population safe," he says. "At this time, we advise people to remain calm. There is no immediate danger associated with these events.

"There are currently no T.W.R.P.s affecting travel." It sounds clunky as McCloy reads out the letters, but government officials never say *Twerps*. Guy wonders if they're forbidden to do so.

McCloy continues. "We believe that conditions may be better in larger cities. If you have the means to get there, you may find power and supplies in Atlanta, Charlotte, or Columbia. If you choose to stay in town, be sure that you have the proper supplies on hand. You should be prepared for this much as you would for a major snowstorm." He goes on, listing supplies—water, canned goods, flashlights.

Guy starts to feel antsy as the gusts build to a sustained wind that tugs at his jacket.

McCloy finishes talking, and he turns his back on the crowd without looking up. He shuffles back in and locks the doors behind him. Thunder crashes loud and close and the crowd begins to disperse.

"Hey, Guy."

The voice comes from behind him, and Guy turns. It's the oldest of the bald men. He stands with his arms crossed, a smug look on his face. It takes Guy a moment before he recognizes him. It's Peter Addison, the history teacher at Guy's school. He has always had gray hair that he wears parted on the side and a little too long. Square-rimmed glasses and a thick mustache. With no glasses and his head and face smooth and white, he's a different person. "Hey, Peter," Guy says.

Peter pulls his lip up in a way that's half grin, half snarl. It curls Guy's insides. "You getting out of town?" Peter says.

"No plans yet."

"I hear it's the thing to do."

Guy thinks back to a winter day months ago, one of those Twerp Wednesdays that floated in the middle of the cold days off, when Peter cornered him in the teacher's lounge. There were other teachers in there, but Peter cut him off from them in a way that made it seem like they were on another planet.

"So you really think this is the last winter?" Peter said.

He was close enough that Guy could see the way that some of the hairs of Peter's mustache turned up and grew into his nostrils. "That's what they say," Guy said, leaning away from him.

"That's what they say. That's what they say." The warning bell rang—two minutes to class—and Peter looked to the door, watched as the other teachers disappeared into the hall. He turned back to Guy. "They're lying, you know. The president. The scientists. All lying."

"Nah," Guy said. He tried to scoot around Peter. "The scientists wouldn't lie. That's why they're scientists."

"What, you believe that Mathiasen guy?"

He was talking about Dagmar Mathiasen, the Nobel laureate the media trotted out to explain what was happening to the sun. He was a celebrity by now—mostly, Guy thought, because he was ridiculously good looking. He was Norwegian, tall, blond, lithe—like a Viking or some Norse god. He was on TV a few times a week, patiently explaining why the sun was becoming the ember, reassuring the world that the Big Bang would reignite the star, making it the sun once again. "He won the Nobel prize," Guy said.

"For physics. Lot of good physics did us. Physics said the sun couldn't die like this, and look at us now."

He leaned closer still. Guy could smell his breath, the greasy reek of fast-food breakfast.

"We've got to be prepared," Peter said. "We've got to take care of ourselves. No one else is taking care of us. Listen," he looked back at the door, "I know some people who've got a plan. We've been meeting. You should come to one of our meetings."

The bell rang. "I'm late, Peter," Guy said, shuffling around him.

"Just think about it, Guy." He kept talking as Guy rushed to the door. "Come to one of the meetings. You'll be surprised what you learn."

He was a Bunker Boy, and he creeped Guy out.

Now he's smiling his weird smile as the crowd swarms around them, people bouncing off of each other like pinballs. Guy feels like he's trapped in the teacher's lounge all over again. "Hey, I've got to take off, Peter. Want to beat the crowd, you know." He laughs hollowly, but Peter just stares back at him.

"You take care, Guy," Peter says.

Guy feels his eyes on him the entire way to the car. He knows now where he has to go. The outage and the police report and now these weird bald men—they're all too much to ignore.

He drives with the windows halfway down and the heater off. Leaves swirl in the street. He loves the way that the world feels right now, in these few moments before the storm. Normally, the ember leaves the atmosphere listless, and Guy has missed the sun-driven squalls. He's not going to waste this one.

The air gets ten degrees colder in a few minutes. Wind courses through the city, between the buildings and through the trees, the breath of a great cold-blooded monster. Everything is thick with an electric tautness as the immensity of what is coming stretches the world in front of it. The first raindrops spatter on the windshield, and Guy breathes in the metallic earthy smell of the rainwater and smiles. The drops are quarter-sized liquid daisies on the glass. They break apart and slither upward like amoebas.

It only takes him a few minutes to make it to the shady and famil-iar neighborhood on the other side of town where he pulls into the driveway of Heather's small house. Before he makes it all the way up the walk, she bursts from the door in an explosion of happy noise and exotic smells, and she throws her arms around him and kisses him hard on the mouth as though she hasn't seen him in years.

HEATHER

SHE'D BEEN IN HIS CLASS THE FIRST YEAR THAT GUY taught in South Carolina.

He taught American Literature to eleventh graders, and he wasn't surprised that the girls flirted with him. He was thirty-two, good looking and energetic, a stark departure from the graying faculty that taught most of the other classes. The girls came up to him after class, leaned their seventeen-year-old bodies over his desk and gibbered on about nothing in the spare minutes at the end of class. Theirs was a harmless game, but Heather was different, more aggressive. Her body was petite but curvy, spilling out of the spaghetti-strap tops she wore, barely contained in her jean skirts. She came in before class and chatted him up, sitting on the desk in front of his with her legs crossed and tons of pink skin showing on her thighs. She watched him during his lectures, the tip of her tongue

37

absently sliding around her lips. She had wavy red hair that spilled across her shoulders, or bounced in a pony tail, or hung in loose pigtails, *good god, those pigtails.*

Guy had scruples. He never touched a student.

Two years later, on a cool and breezy spring day nearly a year after Heather had graduated, she came back into his classroom as he was gathering his things at the end of the day. She hugged him and told him about her life, about working as a secretary at a law firm, about how she was planning to go to college. She needed a letter of recommendation from him. She sat on his desk, her skirt high on her legs, her head back and her chest pushed out, her breasts round and firm under the tight t-shirt.

This was during the darkest part of Guy and Lisa's marriage. They'd had the year of mechanical screwing, the get-pregnant-or-bust mentality taking all the life out of the act. Then the doctor, and that night when she talked of the death of her nonexistent child, and the blame, that heavy, smothering, heart-wrenching blame that hovered over their life and pushed Lisa so far from him, turned her into a ghost that lived in his house. By the time Heather strolled into his classroom, it had been four months since Guy and Lisa last had sex. Four months and Lisa had hardly touched him. She barely spoke to him in the evenings; she watched TV and buried herself in books. At night, his wife lay on the other side of the bed, an icy wall stretching to the ceiling between them. Four months alone.

So Heather sat on Guy's desk and licked her lips, and Guy stood in front of her and glanced over at the classroom door, which was closed, then looked back at Heather. She had on flip flops, and she let one drop off her foot and onto the floor, then she uncrossed her legs and dragged a toe down the center of his chest, and before he even knew what he was doing, Guy had his hand far up the inside of her smooth thigh and her breasts mashed close to his body and his lips locked tight against hers, her tongue darting tentatively into his mouth. He fucked her there on his desk in the eleventh-grade English classroom.

He went home, sure that Lisa would smell the woman on him, sure that she would read it in his face, but she acted no different. She was as cold and distant as usual, that same shell of a woman staring through the TV, the same cold body on the far side of the bed.

Heather gave Guy her number so that he could arrange to get the letter to her (he wrote her a glowing recommendation). When he called her and she said he should bring it by her house, the sex was a given. He drove to the neighborhood on the other side of town, to the small house he assumed her parents bought for her. He showed up that day, and he kept showing up, sometimes several times a week, for all the years since then. It was too easy, with Lisa away at work and Heather at home, so available in those hours of the afternoon.

Heather was never beautiful like Lisa; Lisa was what could be called classically beautiful, with her long limbs and slender body and her delicately-cut face. Heather was all kinds of cute when she was younger, full of youth and life wrapped up in a package that oozed sex. Now she was twenty-four and the youth was gone, but the package was still there—Heather looked like sex, despite her too-big mouth and her hair that was losing its luster and cut into a bob that stole any glamour the redhead had left, and her body, which was still voluptuous, but in a plump way, in an *I've gained twenty pounds since high school* way. She still looked like sex.

Guy had intended it to be only about sex. He needed it, when the affair started, when Lisa was so dark and withdrawn. But as the years went on and Lisa came out of her funk and her sexual appetite became voracious, Guy needed sex less and less. Yet he found himself still drawn to Heather's house. It was an afternoon a couple of years ago—an afternoon when Guy had already made love to Lisa that morning and ended up at Heather's house that afternoon with no intention of sex at all, simply wanting to see her and smell her, whatever it was on her that made her smell like a flower-strewn parade in Rio de Janeiro—that Guy realized he was in love with her. Not that he was out of love with Lisa—he loved her more than ever, damaged or no—but he was in love with Heather too. She was sunlight cutting through the afternoon rainstorm. She was life overflowing. She made Guy feel like the world was something to be enjoyed.

He lay on the couch with Heather that day, her plump body close to his, and he thought to himself, *There is no way that this ends well.*

* * *

Now he's here again, standing in the front yard with this woman who is not his wife in his arms, and she pulls him inside and they have sex on the floor of the kitchen, the tile as cold as the frozen surface of an Alpine lake.

When they finish, he rolls off of her and leans against the refrigerator. He pulls his knees into his chest against the cold. Outside, the rain is coming down at an angle, fat drops moving the grass in Heather's lawn. The thunder crashes close by as the heavy part of the storm draws nearer.

She runs her fingers down his leg. "You've got the goose bumps."

Guy smiles. He loves the way she says it, the girlish lilt of her voice. She still acts like that high school girl he knew, and at times like these, he likes it. She makes it easy to be happy.

She sits up and scoots across the floor and pulls his legs apart, leans back against him as though he's an easy chair. She picks up her jacket and wraps it around the two of them while Guy drapes his arms around her. He cups her breast absently. "Hey," she says. Then she turns her face up to him and kisses him on the chin. "I wish you'd come by sooner. I've been scared."

"You know I can't come by on Sundays. Lisa's home all day. She'd wonder where I went."

"Still." Heather pouts. She rubs her hands on his calves. "It was scary here at night, all alone. I was going to leave, but I thought you might come."

"And here I am." Guy runs his fingers through her hair, and she closes her eyes and breathes deep. "Aren't you glad you stayed?"

She nods. "You were worried about me?"

She's drifted into a babytalk voice, and now Guy is getting annoyed by it. Heather becomes infinitely less interesting for the few hours after Guy has sex with her. The afterglow fades, and the juvenile quirks that were so endearing before become tedious. She's like a child. She looks sad to him now, her legs pale and doughy, her hair a shadow of the beauty it had years ago. She looks pointless. And she is, to some extent. If she was gone, the world wouldn't miss her at all.

But Guy would miss her. In many ways, she's a sexy little waste of space, yet Guy still loves her—a different kind of love, though, than what he feels for Lisa. When the sex is done, what's left between him and Heather is more like a teacher's love for his students.

It's a protective love he feels for Heather. Lisa doesn't need protecting.

So he had worried about Heather. After the news at the police station, he couldn't get her out of his mind. "Maybe I worried about you a little," Guy says. "But you want me to worry."

"It means you care," she says. "What do you think the deal is?"

"What do you mean?"

"With the power."

"Oh. They don't know. I went by the power company, and they just had a sign on the door that said they were working on it. Then I went to the police station." He tells her about McCloy and the reports.

"So are you leaving town?"

"I don't know." Guy stands up and hunts for his pants. "I've got to get back," he says.

She looks small over there, on the floor by the refrigerator, her hands resting on her belly. "I want to talk to you about something," she says.

"Can it wait?" Periodically, Heather decides that she wants to talk. She wants their relationship to go to the next level; she wants Guy to leave Lisa. Guy is sick of these conversations. It's hard to convince her that he loves her and wants her but that he's not going to leave his wife. She doesn't understand any more than Lisa would that it's possible for a man to love two women. "I have to go. Lisa's going to wonder where I've been."

She has the jacket draped over her shoulders. Her stomach is a little soft, but her breasts look great, Guy thinks to himself. "This all just makes me nervous," she says.

"What does?" The rain is easing up now, and the sun's coming through the clouds, painting everything with a greenish glow.

"All this. It's weird. People don't freak out like this just because the power's gone out."

"It's because they've fixed it so quickly when the aurora's knocked it out before," Guy says. "It's happened so many times that the power company's ready for it. It's like aurora, outage, then the power's back on for the morning news. We've gotten spoiled. It's taking longer, but they'll fix it like they always do."

"If they're so used to it, it should take less time."

Guy has nothing to say to this. She's right, and it annoys him. He's the teacher, and *he's* supposed to tell *her* the answers.

She's up now, getting dressed. "I feel like we should leave town."

"And go where?"

"I don't know. I don't feel safe in my house by myself."

"Well, maybe you should go to your parents', then."

"Maybe," she says.

Heather has always been vague about her parents. He knows that they moved away after she graduated high school, and she'd stayed behind. She said it was for her job, but Guy knows that she stayed for him. Sometimes he wishes she'd gone; life would be so much simpler without her. Simpler, but darker. "I can't stay with you, Heather," he says. "You know that. Lisa would find out."

"So what?"

"We've been over this."

Heather makes a pouty face and follows him to the door. "I feel like there's something else going on," she says. "It's weird. I feel like they're not telling us something."

Guy laughs. "You know, Lisa said almost the same thing."

"Don't compare me to her."

"Okay, okay." They step outside and stand on the stoop. The yellow blades of grass hiss as they move in the rain. Guy puts his hand on Heather's hip and kisses her, but she barely kisses back, her lips flat and cold. "Come on," Guy says. "Don't be difficult."

"I want you here with me."

"I know you do. But I can't. Hey." He holds her cheeks in his hands, pushes her hair back from her face. She looks up at him—she seems so short compared to Lisa—blinks her dark-chocolate eyes and smiles. Guy says, "You know I love you, right?"

"I know." She kisses him, harder this time, a kiss with some life behind it. "I love you too."

"You probably ought to go to your parents', just to be on the safe side."

"Okay. I might."

"Just in case." He moves to leave, but she puts her arms around him and holds herself close to his body. Guy says, "Nothing's going to happen to you."

"You'll take care of me?"

"You know I will." He kisses her again and runs through the rain to the car. She waves from the doorstep as he pulls away.

SHELLS

LISA IS THERE WHEN HE GETS HOME. SHE'S SITTING on the porch with Jemi, the sliding glass doors open and the breeze coming in. The condo is the same temperature as the outdoors now, so closing the doors seems pointless. The air moves through the condo and makes everything feel fresh. Outside, the rain comes down through the trees, pattering against the spindly leaves that cling to the branches. Guy feels tense; Lisa is normally at work until nine, giving him hours after a meeting with Heather, hours to calm down and clean up and get ready to face his wife. He heads outside anyway.

Lisa looks up from the porch swing and smiles at him. Guy relaxes. He kisses her on the forehead and sits beside her, puts his arm around her. They watch the rain. The storm is moving away, the thunder fading into the distance like a departing train. The

44

creek flows red with clay. It's fast-moving now and full of sticks and garbage and foam and whatever else has washed out in the storm.

"No work?" Guy says.

"Nope." Lisa nuzzles into him. "We could have gone back to bed. Where were you?"

"What did they say at work?"

"No one was there to say anything. There was a sign on the door that said 'Closed until further notice.' I used my key and went in, but it was deserted. And dark and cold. So I left."

Jemi lies down in front of them and Lisa puts both of her feet on the dog's belly. She rolls onto her back so that Lisa can scratch her with the soles of her shoes. Lisa says, "Where were you all day?"

"I went to the power company. Then the police station."

"Yeah?"

"Nothing at the power company. Nobody was there. They just had a note up that said they were trying to fix it. But the police station was making announcements." Guy tells Lisa about McCloy, and the long announcement, and Peter.

Lisa stares off into the woods while he talks. When he's finished, she sits quietly. Finally, she says, "So what do you think we should do?"

"About what?"

"Do you think we should leave?" She sits up on the bench and crosses her legs underneath her. "I wonder if we should leave. Maybe we should go to your mom's. The power can't be out in Florida too. Plus she's all alone down there."

"That's seven hours away."

"So you think we should just stay?"

"I don't know." Guy gets up and rests his elbows on the railing, watches the creek. "It's not like it's winter. It's not that cold, and if they've fixed the ember, it might even start getting warmer. We could just ride it out."

Lisa nods. "I figured you'd say that. Listen. I went by Walmart on the way home." He follows her inside and into the office. They look at the small pile of plastic bags full of stuff. "Don't be mad," she says. "I'm not being a Bunker Boy. It just—it can't hurt."

Guy kneels and looks in the bags. A couple of gallon jugs of water. Assorted canned goods. A box of granola bars. "The police were saying we ought to stock up," Guy says. He opens another bag and pulls out a box of cereal. It's a type he hates. "Is this all they had?"

"We're lucky I got *that*. It was crazy in there." She sits down in the swivel chair beside the computer. "They had all these heaters and lights running on generators. Everything smelled like gasoline. And it was so crowded. People were crawling over each other to get stuff."

"How did you pay for it?" Guy assumes the credit card system is down.

"I took some of your stash."

Guy has always kept some cash stowed away—a Bunker Boy tendency he's slightly ashamed of. The world has evolved beyond cash; it's antiquated, unnecessary. Still, the cash makes him feel safe. He goes into his dresser drawer and finds the tin that his wallet came in. He lifts back the spongy felt bottom layer and counts the bills that are left. Nine hundred dollars. "A hundred, then," he says to Lisa. "Good haul for a hundred."

"I was going to get more gas too, but the pumps weren't working."

"How much is in your car?"

"Like half a tank."

Guy nods. The Toyota is half-full too.

"There's something else," Lisa says. She reaches into the bag beside her and pulls out a box of shotgun shells.

Guy has a gun. It's a twelve-gauge shotgun; he got it for Christmas when he was sixteen. Guy hasn't used it in years, not since he went duck hunting with a couple of guys from work. Now the gun sits in the back of Guy's closet.

"I wasn't sure if they were the right kind," Lisa says, turning the box over in her hands.

"The right kind for what?"

Her eyes are the color of the dripping woods outside. Guy can read her face. He knows she's reading his.

Guy takes the shells from her. They're twelve-gauge shells, all right. BB shot. "These would do the job," he says.

* * *

46

They build a fire that night and shut the doors and windows tight so that the heat fills the condo, lights it up like an oven.

Firewood had become a precious commodity during the winter. The Twerps limited the temperature on the thermostat, but there were no rules against other sources of heat. Hardware stores and gas stations had firewood for sale outside, huge piles of it stacked along their walls. Men in pickup trucks sat beside the road and sold it straight from their truck beds. It went fast as people burned it up and the woods became saturated with snow; by November, most of the dry firewood was gone and prices skyrocketed. In February you'd pay five dollars a log if you wanted to stay warm. Most people chose the cold.

They don't have much spare firewood, and what they have they ought to save for the next winter, but they burn it anyway. Jemi lies on her stomach a few feet from the fireplace, transfixed by the flames. A pot of soup bubbles on the propane stove. Guy and Lisa sit on the couch and watch the firelight flicker against the walls. It casts dancing shadows, and it feels like they're living out a night that happened a million years ago. On the mantle, Lisa keeps her trinkets from Africa—small carvings of hippos, giraffes, a lion. They seem sinister in the near-dark. The creek thunders by outside, and in the far distance, gunshots echo through the night, flat sounds that bounce against the trees. Hunters, Guy thinks, or cops at the shooting range. Gunshots like these sound in the woods around the city all the time. They carry in the stillness of the night.

Lisa leans her head on Guy's shoulder. The room is warm and she wears a thin, spaghetti-strap nightie. Her cheeks and the tip of her nose are flushed the color of ripe watermelon. "How long do we wait?" she says.

Guy watches the fire. A log burns through and something snaps and the neatly-stacked fire tumbles, becomes a mound of coals. It begins to burn itself out. The room gets darker. "We wait until something happens," he says.

TORNADO

JEMI WAKES HIM UP IN THE EARLY MORNING. LAST night's warmth lingers in the condo; everything still smells of fire. A couple of coals smolder in the fireplace.

The rain is coming down again outside. It falls in neat lines through the trees, making a runnelling sound that flows in Guy's ears. Everything outside is green, the sky and the trees and the rain. It's like he's looking at the world through a sheet of jade. The trees look alive; every leaf is moving under the steady fall of the rain.

There are sounds in the distance. Voices, mumblings and shouts, car doors opening and slamming shut.

Guy puts on his jacket and goes out the front door. The rain is as heavy as a shower, cold on his shoulders, and it coats him instantly. He shakes a hand through his hair and walks to the parking lot. The ember has barely started to come up, and it's behind the clouds, so the only light is that green haze that sits over everything. Still, Guy can see that the parking lot is full of movement. People are rushing back and forth between their condos and their cars. They are carrying suitcases and computers and stacks of books. Couples shout to one another, telling each other what to grab. It's a mad dash, as though a tornado warning has sounded and only a few seconds remain before every earthly possession is swept into the sky.

Guy walks farther down, a few buildings away from his own, where a college kid is trying to close the overstuffed trunk of his car. "Hey, man," Guy says.

The kid doesn't look up. "Hey," he says, mashing down on the trunk.

"What's going on? Where's everybody going?"

"Heading out of town," the kid says. "I'm going to Atlanta. They say it's supposed to be safe there."

"It's not safe here?"

The kid bounces on the trunk a few times and it finally shuts. He stands there for a minute, catching his breath.

Guy is soaked with rain. His jeans sag heavy on his hips and a chill is starting to creep into his middle. "Why isn't it safe here?"

The kid shrugs. "They just said we ought to get out of here. So I am."

"Who said?"

"I don't know who said it first. But that's the word." He looks back at his condo, then through the back window of his car. "I hope I got everything." He opens the door and climbs inside.

Guy puts his hand on the door before the kid can shut it. "Hang on," he says. "What happened that's made everybody so freaked out? Why is everyone leaving now?"

"I told you, man, I don't know." The kid looks up at Guy with sleepy eyes. His shirt is wet and clinging to his chest. He cranks the car. "Everyone else is leaving, so I just figured I ought to go too. You don't go, you're going to be the only one here." Then he pulls the door hard enough that Guy's hand slips off. The door slams shut and the kid pulls out of the parking lot. Guy watches him as he drives off through the rain. Other people are slamming doors, starting cars, driving away. The parking lot is fast becoming empty. Guy feels a hollowness inside him, as though he's missing something, something he can't explain.

Inside he finds a towel and dries off. Jemi bounces around the room. "Go back to sleep," Guy says to her. The rain is noisy and the condo full of that weird green light.

When he's back in bed, Lisa says, "What were you doing?"

"I was outside. People are packing up and leaving."

"Where are they going?"

"I don't know."

Lisa sighs. Her voice is heavy with sleep. "It's too early to go anywhere." She rolls over and puts her hand on his chest. "You're wet," she mumbles, and then she starts breathing the heavy breathing of sleep. Guy listens to the rain outside until he's asleep too.

When he wakes up again the ember is out and the heat from the fire has all seeped away from the condo. He puts Jemi on the leash and takes her outside. The parking lot is almost empty. Only a few cars remain; they dot the parking lot as though stranded, leftovers from the mass exodus.

Ronald Meehan is out on his porch. He lives a few units down from Guy. Guy hates forced conversations, so he's tried to avoid becoming too familiar with his neighbors. Ronald made himself unavoidable. If he has to make small talk, though, Guy figures he could do worse than Ronald. Ronald's a widower, around seventy years old and unabashedly friendly, always smiling a gap-toothed smile, his eyes bright blue holes in his weathered face. He was a fireman once, and his body still seems sturdy and strong, though it's got a hefty coat of fat on it now.

Today, another man, about Guy's age, is standing in the grass in front of Ronald, gesticulating wildly and talking in a frantic, high-pitched voice. The man is tall and skinny, balding on top, like a stretched-out turtle with no shell. When Guy gets close, he can make out the words. The man says, "Come on, Dad, we're leaving."

"Guy's still here," Ronald says, waving his hand at Guy.

"Morning, Ronald," Guy says. "Or afternoon."

Ronald's son looks Guy up and down then turns back to his dad. "That doesn't matter. Everyone else in town is leaving. We want you to come with us. Amy and Ben both want you to come. They want their granddad. Just come on."

Guy tries to avoid them, to let them have their conversation alone, but Ronald's fat old beagle RC comes out on the porch and Jemi spots him. She drags Guy over to the other two men so that she can touch noses and wag her tail at RC. Now Guy is standing right next to Ronald's son, so he sticks out his hand. "I'm Guy. I live in that one down there."

"James," the man says, taking Guy's hand in a weak and hurried shake. "How come you're staying?"

Guy shrugs, looks at the man. His face is tight and red; his eyes seem exhausted. "I'm not sure why I'm supposed to leave?" Guy says.

"But they said we've got twenty-four hours to get out of town." James says this as though it is the most obvious answer imaginable.

"Who says?"

"The Minutemen."

Guy smiles, but James is deadpan. "The who?"

"Minutemen. That's what they call themselves. Haven't you seen those bald guys around?"

Guy feels his insides kink again. He thinks of the man across the creek, of Peter's twisted grin. "A few."

"You've been to the police announcement meetings, right?"

Guy nods.

"I went to one this morning," James says. "We sat there waiting for McCloy to come out, and at eight, one of those bald guys took the stage. He said he was with the Minutemen and that they had control of the town now. He said that everyone had until midnight to get out of town. He said we could go to Atlanta or Charlotte. He said if we went in time, they'd let us go."

Guy shakes his head. "They'd *let us go*? What are they doing to us if we stay?"

Ronald laughs from the porch. "Nothing," he says. "This is a bunch of fuss over nothing. I bet it's just some of those Bunker Boy assholes taking advantage of the power being out. Probably call themselves Minutemen because they think it sounds cool."

"They killed the cops, Dad," James says.

"You don't know that."

"Then how come they were holding the meeting at the police station?" James turns back to Guy. "My neighbor, Mike, was at the midnight meeting. He said that it was crazy. At midnight, McCloy came out to give his talk, and before he could say anything, there was gunfire in the police station. No one was sure what was going on. Then a bald cop came out of the station and shot McCloy in the head. A lot of the people in the crowd ran, but the bald guy put his gun away and started talking, so Mike stayed and listened. He said the Minutemen were taking over. Same thing he said at the eight o'clock meeting. And that we had to get out of town."

"He killed the cop?" Guy says.

"That's what Mike told me."

Ronald puts his hands on his hips. "Was his body still there when you went?"

"No."

He laughs. "I bet Mike's full of shit," Ronald says. "I never liked that guy."

"Why would he make that up?"

"I don't know. Maybe he wants you to leave town so he can break into your house."

James sighs. His lip twitches. He puts a hand on top of his head. "Look, Dad," he says. "We're going. We're heading to Atlanta. We want you to come with us."

"Well, I'm not. I'm not going."

"Fine. I can't make you go." James walks to his car. "I'll call you when the phones work again," he says. Then he gets in the car and drives off. The sound of the engine fades into the distance, and then the only noise is the snuffing of the dogs' noses.

"You buy any of that?" Ronald says.

Guy shrugs. "I don't know. I've seen those bald guys around."

"Yeah, me too." He picks up RC and leans back in his chair. The dog rolls onto its back in Ronald's lap and wags its tail as the old man idly scratches its belly. "I think I'm just going to play it by ear," he says. "Things turn bad, I'll follow them to Atlanta. But I think everyone's blowing this out of proportion."

"Probably so," Guy says. "Stay safe, Ronald."

"Always do."

Guy goes back inside and tells Lisa about the conversation. "It sounds to me like a sort of he said, she said thing. A friend of a friend told me, you know."

Lisa looks concerned. She's sitting sideways on the couch, her arms wrapped around a pillow. "I saw some of those bald guys at Walmart," she says. "They're everywhere." She chews on the corner of the pillow. "Minutemen," Lisa mumbles. "That's from the Revolutionary War, right?"

"I think so."

"Do you think we need to be worried?"

"I don't know."

"Maybe we should leave," Lisa says. "We could go to Florida. To your mom's. Aren't you worried about her?"

"No," Guy says. His mother had taken on a fierce sort of independence after his dad died ten years ago. She'd probably view them as an inconvenience. "I'm not worried about her."

"Well, what about my parents?"

"You want to go all the way down to Miami?" It takes a good twelve hours to get to Lisa's parents' house. Guy's mother lives in the Panhandle of Florida, only about seven hours away.

"I don't know."

"We might not even be able to get the gas. You said the pumps were off."

Lisa drums her fingers on her knee. She sighs.

"Here's what we'll do," Guy says. He gets up and walks over to the couch. He picks her legs up and sits down and lets her legs fall across his lap. "We'll hang out here a few more days. We'll see if the power comes on. We'll treat it like a vacation—like we're camping. Hang around here and relax. We've got the supplies. If the power doesn't come back on soon, or if you don't feel comfortable, we'll take off. We'll go all the way to Miami if you want. But let's not go all that way and have it be for nothing."

Lisa hugs the pillow closer to her. "You think we'll be safe?"

"It can't be any safer out there on the road."

"You're not helping."

Guy laughs and squeezes her leg. He runs his hand along her calf, lifts her leg to his face and kisses her on the knee. "We'll be fine."

That night it takes him a long time to fall asleep. They go to bed early, only a couple of hours after the ember is gone. There's nothing else to do with the power out. Lisa sleeps, but Guy lies awake on his back. He closes his eyes, then opens them and looks at the ceiling. Everything is so black that it's hard to tell whether his eyes are open or closed.

He can't sleep because he's thinking of Heather. He remembers holding her there in front of her house while the rain soaked the lawn. Her eyes sad and young. He told her to go to her parents' house, and he wants to believe that she did. He tells himself that she must have, that there's no reason for him to worry. There's no reason for him to picture her sitting alone in her house, the darkness creeping all around her as bald men stalk through the spongy grass and peer through the windows. She is not sitting on the floor of her living room, her elfish hands choking the barrel of a flashlight. Guy tries to shake these images from his head. He pictures her snug in a bed in the guestroom of her parents' house. Her father probably has a generator. They may even have the heater going.

At last he sleeps, and he dreams. He dreams of Heather surrounded by faceless bald men, on top of her, tearing into her. They are buzzards swarming a carcass, their feathers red to the neck with blood.

MINUTEMEN

IN THE MIDMORNING HE WAKES TO THE SOUNDS
of construction. A saw is whining in the distance. It's quiet for a
moment, then there's a muffled *pop pop* as though someone's ham-
mering. Guy lies in bed for a few minutes and listens. After a while,
he hears the saw again. It's closer this time, and it cuts for about
thirty seconds and then winds down.

"Is the power back on?" Lisa says.

Guy looks at the black face of the digital clock. "No."

She takes an extra pillow and puts it over her head. "Who's
building?"

"I don't know."

Guy gets up and gets dressed and puts Jemi on the leash. He
walks her to the end of the boardwalk and stands in the grass. He
yawns and looks around. It's overcast; the clouds hang low and
heavy, a thick gray blanket over the morning. It looks like November

55

outside even though it's midsummer; the ember is blotted out and everything is shrouded with a stony numbness. The parking lot is empty, save a few cars—his and Lisa's, Ronald's, a couple others. Down near Ronald's condo, a pickup truck is parked in the middle of the lot. In the bed of the truck sits a lot of stuff. Guy squints; he can see TVs and clothes, boxes. He takes a couple of steps forward, but Jemi has stopped, so he stops too. The dog is tense. Her ears are perked forward and her tail sticks straight up. She lets out a low growl, the same growl she gave when she looked across the creek the other night. She's staring.

Guy follows her gaze down the parking lot. Nothing moves. Then, seeming large and out of place, two of the bald men step out from the walkway of the building a hundred yards away, the building next to Ronald's. Two Minutemen. One carries a computer under one arm, the monitor under the other. The second man has his arms full of jeans and jackets. The men are laughing.

Jemi growls again, louder, like she's about to bark, and Guy yanks her collar and pulls her out of the grass. He ducks down behind his car and holds the dog's mouth shut. She looks at him with excited eyes. "Hush," Guy says. He lets her mouth go and she sits quietly, the tip of her tail wagging on the asphalt.

Guy squats near the passenger door of the car. He raises his head and peeks through the window. The men throw the stuff into the back of the truck. One of them is tall and stick-skinny, like a Halloween skeleton with white skin stretched around him. The other is medium-height with a muscular chest. It looks like he spends hours at the gym doing nothing but the bench press. His arms stick out from his sides, a perpetual muscle-man pose. He's got a thick beard on his face but no hair on his head. On a strap across his back rests a gun, a rifle; it looks like a military gun, maybe an M16. Guy looks closer at the skinny man. He wears a pistol on his waist. A cordless circular saw dangles from one hand. The skinny Minuteman hops in the truck and cranks it. He drives forward a hundred feet while the muscular one walks along beside him. Guy can't hear them, but he sees their mouths moving. Muscles laughs at something that Skinny says. Then he takes something from around his neck and hands it to Skinny. Guy squints. Muscles has dozens of necklaces, thousands of dollars of jewelry, dangling from his neck.

They stop in front of Ronald's unit. A dog barks—RC. Ronald is sitting on his porch, the beagle in his lap.

Skinny gets out of the truck and the two Minutemen walk toward Ronald's porch. They hold their guns at ready. Skinny talks first. He has a loud, high-pitched voice, a heavy Southern accent that carries all the way down the parking lot. "What you doing still in town?"

Ronald says something. Guy can hear his voice, but the words are indistinct. RC barks again and Jemi wags her tail.

"We told you to get out by last night," Skinny says.

Ronald talks again.

Now Muscles speaks. His voice is low and gruff. The words come in pieces. Guy hears, "Getting's good." He hears, "You screwed up."

Ronald speaks louder, but the words still fail to form in Guy's ears.

"We're coming in one way or the other, old man," Skinny says.

Ronald starts to stand up and Muscles raises the rifle and shoots Ronald twice in the chest. The shots seem far away, like a pop-gun going off in the deep woods. Jemi jumps and Guy pushes her back down, hushes her. He watches as Ronald steps backward at the impact of the bullets. His shirt has blood spreading across it. He puts his hand on his chest and leans back against the sliding glass door and slumps down to his butt. RC is barking like mad, so Skinny pulls out the pistol and shoots the dog. RC doesn't make another sound; he just flops onto his side and twitches. The Minutemen look at Ronald and then at each other. They lower their guns and head up the walkway to the condo.

Guy realizes that he's breathing as though he just finished a run. He feels like he can't move. "Shit," he says. "Shit. Shit." He catches his breath and gets up and sprints back up the walkway, Jemi running along beside him, the leash in her mouth. He hears the sound of the saw ripping through the morning air.

Lisa is standing in the bedroom in nothing but her sweatpants. She's looking through the dresser for a shirt. Guy puts the leash in her hand and pushes her and the dog into the bathroom. Lisa sits down on the toilet. "What are you doing?" she says.

Guy is still breathing heavy. "They're here. You were right. They're here."

"Who?"

"Minutemen. They killed Ronald. They're going condo to condo."

Lisa's eyes are wide and white as headlights. Jemi's nails click on the tile. She wags her tail and her mouth hangs open in a dog smile. Lisa says, "Then let's get out of here!"

"Can't." Guy looks at her, sitting on the toilet, her breasts hanging bare on her chest. He walks back to the dresser and grabs a sweatshirt and tosses it to her. "They're going in and out. They've got guns. If we go and they're out there, they'll shoot us."

Lisa stands up and pulls the shirt over her head. It's a faded Beatles hoodie with the Yellow Submarine on it. "What are we going to do?"

Guy puts his hand on the door jamb. His breathing has slowed. He feels calmer all of a sudden. "I don't know," he says. "I'm going to get the gun. You stay in here." Jemi barks at him. "Keep her quiet. Hold her mouth shut if you have to. Stay in here with the door locked. Lean up against it. Don't open it unless it's me."

He walks back into the living room and stands with his hands on his hips. He blinks, looks around. Inside of Guy there's a sort of fire, a hot feeling swirling through his arms and legs. He feels giddy, bouncy as he thinks. He turns his phone on and tries to dial 911, but gets nothing but the knocking of the failure to connect. The tips of his fingers tingle and he clenches his fists and lets them go.

The saw starts up at the unit next door to him, and he runs to the closet. He moves the piles of canned goods aside and finds the shotgun. It is heavy in his hands, long and cumbersome, more than half as tall as he is. He puts it to his shoulder and sights on a tree outside of the window. The tip of the barrel seems so far away; it takes forever to swing it from one target to another. He understands now why people saw these barrels off.

Guy breaks open the box of shells and slides one into the underside of the gun and pumps once, putting the shell in the chamber. He slips another shell in, and then another, and tries to add a fourth, but it won't go. *Shit*, he thinks, *the plug*. The regulations say that the gun can't hold more than three shells if you're hunting ducks, and he hasn't used it since he went duck hunting years ago.

Guy wonders if this moment is the one where he dies, if every time he might have died—every close call while driving, every slip on a staircase, every disease his body fought off—just bought him some extra time, enough time for him to live long enough to die here. He wishes he could see the paths unfolding far in front of him. He wishes he held the blueprint to the world.

More than anything, though, he wishes the plug wasn't in the gun. He doesn't have time to take it out and isn't even sure he knows how. If he tries, the gun might end up in pieces, unusable. So he squats down in the living room with three shells of BB shot in the twelve-gauge.

He tries to use the layout of the room to his advantage. He crouches by the door to the office. If someone were to come in through the front door—the only way a person can get in, if he doesn't want to climb up twenty-five feet to the porch—he'd have the living room spread out in front of him. To his left is the kitchen, to his right, the door to the guest bathroom. Pass that door and take a few steps and another door opens to the right, the door to the office. The bathroom opens to the office too, so it's possible to walk straight from the living room to the office, or, if one was inclined, to go through the bathroom, past the sink, and into the other office door. Guy is in the living room on one knee with the office door to his left, the barrel of the gun leveled at the middle of the front door, the bathroom door standing open a few yards in front of him. He waits. He feels his heartbeat in his ears. His forearm strains from holding the gun.

There are voices outside, footsteps on the planks of the walk-way. Guy adjusts the gun, presses the butt into his shoulder. The steps come to the door, stop a moment, and then head to the unit upstairs. Guy breathes. The saw starts up and seems loud and close. Jemi barks and Lisa's muffled voice drifts into the room: "Hush!"

Guy looks at the gun again. The safety is on. "Jesus," he says, and he flicks the safety off, revealing the red bead that means the gun is ready to fire.

He listens as the men clunk around in the condo above him. After what seems like an eternity, their footsteps are on the stairs again, and then they fade down the walkway. Guy sits down and rests the gun across his legs. He realizes he's been sweating. He wipes his forehead with the tail of his shirt, rubs his palms on the front of his jeans. Far too quickly, the footsteps return, and Guy gets back into his crouch, raises the gun to his shoulder, puts the slightest bit of tension on the trigger.

The doorknob turns and the door jerks on its hinges as the deadbolt catches. Guy jumps and begins to breathe heavy again. The door shakes a couple more times, then is still. Skinny says something to the other Minuteman, his voice loud but indistinct on the other side of the wood. Then the saw. It winds up and buzzes like tree frogs crying on a summer night. The door vibrates and then the blade punches through, a single vertical cut to the inside of the deadbolt. The blade pulls out again, and the door quivers as the saw cuts a second slice, this one horizontal, above the bolt, making an upside-down L shape. Sawdust drifts and settles on the carpet. The blade recedes; then it cuts a third time, spinning its way through like a hurricane, unstoppable and loud, until there's a neat box around the deadbolt, separating the door from the lock. The blade vanishes and the saw winds down. Muscles says something and Skinny laughs. Then the doorknob turns, there's a thud and a cracking sound as someone slams against the door and it gives at the cuts, and the door swings open and Skinny is standing there, his mouth open in a grin, the saw ticking in his hand.

Guy pulls the trigger and the gun bucks and Skinny flies backward as though someone has jerked him from behind. His back hits the wall and his mouth opens and closes like a fish's, like the breath has been knocked out of him. Already his shirt is red, his chest bleeding from dozens of holes. The door swings back. Muscles is out of sight and he says, "Fuck!"

Guy ducks into the office. His ears are ringing from the shot and every inch of his body thumps with his heartbeat. He makes his mouth into an O and takes several deep breaths, trying to quiet himself. He stands with his back against the wall, his back to the Minutemen. He can hear Skinny gasping and Muscles cursing. Guy tries to make himself as small as possible, as flat against the wall as can be. To his left is the door to the living room. He can see the sliding glass doors and the porch and the bedroom, but not the front door—that's behind him now. To his right is the door to the bathroom, and the bathroom is behind him too. He waits and listens. Skinny gasps for another minute. Then he's quiet.

There's no sound for what seems like forever. Then there's a faint creaking, the slow groaning of the door being pushed open again.

Suddenly, Guy realizes his mistake, this huge tactical mistake. He doesn't know what he expected to happen—obviously he wasn't going to kill both of them in the first instant—but he hadn't planned at all for a second shot. Now Muscles is coming in, he's coming into the condo, and he won't be surprised like Skinny; Muscles is ready, Muscles has that rifle, that horrible military rifle up on his shoulder. He's tracking the barrel around the room, waiting to explode Guy's head with a single well-aimed shot. And now that he's inside, he's got to go one way or the other. He's got to head into the living room, or he's got to cut through the bathroom. Guy listens. The door is open now, and there are no other sounds. Still, he can feel the presence of the Minuteman, another life pulsing and filling up the room.

If Guy steps into the living room and Muscles is there, Muscles will kill him. There's no way he can get the shotgun up in time. If he steps into the bathroom and he's there, Muscles will kill him. If he waits between the two doors, Muscles will kill him. So he can't wait. He has to go one way or the other, and one direction ends in death, in that instant of light and pain as the bullet tears his brain in half.

He tries to resign himself to whatever choice he makes. Whatever way he picks, it's the only way that it could ever be. Guy believes in the inevitability of the future. The way he figures it, the future was just time waiting to become the past. Everything is possible leading up to a moment, but the closer that moment gets, the more possibilities are whittled away. Maybe those other possibilities exist in other universes with other Guys, but in this universe—*his* universe—when the moment finally happens, it happens once, and it happens a certain way. All those other outcomes become irrelevant. There may be a million ways that something might happen, but there's only one way that something *will* happen.

So Guy will go one way and Muscles will go one way, and one of them will die. Guy was never going to die anywhere else. It might have happened, but it didn't. It couldn't happen, because he had to get here, to this moment now, when he's got to go one way or the other.

Guy steps into the living room. It's empty. He feels a warmth all down his back and a relief like the world has revealed all its secrets to him. The door is half open and Skinny leans against the wall, his eyes glazed with death. Guy takes two quick steps toward the bathroom door, raises the gun, and steps into the doorway.

Muscles is standing in the doorway to the office; he has his back to Guy, the rifle raised. Guy points the shotgun at the back of Muscles's head and pulls the trigger. Nothing happens. Muscles jerks his head.

No, Guy thinks.

He didn't pump the gun.

Muscles grunts and swings the barrel of the rifle to the left in the doorway as Guy pumps the shotgun, a loud sliding metal sound, and the empty shell bounces on the bathroom counter. Muscles spins and the barrel of the rifle goes *clink* as it smacks against the door jamb. Muscles grits his teeth and tries to angle the gun, to lift the barrel clear so that he can finish his turn, but before he can, Guy fires and the dense mass of shot flies the few feet through the bathroom and into Muscles's face and out the back of his head. His body drops to the ground. Blood runs thick across the tile. His head is mostly gone, but his hands still move, slipping in the blood, and his legs twitch; it's as if he's trying to stand back up. Then he collapses and is still.

Guy blinks. The room is full of metallic smells, the sulfur of the gunpowder and the copper smell of blood. He pumps the shotgun and watches the red shell plunk into the sink. He turns and steps out the front door, over Skinny's body, and walks with the shotgun at ready to the end of the walkway. The parking lot is still and quiet. The clouds are shapeless above him. He goes back inside and into the bedroom, then knocks on the bathroom door and says, "It's me."

Lisa opens the door, her eyes red and wild. "You're bleeding."

Guy looks at his shirt. Drops of blood are spattered across his chest. "Not mine," he says.

Jemi wags her tail. It makes all kinds of noise banging against the cabinets. Guy steps into the bathroom and scratches Jemi on the head and looks at himself in the mirror. He looks like someone out of a horror movie. His face and hair are wet with sweat. The shirt caked in blood. The shotgun warm in his hands. He turns back to Lisa. "We've got to get out of here," he says. "Right now."

FLIGHT

GUY GOES BACK INTO THE LIVING ROOM. HE CAN
see Muscles's legs splayed out on the floor in the office. Blood is
seeping into the carpet. Jemi runs out of the bedroom and past him;
she stops a few feet from the office, stares, then goes forward and
sniffs at the blood. "Hey!" Guy says. "Get out of there. Get!" She
looks at him, tail wagging, then goes into the kitchen and sits by her
food bowl.

Lisa comes into the room and says, "Oh god."

"Yeah," Guy says. "There's dead people out here. I should have
told you."

"Well, I figured." She goes out the front door and looks at
Skinny. She crouches, puts herself at eye level with him. "He hardly
looks dead. I mean, look at him! He looks like he could get better."

Guy has horrible thoughts—Skinny, his chest all torn to shreds,
standing up and complaining, bitching at Guy for shooting him. Or

of Muscles getting on his hands and knees and groping around on the floor of the bathroom, trying to find the pieces of his head. Guy shudders and takes two more shells from the box in the office and slides them into the gun.

Lisa goes into the bathroom. "Now *he* looks dead." She turns and grins at him.

Guy's stomach is weak. "We need to get out of here. Get whatever stuff you want to take. Ten minutes. Ten minutes and we're gone."

She's still looking at Muscles.

"Go!"

"Okay, okay." Lisa goes into the bedroom and starts looking through the drawers.

Guy heads into the bathroom and kneels down over Muscles. He doesn't want to look, but he feels compelled for some reason; he can't help but look at the head. The blast hit Muscles on the front left side of his face. He fell with that part down, and the eye that faces Guy is intact, but the white part is deep red. His beard is matted and black with the blood. The back of his head, shaved bald, has come apart in jagged pieces, like a splattered melon. Guy understands why Lisa seemed so fascinated. He stares at Muscles, this man who was alive a few minutes ago and is now a body on the floor, nothing but a body because of the gun in Guy's hands. And if Muscles had been one step farther ahead, or one step back, his gun wouldn't have caught on the door jamb. It would be Guy's head spread out all over the floor of the bathroom.

The ghosts of other realities whisper to him, and the universe is charged with meaning. The blueprint is in his hands, but before he can decipher it, fix it in his brain, the moment is gone. Those other worlds are not the here and now; they are phantoms, lonely planets spinning off into the ether.

He pries the gun from Muscles's hands. It's not an M16, it's an AR-15. He's not sure why he knows the name. He remembers hearing something about these guns—using them to hunt prairie dogs. Small bullets with a huge amount of powder behind them. They move absurdly fast; the target is dead before it can even hear the gunshot. Guy holds the gun to his shoulder and looks at the wall through the scope. The AR-15 is lighter than the shotgun. It seems insubstantial in his hands. He fumbles with the button on the side of the gun and manages to get the clip out, but it's hard to tell how many bullets are left. It looks like there are several. He checks Muscles's pockets for more ammo, but they are empty. He's carrying nothing.

Guy checks Skinny's body next. He takes the pistol—a small, snub-nosed revolver with four bullets left in it—and slips it into the back of his pants. Skinny has a handful of bullets in his pocket, and Guy takes them too. He reaches around to the back pocket, and Skinny's face is inches from his own, his mouth open slightly, his eyes vacant and tired looking. Guy fishes out his wallet and opens it; inside is some cash and a credit card and two IDs—a driver's license and a student ID from the local college. Skinny's name is Stephen Vincent Marquette. In his pictures, he has hair, thick brown hair parted on the side. He wears round glasses and smiles a big-toothed grin. His student ID says he's a sophomore.

Guy sits down beside Stephen Vincent Marquette. Jemi is near the doorway, sniffing the carpet. She's sniffing the footprints that Guy left behind when he tracked Muscles's blood through the house. Guy closes his eyes and breathes deep. He listens to the sound of the creek rumbling by behind the condos. Then he opens his eyes. He puts two fresh bullets in the revolver and slips it back into his pants and walks out into the parking lot, down to Ronald's unit.

Ronald leans back against the sliding glass door, blood streaked in a vertical stripe above him. His eyes are open wide; he looks surprised at what's been done to him.

Guy says, "Ronald?" even though he knows there's no reason to. Ronald's hand is stretched out to the side, near RC, as though he's reaching for the dog. RC lies in the middle of a round pool of blood. Guy looks at the dog and feels tears in his eyes, and then he hates himself. He hates himself at that moment for showing more emotion over the dog than the man, but there's something about that old beagle lying so perfectly centered in the middle of all that blood. The dog is small and his teeth are worn with age. His death is meaningless, and Ronald's death is meaningless, just like every death. Guy looks through the slats of the railing of the porch and into the emptiness of Ronald's eyes. He looks for the answer, but there's nothing in there but withering flesh. Whatever was there that was once Ronald is gone, and where it has gone, or if it has gone anywhere at all, is knowledge lost to the living.

Guy feels electric with life in the middle of the death that surrounds him. The air is moist in his lungs and his heart sends hot blood in rapid circles around his body. He licks his lips and goes back inside his own condo.

Lisa has her bags packed and has put the collar and leash on Jemi. Guy picks up the AR-15, and he and Lisa walk out to his car and put the bags and the rifle in the trunk. They make several trips back and forth, taking everything they can—their small stock of emergency food, the water and juice and Coke, the rest of the emergency cash, a garbage bag full of dog food, some keepsakes: love notes and pictures and Lisa's Africa trinkets. They cram everything they can into the trunk. Guy puts the shotgun sideways across the dashboard, pushed up under the windshield. The shells in the glove box. He keeps the revolver in his pants, the barrel pushed up cold against the skin of his back, the handle jutting above his jeans, easy to grab.

Guy and Lisa stand in the doorway and look back at their condo. It looks like it's been robbed; the condo is stripped of their life. They've thrown their life in the trunk. There's nothing in the condo but replaceable things and dead people. Guy puts his arm around Lisa, a strange sense of bravado flowing through him. For a second, he feels turned on; he wants to throw her down on the floor on top of those bloody footprints and fuck her while Muscles watches through that red eye. Instead, he pulls Lisa to him and kisses her, open mouthed and wet, and he feels her palm moving on his back. Then they leave the door open and go to the car. Guy says, "Hop in," to Jemi, and she jumps into the back seat. Guy looks at Lisa's car—older, less reliable. *Leave it.* He puts his car into gear and they back up.

They drive past Ronald. Lisa looks at him and says, "Poor guy." Then they are gone, out of the parking lot and heading across the creek and up the big hill, the accelerator mashed to the floor and the engine of the tiny Toyota roaring. Jemi stands in the back seat, panting excitedly, her nose leaving gross streaks where she presses it against the window.

"Where are we going?" Lisa says. Her voice is breathless and high, excited, almost happy.

"I guess Atlanta."

"Why Atlanta?"

"That's where they said we can go. Or that's what Ronald's son said. What Ronald's son's friend said."

"You really think Atlanta's safe?"

"I don't know, Lisa." Guy turns onto Main Street and floors it. He blasts through the intersections, paying no attention to the traffic lights. The streets are empty everywhere he looks. "Where do you think we should go?"

She shrugs. "Atlanta's fine."

The interstate that leads to Atlanta is on the other side of town. The empty shops fly by in a blur as Guy pushes the car through downtown. The gas gauge reads a little over half full. From the corner of his eye, Guy sees Lisa looking at it. "I don't know," he says, anticipating her question. Atlanta is three hours away, too far for the gas in the tank. "We'll siphon more, or something."

"I wasn't saying anything."

"One step at a time," Guy says, and then he feels something turn inside of him, some piece of him opens up and leaves a hollowness in his middle, a gap full of uncertainty. He thinks of Heather again. He wonders if she has gone to her parents' house. It's too late to check—she lives on the other side of the interstate, so how can he drive to that neighborhood and explain it to Lisa? How can he justify a detour when he's already rushed enough to leave most everything he owns in the condo with Muscles and Skinny? He crests a hill at seventy miles per hour and his stomach rolls as gravity catches up to the car. Off to his right, a short way into a residential area, he catches a glimpse of another pickup truck full of stuff. He mashes the gas and they head back downhill.

Guy turns the radio on again. Still dead air on every channel; even the Nashville warning has shut off. "Scan through them," he says, glancing over at Lisa, and when he turns back, a dump truck has pulled across the road a hundred yards ahead of him. He slams the brakes and the car skids and he slings forward into the seatbelt. It presses into his chest and he can't breathe for a second, and there's a yelp and a thump as Jemi is flung forward into the back of his seat. They come to a stop fifty feet from the truck.

"Shit," Lisa says. "Oh shit. Go around."

The dump truck is a behemoth in front of them, taking up half the road, and already the Minuteman has gotten out of the driver's seat and leveled his gun at them. He looks young, hardly more than a teenager. Despite the cool air, he wears only a black wife beater that makes his slight frame seem even less substantial. He's no more than five foot three; the long hunting rifle he carries seems bigger than him, and he holds it awkwardly, out away from his body, as if he's shielding himself from Guy and Lisa. He stops a few feet in front of the car, off to the driver's side, and points the gun at Guy. "Hands up!" he says.

Guy puts his palms flat against the ceiling of the car. Lisa does the same.

The Minuteman lowers the gun to a ready position and walks to the driver's side. Guy rolls down the window and the Minuteman peers inside. "Ha!" he says. "Mr. G!"

The kid is grinning at him. He's got gold hoop earrings in each ear; his bald head is flat—the baldness doesn't suit it well at all. The eyes are blue and familiar. Guy blinks at him and smiles and pushes names and faces around in his head until they match up, until the memory clicks into place in the front of his brain. "TJ?"

"Took you half the year to remember not to call me Timothy," TJ says, laughing.

"Yeah. Well, it's on the roll, you know." Guy tries to place this kid in the huge army of students that have come through his class. He feels like it's been a few years since he's seen the boy. Like TJ should be in college right now. TJ is grinning at him still, but the smile is fading. Guy tries to remember something about him. "Still running cross country?" he says. This feels right. *Please let this be right.*

TJ smiles bigger again, and Guy breathes a sigh of relief. "Nah," TJ says. "I had to cut it out. I wasn't any good anyway. Could never get my miles below six minutes." He lowers the rifle, rests the tip of the barrel on the ground, the stock hanging casually from his right hand. He puts his left hand on the door. "You still teaching?"

Guy adjusts his weight, feeling the pressure of the pistol against his lower back. "Yeah."

"You were pretty good, I remember. Not that I cared that much about books."

"Most of the students don't. But I try."

Jemi stands in the back seat wagging her tail. She sticks her face up and out the driver's side window, jamming herself between Guy and TJ

"Hey there, puppy," TJ says. He leans toward the car and scratches Jemi on the head, and that's when he notices the shotgun on the dashboard. His smile disappears. "What you doing with that?"

Guy shrugs. "Protection?"

"You better give that to me."

Guy reaches for the shotgun.

"Slowly," TJ says.

Guy carefully takes the gun by the barrel. He slides it across the dash until TJ can reach it. TJ pulls it through the window and tosses it onto the grass on the other side of the road. The smile returns to his lips and he begins to pet the dog again. He smiles at Lisa. "This your wife?" Guy nods. "You talked about her a lot," TJ says. "She *is* pretty."

"Thanks," Guy says. The car is still on. He looks at the dump truck in front of him, at the rifle in TJ's hand. He tries to decide if he can gun it and get around the truck before TJ can shoot him. He tries to decide if TJ *will* shoot him.

"I'm TJ." TJ sticks his hand out to Lisa, right in front of Guy's face.

Lisa shakes it. "Lisa," she says.

TJ leans forward even more, his whole forearm resting on the door to the car. He puts his right hand and the rifle on the roof. "So let me ask you," TJ says. "What the hell are you doing still in town?"

"We didn't know we were supposed to leave," Guy says.

"Haw haw. We made the announcement a day and a half ago."

"We didn't get it. No phones, remember?"

"Yeah, we figured the phones would go out. But things worked out even better than we thought they would." TJ rocks the gun in his hand, the barrel and the butt of the rifle alternately knocking on opposite sides of the roof. "*Everything's* out! It's crazy!"

"Yeah, like the Dark Ages," Guy says, and he remembers what Lisa had said a few nights ago, about everything being out for good.

It sounded so crazy then. Guy looks at TJ, searches his eyes. "We're leaving now," he says. "We're getting out of here as fast as we can."

"Where you going?"

"Atlanta?"

TJ nods. He looks down the road, off toward the horizon. "Yeah, Atlanta's okay. We're leaving you the biggest cites. You can have Atlanta, Charlotte, New York. We'll take back the smaller cities, the towns, the countryside. They're the new colonies." He looks back at Guy, his face serious. "I'm supposed to kill you, you know."

Guy considers gunning it, taking his chances with the speed of the car and TJ's aim. He considers pulling the pistol from his waist-band, a race with TJ to see who can shoot first. Guy is stunned by his own thoughts. To shoot TJ—barely out of childhood, a kid who spent a year in the same classroom as Guy, goofing off with his friends in the back of the room. Were they in waiting, all those days, biding their time until this moment when one of them kills the other?

The revolver seems to smolder against his back, screaming for him to use it. Instead, he looks at TJ and says, "I wish you wouldn't."

TJ sticks out his tongue and pulls it back. He drums the gun on the roof some more. Then he says, "You were a cool enough teacher. A lot of the teachers were real dicks. And you were a dick sometimes, but not as bad as most of them." He steps back from the car, puts the butt of the gun on the ground and leans forward with both hands on the barrel, Daniel-Boone style. "Go on to Atlanta. I'll pretend I didn't see you."

"Thanks, TJ."

Lisa leans across the center console. "Thank you so much," she says.

"Hey," TJ says as Guy puts the car in gear. "I'm not the only one out here, you know, so I can't say you're not going to run into anybody else." He picks the gun up and gathers Guy's shotgun from the grass; then he starts to walk back to the truck. "They aren't going to let you go," he yells back at them. He gets in the truck and backs it out of the way. He waves to them as they pull past him, and then Guy presses the gas hard and speeds toward the interstate.

TWINS

THE ON-RAMP TO THE INTERSTATE FEELS LIKE A launchpad. Guy floors it and the acceleration pushes him back into his chair as the Toyota revs up to seventy, eighty, ninety miles per hour. The concrete median is a gray blur to his left while the trees form an indistinct green rush to his right.

He's breathing fast. The pistol feels alive in his waistband, like it's glowing and pulsing with warmth. This pistol he almost used to kill his student. A boy. No different than any other.

"Not so fast," Lisa says.

No different than Stephen Vincent Marquette.

The clouds are clearing, and the road is empty and broad and stretches out straight for miles in front of them under a sky pale as melt water. They're over a hundred now and still accelerating. The little car wobbles slightly and the wind is a roar around them.

"Guy."

At 115, the car's governor kicks in. The engine sighs and the car slows. Guy mashes the gas pedal, but nothing happens. When the speedometer reaches one hundred, the car gives control back to Guy. He begins to speed up, but he feels Lisa looking at him, so he takes a deep breath and slows to eighty. He drives in a daze, his brain spinning over the shootings at the apartment, over the flight from the city, the encounter with TJ. What happened to that kid? He was normal. Tame. What sickness has he bought into that he's shaved his head and taken up a gun? What would TJ have done to him if they hadn't known one another? He knows the answer: Exactly what they did to Ronald. What they'd do to anyone.

What they'd do to Heather. She fills his head as she recedes behind him at eighty miles per hour. The Minutemen are sweeping in on her, and Guy is fleeing.

No, he thinks. *She's not there. She's at her parents'.*

Jemi groans and lies down in the back, settling in for a long trip. Lisa is talking beside him. He hears snatches of the one-sided conversation. She's speculating about how far the gas will get them and tossing around ideas about what to do when they run out. She's sorting through her ideas, thinking out loud. She does this sometimes, and Guy knows that she doesn't want an answer out of him. She doesn't want him to try to fix things. She just wants him to listen, and for now, that suits him just fine.

He can't stop seeing Heather; it's like he's stared at a bright image of her too long and her shape is burned into his irises. She's in the trees, the sky, the black asphalt that stretches out ahead of them. And it's not just her: Guy sees her and the Minutemen, their bald heads surrounding her, their greedy hands pulling her apart. The farther they drive, the stronger the images get. It's like there's a rubber band connecting him to Heather, and the more he stretches it, the more she pulls back.

He's got to go back.

He can't go back.

He's got to go back—how far can the band stretch before it breaks?

Guy's skin is hot. He feels like he's going to puke.

He hits the brakes and they come to a stop in the middle of the interstate. The engine rumbles softly, but that's the only sound, and the quiet is startling after the constant roar of the tires on the asphalt and the wind ripping at the doors.

"What are you doing?" Lisa says.

Guy looks up at the ember, which somehow seems to be glowing with scorn. He imagines a child's drawing of the sun, bright and yellow and smiling in a Crayola-blue sky. The ember doesn't smile. The ember is colored with a dusty crayon that's been hidden under a sofa cushion for three years. Its mouth is curled into a scowl, its eyebrows downturned and angry; the sky in which it lives is the washed-out blue of a t-shirt worn by a skeleton found wasted in the desert.

"We shouldn't stop," Lisa says.

A minivan flies past them, the driver laying on the horn the entire way. It's the first other car they've seen.

"We've got to go back," Guy says. The concrete median is gone here, and he begins to pull through the grass between the lanes. The dog is on her feet again, looking out the window, tail slamming up against everything.

"What?" Lisa says. "No fucking way."

"We have to. I have to check something."

"What?"

"It's…" Guy doesn't know what to tell her. What if he tells her that he's going back for Heather, but it turns out she's not even there? He's spilled the secret for nothing. If she's gone—and she's gone, she must be—he can come up with some other excuse and move on. He'll have plenty of time to make something up. For now, though, there's no time. He drives.

"It's what?" Lisa is on her knees in the seat. "Turn around. You turn this car around right now."

"Just give me a minute. Just a minute," Guy says, gripping the wheel. Heather lives just off the interstate. He can be outside of her house in five minutes. He can see if her car is in the driveway and move on; they'll be right back here on the interstate in ten minutes. Lisa can wait ten minutes.

She keeps talking as they head down the off-ramp. "There could be more of them. They're not going to let us go like TJ did. If you get us killed, I swear to god, I will never forgive you."

She's right—there could be more Minutemen. He takes the pistol out of his waistband and looks at the cylinder, at the brassy, flat ass-ends of the bullets. He considers stopping to get the AR-15 out of the trunk, but that will take too much time, and it will look like he's preparing for battle. Lisa will want to know why.

"Turn around," Lisa says. "Turn around or let me out."

"Lisa, can you just shut up? Just shut up for a minute and let me think?"

She scoffs. He feels her eyes on him, her expression some mix of anger and bewilderment. She crosses her arms and sits back in the chair. A stony silence fills the car.

The roads are empty as he pulls into Heather's neighborhood. There are no cars in the driveways, and the windows of the houses are covered with blinds and curtains. The place has the air of a ghost town, a stillness that envelops everything. The wind is blowing softly, and an empty water bottle rolls down the street. Guy drives slowly, looking down the side streets as he passes them.

"You know somebody here?" Lisa says.

Guy cranes his neck and looks down an alley. He watches the road behind him in the rearview mirror. Jemi sits and looks out the window. There is nothing to see, no life anywhere. Guy barely touches the accelerator as he tries to keep the car as quiet as possible.

"I've never been in this neighborhood. You have friends here? Students?"

Students. That will work. He can tell her that some favorite student of his lives here, and he ran into that student the other day at the police station. Some boy—it's a male student in this lie—whose parents were out of town. He seemed so scared.

"Guy." Accusation is creeping into her voice. "Who lives here?"

He's still working out the details of his story as he makes the turn onto the side street that Heather's house is on, and what he sees in that instant flushes the lie out the back end of his skull.

There are two vehicles on the street. One is Heather's car; her stupid little green bug is not at her parents' house, not even on the highway—it's sitting in her driveway at the end of the road.

The other is a pickup truck full of stuff. It's parked on the side of the road fifty yards away, facing the opposite direction, and two

Minutemen are loading a flat-screen TV into the bed. They turn in unison at the sound of the car. They're like reflections of each other, two shadows of the same person cast by streetlights onto the pavement at night. Same height, same build, same face. They must be twins.

"Shit," Lisa says. "I told you."

One of the Minutemen reaches into the bed of the truck and retrieves a hunting rifle. He steps into the road and levels it at the car.

The bullet hits an instant before the bellow of the rifle thunders in his ears. It punches a clean hole in the windshield between Guy and Lisa. He looks at his wife; she's okay. The dog looks frantic and off balance in the back seat, but she too is unharmed. "Get down," Guy says, and he floors it. The engine whines as the car flies forward. Lisa cowers in the seat, her hands over her head, and Guy ducks too, but he can see the men over the top of the steering wheel. One twin is running onto the grass of the nearest lawn. The other, the one with the gun, is working the bolt, feeding another bullet into the chamber.

Then everything happens in an instant. The Minuteman raises the gun and aims it at the car, and he's looking straight into Guy's eyes as the distance between them whittles away, and the Minuteman's eyes go huge as he realizes he's out of time. He tries to jump to the side, but Guy hits him, and his body crashes into the windshield and smashes it into a starburst of glass and blood. The airbags in the Toyota explode and Guy and Lisa are buried in them. There's a horrible *thunk thunk* as the Minuteman rolls over the roof. Guy hits the brakes and the car stops. The air is full of white smoke and smells like burning baby powder. The airbags are deflating and bright lights swim and flash across Guy's vision.

He hears a cry behind him. "Tucker! Oh no. Oh no! Tucker!"

Guy blinks and wipes his eyes. He looks in the rearview mirror and sees the other twin crouching over Tucker's body. The twin has his brother's face in his hands; he pushes the blood-matted hair away from his eyes.

"No, no, no. Please god no."

The Minuteman is crying, mourning there in the middle of the street.

"Kill the other one," Lisa says.

Jemi is barking, an ear-splitting yelp that fills up the car. "Shut up!" Guy says. He looks at Lisa. She has a small cut on her cheek. It looks cool, he thinks, and then he feels ridiculous for thinking it. He looks into her eyes. They are alive with a cold energy. Guy says, "Do what?"

"You have to kill the other one. He's got a gun too. You have to kill him now."

Inside of him is pain and terror and sorrow, but swimming around on top of all that is a crazy burning lust, and he grabs a fistful of Lisa's hair and pulls her toward him and kisses her hard on the mouth. Her kiss is wet and slippery and tastes of blood and sweat.

He pulls away and her eyes are full of indignant fury. "Do it," she says.

Guy roots around on the floor of the car and finds the pistol. He opens the door and climbs out from underneath the airbag. The twins are ten yards behind the car, the living one sobbing over the body of the dead one. Guy raises the gun and pulls the trigger.

The report is sharp and loud in his ears. The gun is so light that it kicks wildly in his hand; he nearly loses his grip. He doesn't know where the bullet goes, but it doesn't hit the Minuteman.

"Shit!" the Minuteman yells, leaping to his feet.

Guy steps forward and fires again. Another miss. The Minuteman starts running toward the pickup. He's scrambling with a pistol that he has jammed into the front of his pants. Guy stands still and aims carefully; this time, when he pulls the trigger, the Minuteman falls as the bullet shatters his knee. He screams and rolls onto his back, still fumbling for the gun. Guy runs forward, pistol raised, and he realizes that he's screaming too, some wordless primal howl that writhes up out of his heart and his spine and his balls and flares into the pastel emberlight. The Minuteman's face is flush with terror. He pulls the gun and points it at Guy, but it's too late. Guy is above him.

Guy shoots him in the center of the chest.

It's like the Minuteman has been crushed by an invisible weight. He breathes once and is still.

Guy looks down at him and catches his breath. "I got him," he says. He feels that same elation he felt before, the impossible thrill that comes with standing on the edge of life and death and coming up on the side of life while the other man comes up death. He feels a rush of history and ancestry, and in that instant, he's certain that in his past lives he was a gladiator, he was a knight, he was a warrior swinging a blood-soaked battle axe in horrible arcs and crushing his enemies, filling them with mortal dread. He was powerful, the stuff of nightmares.

He tucks the gun into his pants. He looks back to the car, and Lisa is watching him, nodding her head.

And behind her, running across the lawns and yelling his name, is Heather.

HER

HEATHER RUNS RIGHT PAST GUY'S WRECKED TOYOTA, right past his barking dog and his wife. It's like she doesn't even know they're there. She's wearing teal sneakers and a pink ski parka. Her hair is loose and curly, and it blows out around her and above her and makes a kind of fiery halo around her head. She stops in front of Guy, and he can see that she's crying. Her face is as red as her hair.

"Oh my god," she says.

"Okay," Guy says. "Listen."

She takes his face in her hands and looks up at him with wide wild eyes, and she says a million things at once: "They were here and I saw them out here and I didn't know what to do, and I tried to call you but there was nothing, no phones or anything, and I was going to run or get in the car but they'd see me, and I don't know what they want, and I am so stupid I should have left but I didn't and I needed you and you weren't here but I wanted you to come and I knew you would, and you came! You're here!" She tries to pull his face to hers so she can kiss him.

"Not now."

Her eyes darken. She's breathing heavily, rapidly, and she takes a few deep breaths and bites her lip.

"We have to go," Guy says. She keeps looking at him with that sad look. "Get in the car." Guy feels like he's talking to the dog. "Get in the car!"

She turns and looks at the car, at Lisa. "Why is she here?" Heather says. "You came back for me."

"We don't have time for this," Guy says.

"I'm not going anywhere with her."

"God fucking damn it, Heather." He leaves her and heads to the car, and now, for the first time, he sees Lisa. She stands beside the car, her arms crossed. The look on her face is impossible to decipher. It's not anger or surprise, and it's not sadness. It's something closer to relief, but that's not it. She's looking into him with those eyes, those eyes like the shimmering reflection of a cliff face in a mountain tarn. Guy can't bring himself to meet her gaze.

He stops a few feet away from her. He can still smell the charred-chemical smell of the airbags.

"This is her?" Lisa says.

Now Guy forces himself to look at her, and she's shaking her head, and Guy can read the emotion on her: it's pity. She feels pity for Guy. She knew that there was someone else out there, and now that she sees that it's Heather—dumb, pudgy Heather, the shooting star that flamed out in high school—she feels sorry for him, embarrassed. Guy is embarrassed too. "You knew?"

"I'm not an idiot, Guy."

"How?"

"Does it matter?"

Jemi is staring at him through the window of the back seat. Her breath fogs up the glass. Guy wants to climb in there with her and pet her and let her breathe her stupid dog breath all over him. Jemi doesn't care who he fucks. Instead, he says to Lisa, "What now?"

She looks at Heather, who's still standing where Guy left her. Heather's got her face scrunched up and is trying her best to look forlorn. "You and I leave," Lisa says to Guy.

"We can't leave her."

"How did you think this was going to work out, Guy?"

"I don't know." He's beginning to feel antsy, like other Minutemen might be on their way. He looks up and down the street. The bodies of the twins bleed onto the asphalt. Otherwise, everything is still.

"Did you think we were going on a road trip? All three of us?"

Heather has taken a few steps toward them now. "I'm not riding anywhere with her," she says, glaring at Lisa.

"Are you kidding?" Guy says. "You don't even know her!"

"I know enough."

Lisa laughs. "Fine," she says. "You two go." She walks up the road, past Heather, to the Minuteman that Guy shot. She picks up his pistol and continues walking up the street.

"Come on, Lisa," Guy says.

She keeps walking.

Heather trots over to Guy and tries to kiss him again. "Leave her," she whispers.

Guy pushes her away. "Lisa!" She ignores him, so Guy lets out a string of curses under his breath and heads back to the driver's side of the Toyota. He looks inside. The car is a mess; the windshield is mashed to the point that it's hard to see through, and the deflated airbags take up half of the front seat. He surveys the front of the car, where the grill and the hood are heavily damaged.

"Can we still drive it?" Heather says. She's practically breathing over his shoulder.

"No." He lets Jemi out of the car and she bounces around in the road for a minute before running onto a lawn to pee. "Go get your car."

Heather looks at Jemi and then up the road at her bug. "The dog can't get in my car."

"Are you being serious right now?"

"She'll slobber all over everything."

"Really, Heather?" Guy jogs to the Minutemen's truck. It's a pickup, small and new. The inside smells like leather. The keys dangle from the ignition. "Get in," he says to Heather. He walks to the back of the truck and begins to clear out all of the useless shit: the TVs, the DVD players and computers, the bags of silverware and jewelry. All this stuff that people saved for, bought, bragged about—it all crashes spectacularly on the asphalt.

"Jemi!" he says. The dog is sniffing around the body of the twin that Guy ran over. She's licking at the blood that trickles out of him and snakes its way toward the gutters.

"Are we leaving?" Heather says. She's beside the truck now; she's got the door open and the truck is making that *bing bing* sound.

Guy breathes deep. "Yeah," he says. "Yeah, let's go." He calls to the dog, and she hops into the space that he's cleared in the bed of the truck. He shuts the tailgate and climbs into the driver's seat and starts the engine. The truck growls with a voice much lower, much meaner than the little Toyota's.

The Toyota. He pulls the truck up beside the car then gets out and pops the Toyota's trunk. He unloads all of the food and other supplies and tosses them into the truck bed. He grabs the shotgun shells and slips the AR-15 behind the front seats. He gathers up Lisa's Africa shit and sets it gently on the floor at Heather's feet. Then he gets back behind the wheel and makes a U-turn and accelerates out of the neighborhood.

Heather is grinning beside him. "Where are we going?" she says, and from the way she says it, Guy can tell she's picturing some fairytale, she and Guy driving that truck off to Fiji or something and living out their lives together on a jungle-lined beach.

Maybe there's some part of him that wants this too. That life would be easy, happy. Each day would be a guilty pleasure. Carefree. Meaningless. "We're going to get Lisa," Guy says.

"Oh." She deflates beside him.

They turn the corner and Lisa is fifty yards ahead of them. She walks down the center of the road, the pistol dangling loosely from her hand. She looks like a cowboy walking into the sunset, an assassin sauntering away from a kill. Guy feels that lust again; all this time he thought that Heather looked like sex, but there's Lisa in front of him: a woman, sex incarnate. He's embarrassed of the child who sits beside him. He wants to kick Heather out, but he can't make himself do it. Despite his embarrassment, he can't shake that feeling he has for her, a feeling of protection, of responsibility, of love. "Don't say anything," he says to her.

She crosses her arms and stares down at the floor.

Guy pulls up beside Lisa and rolls the window down. She doesn't look at him; she keeps walking, her eyes off in the distance in front of her. Guy idles along at walking speed. "Let's go," he says.

Lisa continues to ignore him. Guy can hear Jemi's nails skittering around on the plastic liner of the truck bed. She's standing at the edge of the bed, looking out at Lisa. Her tail thumps on the back window of the cab. Lisa smiles at the dog. "Who's a good girl," she says. She pats Jemi on the head. "What a good dog."

"Come on, Lisa," Guy says. "This is stupid. Where are you even going to go?"

No answer.

"There's nowhere to go. Just come on."

She slows slightly, looks at him, stops. "You can't have both of us, Guy. That's not how it works."

Heather nods.

"I know that," Guy says. He knows the shit he's in. He knows that Lisa is going to rain hell down on him. He knows he'll have to abandon Heather. He'll have to forget her and try to piece together again the marriage that he spent fifteen years building just to smash against the wall. But those are problems for later. He checks the rearview mirror again. "Look. We need to get out of here. Just get in the truck, and we'll go to Atlanta. We'll figure everything out once we get there."

Lisa looks at Guy and then at Heather, then she looks up into the sky, up at the ember, which is dipping toward the horizon. The trees sway as the breeze speaks of evening.

"Let's just get to Atlanta," Guy says.

Lisa tucks the gun into her waistband. "Okay," she says. She opens the door and steps inside.

Heather scoots over on the bench seat and her shoulder presses against Guy. She's a human wall between him and Lisa. This is okay. Guy doesn't know what to say to his wife right now. Lisa shuts the door, and Guy presses the gas, and the three of them jet off toward the interstate.

ROADBLOCK

THEY DRIVE IN SILENCE, BECAUSE WHAT COULD THEY possibly say to each other? There are fights to come, Guy knows this. He's already dreading the conversations: the disappointment from Lisa, the resentment from Heather. He wishes he could have forgotten about Heather, left her in her house and taken off to Atlanta without her, but his guts wouldn't let him; the guilt wracked him and tore up his insides.

And he never could have left Lisa walking alone down that road. Lisa, his wife.

Heather takes her phone from her pocket and tries to send a text. It goes nowhere. She huffs in frustration and puts it away.

Lisa is on the other side of her, her chin resting in her hand as she looks out the window at the trees that fly by. They're going eighty on the interstate again. Jemi is hunkered down in the bed of the pickup. They see few other cars. Those that they do see are loaded down with families and supplies; the passengers wear the worried faces of those who've waited too late.

The ember is sinking toward the horizon. The sky turns glossy and the west begins to fill in with sulfurous yellow. It will be dark in an hour. Guy looks at the gas gauge; they have less than a quarter of a tank left. "We're getting low on gas," he says.

Heather starts to freak out. "Oh my god. What are we going to do? We're out here in the middle of nowhere!"

Lisa sighs.

"We'll find some," Guy says. They've been driving for a little over an hour, and they're nearing the Georgia state line. The fingers of Lake Hartwell stretch out on either side of them as they cross a bridge. "There'll be a pump on somewhere, or we'll siphon some, or, or…" He stops talking as he crests a hill. Ahead of them, a mile or so down the interstate, he can see something blocking the bridge that spans the main part of the lake and separates South Carolina from Georgia. A mass of color and movement. "Shit."

"What?" Heather says. She's looking down the road. "What is it?"

They pull over, and Guy maneuvers them as close to the trees as he can. He cuts the engine. Things are quiet now, and he can hear Jemi pacing in the bed.

Lisa gets out of the car and opens the tailgate to let Jemi out. "You got to pee?" she says. Jemi hops down and pees in the grass, and then she starts tromping around in the woods, sniffing whatever's rotting on the ground back there. Guy gets out and stands next to Lisa. She keeps looking at the dog. "Good girl," Lisa says. Now she turns to Guy. "What's happening?"

"I don't know," Guy says. "There's something going on down there. Something's blocking the road."

Lisa nods and sits down in the grass. Jemi comes out of the woods and trots over to her and buries her snout in Lisa's stomach as Lisa scratches her behind the ears. "What a good girl," she says.

Guy stands in the road and looks down at the bridge. There are several cars lined up on the road; it looks like there's a traffic jam on the bridge, but he can't tell what's causing it. The air around him is growing colder as the ember stretches the shadows of the pines. Guy reaches into one of their bags and pulls out a beanie and slips it over his head. He listens to the sound of the wind in the trees and tries to make out the roadblock. Why didn't he bring binoculars? Why doesn't he *own* binoculars?

Then he remembers. He opens the truck and takes the AR-15 out from behind the seats.

"What are you doing?" Heather says. "Is someone coming?"

Guy ignores her. He leans against the truck to steady himself and looks down at the bridge through the rifle's scope. The bridge and the cars pop into view, magnified ten times or so. There are a dozen cars down there, along with a few large pickup trucks. Concrete barricades span most of the bridge. In the middle of the road is a group of people, their hands on top of their heads. Pacing among them are Minutemen—five, six, it's hard to count—and they carry rifles and handguns. They are yelling, pointing, but their voices vanish before they reach Guy at the top of the hill.

As Guy watches, two of the Minutemen drag a man away from the group. He's a big guy, taller than the Minutemen who hold him, and he's struggling against them. He breaks free of their grasp, punches one, tries to run. He makes it a few feet before a Minuteman raises his rifle and shoots him in the back, the muzzle flashing silent through the scope of Guy's rifle.

A moment later, the report rolls over the top of the hill. Lisa and Heather turn their heads toward the sound of the gunshot.

"We waited too late, didn't we?" Lisa says.

"I don't know," Guy says. He shakes his head. "No. No, we'll figure it out."

They head back up the interstate and turn at the first exit they come to. The ember is almost down, and they're nearly out of gas; trying to figure out what to do about the roadblock tonight seems pointless. Guy is hoping for a working gas station, for an open hotel, and for the Minutemen to be gone in the morning. If he gets even one of those, he'll consider himself lucky.

He's never believed in luck. Sometimes good stuff happens, and sometimes shit happens—it's all random. Still, he can't help but feel that the scales that the world rests on must be slowly tilting against him. How did he kill Skinny, and Muscles, and the twins? Skinny opens the door from a different position, and Guy misses him. Muscles enters the living room instead of the bathroom and Guy is crumpled on the floor of his condo. The twin gets that second shot off. All of these things *feel* like luck, luck that has come up on Guy's side four times in a row. The dice can't keep coming up in Guy's favor forever. He's terrified that at some point his luck—or whatever he has since there is no such thing as luck—is going to run out.

The businesses around the exit are empty and dark. The neon lights of the gas stations and restaurants sit dead in the twilight. There are no cars anywhere; everyone has gotten the hell out of Dodge.

Guy pulls into a hotel and tries the door; it's locked, and it's dark inside. The hotel and everything around it seem like they've been shut down for years. He kicks the door and it makes a cracking sound. He takes the AR-15 and hits the door with the butt of the gun until the glass shatters; then he reaches inside and unlocks the door. Funny—the power's been out for less than a week, and it already feels like the law is meaningless. Anarchy rules the darkened country.

The motel lobby is empty and smells like pine air fresheners. Behind the desk, he searches for keys, but all he finds is a drawer full of unlabeled keycards. He slams the drawer shut. There is a map of the area pinned to a corkboard on the wall. Guy pull it down and takes it with him to the truck.

The next motel they break into is older; it has real, metal keys. He takes two for adjacent rooms and pulls the car around to the back side of the building. They all get out and stand in the parking lot as the last of the emberlight fades from the horizon. The wind is blowing stronger now, making it feel like early winter.

Guy opens a room. "You stay in this one," he says to Heather. "Don't unlock the door until morning."

Lisa laughs. "You think you're staying with me?"

"You *want* me to stay with Heather?"

"Heather," Lisa says. "That sounds about right. Heather or Alexis or Misty or something like that. That's what I figured."

She doesn't know Heather's name. They've been sitting next to each other for two hours, and she doesn't know her name. He wonders if he should have introduced them. What's the etiquette on that?

"Just get your own room," Lisa says. She takes a key from Guy and unlocks the door. "Come on, pup," she says, and Jemi jumps out of the truck and follows her inside. Lisa shuts the door behind her, and then there's the shifting metal sound of the locks sliding shut.

"Just me and you," Heather says. She smiles at him.

Guy closes his eyes, rubs them with his thumb and forefinger. Then he walks past Heather, back to the office, and grabs a third key.

Guy dozes, and when he starts awake, he's out of breath and covered in sweat. The room is pitch black. He feels nauseated, and he stumbles to the bathroom and vomits into the toilet. Now that he's exposed to the air, the sweat seems to turn to ice on his skin.

Guy flushes the toilet. The water goes down and doesn't refill.

Flashes of a dream come back to him. A shirtless Stephen Vincent Marquette, his skinny body perforated, foamy blood spuming through the holes. Muscles piecing his head together with a hot-glue gun. Snowflakes drifting lazily from the gray sky and settling in the twins' frozen eyes.

He has left a trail of death in his wake. There are two bodies lying in the road that, just a few hours ago, were both men. Two more bodies in his apartment. All are probably already entering the early stages of decomposition.

He has killed four men. For thirty-nine years, Guy had never even thought seriously of killing a person. He'd never thought himself capable of it. He could not have been a soldier or a cop or a criminal. He was boring, and death was something that waited at the end of a long, happy life. It was not something that threatened him, and it certainly wasn't something that he would deliver.

Now he's a killer. He wonders if this is murder. This is homicide, yes—the killing of a man is homicide. But is it murder? Did he *have* to kill these men?

Yes, he thinks. Skinny would have killed him if he hadn't beaten him to the punch. Muscles would have shot him dead in the bathroom. The twin with the rifle had already tried, and only his bad aim separated a dead Guy and a living one.

But his brother, the other twin: did he have to kill him? Guy pictures him there, crying over his dead brother. He wonders if that man would have just run away. Was he a killer too, or was he simply doing his job? What went through his mind as Guy charged at him, screaming like a maniac, the pistol in his hand belching fire and death?

There's another voice inside of Guy, one he is scared to acknowledge. It's a voice that says, *Yes. I am fire and death, and they fell before me.*

Guy pushes the thought away and returns to bed. He listens to the wall behind him; he tries to hear Lisa moving around, but there's nothing, just the dull emptiness of the nighttime air. There are no cars droning on the interstate, and there's no hum from electric lights. The silence is complete.

After a while, there's a timid knock at the door. He opens it and Heather is there, smiling up at him. She says, "Thank you for coming back for me."

"I couldn't just leave you."

"I knew you wouldn't." She walks past him and sits down on the bed.

Guy stands in the doorway. He can hear a faint *thump thump* from next door; it must be Jemi's tail, wagging and smacking against the wall.

"Come here," Heather says.

He approaches, and she puts her hand on his chest. She lifts his shirt and kisses his stomach, begins to unbutton his jeans. Guy steps away. "I don't feel like it tonight, Heather."

"Why not?"

"I'm just not in the mood." He gets up and looks out the window at the pickup truck. He locked most of their supplies in the cab; should he have brought them inside?

"You don't have to do anything," Heather says. "I can do it for you."

He turns to her. She has taken her shirt off, and she's leaning back on the pillows with a wicked smile on her face. She twists a nipple between her fingers.

"I killed a bunch of people today," Guy says. "And Lisa's right next door."

She frowns and puts her shirt back on. "Can we just talk then? We really need to talk about something."

"I don't feel like talking." He realizes that he's glaring at her. Guy feels guilty; he feels mean. He doesn't want to treat her like this. He wants to apologize, but the words won't come out.

She narrows her eyes and gets up, walks past him into the cold night. She stomps past Lisa's room to her own and slams the door behind her.

Guy sighs and steps outside. He doesn't have his jacket, and the chill cuts right into him. The concrete feels like ice under his bare feet. It's dark everywhere, and the stars spread out above him in all their millions. He can see the Milky Way, a streak of dust spilled across a black blanket.

He knocks on Lisa's door. He hears Jemi leaping around in excitement, and then the door opens and Lisa is there, a starlit ghost in the dark. She steps aside and lets him in, and he sits down on the bed. She closes the door behind her. Guy scratches Jemi's chest, and then the dog walks to the corner and turns around a few times and flops down to sleep.

Lisa stands in front of the window. She's silhouetted by the stars, a blacker figure in front of the black night.

"I'm sorry," Guy says to her.

"I know you are."

"I didn't mean for it to happen. It just. It just did."

She doesn't say anything. She crosses the room and sits down on the bed beside him.

"You knew about her?" Guy says.

Lisa sighs. "Not her specifically. But I knew there was someone. There had to be someone."

"How?"

"You're not a good liar." He can feel her smirking in the darkness. "'What did you do all afternoon, Guy?' 'Oh, I went for a run.'" Now she laughs out loud. "If you ran as much as you say you did, you'd be a fucking Olympian."

Guy laughs now too. He puts his hand on her leg, and she doesn't pull it away. "You're not mad?"

"Of course I'm mad. I'm mad, and I'm sad. But I'm an adult, Guy. I'm an adult, and you're a man, and this kind of thing happens. It happens to men and women both."

He feels tight inside when she says this. Men and women *both*? He finds himself shuffling through every man he's ever met, putting each in bed beside his wife. *What is she talking about?* But he doesn't push it, doesn't question it. Not now. The mood is shifting in the room, and he feels them drawing toward reconciliation. He doesn't want to ruin it. He'll ask her later.

"But you can't have both of us," Lisa says.

Guy nods.

"So who is it?"

"You know it's you." He squeezes her leg.

She puts her hand on top of his. "We ditch her in Atlanta then."

"Okay." He doesn't know how he's going to do that. He doesn't know if he's capable of that. But Atlanta's a day away, and he can worry about Heather when he gets there. One woman at a time. Tonight is for Lisa.

She stands in front of him. "You listen to me, though," Lisa says.

She pushes him onto his back and takes his pants off. He watches as she slides out of her own. Guy can barely make her out: the curve of her hip, the graceful outline of her face, her hair like the memory of sunlight. Her hands are electric on his skin, and thoughts of Heather, thoughts of the Minutemen, vanish in an instant as he's wrapped up in her.

"You're mine," she says as she climbs on top of him. "You're mine, and she's nothing." She leans forward, her hands on the bed, her face close to his. "That's the way it's going to be."

Her skin is taut and warm on her body and she moves on top of him and the pleasure is overwhelming. Guy rocks with her. He tries to put his hands on her hips, but she pulls them away and pins them against the bed.

"Say it," she says.

"I'm yours," Guy says.

"And her?"

"She's nothing."

Lisa sits up tall, and her eyes spark in the starlight. She says, "You're god damn right."

✳ ✳ ✳

When they're done, Guy pulls back the covers and starts to climb beneath them.

"You don't get to sleep in here," Lisa says.

"What? Why not?"

"You don't get off that easy." Her voice hovers somewhere between teasing and furious.

Guy stands up, naked in the cold room. He feels goosebumps on his thighs as he begins to gather up his clothes. He tries to make out her face in the dark, but the blackness is too complete; she's a shadow amongst other shadows. He can't figure her out—she's all over the place. She's pissed, she's jaded, she's horny, she wants to be alone. She hasn't been like this since Malawi; in those first few months after their training, she was a different woman.

Tonight, Guy doesn't know whether to be angry or grateful. He doesn't know what to say, so he doesn't say anything at all. He gets dressed and pats the sleeping dog on the head and goes outside.

It's colder than before. The moon and the stars have spun overhead and the sky looks different, unfamiliar. He wonders what the sky looks like on the other side of the world, on the bottom half of the globe where they live beneath a different sky. He'd always wanted to go to Australia, to lie in the yellow-brown Outback earth beneath the shadow of Ayers Rock. He wanted to hike the rugged spears of stone that jut from the ground in Patagonia. He and Lisa had planned to go, one day—one day that was always near enough to instill hope but too far away to seem real. A sadness slips over him now as he feels a certainty set in: he'll never see those places. They are too far away, and the world is different now. No matter how he tries to convince himself that the power outage is temporary, that the Minutemen are a passing inconvenience, something about all this feels permanent. There has been a shift in the way of the world; humanity has crested a mountain and has begun the long slide down its steep and rocky back.

Guy shivers. It's winter on the other half of the world. He tries to picture Cape Town or Melbourne covered in a foot of snow. How are they surviving? *Are* they surviving?

He goes back to his room, and the door is locked. The key is inside the room on the bedside table.

Guy stands barefoot in the cold and looks at the empty parking lot. He glances at Heather's door. She's not letting him in. Neither is Lisa. He wants to laugh: two women here, *his* women, yet he's gotten himself locked out of three different rooms. In some other world, this is the stuff of romantic comedies.

It's absurd. It feels like it ought to be funny. But it's not.

LUCK

THE MOTEL ROOM IN DAYLIGHT IS NAUSEATING; GUY can see now that the walls and the bedspread are a sickly shade of pink, like coughed-up lung, like exposed muscle.

He dresses and goes outside. It's shortly after dawn, and the ember has just crested the trees at the edge of the parking lot. The air is crisp and unsoiled. There are no cars, so there's no exhaust, no stirred-up dust, no noise. Birds are chirping somewhere.

Lisa is at the edge of the parking lot. She's talking to Jemi as the dog sniffs around in the grass. Lisa looks over in Guy's direction, and she waves to him. Guy waves back. He can see her face, a goldish pink in the morning emberglow. She's not smiling, but she's not scowling, either.

Guy knocks on Heather's door, and after a minute or so, she comes out. She *is* scowling. She walks past him without speaking and gets into the truck.

Guy loads everything back into the bed of the truck and slips the AR-15 behind the seats. He keeps his revolver—he has put all of the remaining bullets in it, leaving four shots—in his pants. Lisa still has her pistol. Guy locks the doors to the rooms and puts the keys back in the office. Why he does this, he doesn't know; maybe he's leaving it ready for the next desperate traveler. They leave the motel and turn back onto the interstate. This time, Lisa rides in the middle, close to Guy, and Heather sits on the far end of the bench.

He slows as they approach the hill before the bridge. He pulls over to the side of the road and gets out, taking the AR-15 with him. "I'm going to go check it out," he says to the women.

Heather looks at Lisa, and then she gets out of the truck. She sits down near the trees and stares off toward the ember. Lisa leans back on the bench and closes her eyes.

Guy sighs and sets out up the hill. He keeps close to the trees, crouching down, the AR-15 held at the ready. It feels exciting, sneaking along like this. It's like he's in a war movie, or like he's a hit man scouting out a target. It's very cool to have the rifle in his hands. The gun is an extra muscle that fills him with power. It's like a second cock.

I'm a bad motherfucker, he thinks. He understands now why men hoard guns, why they fight so hard for the right to keep them.

He reaches the top of the hill and looks down on the bridge. The roadblock is still there. The cars and the prisoners from the day before are gone, but the pickup trucks remain. A handful of Minutemen lean against one of the barricades. They are smoking, passing a Thermos back and forth.

Guy watches them through the scope, the crosshairs centered on the largest of the men. Even with the magnification, the man seems tiny, impossibly far away. Guy would have to get closer to shoot him. Get close enough and he could do it, if he had to.

But he couldn't get all of them. He'd never drop them all before they spotted him.

He returns to the truck and spreads the map out on the hood. Lisa gets out and stands beside him as he runs his finger along the shore of the lake. There's a small road that crosses it a few miles north, and a highway spans the lake near Clemson. Beyond that, the lake narrows but continues to stretch northward.

"How far can we get?" Lisa says.

"On the gas in the tank? Fifty miles at best." Jemi climbs from the cab and sniffs at his feet. "We've got to keep going, though. We need to get across the lake."

Heather stands up in the bed of the truck and looks down at them. "What are we doing?"

Guy ignores her, continues looking at the map.

"We need gas," Lisa says. She kneels and Jemi buries her head in Lisa's chest as Lisa scratches her neck. "That should be the priority."

"We'll get the gas. We'll get across the lake, and we'll find gas."

"And what if we run out before we get across?"

"We'll look for gas on the way," Guy says. "But we'll make it. Trust me."

Lisa sighs, shrugs.

They drive north. They follow the map, making their way down backwoods highways that are by now completely abandoned. Guy wonders if they are the only people still on the roads. If they are the only people who waited so long.

After a while, they come to a road that crosses Lake Hartwell. Guy pulls the truck to a stop and stares. The way is completely blocked by felled trees. Pines thicker than telephone poles are piled atop each other; the road is littered with branches and needles and sawdust. The air is thick with the sweet smell of sap.

"Why would they do this?" Heather asks.

"They're funneling us," Guy says. "They want us at those road blocks."

"Why?"

He doesn't answer. He doesn't know.

They continue north toward Clemson. The gas gauge reads empty now, but the truck is still running. Guy wonders how far below E that needle will go. They've passed several gas stations, but they are abandoned. One sports a hand-written sign: NO POWER. NO GAS.

"Guy," Lisa says. "The gas."

"I know. I know."

They pass through Clemson. It is as empty and quiet as everything else. They head back toward the lake and stop a half mile away, when they first see the bridge. Even from so far away, Guy can see that the way is blocked. Lisa shakes her head.

Guy gets out and walks farther up the road to where he can look with the AR-15. This roadblock is smaller. There are concrete barriers, a pickup truck, a Minuteman. One Minuteman. He sits on the hood of the truck. Guy can see him well enough through the scope to see his shirt, a Clemson football jersey with the number 10 on it. He's nodding his head rhythmically, and his mouth is moving. Guy squints, and he can see the flash of emberlight on the mp3 player in his hand. He's listening to music and singing along. Guy wonders how much battery he has left and where he's going to recharge it when he runs out. Are these the last songs he'll ever hear? Are they some of the last songs that *anyone* will ever hear? If they are, shouldn't he ration out that battery, save it for just the right moment?

He catches himself and reels his mind back in. *The power is out*, he thinks. *The world hasn't ended. It just feels like it has.*

Guy should be angry, or disappointed, or scared to see the Minuteman, but instead, he's excited. He wonders if this is what he wanted all along, if it's what that shadowy voice inside of him had been pushing him toward. He told himself that he wanted to find an empty road, a clear path across the lake. That way they could just cross the bridge and head on toward Georgia. They could find a working gas station, or at least an abandoned car they could siphon some gas from. They'd be in Atlanta by midday. They'd meet up with others and find out what was going on. They would move forward.

Instead, the Minuteman blocks the way, and Guy has to do something. They don't have the gas to keep wandering the back roads in hopes of circumnavigating the roadblocks. It's through him or nothing. Guy realizes that he's getting what he wanted. He didn't know he wanted it; he didn't want to want it. He wants it, though.

He gets to kill the Minuteman.

He's simultaneously proud and embarrassed of himself. Who is this man who *gets* to kill another man? Why is he aroused at the thought of it? How did that dark side of him so quickly push away the normal man he was yesterday? But he knows: today he holds a man's life in his hands. It is power overwhelming.

Guy lies down in the grass and tries to get into a prone firing

position. He has fired rifles before; when he was a kid, he had a
.22, and his dad would take him to the gun range to practice. Guy
would shoot at metal targets a hundred yards away. He'd pull the
trigger, and the crack of the gun would rock his ears, and a couple of
seconds later—time for the bullet to fly across the yellowing grass,
time for the sound to wave its way back to him—a metallic *ping*
would let him know the bullet had hit home.

That was a hundred yards. The Minuteman is half a mile away.
No chance, Guy thinks. He stands and resumes his crouch-walk along
the treeline. He slows as he gets closer, moves farther into the trees.
After ten minutes, he's near enough that each concrete barricade
is clearly distinguishable. He can see a mug in the Minuteman's
hand; he can read the number on his jersey. How far? Two hundred
yards? One-fifty?

Close enough, he thinks.

"If you can't hit him from here, you can't hit him at all."

Guy leaps a foot in the air at her voice. Lisa is behind him. She
stands behind a tree and peers down at the Minuteman. "Lisa," Guy
says. "You scared the shit out of me."

"Sorry," she says, but she says it in a way that makes it clear she's
not sorry.

"Why did you come down here?"

"I wanted to see."

He groans. "Where's—" He's thinking Heather, but he stops
himself. "Where's Jemi?"

"I shut her up in the truck."

Guy sighs and looks back down at the bridge. The Minuteman
has his headphones on again, and he leans against the grill of the
truck. He drums his palm on the hood in time with the music.
"Okay," Guy says. "Just get down."

She crouches behind the tree with her face sticking out. She
looks like a kid playing hide and seek.

Guy resumes his prone position. Now, the Minuteman fills the
scope. Guy sees him as clearly as if he was standing five feet away.
He's dark-skinned—Hispanic, maybe. He's got the shadow of a
mustache across his upper lip. His eyebrows are too thick; it's like
a fat black caterpillar is climbing across his forehead. His eyes are
closed, and he's singing along with the music again.

Guy breathes, and the crosshairs rise and fall.

He squeezes the trigger. The gun jerks against his shoulder, a subtle kick compared to the punch of the twelve-gauge. The report knocks against the water and echoes around them for what feels like forever.

"Did you get him?" Lisa whispers.

Guy finds the Minuteman in the scope again. He's still leaning against the truck, unharmed. He has a confused look on his face, though. He's taken the earbuds out of his ears and is looking around him.

"No," Guy says. "Hang on." He lines the crosshairs up in the center of the zero on the Minuteman's jersey and fires again.

Another kick. Another bang.

Guy looks through the scope. He has missed again. Why is he missing? He tries to add it up in his head—the rifle must be sighted too short for this; the crosshairs say he's lined up when the gun's really pointed at the ground in front of the Minuteman. Guy makes a mental note to adjust next time.

The Minuteman is scrambling around in a panic. He must have barely heard the first shot; he wasn't sure what it was behind the noise of his music. He heard this one, though. He takes out a pistol and crouches behind one of the concrete barricades, and Guy can't help but laugh.

The Minuteman is on the wrong side of the barricade. He heard the shot, knew what it was, but with all of the echoes, he couldn't tell where it came from. Now he peeks over the barricade and looks off to the west. Guy trains the rifle on the top of the Minuteman's head and fires.

This time he hits him. Guy finds him in the scope and watches as the Minuteman lurches toward the truck. He has blood near his hip on the right side; Guy can see it spreading and staining his jeans. A liver shot? The Minuteman opens the door to the truck and disappears for a moment. Then he stands up and lifts his gun in Guy's direction. He raises the pistol slowly, as though it weighs a million pounds. Guy prepares to shoot him again. Before either of them can shoot, the Minuteman collapses. He falls out of sight behind the barricade.

Guy feels the rush again. It's like someone has heated his blood and sped it up, and now liquid fire is jetting through his veins. "I got him," he says.

"Good shot," Lisa says. She's nodding again, like she was yesterday with the twins. Appraising him. Finding him worthy.

"That's right!" Guy says. He yells it. He pumps his fist on his chest. *Fuck luck*, he thinks. *I'm unstoppable.* He grabs Lisa, and he kisses her hard. She kisses back, kisses as though Heather never existed.

He steps away from her, jittery and elated. "Just try and stop us," he says. He looks down at the roadblock. There's no movement. He looks through the scope; a stream of blood is trickling between two of the barricades; it's where the Minuteman must have fallen. "I'm going to go move that truck. Wait here."

"Okay," Lisa says.

He starts to walk away.

"Guy."

He turns, looks at her. She's youthful and pure with the morning ember shining down on her. She's the woman she was when he met her, before Heather, before the doctor told her about her barren womb, before the long African summers.

"I love you," Lisa says. "I'm pissed as hell at you, but I still love you."

He grins. "Damn right you do."

He descends the hill with a bounce in his step. He walks in the center of the road, the gun at ready. He pauses every dozen yards or so, lifts the rifle and looks through the scope. Everything is empty; nothing changes except for the blood. The stream grows and pools between the barricades.

Soon he can hear the music. It's a tinny sound in the morning, just a warbling scratching coming from the earbuds where the Minuteman dropped them. Guy picks it up and puts a bud in his ear. It's Marvin Gaye. "Let's Get It On." He laughs out loud. *It's perfect*, he thinks. Maybe luck is real, and it all belongs to him. He turns the mP3 player off and slips it into his pocket. He hopes that it has plenty of battery left. He hopes it's full of beautiful music.

Guy looks over at the pool of blood. The truck is in front of him, then two barricades before the crack where the blood seeps through. Guy tries to picture the Minuteman lying behind the concrete; he imagines where his body would have to be for the blood to spill the way it has. The blueprint unfolds before him; he sees where the Minuteman will be lying, dead or near-death. He sees the bullet that will finish him off. This is the way it will be. It is the only way it would ever be, the way it has to be.

Guy raises the rifle and steps around the barricade. The blood is a broad, rusty pool on the asphalt. There are bloody footprints next to it.

There is no body.

Guy blinks. He licks his lips. Behind him, something clicks.

Shit, Guy thinks. He looks over his shoulder. The Minuteman is in the back of the pickup truck, the pistol rested on the edge of the bed.

Guy spins, the rifle at his shoulder, and the world turns and the horizon moves and the ember shines above him and glints on the water. The barrel of the AR-15 moves in a slow arc, painting a graceful path across the gunmetal surface of the lake and the million trees that radiate with their verdant life.

Kill him, he thinks. The barrel moves slowly, so slowly, as Guy turns to the Minuteman. *Kill him. Kill*

LISA

QUANTUM PHYSICS

IT SEEMED LIKE IT OUGHT TO BE LOUDER.

If this was the gunshot that killed her husband and tore her world in half, it should have been deafening, an ear-splitting roar that knocked down the forests and drained the lake and curled back the asphalt on the interstate.

Instead, it was a pop. Just *pop*. Guy was standing down there next to the truck, and he turned, then *pop*, and he fell as if he was a marionette and someone had cut the strings.

Now he's on the ground and he's not moving. Lisa closes her eyes and takes a deep breath and opens them again. He's still there. "No," she says. It's not a cry of anguish; it's a *no* of disbelief. It's a *no* of *That didn't just happen*. She waits for him to get up.

The ember on the water is like a trail of fire falling from a sparkler on the Fourth of July. Lisa has always loved the ember. Its muted warmth is quiet, subtle, far preferable to the gaudy brilliance of the sun. It's the sun late in its career, when it doesn't have to rely on flash and surprise to impress an audience. It can just *be*.

The only sound is the wind moving in the trees. Lisa waits. Guy doesn't get up.

"Fuck," she whispers. Her voice sounds foreign. It's high-pitched and weak. It's the voice of a girl. "Oh fuck."

Lisa has her pistol in the back of her pants. She takes it out and looks at it; it's a semi-automatic, probably a 9mm. It's smaller than the .45 that Chisulo had, the one that he taught her to fire out there amid the baobabs and the scrub grass of Malawi, but the design is the same. She checks that there is a bullet in the chamber. She flips the safety.

She trots along the tree line with the pistol in her hand. She watches Guy, waits for him to get up. He doesn't.

Lisa slows near the roadblock. She crouches near the trees, and then she dashes to the first barricade and ducks behind it. The Minuteman's blood is puddled a few feet from her. The ember's already drying it. It's baking into the asphalt and turning into flaked rust. Lisa steps over the blood and scoots to the barricade nearest the truck. She peeks around. She can see Guy's feet; they're pointed at weird angles: one is turned inward and down, as if in a ballet move. Guy's other leg is bent at the knee, so only his toe is touching the road, like he's begun to jump but hasn't quite left the ground.

His feet don't move.

Lisa stops looking at him. She can't think about him yet. She surveys the truck, its bed. Where is the Minuteman? She listens: no sound.

She steps around the barricade with the pistol raised. The road stretches off in front of her with the trees swaying gently on either side. Guy is there on the ground. She knows he's there, but she won't look directly at him. She's read about that quantum physics mindfuck with the dead cat in the box: the cat is either alive or dead, but until you solidify things by looking, it's both, and it's neither. Nothing is real unless you look at it and lock it down. Until then, every possibility is real at once.

So Lisa doesn't look. She's not ready to turn this into reality.

She scoots along the side of the truck, the pistol pointed at the bed, until she's crouched below the tailgate. She braces herself, pulls back the hammer on the 9mm. Then, in one motion, she opens the tailgate and stands up.

Blood drips from the bed onto the asphalt. The truck is full of stuff, and the Minuteman is sprawled across it on his stomach, his face turned to her. The gun is in his hand, but his arm is splayed unmoving on the bed beside him, and the gun points in the wrong direction. He's breathing shallowly; white, foamy spittle circles his mouth. He stares at Lisa. His eyes are glazed and empty.

Over the course of the last day, Lisa watched her husband morph from a normal man to a soldier. She sat in the bathroom and held her hands tight around Jemi's jaws as two gunshots rocked the condo, and when it was Guy who appeared at the door, blood-spattered and sweaty and victorious, she couldn't help but feel impressed. The bodies outside didn't seem real; it was like she and Guy were playing a game, and they were winning. She approved of her husband, wanted to be on his team, even after seeing death up close with the twins, even after learning about Heather. Guy would pull her through.

But he didn't. He was bested by this Minuteman, and now the gun is in Lisa's hands.

Lisa points the gun carefully. She aims at his side, a few inches below his armpit, where she figures his heart is. She's five feet away. The Minuteman is alive now, but she'll squeeze the trigger, and the bullet will cover the space between them in a fraction of a second, and then he'll be dead. So thin, the ragged edge of life and death.

She shoots him. The breathing stops.

So that's it, Lisa thinks. *I've killed someone.* It was not exciting. There was no rush of victory. She feels blank and empty, and she knows that the game is over. The road she's on is long and paved with death, and she's going to have to travel it alone.

She puts the gun in her pants and walks back around the truck and looks at Guy. He's on his back, looking up at the sky. The rifle is still in his hand, his finger near the trigger. The blood around his head makes it look like he's lying on a red pillow. Lisa takes a step toward him. He's got a concerned look on his face, as if he just remembered something important that he forgot to do. He left his jump drive at work. He didn't pay the water bill.

There's a hole in his right cheek, an inch below his eye. It's a clean, dainty-looking hole; it's not much worse than if he'd popped a bad zit or cut himself shaving.

Lisa knows it's the tip of the iceberg. She knows what the back of his head must look like.

She kneels beside him. "Guy?" she says, and she feels stupid for saying it. What's the point? She touches his forehead and draws her hand back as if she's been bitten. He's cold. He's already cold. How? How can that happen so fast?

And that's when the world caves in.

"You fuck," she says. "You idiot, you idiot." She's crying now. No one's there to see her, but still she's embarrassed. She tries to stop herself, but it all streams out of her: the tears, the words, the emotion. "You cheat. You liar. I loved you, you fuck." She punches him in the chest and his head jerks a little and is still. "I love you. Fuck you. I love you."

RIVER STYX

SHE'S NOT SURE HOW LONG SHE SITS BESIDE HIM.
The ember drifts desolately across the sky, a fiery chariot with a
busted wheel and hobbled horses at the bit. Shadows move around
her. She cusses at Guy, hits him a few more times. Her anger passes
and melancholy sets in; she talks to him of the things they did and
the things they would have done.

Eventually, she's out of tears and out of words, so she just sits.
His blood touches her pants leg and stains it red. She dips her fin-
gertip in the puddle and lifts it up, watches the drips fall onto the
pavement.

After a while, she's embarrassed to find that she's feeling uncom-
fortable around him. It's like an awkward silence on a first date: she
has nothing else to say, and, obviously, neither does he, and the
afternoon of quiet stretches out in front of them too far to handle.

Lisa doesn't want to be around him anymore, Guy with his permanent silence and his look of consternation. She tries to shut his eyes
like they do in the movies, with a quick sweep of her hand. They
stay open. She pushes more forcefully, willing the eyelids to stay
down, but they won't; Guy is determined to watch the sky. Lisa
wishes she had some heavy coins; she remembers this from somewhere, that people once weighted the eyes to keep them closed and
so that the dead could pay the boatman on the River Styx.

Guy has no money for the boatman, but that's okay, Lisa figures.
There is no boatman and no river; there's nowhere for the river to
lead.

The world sharpens around her; she's coming out of a fog now,
and her brain is tuning up. It's a bear awakened from hibernation,
an athlete stretching before a morning workout. She's had all the
mourning time that this new world will allow, so she shifts gears.

She kisses Guy on the forehead, reaches across him, and picks up
the AR-15.

Heather is sitting on the truck when Lisa returns. She's got the
tailgate down, and her legs are swinging back and forth like a child's
whose feet won't reach the ground.

"What took you so long?" Heather says.

Lisa opens the door to the truck and lets Jemi out. The dog is
thrilled to see her, and she stands on her hind legs and puts her paws
on Lisa's chest. "Good girl," Lisa says. "What a happy dog! Why
are you so happy? What have you got to be happy about?" She's
teasing Jemi and her mindless joy, but inside, Lisa is jealous; Jemi
forgot Guy existed the moment he walked away. She'll never miss
him. The dog is as happy at this moment as she's ever been.

The look on Heather's face is somewhere between confusion and
annoyance. "Where's Guy?" she says, accusation in her voice.

Lisa puts the AR-15 back behind the seats. "He's still down
there."

"What's he doing down there?"

"Come on, Jemi. Hop in." The dog jumps into the bed of the
pickup. "Get down so I can close it," Lisa says to Heather.

She doesn't move. "Where is Guy?"

"Get down."

Heather gets down and Lisa slams the tailgate shut. Lisa climbs behind the wheel and starts the truck. "We're going?" Heather says. She runs around and gets into the passenger seat as Lisa starts to drive.

They crest the hill and the lake shines gray like flint in sunlight. Nothing has changed down there: the truck, the barricades, the bodies are all quiet beneath the afternoon ember.

Heather seems to be getting angry. "Is he okay?" she asks.

They stop at the road block and Lisa gets out. She pulls a blanket from one of the bags in the back of the truck. "I'm going to need your help," she says to Heather. She rounds the barricade and startles a crow that was hopping around near Guy's body. It caws and takes to wing, landing in a tree on the far side of the bridge. It caws again and watches them. There are faint, bloody claw prints on Guy's sleeve. Lisa spreads out the blanket beside him.

"Oh my god," Heather says. She's standing beside the truck, frozen in midstride. "Is he okay? He's okay, right?"

"Are you kidding?" Lisa straightens Guy's legs. She folds his arms across his middle.

Heather is shaking her head. She's biting down hard on her bottom lip, like she's trying not to scream. She turns, puts her hands in her hair. "God damn it," she says. "God *damn* it!" Her face is bright red. She kicks the tire of the Minuteman's truck, and then she sits down on the asphalt and pulls her knees up to her face.

Lisa is about to yell at her, to tell her to get her shit together. *This is* my *husband*, she thinks. *You can't cry over him.* Then she remembers that she too, cried over this body, that she was overcome and took time to regroup. Legitimately or not, Heather loved this man. Lisa waits.

After a while, Heather looks up. Her eyes are wet pools in her face. "Can I see him?"

She's asking permission. She knows who he belongs to. "Just for a minute," Lisa says. "Then we have to go." She steps away.

Heather kneels beside the body. She runs her fingers down his arm. As Lisa watches, she speaks softly, her voice a breath, barely a whisper. Lisa can't make out the words. Heather touches his hair where it lies in the pool of blood. She adjusts it, smooths it on his head as if she's getting him ready for work in the morning.

She looks at Lisa, then back at Guy, like she wants something more—to kiss him? "Time to go," Lisa says.

They pick Guy up and move him to the blanket. It seems like he weighs twice what he should. They drop him harder than they mean to and his head bangs on the asphalt.

"Shit," Heather says. "Sorry."

Lisa reaches into Guy's pocket and takes out his wallet. The emergency cash is in there—nine one-hundred-dollar bills. Guy's driver's license is visible behind its plastic sheath. It's a bad picture of him; the camera is too low, and the angle and the shadow make it look like he has a double chin. Lisa smiles. He hated that picture.

They roll him up in the blanket, and the blue cloth turns red at the end where his head is.

"What now?" Heather says. She's looking down at the blanket with tired red eyes.

Lisa shrugs. "I guess we take him to Atlanta. Things will be normal in Atlanta. More normal than this. We'll find a funeral home."

Heather nods. "In the back of the truck?"

"Yeah."

"With the dog?"

Lisa looks over the barricades at Jemi, who is standing in the truck bed, wagging her tail. Will she know who this is? Will she try to roll around on him like she does the dead animals she finds in the woods? Will she lick the blood? Will she try to *eat* him? "We'll put the dog in the cab with us," Lisa says.

After a lot of grunting and shuffling and cussing, they get the body into the back of the truck. He's lying on his back on one side of the bed, and the supplies are stacked on the other. He's as immobile as the bags of clothes. He could be a rolled-up blanket with rocks inside. There is nothing left in that body. Guy is a husk now.

It seems like he's been dead forever, like he never lived. It's impossible that he was driving this truck a couple of hours ago.

Lisa wishes she still believed in heaven.

✳   ✳   ✳

They loot the Minuteman's truck. He was out for the long haul, apparently. He had food and water of his own, and beer—two cases of premium beer. His pistol is a .45, almost like Chisulo's, but black where Chisulo's was brilliant polished chrome.

Better, the Minuteman was prepared to drive. There are four five-gallon gas cans in the bed, so Lisa pours two of them into their truck and stores the others. Then she gets into the Minuteman's truck, pulls it out of the way, and climbs back into her own. Heather stands beside the barricades. She looks at her feet, then out over the water. She finally looks at Lisa.

Lisa nods. Heather gets in the truck. They drive.

Jemi sits in between them. Her jaw hangs open and her tongue lolls from one side of her mouth. Sometimes she turns and nudges Lisa with her wet nose. It's gross, but it's still better than having nothing between her and Heather.

They make their way back south to the interstate. The roads are empty at first, but as they get closer to Atlanta and the road spreads out from four lanes to eight, other cars appear. They are loaded down with supplies; pickup truck beds are packed dense and high, SUVs and cars have piles of stuff strapped to their roofs. When Lisa can get a glimpse through a window, the people all have the same looks on their faces. It's desperation and fear. All of them have waited too long, just like Lisa and Guy did. She wonders what they saw on the roads before they made it this far. Are there other cars ferrying dead husbands to the city?

She looks in the rearview mirror. The tail end of Guy's blanket flaps around in the wind. Lisa wonders how cold the body has gotten.

"I wanted him to leave you," Heather says.

"What?" Lisa heard her, but she's stunned at this. Why would this girl say that to her while her dead husband lies five feet behind her?

Heather leans forward so that she can see around Jemi. "I always hoped he would leave you," she says with a weird intensity. "He'd leave you, and he and I would run away together."

Lisa is quiet. What is there to say in response to this?

"I'd try to get him to say he'd leave you. Even if he didn't mean it, I just wanted to hear him say it." Her face softens, and she smiles and shakes her head. "He would never say it. He never told me he'd leave you. Not even to placate me."

"Why are you telling me this?"

"Because he loved you." She puts her hand on Lisa's knee, and Lisa cringes. Heather pulls her hand back. "You should know how much he loved you. I know he was with me sometimes, but it was never real." She folds her hands in her lap and looks at them. Her voice is quiet now. "He never loved me like he loved you. I could tell that what he had with you was real."

What is her angle? Lisa tries to read Heather's voice. It's impossible to tell if she's being sincere.

"I knew he would never leave you," Heather says. "I don't know why we kept it up. It was stupid. It was a waste." Heather sits back in the seat and stares out at the road. After a while, she speaks again. "I'm sorry for what we did. We shouldn't have done that to you. I never thought of you as real, and that made it easy. Now that I see you, I wish we'd never done it. I'm sorry, Lisa. I'm sorry."

It's the first time Heather has said her name. It sounds weird coming from her lips; it's like a word spoken in a foreign language: the sound is there, but it doesn't carry meaning. When does your name mean something? Is it anything other than noise when it's spoken by strangers?

Heather has her hand on Jemi's head, and the dog's ears are pressed back in happiness, her eyes half closed. She turns to Lisa and smiles, her face blank and innocent. Friendly.

Lisa sighs. "It's okay," she says.

"But it's not okay. It was screwed up. We screwed up. He might not be dead if not for me. The two of you might be in Atlanta already."

"Heather," Lisa says. Her name has that same foreign feel on her tongue. "It's okay. You fucked up. It's okay."

"Can you forgive me?"

"No. But that doesn't mean anything," Lisa says. "I don't have to forgive you. We don't have to reconcile everything we ever do. Sometimes we can just move on. The past is done, and we focus on now."

"So we're okay?"

"Are you wanting to be buddies or something?" Lisa glares at her and Heather looks down at the floor.

"We don't have to be buddies," Heather says. "I just don't have anyone else. I don't know what to do next."

Lisa nods. She doesn't want to admit it to herself, but since she has no one else either, Heather's presence is comforting, a tiny reassurance. The girl is a dim light in a dark world. "You and I are okay for now," Lisa says. "Guy fucked up. You fucked up. We all fuck up eventually."

"Everyone?"

"Everyone."

Ahead of them, the skyscrapers of Atlanta rise from the earth like the teeth of a crocodile.

ATLANTA

SHE DOESN'T KNOW WHAT SHE EXPECTED OF ATLANTA.
Things had gone to shit so rapidly and so completely back home
that she expected anarchy and chaos. Atlanta would be aflame; fingers of thick black smoke would reach skyward, and the night would
burn orange from the million fires that raged beneath it. Terrified
people would circle their cars like pioneers circling wagons, and
they'd crouch around a feeble bonfire and pray that the gangs would
not descend on them tonight. She would have to fight and kill for
food and shelter.

No. Atlanta has not succumbed to the chaos. The city is humming along peacefully, even happily. Traffic moves slowly, but it
moves; the lines of abandoned cars Lisa had pictured are not there.
There's no sign of electrical power, but Atlanta has not reverted
to the Stone Age. Rather, it's more like the world's largest tailgate

party. From the elevated interstate, Lisa can see down into parking lots and vacant fields. Cars are parked in orderly lines on the outer edges of the lots, and RVs and campers are clustered toward the center. People sit on their cars or in lawn chairs. They're talking, laughing. Some kids are playing tag. A guy is grilling hotdogs on a propane grill next to his RV.

Lisa is embarrassed. The power went off, and she became an animal. They broke windows and stole. She killed a man. Guy killed four, and now he's dead too. They let their ids rise up inside of them and control them. They were golems serving their ancient master. Here, people are civil; they're waiting reasonably for the world to return to normal.

"Those bald assholes ruined everything," Heather says.

"What do you mean?" Lisa says.

Heather gestures out the window. "Everyone's doing just fine here. The Minutemen said we could come here, and without them, everyone's happy. The power's out. Big deal. There's no reason we should be killing each other. Those psychos are the ones turning everything to shit."

Lisa can hear the strains of music coming from another car. It's country music, and Lisa hates country, but any music seems good now. It's a sign of the normalcy of the world.

"What do we do now?" Heather says.

Lisa looks at the clock on the dashboard. They've got a few hours before it gets dark; it's summer, but night seems to rush in more quickly after emberset than it did after sunset. The cold star doesn't light the horizon like it used to. "Find a hotel, I guess?" Lisa says.

"Maybe someone's got a phone that works. Maybe a satellite phone? Would that work?"

"I don't know," she says, but she knows the answer. There's a certainty inside of her, a terrible knowledge: none of it works. The Electric Age is over.

They exit the interstate a couple of miles from downtown and pull into a cheap motel. The parking lot has a festival atmosphere. It feels like it's the Fourth of July and everyone is waiting for the fireworks. Lisa parks on the edge of the lot and gets out with Jemi. She watches the dog run around in the grass median that separates the motel from the fast-food place next to it. Lisa takes a few of the most valuable things from the bed of the pickup and puts them in the cab. She puts her hand on the blanket; she rubs Guy's leg, the muscle of his calf. Is he the most valuable thing in the bed or the least valuable? What can he do for her now? What is she supposed to do with him?

They go into the lobby, and it's full of people too. A family is napping in the corner, five of them in matching blue sleeping bags. A group of teenagers plays Monopoly. Lisa talks to the clerk, who wants three hundred dollars a night for a room. Fifty to sleep in the lobby, twenty-five to stay in the parking lot.

Lisa wants two rooms. She wants to put Heather away behind four walls and a door, somewhere she won't have to see her or think about her for a while. Then Lisa wants to shut herself in her own room and do nothing. She wants to sit in darkness and silence and give the world time to sort itself out.

She has the nine-hundred dollars in Guy's wallet. She doesn't know what else she'll need it for or how long it will have to last her. "You have any money?" she says to Heather.

Heather shakes her head. "We left too fast."

"We'll stay in the parking lot," Lisa says to the clerk.

Lisa and Heather sit on the edge of the truck bed and eat cold soup from the can. Jemi stands between them eating her dog food straight off the bed.

Lisa has her legs stretched out over Guy's body. They are sitting a bizarre Shiva.

"How long before he starts to smell?" Heather says.

"I don't know," Lisa says. "I don't know how that works. We'll find somewhere for him tomorrow." She opens one of the cases of the Minuteman's beer. It's a stout from some microbrewery, a dense black beer that tastes of coffee and chocolate. She sips it slowly; it's nice and cool from the evening air. She pulls another beer from the case and holds it out to Heather.

"No, thanks."

"You don't drink?"

It takes Heather a moment to respond. "I drink sometimes. Just not right now."

Lisa shrugs and takes another pull. The ember has disappeared behind the trees but hasn't yet gone over the edge of the earth. The scattered puffball clouds in the sky are colored like marshmallows set alight over a campfire. Around them, people build fires in the parking lot. They stack wood—priceless, precious firewood— straight on the asphalt. They douse it with lighter fluid and the flames shoot up like dancing demons.

It's nearly dark and the stars are blinking to life when the two men amble over to the truck. They are young, one white and one black. They introduce themselves. Brett and Richard.

"Y'all here alone?" Brett says this with a Southern accent that's strong even for Georgia. He is the stereotypical frat boy: longish brown hair swept across his forehead, a pastel-pink polo shirt, a visor. He scratches Jemi behind the ears.

Lisa looks across at Heather and down at Guy's body. "Sort of," she says.

Richard is at least a hundred pounds overweight, and he wears glasses and has a nerdy look about him, like he gained all that weight while sitting behind a computer. He holds a beer in his hand. "You got news?"

"News?" Heather says.

"Everyone here's spinning the same shit. You're new, so we thought you might have some new news."

"We don't know anything," Lisa says. She's skeptical of these men. The last several strangers she's come across have wanted to kill her.

Richard shrugs. "We've got a fire going," he says. "You want to join us?"

They are young, smiling. Lisa tries to see inside of them. There are still normal people in the world, right?

"We've got hot food," says Brett. He's eyeing the empty soup cans. "We're grilling sausage. You can trade us some of those good beers. All we've got is Milwaukee's beast." He looks at the can in Richard's hand with mock disgust, and Richard shrugs and downs whatever's left in there.

Heather laughs. She looks over at Lisa and raises her eyebrows.

Is she asking for permission? Lisa thinks. She doesn't want to end up as some sort of mother figure to this girl. It's only been a few days since Heather was fucking Lisa's husband. Regardless, she doesn't want to spend the night sitting in the truck with Heather and what's left of Guy. She looks down at the blanket. He'll be fine while they're gone, right? "Yeah, we'll come," Lisa says. "This is good beer, though, so it better be good food."

Ten minutes later, they're sitting around a warm fire eating hot sausage sandwiches. The bread is drenched in garlic and butter, and the sausage is spicy and salty and gets grease on Lisa's chin. She washes it down with the cool dark beer. It may be the best meal she's ever had. Jemi lies beside her, gnawing contentedly on a T-bone.

They talk. The men go to school at Georgia Southern, in Statesboro, three hours away. There were Minutemen in Statesboro too, and the two of them got out of town as soon as they were told. "I sure as hell wasn't hanging around," Richard says. "Those guys had guns. Had their heads shaved like they were some sort of white-supremacist motherfuckers. Nah, man. I'm out."

Lisa is on her second beer now, and she's beginning to feel buzzed. She's warm and the food is good, and she almost forgets about Guy. Is she supposed to be mourning still? It already feels like he's been dead forever. He was alive this morning. He was walking around just a few hours ago. How is that possible?

"You tried to ride it out in town then?" Richard says.

"Yeah," Lisa says. "We didn't think it was a big deal. I guess we just didn't believe them."

"Glad you made it," Richard raises his beer, and Lisa reaches across and tinks the neck of her bottle against his. He gets up to make himself another sandwich.

"How many of those you going to eat?" Brett says.

"Many as I can." He laughs.

Lisa laughs too, and she feels guilty for it. She ought to be blank, numb with grief. She should be in agony. It feels wrong to be happy and full while Guy lies cold not fifty feet from her. She thinks of telling them about him, but this night is so close to normal that she doesn't want to spoil it with the body in her truck.

"So, y'all don't have any new news," Brett says, "and you just got into town. You probably don't even know the old news."

Richard sits down and goes to work on his new sandwich. "Not that we know that much," he says between bites. He scoots his seat closer to Heather.

"We don't know anything," Heather says. She's nursing a bottled water. "The power went out, and the Minutemen started killing people, and we got out of town." She crosses her legs and leans toward the men. "What's there to know?"

Brett and Richard spend the next half hour filling them in on all that they've missed since they lost contact with the world. They take turns relating the story as they've heard it. News is sparse, and it's hard to tell the gossip from the truth. Only a couple of things seem certain.

The Minutemen are everywhere.

"Minutemen, like from colonial times," Brett says. "Revolutionary War, Boston Tea Party, all that."

They're a Bunker Boy organization, and they've taken over small towns and cities across the whole country. The National Guard is supposedly fighting back, but the going is slow; the Minutemen are organized and well armed, and the military has no reliable way to communicate between ranks.

Other than places that are running under generator power, there is no electricity anywhere in the country. Whether this happened because of the Big Aurora—they refer to it as though it's a proper name—or because the Minutemen rigged it is unclear, but most people suspect it was a combination of both. "Supposedly someone's working to fix things," Richard says. "No one can say *who's* doing it, but they say it's being done."

"So what are we supposed to do now?" Heather says.

Richard shrugs. "Wait. Hope they turn the world back on."

It's late at night when they stumble back to the truck. Lisa stumbles, anyway; Heather didn't have a single beer, while Lisa had five.

"Where do we sleep?" Heather says.

"You can take the cab if you want," Lisa says. "You can use a blanket. We brought a bunch of blankets."

"Where are you going to sleep?"

"I'm going to sleep in the back." Lisa is too tired and drunk to lie. "I want one more night with him."

Heather nods. She takes a blanket from a bag and gets into the truck. "Okay. Goodnight, then." She shuts the door.

Lisa climbs into the bed and spreads out a blanket and sits down. "Hop in, pup," she says to Jemi, and the dog leaps into the bed and curls up beside her. Lisa adjusts one of the bags of clothes so that it can serve as a pillow, and then she wraps herself up in the blanket like she's a burrito. She lies on her side and looks at the blanket that holds Guy's body. She puts her arm around it and scooches herself close to him. The part of the blanket near his head is dirty brownish-red, crusted with blood. She peels it back. She wants to see him again. She needs to see him.

Guy's eyes are still open, and they look dim and a little sunken. His face is a sickly gray, his lips blue in the moonlight. The hole in his cheek is clean and dry.

Lisa nuzzles close to him. She puts her face in his hair; it still smells of the cheap shampoo that he liked. She bought the twelve-dollar-a-bottle stuff, and he used the kind that sat on the bottom shelf and cost eighty-nine cents. That cheap shampoo smells like Guy, and she feels memories flood through her: her face pressed against his chest as she lay in bed with him on the long mornings, his mouth on her neck as they made love, the time they shared a sleeping bag beneath the huge African sky on that safari in Malawi.

It's too much for her. She's crying and shuddering in the back of the truck. "I miss you," she says. "Even the bad stuff. I miss you." Jemi grunts and rolls closer to her, and the dog's back feels warm against her own. She's drunk in the back of the truck with what's left of her family. She wants Guy to talk back. She at least wants him to hear. "You were more good than bad, Guy," she says. "You made me happy."

Guy doesn't answer. Lisa cries until she falls asleep.

BURIAL

LISA WAKES UP SHIVERING WITH THE EMBERLIGHT slanting in from the east. The parking lot is beginning to stir; she smells coffee, cigarettes. Jemi snores beside her.

She has her hand on Guy's chest, her leg wrapped across his. He feels stiff and cold. His face is ghastly; his eyes are wilting like jellyfish stranded on the beach. The blood has leeched away from his face, leaving it a mottled blue and gray. She can't look at him anymore—whatever comfort he gave her last night, in the drunken darkness, is gone in the yellow hangover of morning. She pulls the blanket back over his head.

Jemi wakes up and presses her nose against her, and then the dog jumps down and runs into the grass. Lisa gets out of the truck bed and looks through the windshield; Heather is lying on her side, her knees pulled up close to her chest, a jacket wrapped tight around her. It looks like she's grinding her teeth. Lisa taps on the window, and Heather blinks, looks up at her.

Heather stretches and sits up and opens the door. "Hey," she says.

"Hey."

The parking lot is waking up, and smoke is in the air from a nearby fire. It's cold out, colder than it's been for days. Heather gets out and puts the jacket on and zips it up. "Brr," she says. She smiles up at Lisa. "What are we doing today?"

"I don't know," Lisa says. "The plan kind of ended with Atlanta. That was as far along as Guy had it figured out. I haven't really thought about what's next, either."

"We ought to try and find a phone."

"It's not going to work."

"I still want to try." Heather digs around in the bed of the truck and finds a bottle of water. She opens it and takes a long drink.

Lisa watches her. The girl seems so small, so young. "Where are your parents?"

Heather screws the lid back onto the bottle and watches the dog. After a while, she says, "I think they're in Alabama."

"Where in Alabama?"

"I don't know."

"How could you not know?"

Heather doesn't look at her. "It's complicated," she says.

Lisa wants to push her for answers. If she could dump her at her parents, the Heather part of her life would be over. Lisa wants to be rid of her, this husband-stealing girl, but there's something inside of her that won't let her simply abandon Heather. There's a kinship there, a bond forged through the man they shared.

Lisa gets her own bottle of water. Her head is pounding from the beer. She feels like she needs to drink a gallon of water to flush it out of her.

Heather looks over at the blanket. "What do we do with Guy?"

Lisa has been thinking about this. If she notifies some authority figure—police, paramedics, whatever—won't they ask questions? Who shot him? What happened to the killer? She's decided not to talk to the cops but hasn't ruled out finding a morgue. But the power's out. Is the morgue full of defrosting bodies? Is Guy just going to rot in a metal tube until the world comes back to life? What if she has to move on—will she ever get him back? The whole thing's a burden and a hassle. "I don't know," Lisa says.

"We could take him to the morgue?"

"I'll figure out what to do with him." Lisa feels the sharpness in her voice and regrets it. The girl is trying to help. Heather loved Guy too, but he is Lisa's burden.

"Okay," Heather says. She looks hurt, but she puts her hands in the pockets of her jeans and smiles at Lisa anyway. "I'm going to go pee," she says, and she heads off toward the lobby of the motel.

Lisa watches the ember as it crawls above the treeline. It's the faded yellow of a low-quality diamond, and its light is as insubstantial as vapor on her skin. Lisa likes the ember, but she misses the way that the sun could radiate heat into you even when it was cold outside. She misses the smell of sun on her skin, the smell of beauty and cancer baking.

Why is it still so cold? If the Big Bang worked, shouldn't that warmth be coming back?

"What now?" she says to Guy. "What do you want me to do?" She looks at him and up at the bluing sky. Jemi sits beside her and wags her tail. Lisa looks at the bottle of water in her hand, and then she knows.

When they'd made their will, Guy tried to have it stipulated that he would be buried at sea. "It sounds perfect," he said. "You'll sink to the bottom, and then crabs and fish will eat you. You'll be inside of them, and you'll just be part of the ocean forever. Maybe your bones will be the start of a reef. So much life."

What he definitely *didn't* want was a traditional burial—embalming, coffin, graveyard. He hated the idea of his body being artificially preserved in an expensive box for all of eternity. Lisa didn't know exactly what Guy thought would happen after he died, but one thing's for certain: he didn't think he would need his body.

The lawyer squelched the burial-at-sea idea. Too complicated, too expensive. Guy had settled on cremation with the ashes scattered at sea. He wouldn't be eaten by crabs and fish, but at least he'd be out there on the water.

This is something Lisa can give to him, one last thing.

She loads Jemi into the truck and tells Heather that she's going to the morgue, and then she gets back on the interstate and heads out of town. She remembers some bridges on the way into Atlanta; surely one of them will work. She crosses a bridge and looks down at a fast-flowing creek. *Too small*, she thinks. She drives on, the traffic into town thinning, the traffic out nonexistent.

After fifteen minutes, she sees a turnoff for Stone Mountain State Park. She takes the exit and heads south through woods and rural subdivisions until she reaches the park entrance. There's no one at the gate, and the park is closed. She drives around the barricade and follows the road as it winds through towering pines and ancient oaks with sprawling canopies. She eventually comes to the lake, a flat span of water that reflects the bald mountain itself. It's not the sea, but it will do. She turns the truck off and breathes deep the clean air. The place is deserted; the only sound is a squirrel that sits in a tree, chewing on a pine cone and watching her.

She lets Jemi out and the squirrel rushes to the top of the tree and cackles down at them. Jemi barks and runs to the base of the tree and sniffs around, then steps into the lake up to her ankles. She dips her nose in and jerks it out, shaking her head. "Cold?" Lisa says. It must have frozen over in the winter. This must have all been white. It will all be white again.

There's a boat ramp at the end of the parking lot, so Lisa turns the truck on and backs it down the ramp. She finds some rowboats beached behind a boathouse near the trees. She drags one into the water then rows over to the boat ramp. Lisa gets out and pulls the boat up in the mud, getting her shoes wet and dirty. She opens the tailgate and grabs Guy's body by the ankles and pulls. It takes her ten minutes and exhausts her, and she drops him in the mud, in the water, generally ruining him, but she gets him in the boat.

She catches her breath. There are rocks scattered around the edges of the parking lot, so Lisa gathers several of them and loads them into the rowboat. She unwraps the middle of the blanket and sets them on Guy's chest. Then she wraps him back up and ties the blanket tight with t-shirts. "You coming?" she says to Jemi, and the dog steps timidly into the boat. She stands with her paws spread wide as if she can't keep her balance. Lisa begins to row.

When she reaches the middle of the lake, she stows the oars and floats. She looks into the sky. There are no clouds up there; it's just that endless blue, not as brilliant as it was before the ember, but deepened still by the infinity that stretches out beyond it. Lisa wonders if Guy is up there somewhere. She knows in her heart that he's not, but she likes to wonder about it anyway. He liked to talk about other universes: for every possibility, there's a universe where that possibility is reality. So maybe he's out there in one of those universes where the Minuteman's bullet missed him. Not like it matters in this one.

She pulls the blanket back and looks at him again. This could all be very stupid, she knows. The power could come back on soon—it could be back on right now. She might toss him into the water and find that tomorrow the Minutemen are defeated and everything's back to normal. Then, some camper will find him washed up on the shore, and he'll become a John Doe. They'll check DNA and dental records to find out who he is. They'll search for his murderer, and they'll track Lisa down, a suspect. She'll have to explain it. How will she explain it?

Or the ember might die, and this lake will become a block of ice. *Try finding him then,* Lisa thinks.

She strokes his hair. She tries to close his eyes again, but still they won't budge. He's going to look up at the ember forever.

Jemi has noticed him for the first time. She sniffs at him, licks his face. Then she looks up despairingly at Lisa. "It's okay, girl," Lisa says. "We'll be okay."

She kisses him, and his lips are cold but soft. She presses her hot forehead against his cold one. "You're my love," she says, and then she covers him with the blanket. She nearly tips the rowboat over as she hefts him over the side; his legs go first, then his middle, and then gravity works on the rocks and pulls his chest and shoulders and head along behind them. There's a splash, a *plunk* sound, and then the water closes around him, and he's gone.

Jemi whimpers as she looks into the water where he sank. "You'll forget him in a minute," Lisa says to Jemi as she rows toward shore. "Lucky."

WIND

HEATHER IS SITTING WITH RICHARD AND BRETT
when Lisa gets back from Stone Mountain. They're playing cards—
poker, using acorns as chips. Richard seems to be winning; he has a
hundred or so acorns lined up in front of him in geometric patterns.
He's wearing an *Evil Dead* t-shirt, a bloody hand reaching up from
the grave. He's the first to see Lisa, and he opens one of his cheap
beers and hands it to her. He pours some water into a Tupperware
and sets it in front of Jemi, who slurps noisily.

Lisa drinks the beer. It tastes of metal and corn, but it's a clean
flavor, refreshing. "Thanks," Lisa says.

"Deal her in next hand," Brett says without looking up from his
cards. "Shit, I'm out."

Richard wins the hand, and Brett deals a new one. Clouds have
begun to move in from the north, and shadow falls over them as the

ember is swallowed up. Lisa has been wearing her Yellow Submarine hoodie since they left South Carolina, and now she pulls the hood over her head and tucks her hands into her pockets.

"Y'all ready?" Brett says. He's wearing a blue-pastel polo today, along with a different visor. Today's variant of the fraternity uniform. He deals the flop.

"I spent half the day looking for a phone," Heather says. She folds, daintily setting her cards on the asphalt beside her foot. Richard mimics her as he folds, taking exaggerated care with the cards. "Dick," Heather says, kicking him playfully in the shin. "Anyway, everyone has a cell phone, and none of them work. All the towers are out, supposedly."

Brett scowls at his cards. "Raise," he says.

"I even found a guy with a satellite phone," Heather says. "He couldn't get a signal, either. He thinks that the satellites are all dead. The Big Aurora killed them all."

"So what, then?" Brett says. "They have to send spaceships up there to fix them all?"

"They'd probably just launch new ones," Richard says. "A lot of those satellites are in geosynchronous orbits, way the hell out there. Thousands of miles. They're not getting out there. Of course, they're not launching new ones any time soon, either."

Brett turns over another card. "Aw, shit," he says, tossing his cards. Lisa piles the acorns in front of her chair as Brett deals again.

The clouds cover the sky as they play and talk. After a while, they put the cards away and Richard begins to prepare dinner. Heather stands beside him, watching him cook. He's making a simple chili—a green pepper and an onion, some cans of beans and tomatoes, seasoning. Richard says something, and Heather touches his elbow and laughs.

Lisa goes to the truck to fetch the other case of the Minuteman's beer. Heather follows her. "Did you take care of him?" she says.

Lisa nods. She searches through a bag and finds Guy's heavy winter coat and puts it on. She digs out her own down coat—thicker and warmer than Heather's parka—and gives it to Heather.

Heather puts it on. It fits her too well. "Thank you," she says.

Lisa offers her a beer, but Heather shakes her head. Lisa opens the beer and drinks. "You and Richard," she says.

"Yes?" Heather cocks her head.

"You know."

"It's not your business."

Lisa steps toward her, but Heather doesn't move. "He *just* died, Heather."

"I know that," she says. The girl is looking up at her, focused and indignant. "And it tears me apart. I loved him too, you know. But he's not here to take care of us anymore, Lisa. And we're going to need someone."

"You don't think I can take care of myself?"

"That's not what I mean." She looks back to Richard and Brett. Brett has started a fire, and he's scooting the chairs closer to the heat. "Those guys are feeding us. And they're nice. It helps to have people on your side." Heather looks at the ground, softens her voice. "You're going to leave me eventually. I know you are. And yes, I know you can take care of yourself. I take care of myself too. I just do it differently."

Lisa wants to be angry. Heather's right: part of Lisa does want to leave her, move on without her, but Heather looks helpless standing there in front of her, a girl alone in a cold world. She shouldn't have to latch onto random men simply to stay alive. Lisa sighs. "I'm not going to leave you."

Heather smiles at her.

Lisa can't bring herself to smile back. Not yet. Not when the Heather-and-Guy affair just ended, and ended only because Guy got killed. Instead, Lisa nods. "We'll take care of each other," she says.

They head back to the fire and pass out the beers. Lisa warms her hands over the fire. She drinks her beer, and the taste is bitter and rich. "This feels like a hurricane party," Lisa says.

"You celebrate hurricanes?" Richard says as he stirs the chili.

"You're not celebrating, really."

"But it's a party?" Brett adjusts the wood and the flames go higher. "Enlighten us."

"It was in Florida, where I grew up. There were hurricanes every couple of years, and they'd cancel school and work and everything. The storm would come in, and the wind would blow and the waves would come up over the street. The power would always go out, and my friends and I would get together and sit in the dark, drinking beer and watching the storm. It feels like that now. Without the storm."

"Oh, there's a storm," Richard says. "It's just not a hurricane."

This sits heavy over the group. The ember is setting behind the clouds, and its dim light casts everything in a sepia tint. It's like they're living in a memory.

"It was weird, though, after the parties," Lisa says. "You'd wait for the power to come on, but until then, there was nothing to do. You'd party at night and wake up the next morning, and the storm would be gone and the beers would be empty, but the power was still out. You couldn't go on with life. It was like you were in limbo, like you were living after the end of the world." She finishes her beer, and she wonders if she should slow down. *What the hell*, she thinks, opening another one. "But then they'd turn it back on, and everything would be fine."

"They'll turn it back on this time too," Brett says. His words feel hollow. The specter of the future hangs over them; they're all thinking the same thing: *No they won't.*

Heather's the one who says it. "What are you guys going to do if they can't turn it back on?"

The men look at each other. "Should we tell them?" Richard says. He's spooning chili into bowls. He hands them around the fire. Lisa takes a bite, and it's rich and dense and spicy. It tastes like it was made to go with the beer.

Brett looks at Lisa, then at Heather. "Don't see why not," he says.

"Okay," Richard says. He lowers his voice, and they all lean in toward the fire as he talks conspiratorially. "We actually talked to some guys who work for Georgia Power. They had them working nonstop since the power went out. They were replacing transformers and restringing lines and all that. Then, yesterday, they sent them all home."

A concerned look slips over Heather's face. "They just stopped trying?"

"They decided trying wasn't doing any good. Whatever's broken is bigger than they can fix. It's worldwide. The power guys said that they're sure it's sabotage, maybe even an inside job. The Big Aurora started it, but the Minutemen made it permanent. They don't know how, but that's what they're saying."

"So the point is, it's not coming on any time soon, and we can't stay here forever," Brett says. "It's going to get cold again, and soon. Tell them, Richard."

"It's too cold," Richard says. As if answering him, a wind comes out of the clouds and stings their skin. "The government says that the Big Bang worked, but if it did, it's not working as fast as they thought it would. We're going to have another long winter."

"We're all going to freeze here in this parking lot," Brett says. "We can't stay here."

Lisa jumps in. "My parents live in Miami. We could go down there."

"Maybe," Richard says. "But that's where everyone's headed. If we could even get down there, there may not be enough resources. Or enough space."

Heather has her water hugged against her belly, as if clinging to it will keep her warm. "So where are we supposed to go?" she says.

"Okay, here's the rumor," Brett says. He lowers his voice, and they all lean closer to hear him. "Asheville had problems for years with their coal plant. Pollution messing up the water supply. So last year, they started building windmills on the mountaintops. They were supposed to turn them on next summer. They weren't on when the Big Aurora hit." He sits back in his chair and smiles.

"So?" Lisa says.

"So they weren't damaged by the aurora. And the Minutemen didn't get to them."

"And now they've turned them on," Richard says.

Heather is beaming. "Asheville has power?"

"Shh," Richard says, and then he laughs and puts his hand on Heather's knee. He smiles over at Lisa. "That's what they say, right, Brett?"

"That's what I heard," Brett says. He bites his lip, nods. "We're going up there when the time's right."

"You two could come with us."

The wind gusts again, and an eerie silence falls across the parking lot. It's nearly dark, and Lisa looks around her, at the hundreds of faces lit by campfire light. The faces are turned skyward, where the clouds are slinking by. Lisa looks up.

It lasts only a moment, but it's there. A flurry. Snow.

It's the first week of August.

NORTH

LISA AND HEATHER SPEND TWO MORE NIGHTS IN THE parking lot. They drink, they eat up their supplies, they play cards and talk and laugh with their new friends. They discuss the rumors—rumors of the power, the Minutemen, the ember. The news is always vague and never encouraging. There's a feeling of unrest in their makeshift camp, and it is growing: something is wrong out there beyond the borders of the parking lot, out in the hinterlands that surround Atlanta.

And it's getting colder. The ember rises a few minutes later each morning, sets a few minutes earlier at night. What little warmth it has shines down on them from lower on the horizon.

It's their fourth day in the parking lot when Heather pulls Lisa aside after lunch. "Richard told me this morning," Heather says. "They're leaving tonight."

"For Asheville?"

"Yeah." She looks over at Richard and Brett. They're quietly packing stuff into the back of Brett's Mustang. "We're not going until late. He says that we have to wait until people are asleep. Otherwise, everyone might try to go."

Lisa looks around the parking lot. There are fires burning, but not as many as before. There is no music. Few people talk, and those who do speak in low tones, as if their voices might trigger an avalanche.

Heather turns back to Lisa, and Lisa can see the indecision swimming in the girl's eyes. Heather says, "Do you think we should go?"

"I don't know," Lisa says. "I don't know what else to do."

"Me neither."

Brett shuts the trunk of the Mustang and looks in their direction. He spots Lisa and smiles at her, winks.

"Do you trust them?" Lisa says.

Heather looks their way and waves. "They've been nothing but nice to us," she says. "Richard is really nice. I think he likes me."

Lisa watches them as they lean against the car and talk. They laugh, and Brett punches Richard in the shoulder. They're practically boys. They're not Minutemen.

"Do *you* trust them?" Heather says.

"Yeah," Lisa says, and she does, but she's not ready to rely solely on trust. "Come here," she says, and she and Heather head to the truck. Lisa opens the glove box and takes out the pistols: the roadblock Minuteman's .45, the twin's 9mm, the revolver Guy took off the skinny guy at their apartment. She slips the .45 into the back of her pants and hands Heather the 9mm. "Can you shoot it?"

Heather turns the gun over in her hands. "Is it like in the movies?"

"Pretty much."

"Then yeah, I guess I can. I don't want to."

"No one does," Lisa says. She finds a roll of duct tape in the bed of the truck and tapes the revolver around her ankle and covers it with her jeans. "Let's hope we don't have to."

They meet after midnight. A small line of cars pulls up beside the parking lot. There are two pickups, an SUV, a minivan, and a few economy cars. They idle with their headlights off, exhaust floating into the air like white tails.

Brett trots over to the truck at the front of the line. Whoever is inside rolls down the window; they exchange some words, and the window goes up and Brett comes back. "We ride in the middle," he says. He speaks quietly; they're trying not to alert the rest of the parking lot. "We're taking the back roads, through the mountains. Supposedly the Minutemen have roadblocks set up on the interstate."

"They do," Lisa says. "We saw one."

Brett nods, but he doesn't ask her for anything more. "We go into the Chattahoochee Forest, then up into Asheville. Everyone's full on gas, right? Because we're driving fast, and we're not stopping until we're there." He looks around the group, smiling with nervous eyes. "Y'all ready?"

Everyone nods. "Tired of this parking lot," Heather says.

"Good," Brett says. "Let's roll out."

They get into their cars. Lisa follows the Mustang through the sleeping parking lot. Heather has her jacket on and zipped up tight despite the heat blasting from the dashboard. Jemi sits between them, a thin trail of drool hanging from her mouth.

Lisa puts her hand behind the seat and touches the smooth stock of the AR-15. She feels the cold pressure of the Minuteman's .45 against the small of her back, the weight of the revolver on her ankle.

The truck at the front of the line moves forward and Brett pulls in behind it. Lisa follows, and the rest of the line closes in behind them, the other pickup bringing up the rear.

They get on the interstate and drive a few miles northeast. The moon casts a ghostly light on everything, and the blacked-out skyscrapers of Atlanta cut into the stars behind them. They exit onto a narrow highway and turn north. There is no one on the road, and it's pitch black as they wind through the darkened shopping centers and abandoned subdivisions. Lisa mashes the gas in order to keep up with Brett. They're going over seventy, and it makes the winding road feel like a racetrack. She white-knuckles the wheel and keeps her eyes tight on the taillights in front of her.

After an hour, the mountains rise up from the horizon like a black-backed monster. The buildings disappear and vast woodlands stretch out on either side of them. The road begins to ramp up. Lisa pictures Asheville, the turbines spinning high up on those green mountains, cranking out power and warming the bright-lit city below. Richard and Brett, delivering them to safety. "You were right about them," Lisa says.

"I told you."

"Why go for Richard, though?" Lisa laughs. "Brett is much better looking."

Heather sits up and grins. "Not my type."

"You don't go for frat boys?

"It's the way they dress. They look like they're going to Easter breakfast."

They laugh, and it makes the car feel warmer. "So what is your type, then?" Lisa says, and then she remembers. She knows Heather's type. Tension fills up the space between them.

Heather looks away. "I can't stop thinking about him," she says. "I'm sorry. I know I shouldn't say that to you, but I don't know who else to talk to."

Lisa closes her eyes. "Me neither."

"It doesn't feel like he's dead."

This is how Lisa feels too. It seems crazy that he was alive and well at this time last week and is now at the bottom of a lake. Still, it feels pointless to say.

They pass an overlook and look out at the valley beyond. The trees stretch black and infinite toward the horizon, undulating gently with the lay of the land. The moon hangs above them like a chunk of a golf ball and gives them a gauzy glow.

"He said he didn't believe in heaven," Heather says. "You know that, I guess."

They talked about these things? Lisa feels a new pang of jealousy, a rush of anger at the thought of it—the two of them, lying in bed on a summer afternoon, talking about life and death and the great mysteries of the world. Heather and Guy were supposed to be solely about sex. The philosophy and the long, winding conversations were for Lisa and Guy alone. "Of course he told me," Lisa says, but she's lying. Guy was never clear on his afterlife beliefs. As often as they talked about it, he'd never just come out and say what he thought. She thought he was an atheist, told him so, but he denied it. He definitely wasn't any classifiable religion, and he certainly didn't believe in *heaven* heaven. He was vague with Lisa, yet he told Heather outright.

"That's what makes me the saddest, I think," Heather says. "He's dead, and if he didn't believe in it, then he's not there. He's just dead. Just nothing."

"That's what happens to everybody, Heather." Lisa doesn't mean for it to sound mean, but that's how it comes out.

"You don't know that. People have been to heaven and back. Near-death experiences."

Lisa sighs. "There are scientific explanations for all of that."

Heather is quiet for a while, and then she says, "There's more to life than what we see, Lisa. There are things that science can't explain. There are things we're not meant to know." Her voice is confident now. "Science was supposed to have all the answers, but they can't solve everything. They can't fix the ember. So it's good to know that there's someone else looking out for us. And someone's waiting for us when we're gone."

Lisa is annoyed and depressed by her at the same time. She doesn't know what to say, so she just says, "If it makes you feel better."

"You don't believe in anything?"

"No." Lisa realizes that she, like Guy, has never come right out and said what she knew inside—that she knew that this life was it, that there was nothing else out there. It feels good to say it now. "But I don't need it. Life can be great while you're here. You don't need the supernatural for that. You don't need heaven."

Heather sits up and looks at her. "I just don't see how you can't believe in *anything*. I mean, there's so much beautiful stuff out there!" She gestures at the shadowy mountaintops that ridge the horizon.

She's a kid, Lisa thinks. *Give her time, and she'll see.* Everyone has to see it eventually, even if they don't admit it to themselves. "The world is full of so much good *and* bad stuff," Lisa says. "It's all random. Sometimes you get the good and sometimes you get the bad. And if you try to say that someone's in charge of it, you have to do all these explanations and loopholes and bullshit to make it add up, and even then it doesn't add up well."

"But you had too much good for it to be random. You had Guy. Even though he was with me, he loved you. He was happy. Weren't *you* happy?"

Heather's waiting for an answer, but Lisa just wants her to shut up. It's too late now, though—Lisa can feel the memories boiling up inside of her, her stomach wrenching with guilt. "I was. We were. But shit happened," Lisa says. "It always does."

"I don't understand."

Lisa looks at her. She's patient, waiting for an answer, but her face is open, kind. *What the hell*, Lisa thinks, and she tells her about Chisulo.

It seemed to Lisa that she and Guy had just arrived in Malawi when the Peace Corps split them up.

Sure, they spent two weeks in Lilongwe doing introductory training, where their instructors drilled them on culture and dress and religious customs and taught them basic phrases in Chichewa and Chitonga. The Corps took the volunteers on a weekend safari. They watched elephants bathe in the shallow muddy lakes and took pictures of lionesses as they slept in the tall grasses of the savannah.

It was like a vacation, a dream. Then they split them up. Guy stayed near Lilongwe, but Lisa was sent south to a village near Mangochi, a cluster of fifty or so shacks and concrete buildings on the sun-blasted shore of Lake Malawi. This was community-based training in their specialties, and because Lisa's program was different from Guy's, they trained in different parts of the country. They knew this was coming, and they had braced themselves for it; three months apart—they could do it, it would be worth it. They'd see each other for a weekend at the halfway point.

It was difficult at first. Lisa and Guy had scarcely spent a night apart since they began dating, and now, Lisa spent her nights desolate and wracked with loneliness in a single-room hut. She cried herself to sleep and felt like an idiot, like a coward, for doing it. She wondered what Guy was doing up in his village. He was less than a hundred miles away, but it felt like he was on the other side of the world.

Maybe it was the loneliness. Maybe it was the foreignness of the country or the haze that the long days and hot nights seemed to cast over everything. Something there on the banks of that lake made it easy to fall for Chisulo.

He was the son of her instructor, and he came to class from time to time to help out his father. Chisulo was young, early twenties, and he worked on a cattle ranch outside of the village. He was tall and thin, but he was dense with lean muscle that coiled like hard ropes beneath his skin. The skin itself was a beautiful shade of brown, like roasted pecans; he stood out from the midnight-skinned villagers, and Lisa wondered if some British had leaked into his bloodline back during the colonization of his country.

He had black eyes that shined silvery in the sun, like polished hematite. When he looked at her with those eyes, Lisa felt like he was dismantling her. She came apart like dandelion seeds on the wind.

Chisulo invited her to swim in the lake with him after class. Lisa only got in up to her knees—she'd read that there were parasites and bacteria in there, and she didn't want to take any chances—but Chisulo dove and splashed like a seal. They laughed like children beneath the African sun.

She'd only been in the village for three weeks when she slept with him. They went for afternoon coffee in Mangochi, and they sat at a picnic table and watched dusty kids kick a soccer ball around in an empty lot. The heat gave everything a languid, sleepy feel, and as coffee turned to drinks, she leaned into Chisulo, touched his elbow, laughed at his jokes. She lost count of how many of the watery Kuche Kuche beers she drank. As they walked back along the river with the setting sun trembling on the horizon like a drop of spilled paint, he put his hand on the small of her back, and it felt as natural as anything she'd ever done. She couldn't stop him from following her into the hut. She didn't want to.

Lisa felt evil. She was heartless and selfish. How could she do that to Guy? It was less than a month since she saw him last, three weeks until she'd see him again. Yet she'd turned to Chisulo so easily, as if her time with Guy meant nothing.

She felt evil, but she didn't stop.

❊   ❊   ❊

The memories keep coming, but Lisa can't talk anymore. She feels tears forming in her eyes, a knot twisting tight inside of her. She puts her hand on her stomach. "I was so horrible to Guy," she says. "The things I let him believe."

They've crossed some sort of peak and begun to head east. Roadside signs say that Asheville is ahead. Lisa shakes her head, blinks away the tears. "We're almost there."

The truck is silent except for Jemi's panting.

"I cheated on Guy too," Heather says. She puts her hand on Lisa's knee.

Lisa lets her keep it there. Heather's touch is warm, her eyes friendly. "With who?" Lisa says.

"Everyone." Heather laughs, a sad little laugh.

Lisa finds herself chuckling too. In spite of everything, Lisa finds it hard not to like her. She understands why Guy was drawn to Heather, and for a moment, Lisa can see why he needed them both. Lisa has always been the ember, but Heather is the sun.

"I mean, I don't know if it's really cheating," Heather continues. "We weren't together. Sorry. I mean, you know what I mean. But I would see other guys, and I wouldn't tell him about it. So it was kind of like cheating."

"Maybe it's what we do," Lisa says. "It's how we're wired. We all do it, and if we don't do it, we want to."

"Everyone lies in their own way." Now she smiles at Lisa, and Lisa smiles back. "We lie to each other," Heather says, "or we lie to ourselves."

Brett's brake lights flare red in front of her, and Lisa slows.

"Why are we stopping?" Heather says.

"I don't know." Lisa tenses, focuses. The conversation is forgotten.

The caravan comes to a stop. The pickup in front pulls forward at an angle, then backs up so that it's sideways across the road.

"What's he doing?" Heather says. Jemi begins to whine.

Lisa looks in the rearview mirror. The truck in the back of the line has done the same maneuver. "Oh shit," Lisa says.

The door to the truck opens and a huge man gets out of the passenger seat. The truck is one of those lifted monsters with giant wheels, and he's taller than it, and built like an offensive lineman.

Overweight, but heavy with hidden muscle. He's a bull. He's got a Braves ball cap on. "Turn off the cars!" he yells.

The night goes quiet as the cars in front of and behind her shut down.

Heather looks over at Lisa, confusion on her face. "Are we in trouble? Is someone coming?"

Lisa looks into the mirror again. Two men lean against the pickup in the back of the line. They're fifty yards behind her, but she can see them clearly. She can see the white glint of moonlight on a bare skull.

Richard gets out of the Mustang. "What's going on?" he says to the Bull.

"Get back in the car," the Bull says.

Richard is walking toward him now, his arms out, questioning, aggressive. "No! We've stopped. We're not supposed to stop here. Tell us what's going on!"

"Back in the car!" The Bull reaches for his pocket, but Richard is rushing him. He crashes into the Bull and they slam against the side of the pickup with a metallic thud. The Bull falls onto his back, and Richard is on top of him, his fists gripping his collar.

"You've fucked us, haven't you?" Richard screams.

The Bull says something, but Lisa can't make it out.

Whatever he says shakes Richard visibly. He lets go of the Bull and looks back at the Mustang, back at Brett.

Brett stands beside the car. "I'm sorry, Richard."

Richard stands up. His eyebrows are scrunched in disbelief as he shakes his head. "*You* did this?" he says.

"It wasn't supposed to happen like this."

"You son of a bitch," Richard says, and then the gunshot shatters the thick silence of the mountain night. Richard staggers backward and slumps against the truck. He touches his chest, looks at the blood on his fingers, then back at Brett. His legs give out and he crumples on the pavement.

Lisa covers her mouth with her hand.

The Bull stands up. The pistol dangles from one hand, his hat from the other. His bald head shines in the moonlight. "Everyone just stay put," he says.

Headlights appear on the highway in front of them, too many sets to count. More are arriving behind them.

"Oh shit, oh shit," Heather says. "What do we do?"

Jemi is barking now, a yelp that enters Lisa's ear and cuts through her brain. Lisa looks forward, then back, and then she opens the door. "Run."

Lisa grabs Jemi by the collar and darts for the woods. The pavement is behind her in an instant, and she hears the Bull shout, and more car doors open and slam shut. Jemi is barking still; she's sprinting behind her, her voice carrying clean in the night. Lisa crosses the grassy shoulder and looks back as she breaks into the line of trees; the Bull is chasing, the pistol in his hand. Other bald men are there too, among the cars—where did they all come from?

She sprints, dodges trees, leaps over bushes. Thorns tear at her, and she stumbles, falls, gets back up. She's lost Jemi, but she still hears her, barking and growling back on the road. There are gunshots. She hears a woman scream—Heather?

She can hear the Bull behind her. He lives up to the name she's given him; he plows through the undergrowth like it's nothing. He grunts and curses Lisa as she runs.

The ground begins to slope upward, and she falls again, rolls backwards, regains her feet. The Bull is close enough that she can hear him breathing. She realizes that she's breathing frantically too. Guy always wanted her to run with him, but she never cared about exercise. She looks good; why should she work out? Now she'd give anything for the lungs and heart and powerful legs of a runner.

Out of nowhere, the hill becomes a muddy cliff. She climbs it on her hands and knees, but she slips back down. She tries again, grabbing roots, tearing her skin, jamming dirt and gravel under her fingernails. When she slips again, she's exhausted, and she slides down the cliff and comes to a stop in a bed of rotting leaves. She looks back into the darkness behind her and pulls the .45 from her pants.

For an instant, she's back in Malawi with Chisulo, standing beneath a scorching sun in the rambling grasslands on which his cattle feed. He stands behind her, steadies her hand as she holds his pistol. She fires at a tin can, misses. "You can't miss when it's a lion," he says. She fires again. Again.

It's not a lion now, but a bull. He steps out of the trees and looks down on her. He leans forward, hands on his knees, and catches his breath. "Bitch," he says. He notices her gun. "You know how to use that?"

Lisa levels the pistol at his chest and fires.

"Ahh!" the Bull screams. He hops up and down, gripping his left biceps. "You fucking shot me!"

Before Lisa can fire again, he steps forward and pistol whips her. The world explodes in a flash of white light that sparks and fades into blackness. The pain is excruciating, nauseating, and she curls on her side, her head clasped between her palms. A high-pitched whine drowns out all the other sounds. She blinks, spits, reaches for the gun. It's gone, lost somewhere among the dead leaves.

The Bull is looking at his bleeding arm. "I'm going to have to get stitches," he mutters. He sighs and beckons with the pistol. "Let's go."

Lisa wobbles to her feet and walks back toward the road. The revolver sits heavy on her ankle, and she thinks about going for it, but the Bull is right behind her, his gun at the ready. The woods are dark and deep, and the noise from the road seems far away. Lisa can hear the voices of men. They shout commands; they laugh. She can hear Jemi, her bark frantic and high, a desperate bleat. The headlights peek between the branches like spotlights, and they cast skeletal shadows across the forest floor. Lisa slips and braces herself on a tree trunk.

"Get moving," the Bull says. He prods her in the back with his pistol. "We don't have all—"

Lisa turns. The Bull is frozen, staring off into the dark. He raises his gun, and then the woods explode around them.

The gunfire is close; the muzzle flashes light up the night. From somewhere to their right, the bullets fly. They slice through the air in a high-pitched rush of sound and speed. There's a smacking sound, and the Bull grunts and falls forward. He grabs Lisa by the elbow and pulls her down with him.

The woods fall silent. Lisa can smell gunpowder on the air.

The Bull drags her along as he scoots behind a log. "Stay put," he says. He's been hit in the same arm where Lisa shot him. He touches the wound. "Son of a bitch," he says. He lets go of Lisa and peers out over the log, and that's when the guns erupt again.

This time, Lisa doesn't wait. The Bull is shouting and shooting back, so Lisa leaps to her feet and runs. She's bent double, her hands over her head; the woods are shattering around her as bark and leaves and dirt fly at the impact of the bullets. Somewhere behind her, the Bull is yelling at her, but she ignores him. She forgets the Bull. She forgets the revolver taped to her leg. She forgets the road and the cars and her dog.

She runs.

She doesn't know how long it's been or how far she's gone. She comes to a shallow creek and splashes through it, the icy water soaking her shoes and stinging her toes, and when she gets to the other side, she finds she can't make it up the bank. She's too exhausted. Her legs won't do what she tells them. Lisa stands on the shore of the creek and breathes and listens to the silence of the forest night.

She can't hear the Minutemen or the gunshots. She is alone.

Lisa drinks from the creek. The water is cold and has the heavy taste of minerals. Her breath rises in thick white puffs. Her ears are still ringing from the gunshots. The look on Richard's face is burned into her memory. *You did this*, he had said to Brett. Brett, a Minuteman, tricking them, luring them into an ambush. And for what? What are the Minutemen doing with these people they take from the roads—the ones they took at the roadblocks on the bridges, the ones they took in the mountains in the dead of night?

When she's rested, she climbs the bank and walks. There is nothing but blackness around her. The woods look the same in every direction. She tries to picture the area from above. Is she still in the Chattahoochee forest? Are there roads and houses nearby, or is she lost—is she walking farther into the endless wilds?

She turns and walks back to the creek. Near the water's edge, a huge tree has fallen over. Its roots are caked with mud and overhang the crater where the trunk once stood. Lisa climbs down in the hole beneath the tree. She pulls her jacket tighter around her and tucks her hands deep in her pockets. Her toes squish in her shoes, and her feet are beginning to feel numb. She takes her shoes and socks off and tries to cover her skin with her jeans.

Lisa wrests the revolver from her ankle. It's wet. Will it still fire?

She hunkers down in the hole and watches the woods, the revolver gripped tight in her fingers. After a while, the snow begins to fall.

DANTE

THE WORLD TURNS WHITE. FLAKE BY FLAKE, THE SNOW gathers in the nooks between branches; it clings to the withering leaves of the trees and spreads across the forest floor. By the time the ember begins to rise and change the shadows from nighttime black to the blue of morning, everything is dusted in a thin layer of powder.

Lisa rubs her feet between her hands. They have a blue-gray tint to them; her toes have been numb for hours. She squeezes them and forces them to bend.

The snow stops. Lisa sticks her head up out of the hole and looks around. The layer of snow is thin with grass and twigs sticking out of it. It's already melting in the emberlight; the pristine smoothness of it falters as the flakes collapse in on themselves.

Her socks still hang from a root where she left them to dry. She touches them, but they feel almost as wet as they did last night. She tries to put one on, but she can't get it over her toes. It's like her feet are attached to someone else's body. Lisa realizes that she's shaking. Her hands are quivering in the cold. She can't stop her teeth from chattering. "Come on," she says, and she forces the sock onto her foot. It's damp, but her foot seems warmer than before. She puts the other sock on and slips on her shoes. The laces are impossible for her frozen fingers.

Lisa climbs out of her hole. The snow clouds are pulling back, and the ember is shining down from a clean blue sky. She climbs down to the creek and drinks. She's crouching there, deciding what to do next, when she hears the singing.

It's a man's voice, and he sings in a smooth baritone. He's singing "Ring of Fire."

Lisa scrambles back up the bank and dives beneath the tree. She squeezes the revolver between her palms; she has to concentrate to position her finger over the trigger.

The singer is coming from behind her, following the creek. A flight of birds cackle as he scares them to wing. They fly over Lisa and disappear into the trees in front of her.

Lisa backs up against the muddy roots of the tree and makes herself as small as she can. She forces herself to breathe quietly as she holds the gun at ready. She hears the snow crunch beneath his footsteps, and then he is there. He walks past the tree, still singing. Lisa can only see parts of him through the roots: a dark gray jacket, a blue scarf. A rifle over his shoulder. And heavy, fur-lined boots on his feet.

He stops singing. He's looking down at the creek. He kneels, lays the gun beside him.

Shit, Lisa thinks. Her footprints.

She steps out of the hole. "Stay on your knees," she says. He reaches for the gun and Lisa pulls back the hammer on the revolver. "Don't touch it."

"Okay," he says. "I'm not touching it."

"Just put your hands on your head," she says, and he does. Lisa holds the gun on him and approaches. He watches over his shoulder, and she can see part of his face: his smooth, brown skin; his eyes so dark brown that they seem black even in the morning ember. Lisa grabs the butt of his rifle and tosses it away. "Your boots," she says. "Give me your boots."

The singer looks at his feet. "I need my boots."

"I need them more. And I have the gun."

"They wouldn't fit you, anyway." He stands up.

"Stay down!" Lisa says. She points the gun at his chest. "I'll shoot you. I swear I will."

"Why?"

He turns to her, and for an instant, Lisa is certain she's looking at Chisulo. He's got the same build: tall and lean, like a swimmer. His skin like polished sandalwood.

"Why you want to shoot me? I didn't do anything to you."

Lisa realizes he's right. He was minding his own business, and she climbed out of a hole and pointed a gun at him. But it felt like the only thing to do. Since the Big Aurora, half the people she's met have tried to kill her. The singer had a gun. Pointing her own gun at him seemed logical. "Just give me your boots," she says. "My feet are going to freeze."

"I can get you some boots," the singer says. He takes a step toward her, his hands in front of him, palms out as if he's approaching a frightened animal. "Boots, and food. We can help you out."

Lisa aims the revolver at his face, and he stops, steps back.

"You don't need the gun," he says. "I promise I'm not going to hurt you. Just trust me."

Trust. What good is trust in this world? She trusted Guy, and he cheated on her. She trusted Brett, and he tried to deliver her to the Minutemen. "If you don't give me your boots," Lisa says, "I'm going to kill you and take them from you."

"She won't. She won't." The singer's looking past her now, and Lisa turns her head.

He's standing on the fallen tree. A boy, a skinny teenager. He holds a shotgun that's nearly as big as he is. He's got the barrel trained on Lisa's back.

"It's okay, Virgil," the singer says. "She's not going to do anything."

"She better put that gun down," Virgil says.

"She will. She will." The singer is smiling at Lisa now. "You will, right?"

Lisa looks at the singer. His face is open and warm. The creek bubbles behind him, and around them the birds are waking up, flitting from tree to tree. She lowers the gun and looks at the ground.

She realizes she's out of breath, and she kneels. Her feet feel like blocks of concrete.

The singer crouches in front of her and puts his hand on her shoulder.

She looks up at him. He's young—twenty-five, maybe—and beautiful. Lisa is suddenly self-conscious, and she wipes a trail of snot away from her nose.

"I'm Dante," he says. He smiles again. "Come on. Let's get you some boots."

They live a mile down the creek, not far from the highway. The trees open onto a small trailer park, where a dozen trailers sit around a cul-de-sac with a run-down office in the middle. Their trailer is at the far end of the lot. It's the biggest—a double-wide—and the inside is comfortably furnished. The floor is thick gray carpet that feels like a cloud beneath Lisa's feet. Dante guides her into the living room and sits her in front of the small fireplace in the corner. He puts a handful of charcoal in it and lights it. Virgil watches them from the doorway, and then he disappears into another room.

In a few minutes, the coals are warm, and Lisa takes her shoes off and puts her feet near the fire. She feels nothing at first, but then her feet begin to tingle, then burn, until there are stinging hot wires of pain shooting through her bones and up into her ankles. She grits her teeth.

"Yeah, it's going to hurt," Dante says. He boils coffee on a propane stove and brings her a cup. He sits down beside Lisa and says, "What were you doing out there?"

She spares him the whole story and starts with the drive to Asheville. She tells him about the blocked road, the Minutemen, and the Bull. "And he had me," Lisa says. "And then someone started shooting."

Dante's eyes get wide. "That was *you*?"

She's confused at first, and then the gears click into place in her head. "That was you?"

This wasn't the first time the Minutemen had staged an ambush, Dante says. He found bodies in the road the week before. The Minutemen use the same spot every time, a bend in the road about a half mile from the trailer. This time, when they heard the gun-shots, Dante and Virgil gathered their own weapons and ran to the caravan. "We got there too late," Dante says. "We could see from the woods. One guy was already dead. Black guy."

"Richard," Lisa says.

"Your friend?"

She nods.

"I'm sorry," Dante says. "We were going to leave. Too many to fight. But then we heard someone in the woods. We saw that big bald motherfucker, and we were going to get him. We couldn't get them all, but we'd get him." He sips his coffee. "We didn't know you were there until we saw you running."

"Did you kill him?"

"Nah," Dante says. He looks frustrated. "I emptied two clips at him, but he wouldn't go down. The others started to come up from the road, so we had to bolt."

Lisa's feet are starting to come back to life. The pain is subsiding, and a glowing feeling swims beneath her skin. "You hit him," she says. "You got him in the shoulder."

Dante nods. "That's something, at least." He finishes his coffee. Then he reaches down and touches the sole of her foot with his fingertips. "You feel that?"

"Yeah."

"That's good," he says. "You sure don't want frostbite." He prods at her a moment more, and then he lets his fingertips hang there, runs them down the center of her foot.

She tingles beneath his touch.

Dante pulls his hand away. "You ought to nap," he says. "You can take our dad's room. He's not using it."

A few minutes later, she's wearing a pair of Dante's sweatpants, and she's swapped her Yellow Submarine hoodie for one of his plain black ones. She crawls beneath the covers of the bed, and in a moment, her body heat has filled the space around her. She feels truly warm for the first time since the power went out. She realizes that she hasn't slept in a bed since that night in the hotel.

The last night of Guy's life. He slept alone.

She wants to cry, but she's too tired. Instead, she sleeps.

✳   ✳   ✳

151

In her dreams, she sees the face of the Bull. She hears gunshots, dogs barking, a woman's scream.

She wakes thinking of Heather.

Lisa opens her eyes, and she can see out the window. The sky is turning the dusty blue of late afternoon, and hints of yellow are creeping into the western horizon. A few patches of snow cling to the trees that mark the back edge of the property. Most of it has melted.

She gets out of bed and looks around the room. On the wall hangs a family portrait: a younger Dante stands tall between his parents. His mother is heavy-set in a way that suggests not sloth, but grit and determination; his father is an older, thicker version of Dante. A tiny Virgil stands in front, his hair in an afro that sticks out six inches from his head, his smile missing half its teeth.

The picture hangs beside a bookcase, the dominant feature of the room. It's built of heavy, dark wood, and intricate swirls are carved into the sides. The shelves are crammed with books. They are titles that passed through Lisa's hands time and again at work: Shakespeare, Milton, Chaucer—two whole shelves that look like the classics section in the library. She's read many of them herself.

Below the classics are two more shelves, these stuffed with science texts. Lisa sees everything from Darwin to Dawkins, from Newton to Hawking.

"He liked to read," Dante says. He's standing in the bedroom door. He has changed clothes, and now he wears a snug gray t-shirt with Duke's blue devil on it. Long, tight muscles run up his arms.

Lisa realizes that she's staring at him, and she turns back to the books. "My husband would have loved this," she says.

"A reader?"

"A teacher." She takes *On the Origin of Species* from the shelf and sits on the bed. She read it once years ago. She opens it now and looks at the delicate sketches, birds as fragile and varied as the snowflakes outside. These, the creatures of the Galapagos, each suited to its specific island, its place in the world. Each carved for its purpose by time and death.

"This is why Dad was so smart," he says. "He dropped out of high school. Said it wasn't for him. But he was the smartest man I knew. He knew about everything. He knew the Big Bang wasn't going to work."

"But they said it worked."

"They said a lot of things." Dante sits down beside her. "Don't mean it's true."

The snow, the cold—it will end. It must end, Lisa thinks. They said the Big Bang worked, that it restarted the sun. She looks at the book and wonders what the finches are doing now. Are they alive down there on those rocky islands? If the ember keeps dying, will they evolve? "Your dad," she says.

"He didn't make it." He folds his hands and looks at the floor. "And your husband?"

"No."

They sit quietly for a while, and then Dante begins to talk. He speaks softly but quickly, and he tells her everything.

His dad was a Bunker Boy—one who had no interest in the Minutemen. After the first aurora, he'd begun researching the sun, formulating his own theories. He dug up old scholarly articles that had been dismissed by most of the scientific community. Dante pulls them off the shelf and shows them to Lisa; they have titles like "Retrograde analysis of future solar energy given a zero-energy endpoint" and "G-type main sequence stars in Milky Way emitting unexpected radiation levels."

"I didn't understand it," Dante says, "but he wouldn't shut up about it. He said the government was lying. They weren't restarting the sun. It's all downhill from here."

He'd stocked up on food, guns, ammunition. A year ago, when Dante's father decided he wanted to build a bomb shelter, his mother declared she'd had enough. She left in the middle of the night, a week before the first snowfall of the long winter.

After the Big Aurora, the other residents of the trailer park fled, but Dante and his family stayed behind. It was only a few days before the Minutemen came through. Two of them, in a pickup truck, looting the trailers.

"That's what happened at our place too," Lisa says.

"I don't know what they're doing with everything," Dante says. "What are they going to do with a TV? With a computer? Power's out everywhere."

The Minutemen tried to get into Dante's trailer, and it ended in a shootout. When it was over, one Minuteman was dead, and the other fled. Dante's father had a bullet in his stomach, and he died within an hour.

"We buried him out back," Dante says, his voice barely a whisper. "I don't know whether to hate him or love him. We could have left, but he wanted to hold out. Got himself killed. But if he hadn't been ready, hadn't gotten all the supplies, then we'd be dead too." He shakes his head. "I don't know. I've just seen too many bodies, you know?"

Lisa knows. The dead men in her apartment. The twins. The man she killed at the road block. And Guy. She pictures him on the bottom of the lake in the shadow of Stone Mountain, minnows picking at his skin, algae growing beneath his fingernails.

And then Richard. "You said they left the bodies in the road last time?" Lisa says.

"Yeah. But me and Virgil moved them."

Lisa shuts the book and stands up. "We've got to go check," she says. She looks out the window, where the ember is just touching the tops of the trees. That scream echoes in the back of her head. A woman, in terror. She sees Heather sprawled on the asphalt, her eyes gazing upward with the blank stare of the dead.

"It's almost dark," Dante says. "It's getting cold."

"So we'll walk fast."

Shadows are stretching down the highway when they reach the road. It seems different than it did the night before; it's serene, quiet. The emberlight that slants between the trees pools on the blacktop like the glow of street lamps. There's a light wind, and the treetops sway and whisper to each other.

A man lies on the shoulder of the road. He's got two bloody bullet holes in his back. Dante kneels beside him, turns him over. The man is old, with wispy white hair combed across his pink skull. His eyes are closed, and he smiles. They drag him a few feet into the woods and lay him beneath a tree, his arms crossed over his chest.

Farther up the road is Richard. Other than him and the old man, there are no bodies. No women. Lisa is relieved. She doesn't know why—she ought not to care about Heather—but the thought that the girl isn't dead fills her with hope.

There are no dogs, either. Lisa listens to the quiet sounds of the forest. "Did you see a dog last night?" she says.

Dante shakes his head. "No dog."

Jemi was right there with her, and then she was gone. Did they catch her? Kill her? Is she still around here somewhere? "Jemi?" Lisa calls. Her voice is lost among the trees.

They walk over to Richard and look at him. He still wears that look of outrage.

"He was pissed," Dante says.

"It was his friend who sold us out." Lisa looks ahead, where the road curves out of sight behind the trees. "How far are we from Asheville?"

"Not far. Fifteen minutes."

"We were so close."

"Why were you going to Asheville?"

She tells him about the plan. The windmills, the power.

"There's no windmills in Asheville," Dante says.

He's backlit by the setting ember, and the hood of his jacket moves in the breeze. His eyes are like fine points of coal. Lisa sits beside Richard and puts her head in her hands. "We're so stupid," she says.

Dante sits down behind her and leans his back against hers, and she leans into him. They sit, propped against each other, while the light fades from the sky. "You're not stupid," Dante says. "Ain't none of us knows how to play this. We're all just doing it as best we can."

It's nearly dark when they carry Richard into the woods. They lay him in a clearing and cover him with pine straw.

It's the best they can do. There are no funerals in the age of the ember.

It's dark by the time they get back to the trailer. Virgil is sitting on the couch with headphones on. He's nodding his head to the music.

"You're going to run the battery down," Dante says.

Virgil takes the headphones off. "It's going to die now, or it's going to die later. I'm going to listen to it when I want to."

"Fine. Do your thing. But once it's gone, it's gone." He turns to

Lisa. "Dad got us lots of batteries, but there's no recharging that thing." He leads her into another room of the trailer. There's a small bed in the middle, but the rest of the space is taken up with supplies. There are piles of boxes and cans of food, giant jugs of water. Clothes and cooking utensils and medical supplies. It's like Lisa's stash back at the condo, but multiplied by twenty.

Lisa picks up a flashlight and turns it on and off. "So much," she says. "How long will it last?"

Dante shrugs. "He was preparing for four of us, but now we got his share, and Mama's. We ought to start eating it, get some more space in my room."

"Why put it all in your room?"

"He never got to build the bomb shelter," Dante says, "and I wasn't here. I was off at school while he was buying it all. I only came home to help with Virgil after Mama left."

Lisa looks back into the living room, where Virgil sits with his eyes closed, lost in his music. "You're going to try and stay the winter here?"

"Don't know where else to go."

"They might come back. The Minutemen." Lisa moves to a corner of the room and checks out the collection of weapons: rifles, pistols, boxes and boxes of ammunition. "You said you killed one of them. And they know someone was shooting at them last night. They'll put two and two together."

"We've got the guns."

"There's too many of them," Lisa says. "They'll come for you, and you'll get killed. You and Virgil both."

A shadow crosses over his face. "They won't get Virgil," he says. "I won't let that happen." He grabs a couple of cans and heads into the kitchen. Lisa can hear pots clanking around as he prepares dinner.

They eat in silence, the three of them at the kitchen countertop.

Afterward, Virgil goes into his room, and Dante steps outside. "Come here," he says to Lisa.

She follows him out there and they sit on the steps of the front porch.

"You seen the stars since the lights went out?"

Lisa looks up. The night is brilliant in this world without electricity. The Milky Way stretches across the sky above them, a cloudy white band tinged with hints of pink and blue. Around it are the billion stars, jewels of every color. They can see red Betelgeuse burning at Orion's right shoulder. Sirius glows below him, the bright blue dog star. And between them, the infinite points of light that signal other stars hidden by the glare of the lights of man. Other stars, other solar systems, other worlds. "It's incredible," she says.

"One of the only perks."

She looks at him, his profile a dark shape cut into the night sky. He turns to her, and his eyes seem as black as the spaces between the stars. They cut right into her, melt her inside. She knows she shouldn't be feeling what she feels: attracted to the man, flattered by his attention, a little turned on. *I am a terrible person*, she thinks. *Guy lives a hundred miles away in Africa, and I immediately betray him for Chisulo. Now, he's not even been dead a week, and I'm looking at another man.* She turns away, embarrassed.

"You want to stay with us a while?" Dante says. "You can share our food. Sleep in Dad's bed."

"I want to. It's not safe, though. They'll come back. I'm not going to stay here and wait for them." Lisa shakes her head. "I'm going to leave. You and Virgil should too. We should all leave. Pack up the supplies and go."

"We can't," he says.

"We have to."

"I can't do it to Virgil." Dante stands and walks to the edge of the porch. "He thinks if we leave, Mama won't be able to find us."

Lisa stands beside him. She puts her hand on his elbow. "Is she coming back?"

"Nah," he says. "She's gone."

She squeezes his arm. Lisa looks up into the sky. A star detaches itself from the rest and coasts across the blackness, gliding silently from west to east. It's the brightest thing in the sky. "Look," she says. She points up at it. "A satellite?"

Dante watches it, and a smile spreads across his face. "It's the space station," he says. "Dad used to make us come out to look at it. Sometimes he woke us up before dawn so we'd see it."

The bright spot seems to move impossibly fast. It streaks across the stars. "Are there people on it now?"

"I think so."

Lisa tries to imagine those people on the space station, spiraling endlessly around the dark Earth. They are castaways on a lifeboat in the middle of the ocean. Coal miners buried beneath a mile of rock. Their desolation knows no end.

Lisa doesn't want to be alone beneath these skies. She doesn't want to come untethered, to float aimlessly like the men up in space. She turns to Dante. "I'll stay a little while," she says.

INFERNO

IT'S ONLY A FEW DAYS BEFORE THE MINUTEMEN come back.

Virgil and Dante spent the morning hunting. When they return, Dante goes inside to clean the guns, and Virgil sits down on the porch steps, two rabbits at his feet. Lisa sits beside him. It's nice outside, the midday ember warm on her shoulders.

"You know how to skin them?" Virgil says.

She'd see Chisulo do it once: a savannah hare he'd shot at the edge of his father's property. He made it look so easy, as if he was simply pulling a coat off of the hare. "I've never done it," she says.

"Dad taught us." He picks one of the rabbits up and pulls a knife from his pocket. "Like this," he says, and he cuts a notch into the hide near the rabbit's neck and puts two fingers inside and pulls. It's just like the hare in Malawi; the skin comes off like a glove. It's clean, nearly bloodless. Some fur remains on the feet, so Virgil cuts them off, and then he removes the head. He guts the rabbit, spilling its slick innards into a bucket, and then sets the cleaned rabbit on the step in front of them. Skinless, it looks like a creature that stalks the floors of hell.

"You're good at it," Lisa says.

"You want to try?" He hands her the other rabbit.

Lisa touches its fur, soft and a delicate sandy brown. She hated hunting before, yelled at Guy the time he went duck hunting years ago. Such a waste; killing these animals for sport. Now, though, it feels essential. The rabbit is serving a purpose, and its death has some small meaning. Everyone working to survive beneath the ember, and to survive, some must live, and some must die.

Virgil wipes the knife on his pants and presses it into Lisa's hand. "So cut him here," he says.

She does what he says. He guides her through the whole process. It ought to be gross, but she finds herself exhilarated by it. It is raw and primitive and what she was meant to do. She pictures a distant ancestor of hers, some sun-darkened woman in the vast plains of Africa, crouching beneath a strong sun, cleaning her dinner. An ancient kinship.

"You're good at it too," Virgil says.

"Thanks." They look at the two clean rabbits at their feet.

"So we'd hunt with Dad," Virgil says, "and we'd bring the stuff home and Mama would cook it. She'd make stew with the rabbits." He's rubbing his hands on his thighs, looking off into the distance.

"Was she a good cook?"

"Lot better than Dante." He smiles, and they both laugh.

He's fourteen, but as Lisa looks at him now, Virgil could be ten. He's biting his lip, fighting back tears. "She'll come back, Virgil," Lisa says. "I'm sure she will."

He nods, looking his age again. "Yeah. Maybe."

Lisa knows it's not true. She knows that Virgil knows it's not true. Still, they let the lie hang there between them. It feels good to have hope. She lets the hope wash over her too, as she pictures Dante cooking the rabbit. A hot stew, a warm bed, the three of them comfortable in the trailer. It could work. It could last.

And then the fantasy is over. There's a sound in the distance: engines, trucks on the highway. Virgil's eyes go wide.

Dante steps outside and stands still, listening. "They might pass," he says.

The noise fades into the distance, and for a moment there's nothing but the empty silence of the late-summer afternoon. Then the sounds return. The rumble of a diesel engine. The crunching sound of gravel beneath heavy wheels.

"We drive?" Virgil says.

Dante has an old SUV parked in front of the trailer. He rarely drives it—saving gas. "No time," he whispers. "Inside."

They carry the rabbits into the trailer and lock the door behind them. Lisa crouches in front of the living room window. From here, she can see most of the park. The driveway leads into the cul-de-sac and loops around the office building, and the other trailers stand abandoned, some of their doors ajar, the way the Minutemen left them.

Dante goes into his room and comes back with his arms full of guns. He hands Virgil a pistol and keeps one for himself. He sets two rifles on the coffee table. "You got your revolver?" he says.

Lisa nods. She hasn't let it out of her sight since she taped it to her leg in Atlanta. She hasn't fired it, either; she has no idea if it will work or if it was ruined when she stepped in the creek. Still, she takes it from her pants and holds it at ready.

The trucks come into view. The first is a huge, double-axel pickup. A flag is mounted in its bed: a deep blue field with two white muskets crossed behind a red tri-corner hat. There are two more regular pickups behind it, and then the truck that Guy and Lisa took from the twins what seems like a lifetime ago. Lisa wonders what the Minutemen did with all of her stuff. Her entire life was in there—clothes and keepsakes, the material representation of forty-one years of life. The only things she has left are the clothes she wears and Guy's wallet. The wallet is useless at this point; she can't imagine getting anything out of the money or the credit cards. She keeps it anyway. It's all that's left of him.

There are five trucks in all. The last is the lifted monster that belongs to the Bull.

"Of course," Lisa says.

The trucks pull up in front of Dante's trailer, the engines stop, and the men get out. There are twelve of them, all bald, all armed.

The Bull gets out last. His arm is in a sling, but he holds a sawed-off shotgun in his other hand.

"That's the one from the woods," Virgil says. He kneels at another window, his pistol rested on the sill. "We're going to get him this time."

The men huddle at the road in front of the trailer. They talk and point. The quiet of the afternoon is complete. Lisa can hear the gravel move beneath their feet as they walk. "There's too many of them," Lisa says.

Dante watches the men. He licks his lips.

"Dante," Lisa whispers. "Too many. We have to go."

Outside, the Bull pumps his shotgun. "You fuckers in there?" he yells. His voice reverberates against the empty trailers. "Come out, come out!"

"We can get them!" Virgil says. He pulls back the slide on his pistol.

"No," Dante says. He takes Virgil by the wrist and forces the gun down. "She's right. There's too many. We got to get out of here." He slips his gun into his pocket and runs back into his room. Lisa follows. Dante stands in the doorway, scanning the supplies. "We've got to take it with us," he says. "Get a bag. Get something."

"There's no time," Lisa says.

"No. We'll need it. He spent so long getting it all together. All for us."

Outside, the men are fanning out. They're going to surround the trailer.

"Dante." She takes his hand.

Dante looks younger than he ever has. Virgil is still a child, and Dante's only a few years removed from being a child himself. His eyes are desperate. He looks at her, and Lisa can see inside of him; he's looking for an answer. He's looking for someone to tell him what to do.

"Now," Lisa says.

He nods. He runs into the living room and grabs Virgil by the arm. Lisa picks up one of the rifles, and Dante grabs the other, and they go out the back door. The tree line is fifty yards away. "We run?" Dante says.

From the side of the trailer comes the sound of footsteps. Voices.

"No," Lisa says. "It's too far." She looks around. The trailer is raised three feet off the ground, and behind the back stairs is an opening to the space below. "Under," she says, and they duck beneath the house just as the man turns the corner.

It smells like the earth under there, and the smell rattles memories loose in her brain: her night beneath the tumbledown tree, Guy's body caked in mud at Stone Mountain, the floor of her hut in Malawi. She and Dante and Virgil crouch together and watch the legs of the Minutemen. There are three of them spread out around the back side of the trailer.

Virgil crawls forward and peeks out from beneath the stairs. When he comes back, his face is wild with fury. "That's the one," he whispers. "That's the one who shot Dad."

Lisa looks. He's an older man, dignified looking. He wears black horn-rimmed glasses.

Virgil lies on his belly and points the gun at him. "I can get him."

"Get your ass back here!" Dante says. He's whispering and yelling at the same time.

Virgil pulls the hammer back. "He's right there."

"Virgil!"

And then there's a crushing sound above them. Three loud slams as a Minuteman breaks down the front door. Then footsteps moving through the trailer.

Dante grabs Virgil by the leg and pulls him farther under the house. He wraps his arms around the boy and they lie looking at the floor above them. Lisa crawls to them. Above, the footsteps track through the different rooms. There are several pairs of feet, several Minutemen. When they get to Dante's room, they stop.

"Whoo!" one of them says. His voice is muffled but clear. "The mother lode!"

There's another voice. Lower. The Bull. "No shit," he says. "Ours now."

For half an hour, the three of them lie beneath the house and listen to the Minutemen as they unload the supplies. Back and forth they go, carrying everything the boys own back to their trucks. Guns and food and water. Everything. Finally, the footsteps stop. "So where they at, then? They bugged out?"

"They'll be back." The Bull. "They wouldn't have left their stuff."

"We wait for them?"

There's a heavy silence, and then the Bull says, "No. Better. We leave something for them."

The footsteps vanish, and truck doors open and close. A moment later, the feet return and pace deliberately through the house, stopping in each room.

"What are they doing?" Virgil says.

Then she smells it. Gasoline.

"No," Dante says.

In back of the trailer, the three men have gathered together. Lisa can see their hands as they pass a cigarette back and forth.

She feels the heat before she sees the flames. It seeps through the floor and, for a moment, feels magical as she lies against the cold dirt ground. After a few minutes, flames begin to lick around the underside of the trailer near the front door. A hole opens in the living room floor, and the red-orange firelight burns through the shadowy crawlspace. Lisa can see the flames reflecting in Dante's dark eyes, eyes full of fear.

The men finish their cigarette and stomp it out in the grass. One of them lights another.

A crash, and the bookcase falls through the bedroom floor. It stands upright in the dirt, half of it obscured as it sticks up into the trailer. The entire thing is encased in flames. The pages curl and the red-rimmed ashes flutter into the air.

Smoke fills the crawl space. Virgil coughs, and Dante presses his hand over his brother's mouth.

Lisa watches the men. *Go*, she thinks. *Just go.*

The trailer groans and shifts. It is supported by concrete pillars, and the entire structure lists as a corner burns away and the pillar punches through. The hole into the living room grows wider, a gaping mouth into the inferno. The couch falls through, and then the refrigerator crashes down a few feet from Lisa's head. *Please*, she thinks. *Go.*

The fire roars like a beast out of hell.

Somehow, she can hear the men laughing. Lisa looks again, and they toss the cigarette to the ground, and then the legs are moving, heading back to the front of the house. Then they're gone. She hears engines starting, gravel flying as the trucks peel out.

"Go," she says. "Go!" Dante and Virgil crawl out from behind the stairs, and she follows, and they sprint for the trees. She looks behind her. The trucks are gone. The trailer is a fireball.

At the trees, they stop. They kneel in the undergrowth and watch the trailer burn. It glows from within, and the windows belch smoke. The other trailers are on fire too. The park is a wheel set aflame, the trailers bright points affixed to each spoke.

"Why would they burn them all?" Virgil says.

"I don't know, man," Dante says. "I don't know."

After a few moments, Dante's trailer collapses in on itself. It is nothing but a smoldering heap. The smoke rises half a mile into the still afternoon air. The ember hangs above it all, burning with its own cold fire.

MARGOT'S

THE FIRES ARE STILL BURNING AS THE EMBER SETS. The smoke is tinted orange as it floats above the trailer park. The Minutemen burned the office too. They took Dante's SUV.

There is nothing left, so Lisa, Dante, and Virgil walk.

They follow the gravel road back to the highway. Clouds are coming in and covering up the moon.

"More snow?" Virgil says.

"Maybe." Lisa looks both ways down the road. It curves into blackness in either direction. She sets off in the direction of Asheville. She holds the rifle against her chest. Dante follows, a few steps behind her. Virgil trails them. He shuffles his feet, his head down.

"Where you want to go?" Dante says after a while.

"I don't know." Lisa isn't sure what she's looking for. She has vague ideas: find a car, hotwire it, drive back to Atlanta. Drive to Miami. Drive to Ecuador if she has to. Wherever it is warm. "What's down this way?"

"Not much the next few miles. Then it's I-40. Then Asheville. But we don't want to go there. They're in there somewhere."

She nods, keeps walking. Beside them are woods broken up by broad pieces of farmland. Bare peach trees claw at the sky with their bony limbs. The farmhouses sit vacant at the edge of vision. Somewhere, a cow lows, a haunting sound in the night. The roads are surprisingly empty; there is no trace of the thousands who fled Asheville. Their evacuation was orderly, calm. People behaving sensibly, like the refugees in Atlanta.

They walk for an hour as the clouds cross from horizon to horizon. They close the sky up like the lid of a roll-top desk. From somewhere far away comes a low rumble of thunder, and the wind picks up. Lisa was wearing her hoodie and her jacket when the Minutemen showed up, but Dante wears only a loose-fitting sweater. Virgil has on the brightly-colored jersey of a soccer goalkeeper. No one has a hat. No one has gloves.

The thunder rolls again, and rain begins to fall. The drops rush down the road; they are funneled by the wind, and they come at them not from above, but from the front, blowing straight into their faces, into their eyes.

"We've got to get out of this," Lisa says. Shapes appear out of the darkness far ahead. Buildings, an overpass.

The rain has turned to sleet by the time they reach the interstate. It's already piling in a slushy mess in the gutters; it freezes on the windshields of abandoned cars. The asphalt becomes slick beneath her feet. Lisa walks with the gun in one hand, the other hand in her pocket. She swaps hands every few minutes. Her fingers are beginning to take on that same numbness that her feet felt after she stumbled through the creek. Her jacket is damp, and the cold is leaching into her skin.

They take shelter beneath the overpass. Lisa crouches behind a pillar and looks out at the darkened buildings, the remnants of the microcity that crops up at every interstate exit. Gas stations, restaurants, hotels. A few abandoned cars at a gas station that still sports hand-written signs reading NO GAS. She's reminded again of her last night with Guy. She wonders if the three of them can break into a hotel—this new group of three survivors. She remembers the keycards at the first hotel Guy had broken into. Doesn't every hotel have keycards now? How lucky they'd been to find a hotel with actual keys. She knows she won't get that lucky again.

Plus, they'll need water. They'll need food.

Just past the interstate are a handful of restaurants. "Let's go," she says.

They lean into the wind and move on. They pass a McDonald's with the windows all busted in. The next restaurant is a diner built in the fifties style; it resembles a silver train car snatched off the tracks and plopped in the middle of a parking lot. The sign on top reads MARGOT'S. Neon lights wrap around the edge of the roof. They must have been brilliant before, but they're all black tonight.

Everything dark, empty. The interstate exit is a wasteland freezing in the storm.

The three of them are almost past the diner when Lisa hears a voice above the squall. "Here! Over here!"

She looks back. The door to the diner is open, and a woman stands there. She is old, black, with short white hair. She's waving to them. Beckoning them inside.

The woman is Margot, and there are fifteen people living in her diner. When Lisa enters, they're all crouched down behind the counter or hiding back in the kitchen. They come out one by one; they're jittery, scared-looking people: women, children, teenagers, a couple of men. Some of them seem to be related to each other, but it's impossible to tell where one family ends and another begins. Each person seems an island, wary of everyone.

"They've come from all around here," Margot says. "Some of them alone. Some of them with their brothers or their moms. All of them lost someone."

A little boy—four years old, maybe—crawls out from under a table. He walks barefoot across the tile and grabs ahold of Margot's hand. He looks up at Lisa, and Lisa tries to smile. The boy shies away, steps behind Margot's leg.

"They were hungry," Margot said. "And I have food." The

wind is howling outside, and the rain is pelting the windows. "Y'all want some food?"

Lisa, Dante, and Virgil sit at the counter and eat cold blueberry pie. The rain is turning to ice outside, and dagger-like icicles stretch down from the rooftop. The other people sit in the booths at the far ends of the diner. They watch the three of them warily, whispering amongst themselves. After a while, a man approaches them. He wears a pistol on his belt. Dante puts his hand on his rifle and the man puts his hands up. "No. It's not like that, friend," he says.

Dante relaxes. "Sorry, man. It's just been a long day."

"I know what you mean." He sits down at the counter beside Dante. The man is about Lisa's age, but he seems much older. He's got a gaunt look about him, and his gray hair is going white at the temples. "I've never fired the thing, actually. I bought it the day things went bad. Been carrying it ever since, praying I don't have to use it." He gestures toward the other people in the diner. "We've only got two guns between all of us."

Lisa looks at her own rifle, which is laid out on the counter in front of her. She touches the butt of the revolver where it juts above her pants. Strange—guns are already a form of currency, and she is the richest person around.

"You folks have plenty of guns," the man says.

Lisa pulls her rifle into her lap. "You can't have our guns," she says.

"Don't want them. Just want you."

Margot quietly takes their empty plates away and vanishes into the kitchen. The rain has turned into pellets of ice, and it drums on the metal roof of the diner.

"What do you want with us?" Lisa says.

He looks at Dante, but Dante is staring straight ahead. He still has his fork between his fingers. The man moves to the stool next to Lisa. He sticks out his hand. "I'm Tom, by the way."

"Lisa."

"Anyway, Lisa, here's the thing. We're not going to last long in here. We've got food, all right, but look at us. We're like stowaways on a spaceship, so many of us crammed in here. And the place could blow away in a minute. Look." He points at the windows, which are shaking in their panes as the storm blows outside. "It certainly won't hold up if the Minutemen come. And the others out there. They find out we have food, they'll come for us."

Dante leans forward and looks past her to Tom. "What others?"

"Other survivors. Bunker Boys. They're not all Minutemen, you know." Tom takes out his pistol and sets it on the counter in front of him. It's a revolver, larger than Lisa's. He spins it, and the barrel ends up pointing right back at him. "Some of them came by a few days ago. We saw them loot the gas station across the street. It's only a matter of time before they come back for the diner."

"So what," Lisa says, "you want us to kill them? Do you think we're mercenaries? We're barely surviving ourselves."

"No," Tom says. He pops open the revolver's cylinder, spins it, snaps it shut. "I just want a better place to stay. I want to stay where the Bunker Boys are staying."

"Where?"

"The library." Tom tells them about the night he spent in the library. He'd ended up there after the Minutemen raided his neighborhood. He headed for the library hoping for some sort of emergency shelter, but instead he found three armed men camped out inside. They let him stay with them for a night, but they kicked him out the next morning. Not enough food, they said. Tom wandered until he ended up at Margot's. "There's only three of them," he says. "There's a lot more of us. And now we've got," he points as he counts, "five, six, seven guns. We can take them."

Lisa is so sick of the death. How is it already such a huge part of her life? Two weeks ago—*two weeks*—she was on her couch, watching TV. Guy had his arm around her, and Jemi curled on the floor at their feet. It's like a scene from another universe.

"We can take them," Tom says again. His eyes are ravenous. The gun gripped tight in his hands.

"Not like that," Lisa says.

When the ember rises in the morning, the world shines like it's coated in glass. The storm has left a layer of ice over everything. It wraps the sagging telephone wires like glass tubing. The branches of the trees are sparkling silver knives that stab into the sky. Bushes look like brittle sea urchins made of diamond.

"You shouldn't go alone," Dante says.

"It won't work if I don't go alone." Lisa has her revolver in her pants. She's debating whether or not she should take the rifle. *No, she thinks. Too obvious. Too imposing.*

"It's dangerous."

"Everything's dangerous, Dante." Lisa sets off for the library. According to Tom, it's another half mile in the direction they were headed the night before. She moves slowly; it's like walking on an ice-skating rink.

No, it wouldn't work if Dante went. There are men in the library, and Dante is a man, and all those men and all those guns can only lead to trouble. This has to be subtle. It has to be peaceful. It will only work if she goes alone.

The air is clean and cold in her lungs. It feels like she's just eaten a peppermint. Today, it feels good to be outside. The ember is still rising in front of her, and it looks happy up there in its cloudless home. Lisa feels like she knows the ember. It is an old friend with whom she has a conflicted relationship. When it's gone, when the storm clouds roll in, she misses it. When it returns, the very sight of it fills her with joy. For a while. Soon enough, though, she remembers. Her friend is dying. Death haunts it, hanging over it like smog, and then she hates the ember. She hates it for what it's doing to the world, for what it's doing to her.

It takes her half an hour to reach the library. It's a small building, some satellite division of the main library in Asheville. She stops a few feet from the door. What now? Knock?

"What do you want?"

Lisa looks up. There's a man on the roof. He's tall and bearded. He holds a rifle with a large scope, and he's got it pointed at her head. "To talk," Lisa says.

"About what?"

"Food."

He lowers the gun and scrutinizes her for a moment. "You armed?"

"I have a pistol," she says. No sense in lying.

"Get rid of it."

She takes the revolver from her pants and tosses it into the bushes. She puts her hands in the air.

The man on the roof says something to someone that Lisa can't see, and a minute later, the door opens. Two other men come out. One looks similar to the man on the roof, but he's shorter and clean shaven. The third is older, fatter; he looks like he could be their father. He wears a camouflaged jacket and a rainbow-colored wool scarf. He looks Lisa up and down, and then he looks past her, back up the road where she came from. "You alone?" he says.

"Yes," Lisa says. "Can I put my hands down?"

"No one told you to put them up." The son goes to the bushes and brings Lisa's revolver to his dad. The old man looks at it for a moment, and then he holds it out to Lisa. "You're not planning to use this on us, are you?"

"Not if I don't have to."

He smiles, and his teeth have the yellow color of age. "Tough girl, huh? I like it." He holds out his hand. "Abe."

"Lisa." She takes the pistol from him and puts it back in her pants.

"What do you know about food, then?"

Lisa tells him the story. She tells him about Tom, and the diner, and the stockpile of food. "We've got more food than we need," she says, "but no good place to stay. You've got a place to stay, but not enough food. We can make a deal."

"A deal," Abe says. He whispers something to his son, and then he looks up at the other man on the roof. "You want a deal, but you've got nothing to deal with."

"We've got the food."

"Yeah, but we've got the guns. And we know where the food is. What's stopping us from just going and taking it? Tom going to stop us? That pussy's not stopping anybody. Why shouldn't we just go get it?"

"Because I lied," Lisa says.

Abe blinks. "About what?"

"About coming alone."

"No you didn't."

She takes a step toward him. "There are guns on you right now.

On your boys. And I've got you out of the library. Out in the open. They're just waiting for my word."

He looks around. The emberlight on the ice makes everything bright and blinding. The world is cast in the shade of ice, and there are a million places to hide. "I don't believe you."

"You want to bet?" Lisa stares him down. She is alone. She knows that there is nothing to stop him from shooting her and looting the diner. Nothing but the look in her eyes.

Abe slowly begins to nod, and then he's smiling again. "All right, tough girl. All right. You got us pegged, then. Let's make a deal."

WHISKEY

IT DOESN'T OCCUR TO HER UNTIL LATER THAT SHE actually could have had Dante and Virgil hiding somewhere with guns trained on Abe. She wouldn't have had to bluff. The bluff seems incredibly stupid in hindsight, incredibly risky, but it worked. Whatever works. Lisa is figuring things out as she goes.

Abe and his sons have two pickup trucks, and the day is spent ferrying food and people up and down the hill from Margot's to the library.

They clear the books off of the shelves in the science fiction section and use them to store the food. Lisa finds a ledger in one of the offices, and she keeps track of everything as it comes in. Eight cans of spaghetti sauce—industrial size. Three twenty-five-pound bags of rice. Blocks of frozen spinach and collard greens; these, they store in the shade behind the library, buried beneath chunks of ice.

At night, it's like a freezer out there anyway, and the days aren't much warmer. It's only August, but already the highs are maxing out around forty degrees.

Lisa records diligently. This is the kind of stuff that Lisa has made a career out of doing. To most people, it would be boring, but Lisa has always liked it. A place for everything, and everything in its place. The world neater and more useful because of her.

"How long's it going to last us?" Dante says as he tosses a fifty-pound bag of flour onto the bottom shelf.

Lisa looks at the numbers in the ledger. "I'd have to add up the calories to know for sure," she says. She's been trying to do the numbers in her head: twenty or so people, three meals a day, one winter—five months? Seven? More? She remembers reading about rationing in a historical novel set during World War II. People can survive off of very little. The body adjusts. "A long time, I think. If we're careful."

Dante leans against the shelf. "You're going to hook a brother up, right?" He grins at her. "Little something extra for my hard work?"

She jabs him with her pen. "You'll get your share, just like everyone else."

"He's right, though." Tom is standing in the doorway with a case of bottled water. "Some of us have been working all day. Some of us haven't." He puts the water on the shelf and peers over her shoulder at the ledger. "How are you going to divvy it up?"

"I haven't done the math yet," Lisa says.

"I'm just saying," Tom says, "you should earn it. You get out what you put in."

Lisa closes the ledger. "Everyone will get a fair share."

"I hope so." He heads out the door, muttering to himself.

Dante looks at her, raises his hands, mouths *What the fuck?* Lisa shrugs.

The last load of food is the perishables. There are bags of bread sliced for sandwiches. Several crates of fresh vegetables—carrots, onions, tomatoes beginning to go soft. There's fruit too: a big box of apples and a basket of peaches that Margot carries in herself. "I picked these," she says. "My cousin grows them. They were part of the summer harvest. What little harvest it was."

Lisa picks one up and smells it. Its creamy sweet smell hovers in the front of her brain; she touches the velvety skin of the fruit to her cheek and remembers cobbler and ice cream on a cool fall afternoon.

Margot scowls at the basket. "They going to go bad soon."

"We can't waste them," Lisa says.

"We could can them," Margot says. "But we don't got the supplies."

Lisa nods, looking at the supplies. "We eat them, then."

So they have a banquet.

Abe has a large propane stove, and he lights it near the doors of the library. Margot sets to chopping, and after a while, she's got a stew going. She uses the vegetables and some ground beef that's a few days past its expiration date. She breaks chunks of ice off of the eaves outside and puts them in the pot to melt, and she flavors the water with bouillon cubes and thyme. It's not long before the smell of it drifts to the far corners of the library, an intoxicating aroma, salty and sweet and dense.

Dante toasts the bread over a grill—also propane powered. Abe has propane everything—stoves and space heaters and grills and more—and one of the library's storage rooms is stocked with spare bottles of the gas.

In the center of the library are a dozen tables set up for studying. Lisa and some others push a few of them together and surround them with chairs. It's getting dark outside, so Abe hangs a lantern above the tables, and the light spreads out and ends right where the bookcases begin. From the table, it seems like the world is nothing but the food and the other people. It feels like they're dining at an English castle in the Middle Ages, the guests of a king. Abe sits at the head of the table, and one of the heaters burns at the other end, blasting its warmth across the faces of those gathered.

They brought the dishes from the diner too, and Margot serves the stew in deep yellow bowls. Lisa takes a bite. It's the best thing she's had since Richard's sausage sandwiches in Atlanta. She dips her bread in the broth and chews.

"It's delicious, Margot," Dante says. He sits beside Lisa. Dante raises his bottle of water, one of hundreds in the combined stock-pile of Margot and Abe. "To Margot, for cooking, for sharing. For taking care of us."

They tap the plastic necks of the bottles together. "And to Abe," Lisa says. "For putting a roof over our heads."

Now Abe stands. He looks around the room, his features hard-ened in the lantern light. He's got a large nose but a delicate mouth, and his eyes are the pale cerulean of the sky near the horizon. "We're here tonight, each of us, because we didn't leave," Abe says. "All around us, people fled: to Atlanta, to Miami. Things went sour, and adios. Some left on their own, and some were chased out." He sets his water down on the table and looks into his empty bowl. "Some are not here because they didn't survive. Each of us has lost someone. I lost my wife." He reaches his hands out, touches each of his sons on the shoulder. "My boys lost their mother."

"We lost our dad," Virgil says. His eyes are wet, and he looks at Dante, who nods to him. "Our mama too," he says.

"I lost my daughter," says a woman at the other end of the table.

"My brother," Tom says.

"My dad," says a girl.

"Me too," another says.

They go around the table, each naming a person gone from the world. So much loss. It comes to Lisa, and she says quietly, "My husband."

Abe looks into her eyes, and then he scans the table. "We've all had loss. But we've found something too. We've found each other, and we'll take care of each other." He points in the direction of the doors, out toward the cold and the dark. "We're not going to let them get us. We're not going to let the cold get us. We're going to brave it together. Together." He raises his bottle. "So we raise our glasses to Lisa, for bringing us together."

"To Lisa," Dante says, and they drink.

The table is lively now, and conversation flows as the evening turns to night. The survivors talk of where they've come from, where they're going. They talk of those they've lost, share old memories. Laughter and smiles and tears. The food is good and the library is warm.

The children grow tired, and one by one, their parents take

them to bed. The table empties as people claim their corners of the library, small places to make their own.

"You going to sleep with us?" Virgil says to Lisa.

"Yeah," she says. "Pick us out a good spot."

Dante smiles at her, touches her knee. Then he and Virgil leave, and it's just Lisa and Abe. He watches her from his seat at the head of the table. The lantern hisses as it burns, and from the shadows around them come the hushed voices of people bedding down.

"We have to talk," Lisa says.

Abe raises his eyebrows. "Oh?"

"About the food."

He clicks his tongue and nods. He takes his napkin from his lap, folds it, and sets it on the table in front of him. "All right," he says. "Have a drink with me then."

They go behind the circulation desk into the main office. Abe carries the lantern with him, and he turns it down when they're inside; its glow shudders against the corners of the room like campfire light. Abe has put his personal stuff in here. On the desk is a picture of him and his boys—they are young here, teenagers—and his wife, a pretty woman with long brown hair. They're at Disney World, posing with Mickey Mouse.

Abe sits behind the desk, opens a drawer, and produces a purple sack. He peels the cloth back and reveals a bottle of Crown Royal, and he pours two inches of the amber liquid into a glass and passes it to Lisa before pouring a glass for himself. He raises his glass. No words for this toast. They clink their glasses together.

Lisa drinks. She has always hated whiskey, and this stuff burns her throat, but tonight it feels good. It's a good burn that warms her inside. She licks her lips and sits down across from Abe.

They drink quietly, watching each other across the desk.

"They listen to you," Lisa says after a while.

Abe nods. He looks off into the middle distance as if he's waiting for something to appear out of the darkness. "They do," he says. "But they'll follow you."

Lisa blinks. "No they won't."

"They will."

"They have no reason to."

"They have no reason not to." He finishes his whiskey and pours himself another. He reaches across the desk and pours another inch into Lisa's glass. "Look at them out there. You saw what they're like. Not a one of them can make a decision. They were all sitting up at that diner waiting for someone to come and save them. They were waiting for someone to tell them what to do. If you hadn't shown up, they'd have sat there until the place froze solid."

There are windows in the office that look out on the library. Through them, Lisa can just make out the shapes of a few people clustered in the young adult section. A woman and two children.

"Some people are like golden retrievers, Lisa," Abe says. "They're soft. Indoor animals. Nothing more than pets. But some people are huskies. No one tells a huskie what to do. A husky leads." He points at her. "You and me, we're huskies."

"I've always thought of myself as more of a boxer," Lisa says. She thinks of Jemi, wonders where she is. She hopes she's found a warm spot out there in the woods.

Abe laughs. "A boxer. That'll work too," he says. "But you're no lapdog."

She smiles at him and drinks her whiskey. It's making her feel light, a different kind of buzz than she gets from beer. Lisa looks at Abe, at his camouflage jacket. "You were military?" she says.

"No. We were stockbrokers. My sons and I, we had a firm. Never spent a day in the military among us." He finishes his whiskey and looks into the empty glass, then at the bottle. He sets the glass on the table and puts the bottle back in its sack. "It's fun to pretend, though. Who doesn't love to play soldier?"

Lisa sets her glass down. She's got a few sips left, but she's not sure that she can finish it.

"It's not just my wife I lost, Lisa," he says. "I've got a daughter. She's about your age." His eyes twitch a moment, and he puts his hand over his mouth and rubs the stubble on his cheeks. "She's one of them. She and her husband both."

"Minutemen."

He nods. He stares at his empty glass for a long time.

"The food, Abe," Lisa says quietly.

"Ah." He clears his throat. "You catalogued the supplies, then."

"As best as I could."

"And we don't have enough to make it through the winter, do we?"

Lisa has done the math several times. They can make it a few months. By the new year, they'll be running low. They'll be out entirely long before spring. "No," she says. "Not even close."

Abe nods. "Figured as much. But they don't know that. They don't need to know."

"And what do we do—"

"When the time comes, we'll decide."

"I have to ask you something, Abe," Lisa says. She'd seen Abe's stockpile, which held enough for him and his three sons to last the winter and more. "You didn't need food. You didn't need us. So why did you let us in?"

"Well, you put a gun to my head!" His face brightens back up. He's smirking at her, his eyes narrow and knowing.

"You knew there were no guns."

"I did," Abe says. "But you knew I knew."

"I did." Lisa picks the glass back up and finishes the whiskey in a single swallow. It hits her stomach and coats it in fire. "Why, then?"

Abe shrugs. "Maybe I wanted the company."

Lisa runs her finger around the rim of her glass. She sets it carefully on the desk. "Thank you for the whiskey, Abe," she says, and she stands up.

"You sleep tight, tough girl."

She shuts the door behind her and leaves him in the quiet glow of the lantern.

RATIONS

IT'S A WEIRD TIME WARP IN THE LIBRARY: THE DAYS drag, but the weeks go quickly.

It's getting colder. Lisa stands outside in the evenings and looks up at the ember. It's so feeble, a single star in the midst of the infinity of the universe. She imagines that she can hear its voice, the high-pitched whine of microwaves and radiation cutting through the void. It gets weaker as she listens, she loses it among the cries of the billion stars of the galaxy.

The entire sky seems dimmer than before. Midday has the dusky weight of late afternoon.

After a while, a certainty begins to set in: the Big Bang did not work. There is nowhere to go but down.

Snow falls, and it melts, until one day it doesn't. It coats the roof of the library and the surrounding buildings; it turns the trees into white-armed giants. The ember rises later in the morning and sets earlier in the evening. It seems hopeless there on the low horizon, its heat radiating uselessly on the snow-slicked world.

They see Minutemen from time to time. In the library, the people crouch in silence behind the windows and watch as the pickup trucks rumble by, the thick tread of their tires chomping through the snow. The survivors hold their collective breath; they wonder if today is the day they get captured, or if today is the day they die. Each time, the Minutemen move on.

Lisa leans her forehead against the glass. Ice crystalizes and cracks on the windowpanes. The planet is not the one she knows.

The survivors settle into a routine. Lisa speaks to everyone, asks them what they did before. She wants everyone doing what makes them most useful. One woman was a hospice nurse, one taught at an elementary school. A man was a mechanic. Their jobs are obvious. The rest are obsolete—office workers, an editor at a newspaper, a taxi driver. Tom was a software engineer. These jobs may never exist again. Lisa puts them to work where she can: preparing food, caring for the children, keeping the library clean.

A few search for more food—the rangers, they call themselves. They scour the nearby buildings and houses one by one, sorting through what was left behind, taking anything that might be useful. Sometimes, they stumble upon a wild deer or a duck, and when they're lucky enough to shoot it, Margot cooks it over the propane grill.

Lisa ranges. She loves the silence of those long, cold afternoons beneath the cornflower sky. She likes the way the snow crunches beneath her boots and the roads stretch out empty in all directions, black paths to forgotten places.

Often, Dante goes with her. They walk side by side, their shoulders brushing occasionally, their guns hanging loose from their gloved hands. They talk. Early on, they reached some unspoken agreement: there are certain things about each other that they don't need to know. Dante talks rarely about his father. He never mentions his mother. He knows that Lisa was married, but she's never spoken Guy's name in his presence. These days in the snow are for

Lisa and Dante alone, and the people they were before—and the people they left behind—are not part of this new life.

Instead, they talk of pointless things. TV shows they liked, songs they used to listen to. The places they'd been, the places they'll go if the power comes back on. These things are easy. They tease each other, and their laughter echoes against the ice-clad walls of the empty buildings. Their voices visible in clouds of vapor that appear before their faces.

Lisa likes the quiet of the library at night. She tiptoes between the darkened rows of bookcases, running her finger along the spines; each is different, each has its own texture: the slick glossy edge of a new hardcover, the wrinkled roughness of a well-worn paperback, the matte-finish spines like ultrafine sandpaper. She can smell them. It's an earthy smell, a mix of the woody paper and the sour ink, the oil of a thousand fingertips. The hint of mildew and mold from those books that got splashed in the bathtub, or the distant smells of coffee or Coke spilled onto a page at a diner a decade ago. The books smell like work, like home. They smell like life.

They bring back memories. She misses Jemi. She wants a dog to follow her around, tail thumping against everything, tongue lolling and drool splatting on the floor. She even misses Heather; for all the hurt she brought into Lisa's world, the girl kept her afloat in those first mad days after Guy's death. Lisa wonders where Heather is. She wonders if she's alive, if she's warm.

Most of all, Lisa misses Guy. She thinks of him constantly, but his loss, the weight of his absence, is something she keeps for herself. There are nights when she stays up talking to Dante, and others when she drinks with Abe. But most nights, she sits alone in a dark corner of the library, and she takes Guy's driver's license from his wallet and runs her fingertips over his picture and remembers. It's never big things she thinks of—their wedding, the day they flew to Africa, the move to South Carolina. No, it's the small things. She lies on a couch in the library's reading area late in the night while the other survivors sleep around her. She remembers a day, not even a year ago, when she lay on the couch in her own condo. It was a Twerp Tuesday, and Guy sat on the floor beside her, the laptop open in front of him. He was reorganizing his music library.

"Come here," Lisa said.

"Hang on. I'm in the middle of this."

"Come here." She held her hand out, and he looked up at her and smiled. Lisa scooted forward on the couch and he climbed behind her, laid his body out alongside hers, wrapped his arms tight around her. She felt him press his nose into her hair and breathe.

"You smell good," he said.

Jemi stood in front of them, mouth open, tail wagging. "All right, pup," Lisa said. She never let the dog on the couch, but today she wanted her there. She wanted her whole family there. "Hop up." Jemi stepped onto the couch and collapsed half-on-top of them. Her tail thumped for a moment, and then she was asleep.

Outside, the woods were full of the white quiet of winter. The snow clung to the branches of the trees, and the pine needles poked through like sprouting grass. The heater cut off, and the silence was complete. Lisa was warm with her husband and her dog, and that warmth melted from her skin right into the heart of her, and she listened to their breathing and shut her eyes and slept.

She never lay with them both like that again.

There are other survivors asleep all around her, yet she feels like she's adrift on that space station. She's just a point of light moving through the blackness.

She longs for closeness, for contact. She watches Dante as he sleeps. Lisa wants to pull his arms apart and lie against his chest and listen to the sound of his breathing.

She wants to feel his hands on her. She wants to know the taste of his skin.

And she feels sick for the wanting. She imagines that Guy is standing close by in some ephemeral form. He watches her through the warbling panes that separate the universes. He presses his palms against the barrier, and it shimmers and pushes him back, and his mouth moves with words that no one can hear.

So Lisa sleeps alone.

She's long since lost track of the days, but Lisa figures it's late October, maybe early November, when the ledger stops adding up. She spends some time each morning cataloging the food. She meets with Margot and they plan the meals: a day's worth of breakfast, lunch, dinner, and snacks for everyone in the library. She crosses things off as they're eaten, adds in the food they find while ranging. One morning, there's a can of beans missing. "Did you use an extra one yesterday?" Lisa asks Margot.

"No," Margot says. "Used six, just like we planned."

Lisa chalks it up to an error, ignores it. Then, two days later, a box of cereal goes missing. Later it's a candy bar from Abe's stash, then a six pack of Coke.

She talks to Abe about it. "You're here more than I am," she says. "Is someone getting into the supplies while I'm ranging?"

"I don't know," he says. "Then again, I'm not exactly guarding them."

"Should we have someone guarding them?"

Abe shrugs. "We can do that," he says. "It would probably work too. But you know what kind of message it sends."

Lisa nods. A guard means a lack of trust. Suspicion. "What do we do, then?"

"You know what we do."

Lisa gathers everyone together before dinner. It's late afternoon, and the ember floats above the horizon at an angle that fills the library with its light. The color flows through the glass doors and the windows and spills across the bookcases, splashing them with an orange like molten metal.

Lisa looks at the faces of the survivors and realizes that she barely knows them. She has spent her time with Abe, or with Dante and Virgil. The rest of them are barely more than strangers. They are a ragged bunch, and they form a half circle around her. They sit on the floor or in chairs; they lean against bookcases or stand with their arms crossed. Some look confused, some look annoyed. A few are armed; those with guns tend to wear them at all times. Lisa runs her finger along the wooden grip of her own revolver.

Abe stands beside her. Lisa looks at him, and he nods.

"We're all in this together," Lisa says. "We've been in it together from the beginning. We've worked together, and we've survived.

Things have gone well. And it's because we've shared, and we've been fair with one another." She pauses, looks from face to face. "Someone is not being fair."

The crowd stares at her. "What do you mean, Lisa?" Virgil says.

"We've got enough food to last us the winter." She speaks slowly, letting the weight of the words carry them to the dark corners of the building. "But only if we pace ourselves. Only if we ration. But someone is eating more than his share." Lisa waits a moment. She doesn't know what's going to happen next. She tries to feel the mood of the people. Where do their loyalties lie? "Who has been taking more than his share?" She waits.

They look at one another. Silence.

"If you speak up, you'll be forgiven. We'll go back to sharing, and everything will be fine."

A few of them are looking at Abe. Abe watches Lisa.

"If you don't speak up, and we catch you, you're done. We can't abide cheaters here. We can't allow it."

More silence.

Lisa can feel the moment slipping away. She is losing them. For weeks, months, people have cooperated; Lisa was not a leader, exactly—she never wanted to be—but she planned, and people followed her plans. Her plans had worked. They were neat, orderly: like her ledger, like the books on the shelves around them. Cleaners cleaned, cooks cooked, rangers ranged. Life more organized, easier, because of her.

And now she speaks to them, and there is no answer.

"You need to speak up," Lisa says, her voice feeling hollow. "Speak up or else." She looks at Dante. He's urging her. It's like Lisa can read his thoughts: *Come on, girl. Come on!* "Please," Lisa says.

And then a boy stands. He's younger than Virgil, probably nine or ten years old. "That guy," he says. "That guy took my candy bar. He got a whole bunch of them."

He's pointing at Tom, who's leaning against the front door.

"Don't listen to that kid," Tom says, but already, the crowd is looking at him. The momentum in the room shifts in an instant, and the weight is lifted from Lisa and falls crushing on the man.

"Tom," Lisa says. "Are you taking more than your share?"

"No," he says. "I'm fair as any of you."

Abe turns to his son. "Go check his bag," he says. Abe's son walks off to the far side of the library.

Tom watches him go. "I'm no cheater," he says, but his voice is quiet.

Abe's son returns with the bag. He dumps it out on the ground. Among Tom's clothes are two Cokes, a candy bar, and a can of green beans.

"I got that ranging," Tom says.

"You're not a ranger," Lisa says. She picks up the candy bar. "This is one of yours, right?" she says to Abe. He nods. Lisa walks toward Tom. The crowd parts and lets her through. She stops a couple of feet away from him. His head is haloed in the fire of emberset. Lisa speaks quietly. "Tom," she says. "We trusted you. We trusted you, and you stole our food. And then I gave you a chance to make up for it, and you lied. You stood there and lied to our faces. You lied to me."

Tom stands up straighter. His face is six inches from Lisa's. "It's a goddamn candy bar," he says. The words come out like a growl.

Lisa doesn't blink. "A candy bar today. Who knows what you'll take from us tomorrow." She looks out the window, out into the dying light. "How can we trust you? We have to have trust. Without it, we're nothing. You have to go, Tom."

Tom laughs.

"Go. I'm not asking."

He grins at her, and then he turns to the others. "She thinks she's in charge!" he says. "I don't remember voting her in charge. Way I remember it, she's the last who showed up. We were all doing just fine before she and her little boyfriend rolled in."

Dante stands up behind her, but Lisa holds out her hand: *Wait*.

"Way I remember it," Tom says. "It was *my* idea to come to the library in the first place. Seems like if anyone should be in charge, it ought to be me." He waits. The momentum has shifted again. It flows through the room like a slick of oil. "We don't have to listen to her!" Tom says. "We can do it our way! Aren't you sick of eating when she tells you to eat? Eating *what* she tells you to eat? I say we make our own goddamn decisions." He's worked up now, a sort of calm rage burning in his eyes. He keeps touching his pistol with his thumb.

187

"Tom." Lisa points at the door. "Get out of our library. Now."
"Make me."

Lisa pulls the revolver from her pants and points it at him. "Go."

Tom smirks, shakes his head. "You're going to shoot me?" he says. He laughs again, a manic cackling sound. "Abe, you're going to let her do this?"

Abe shrugs. "I'm with the tough girl on this one, Tom."

The smile leaves Tom's face. Slowly, he begins to nod.

Lisa is watching his hand, watching his gun. She's never fired her revolver. Guy was the last to fire it, way back when he killed the twin. Since then, it's been soaked in a frigid creek and dried again. What happens to bullets when they get wet? Will the gun fire?

And she wonders if she can make herself do it. She'd killed the Minuteman at the roadblock, but really, she was just finishing the job Guy started. Putting the Minuteman out of his misery. Tom is alive and well and standing in front of her. To strike him down, to end his life, is different. The thought fills her with terror and wonder.

Lisa licks her lips. She pulls back the hammer.

"All right," Tom says. "All right. I see how it is." And then he goes for the gun.

Lisa's revolver works. The library is full of the sound of the report and the smell of gunpowder. The noise pounds in her ears. Her eyes water. A woman screams, and a few people duck behind bookcases.

She's hit Tom in the throat. "Fuck," he says, but it comes out more as a gurgle. "Oh. Oh." He falls.

A little girl begins to cry, and her mother drags her to the far side of the library. The rest watch in silence as Tom bleeds out.

When he's still, Lisa puts her gun away. She turns to the crowd. Some are trembling, some stricken with horror. Every eye is on her. "We have rules," she says. "We have them for a reason. If we follow them, we'll survive. We'll make it through this. So we're all going to follow them."

Dante is watching her, awe on his face. Abe smiles, nods.

Lisa points the gun at the door. "If you don't want to follow them, then you can get the fuck out of our library."

After that, the ledger starts to add up.

JEEP

BY DECEMBER—LISA ASSUMES IT'S AROUND DECEMBER, though no one has bothered to count the days—the snowfall has nearly stopped. It has done its job though, and what has accumulated refuses to melt. The world is cased in white. Abandoned cars wear the bleached shells of giant tortoises long dead. The buildings look like gingerbread houses heaped with vanilla icing.

At midday, the ember slickens the top layer of snow, and at night it refreezes, harder and stronger than before. The weather is an architect, and it carefully shapes its village of ivory.

Lisa wonders how long it will last, how much worse it will get. She reads about the weather in the barren reaches of the world. In Mongolia, they call it a white *zud*. The snow falls, and it falls, and it buries the boundless grasslands for months on end. Millions of animals die. Entire herds are lost.

She wonders about life outside of the library. Does Mongolia exist anymore? What about northern America, all those places even colder than Asheville? Can anything survive?

Lisa sets new rules as the deep freeze hardens. She has to after they nearly lose both of Abe's sons.

They'd set out late, after lunch, and the clouds were already draping the sky. The storm blew in during the late afternoon, and the high winds came out of the north and rattled the walls of the building. Lisa and Dante had to fight to keep Abe inside. He paced back and forth in front of the doors as the night came on, speaking softly to himself: "My boys. My boys."

They came back around midnight. They appeared out of the dark like zombies, lurching forward, their skin blue as corpses, their lips frosted with ice. The nurse treated their frostbitten skin. One son lost the tips of his pinky fingers, the other the point of his nose.

So now they only range on clear days. Rangers must be back an hour before emberset.

Lisa and Dante leave early on one of these clear days. They head south, following the highway back under the interstate and veering off into a subdivision on the edge of the forest. Their boots sink an inch or two into the refrozen snow before they hit its dense-packed heart. The ice splinters and crackles as they walk.

The Minutemen have already been through this neighborhood. Some of the houses stand with doors open or windows busted out. Snow drifts into the dark hallways.

At the back of the subdivision, a road leads up a hill. It winds skyward, and beyond the bare branches of the trees that line the road is the endless sprawl of the forest. For miles and miles, the leafless trees scratch against one another like the bones of fingers cleaved of flesh.

The silence is annihilating.

Dante walks a few feet in front of her. He stops, raises his fist. He pulls his pistol from his pants.

Lisa takes her gun out, and she looks past him, up the road. There is something up there, a darkness against the dark trunks of the trees. They walk quietly, guns at ready. The shape comes into focus: it's an old military jeep. It's painted an olive green that's so tarnished with dirty snow that it appears black. The tires have a menacing, rugged tread on them. There are no doors or windows, no windshield. A thin layer of snow dusts every surface.

Someone sits in the driver's seat.

Dante points his gun at the person and whistles, but the person doesn't move. Dante looks back at Lisa. They move forward.

There are no trees in the area around the jeep. There's a broad clearing at the end of the road, and the backrests of a couple of benches stick up above the snow. A short railing runs the length of the clearing; beyond it is a cliff, and beyond that, the rambling forest. It's a park, an overlook. It's a relic of that time that already feels so distant, a time when life was so easy that people could spend an afternoon doing nothing more than sitting and looking out at something beautiful.

The jeep is pulled right up to the railing. The man inside is still. He too is dusted with snow.

"Oh," Lisa says. She puts her gun away and walks around to the driver's side. The driver is younger than Dante, maybe only a few years older than Virgil. He wears a National Guard uniform. The name tag on his chest says *Leonard*. There's a pistol in his hand and a hole in the side of his head. He looks out over the forest through eyes frozen solid in his skull.

"It's a nice view," Dante says.

"He's so young." Lisa touches his hand, and it's as solid as a block of stone.

Dante stands a few feet away. He's looking out over the trees, where the ember has passed its apex and is slouching westward. "None of us are young anymore."

Lisa stands beside Dante. The trees below them are like a scatterplot of gray and black against a blank sheet of paper. Somewhere near the horizon, a frozen lake glints with emberlight. "It's still so beautiful," Lisa says. "I know it's hard. Everything is harder now. But look at it all. How could he let it go?"

"Beautiful's not enough," Dante says. He takes her hand. "You got to have someone to share it with."

❄   ❄   ❄

They take Leonard from the jeep and carry him into the trees. They position him on his back. He lies staring into the sky like Richard, like Guy; empty, like all those other bodies.

There's a camo cover over the bed of the jeep, and Lisa pulls it back. Beneath it is a huge stash of supplies. There are pre-packaged military rations, blankets, and clothes. A few frozen jugs of water. And weapons; Leonard had an M16, two pistols, and plenty of ammo for both. Lisa opens a metal toolbox. Inside are three grenades.

"No shit," Dante says.

Lisa brushes the snow off of the driver's seat and climbs in, and Dante gets in beside her. The keys are in the ignition. She smiles at Dante. "Cross your fingers."

"Clutch," Dante says.

"What?"

"Got to mash the clutch."

Lisa looks down at the three pedals beneath her feet. The stick shift sticks up to her right; she doesn't know why she didn't register it before. "Oh," she says. She looks away. "You should drive."

"For real? You can't drive a stick?"

"I'm sure I could." She's feeling defensive. "I've just never tried. And we need to get this stuff back."

"Oh no. You're learning."

"Not now."

"This is happening, Lisa."

He's grinning at her, and she finds herself smiling back. The ember is still high overhead and there isn't a cloud in the sky. "Okay," Lisa says. "Driver's ed."

"All right then." He lets some cockiness seep into his voice. "Press the clutch."

She presses the pedal and turns the key. There's a terrible sound like metal scraping on metal, but the engine does something. The jeep shudders a moment and is still.

"Easy on it," Dante says.

She tries again, and this time the engine turns over and the jeep roars to life.

"Keep the clutch down. Gas. Gas. Get her going."

Lisa revs the engine.

"All right. Reverse."

She reads the diagram printed on the end of the stick and shifts. She can hear things sliding around in the transmission. Dante tells her to ease off the clutch and give it some gas, and she does, and the jeep jerks and tosses them around, and then the engine dies.

Dante is laughing. "That's normal," he says. "You'll get it."

After five minutes of jerking and restarting, she's got the jeep out of the park and onto the road, and she shifts it into first gear. They move slowly, the tires digging deep into the snow and muscling through it.

"Put her in second," Dante says.

Lisa speeds up and throws the jeep into second gear, and now they're moving. The wheels seem to glide across the top of the snow, and the trees tick by beside them as they descend the hill.

"Easy. Easy."

Lisa tries to shift into third, but again the jeep jerks, throwing them around in their seats, and the engine stops. The jeep keeps moving, sliding out of control down the hill. "Whoa," Lisa says. She mashes the brakes, but nothing happens. "Oh shit. Oh shit!" The jeep turns sideways in the road and crashes into a snow bank with a soft *thud*. The impact rattles a tree and shakes loose a shower of snow. They are coated in white.

Dante is quiet for a moment, and then he looks at her, and he erupts in laughter. He's laughing with his eyes closed and his head back, and the sound knocks off the vacant houses and recoils through the valley below. "You look like a damn snowman, girl!" he says.

Lisa is laughing too, so hard that the cold stings her teeth.

And then Dante puts his hand on the back of her neck and pulls her to him and kisses her. His lips are like sunlight, and Lisa feels heat running up and down her spine. She closes her eyes. The frozen forest seems to spiral away into a balmy fog.

Dante pulls back and looks at her, intense, smiling. He leans back in, but Lisa stops him.

Behind him, at the bottom of the hill, is a Minuteman.

DEFECTOR

DANTE LEAPS FROM THE JEEP AND DRAWS HIS PISTOL. He points it at the man. "Hands up!" he yells. "Put your fucking hands up!"

The Minuteman throws his hands into the air. "They're up!" he says.

"Keep them up!" He turns to Lisa, whispers, "What the hell is he doing?"

"I don't know," she says. She's looking around. They've never seen the Minutemen anything less than heavily armed. They're never on foot. Never alone. The whole situation screams trap.

The Minuteman starts to walk toward the jeep.

"Stay put!" Dante says. Then, to Lisa: "You want me to shoot him?"

Everything is still around them. The houses look as though no one has been in them for months. The woods are deserted. She can see footprints in the snow: hers and Dante's, the Minuteman's, but no others. The three of them are alone. "No," she says. "Don't shoot him. Just wait."

Nothing happens for what feels like a long time. Finally, the man says, "Can I put my hands down?"

"No," Lisa says. "Keep them up, but come up here. Slowly."

The Minuteman begins to climb the hill. He's an older man, his bald head darkened by a layer of peach fuzz. He wears horn-rimmed glasses.

"Motherfucker," Dante says. He strides forward, meets the man, and punches him in the face. The Minuteman falls to the ground, and his glasses go flying. Dante climbs on top of him and pulls him up by his shirt. "Mother*fucker*!" He punches him again.

"Dante!" Lisa says. She gets out of the jeep.

He's not listening. Dante punches the man once, twice more, lost in rage. He's oblivious to Lisa and everything around him. "Killed my dad!" he yells. "Burned our house. Son of a bitch!"

"Dante!"

Now he stops. He looks up at Lisa dazed, as though he's just been woken up.

The Minuteman is gasping. He spits blood onto the snow. He reaches out and grabs his glasses and puts them back on. "I'm sorry. It's not the way I wanted it." He's got a neutral accent, the polished speech of an academic. "Truly, truly I'm sorry."

Dante lifts him up again, stares into his eyes. Then he lets him drop and walks away, shaking his head. "Bitch deserves to die," he says.

"Not like that," Lisa says. "Get up. Turn around. Hands behind your head."

The Minuteman stand ten yards in front of the truck. He looks out over the abandoned houses below.

Dante picks up the M16. "We doing this?" he says.

"No," Lisa says. "Sit down."

He glares at her, but he climbs into the passenger seat.

Lisa gets behind the wheel. "Walk," she says, and they creep along behind the man, the engine purring as twilight arcs across the land. They're back at the library before dark.

The eyes of the survivors are on the Minuteman as Abe and his sons duct tape him to a folding chair. The snow glows orange and the ember disappears; darkness slips across the land. Abe lights the lantern and sets it on the ground in front of the Minuteman.

Virgil watches from a corner, his face warped with hate. Dante had sought him out the moment he and Lisa returned. "It's him," he said. "And he'll get his. But wait. You got to be cool for now. Just be cool."

Lisa pulls a chair in front of him and sits down. Dante, Abe, and a few others stand behind her. She looks at the Minuteman. He's nearly Abe's age. He has dried blood around his nose; his right cheek is swollen and the skin around his eye is turning purple.

"What were you doing?" Lisa says.

He blinks at her. "I left them."

"Left them?"

"The Minutemen. I'm done."

Lisa looks back at Abe. He raises his eyebrows and shrugs. Lisa turns back to the men. "Why?"

"It's not what I signed up for."

She watches him, tries to read his face. Behind his glasses, his dusty-brown eyes are dry and tired, and he speaks slowly. He seems worn down by life. He doesn't look like he's lying. "What's your name?" Lisa says.

He sighs. "Walter."

"How long have you been with them?"

"Since the beginning."

"And you leave now?"

Walter nods.

"Why?"

And then, the Minuteman talks.

He joined because he wanted to be part of the Refounding. The Minutemen had formed in secret in the months following the launch of the missiles. They'd grown slowly, a movement that started with online message boards and moved to secret basement meetings as organization improved and leaders arose. The group was ostensibly meant as a response to the government's position on the ember, but it ran much deeper than that. The Minutemen were driven by an anti-government sentiment that had been growing for years, generations.

"The country's been going in the wrong direction for so long," Walter says. "This was a chance to change direction. This was a chance to fix things."

That was what was promised by the New Founding Fathers. The leaders of the Minutemen were well organized. They had a plan. There were seven of them, and they took the names of the original founding fathers: Washington, Franklin, Adams, Jefferson, Madison, Hamilton, and Jay.

"Franklin's the smartest of them all. He might be the smartest man alive," Walter says. "He knew about the ember, somehow. He knew what was going to happen before the first aurora, before it was on the news or anything. And he knows what's best for New America." An anxious look comes over his face. "It's Washington who's behind the wheel, though. He's the one most of them look up to. And he is pretty inspiring."

"He's in charge here?" Lisa says.

"No," Walter says. "It's Jefferson in charge here. The others are spread out around the country. Franklin's up in the Northeast somewhere, and Washington's in Texas."

The New Fathers began recruiting while the missiles soared through space. They wanted everybody, but they went hard after certain types of people: men and women essential to the country's infrastructure. Police officers, utility workers, soldiers. By the time the missiles hit, the Minutemen were a million strong, and they were everywhere. They were inside the power companies where they brought down the electricity in the wake of the Big Aurora. They were among the cops, sabotaging efforts to keep the peace. The military members kept the troops disorganized. They stole weapons. They made a response impossible.

"And it really worked," Walter says. "We took the country. It was the first stage of the Refounding. The first step toward New

America." He pauses, takes a deep breath. "But it didn't happen the way it was supposed to. The way it was promised."

The Refounding was supposed to be carried out with no bloodshed. This was Franklin's plan. He had it mapped out: with the right Minutemen in the right places at the right times, the transition could be quick and painless. The world would barely know that anything had changed. They'd take the Capitol, drive out the old government, and turn the power back on. New America would be born peacefully, and life would finally be on the right track.

"But Washington changed the plans," Walter says. "A couple of days before the power went out, he sent a message to all of us. It was one sentence: *Blood alone moves the wheels of history.* I looked it up. Mussolini said it. It got everyone pretty riled up. I'll admit, I was caught up in it too. The looting, the stealing. We were taking the food and supplies, obviously, but we were taking things we didn't need. What am I going to do with a laptop?"

"It never occurred to you to be civil?" Lisa says. "To act like a human?"

"I think we were acting like humans," he says, shaking his head. "That's the sad thing. It's so easy to get caught up in it. There's something inside you that you didn't know was there, something dark, and when the looting turns to killing, it comes out. Something animal." He pauses, looks at the ground. "We did a lot of horrible things. There's no excuse for it. It's just, things get rolling, and everyone's shooting and fighting and it's, it's hard to stop." Walter turns to Dante. "I'm sorry for what I did. I'd take it back if I could."

"Can't, though," Dante says. "Dead is dead."

"I know. But there's nothing I can do besides apologize."

Everyone is quiet for a few moments. They can hear the sound of Margot cooking at the other side of the library. The knocking of the blade on the cutting board as she chops. The faint roar of the propane stove. The smell of garlic hangs in the air.

"Things calmed down after the first week or two," Walter says. "And I thought it would get better. But Jefferson. He's…" Walter stops, unsure of what to say. After a moment, he continues. "We saw some terrible things back at Biltmore."

Lisa stops him. "Biltmore?"

"Yeah. That's where they stay."

The Biltmore House of Asheville. The famous home of the Vanderbilts, barons of the Gilded Age. It's a tourist trap. Lisa and Guy went there once, back when they'd first moved to South Carolina. They stood in lines and trudged through room after room of old stuff. Lisa was bored out of her mind.

She pictures it now, swarming with bald men. The Minutemen have turned an attraction into a fortress.

"I couldn't take any more of Jefferson," Walter says. "I was sick of Biltmore. Sick of blood. So two days ago, I left. I wandered." He shudders. "There's no one else out there. I thought I was going to freeze."

"Why didn't you just go back?" Dante says.

Walter's eyes widen. "Can't go back. I can't ever go back. The things they do to defectors—no. Can't go back."

Lisa sits with Abe in his office after they're done with the Minuteman. He pours her a glass of scotch. It's Johnnie Walker Gold Label, and it tastes smoky and warm.

"What do we do with him?" Abe says.

Lisa looks out the window. The Minuteman is still taped to his chair, and now he has tape over his mouth. She didn't like the idea of him talking to the others in the library. "I don't know," Lisa says. "Depends on if he's telling the truth."

"What's the motive, though? If he's lying."

"To get inside? Open the library up and let the others in to take our stuff?"

Abe swirls the whiskey in his glass. "But they're in Biltmore. They've looted the town. What's the point in taking one more little batch of stuff? Especially if they'd have to fight us for it. It wouldn't be worth it."

Lisa nods. "Even so, he does nothing for us. He's just another mouth."

"So you'll just push him out the door?"

She closes her eyes and tries to see the future. Lisa sees Walter forced out of the library, wandering the snowscape. His fingers and toes blacken with frostbite, and he slows until he moves no more, a corpse as stiff as Leonard in his jeep. Or she keeps him in the library, and he turns on them. He opens the doors in the still of midnight and lets his fellow Minutemen inside. They stalk between the bookshelves, executing the sleeping survivors. They corner Lisa, and in the moment before the bullet cracks her skull open, she sees the dead around her—all those people who looked to her, listened to her, trusted her—dead because of her weakness.

Or a third option: he's not evil. Walter really is a defector. He lives peacefully with the other survivors. He knows things: where to find food, how to avoid the other Minutemen. He helps keep them alive.

"He stays for now," Lisa says. "He stays in the chair."

An hour after she goes to sleep, Lisa wakes from the cold. Dante is gone. She can hear his voice at the front of the library. He's speaking quietly, but forcefully. Lisa pulls her gun and creeps along the bookcases.

The moon is out tonight, and its light comes through the windows and makes everything look like it's plated in chrome.

Dante stands in front of her, his back to Lisa, and in front of him is Walter's back, taped to the chair. Beyond him is Virgil. He has the machine gun they found in the jeep. He's got it pointed at Walter's face.

"Come on, Virgil," Dante says. "This isn't what we do."

Virgil is crying. "He killed our dad, Dante," he whispers. "He shot him."

"That doesn't mean you get to kill him." Dante is holding his hands in front of him, pleading, his voice low. "We're not like that. We're not eye for an eye. That's not what Dad wanted from us."

Lisa puts her gun away. She steps into the shadows of the bookcases, afraid that if she goes any farther, she'll spook the boy.

"We're supposed to just let him go?" Virgil says.

"He knows what he did," Dante says. "He's sorry. He said he's sorry. Ain't nothing else he can do."

Virgil is sniffling. He wipes his nose with the back of his hand, and then he raises the gun again. He takes a step toward Walter.

Lisa can't see Walter's face, but she can see his hands where they're taped behind his back. His fingers are laced together, and he's squeezing so tight that his knuckles have gone white.

"Virgil," Dante says. "You're better than this. We're better than this." He walks around Walter, talking the whole time. "This isn't the world we're going to live in." He reaches out and touches the barrel of the gun. He presses it down, gently, until it's pointed at the floor, and then he takes it from Virgil. His brother is bawling now, and he collapses into Dante's arms. "It's all right, brother," Dante says. "You did right. You did right."

Lisa returns to her place and lies down.

A few minutes later, Dante and Virgil return. Dante covers his brother with a blanket, and then he settles down beside Lisa. Their faces are inches apart, and she can see his eyes, darker spots in the dark night. She touches his cheek, and then she leans in and kisses him softly on the forehead.

He wraps his arms around her and pulls her close to him, and his warmth flows from his body to hers, and Lisa feels like she's squeezed in the fist of life itself.

HORIZON

LISA WAKES AS THE FIRST FRAIL FINGERS OF LIGHT reach through the windows. The rest of the library is asleep. She slips from Dante's arms and goes to Walter, who sleeps tied to his chair. She shakes him; he starts awake and blinks at her from behind his glasses.

Lisa pulls the tape off of Walter's mouth. "How many of you are there?" she whispers.

"Huh?" His voice is heavy with sleep.

"Minutemen. How many Minutemen are at Biltmore?"

He shakes his head. "A hundred? More? It was hard to tell. Jefferson kept us working, everyone in his place, working his job. We were never all together."

"So you don't know everyone," Lisa says. Maybe it was too much to hope. She crouches in front of him. "Is there a girl there? A redhead."

"There are some redheads, yes."

202

Lisa feels her heart flutter in her chest. She has worried about Heather, though she can't say why. She barely knows the girl. Still, Heather is some connection to her old life, to Guy. Maybe Lisa feels like she owes it to Guy to see that Heather is safe. "A red-headed girl was with me when your people attacked us. A couple of weeks after the Big Aurora. She's…" Lisa's not sure what to call her. "She's my friend."

Walter shrugs. "There's a redhead who works in the kitchen. She's old, though. There's another one who came late. She's about your age. She cleans, I think." He looks up at the ceiling, deep in thought. "Oh, and there's Jefferson's girl."

"What's her name?"

"I don't know."

"Is it Heather?"

"I don't know her name."

Lisa looks into his eyes. Walter's face is passive, even bored. He doesn't know anything else. Maybe it's Heather he's talking about, maybe not. Lisa thinks back to the last time she saw Heather, there on the road to Asheville. "Why the road blocks?" she says.

Walter sighs. "Jefferson sets them up when he needs more work-ers. He has spies in the field who arrange the whole thing. Convince people to get on the road, drive to the right place. Then they take them. The worst jobs—he saves them for the people they take."

She thinks of Brett, playing her and Heather and Richard, set-ting them up for capture from day one. "All for Biltmore? How many slaves do they need?"

"Biltmore's just the biggest stronghold around here," Walter said. "They've got outposts all over."

Slaves, taken captive on the roads, toil for the Minutemen across the country. Lisa feels something sink inside of her. Heather could be anywhere.

Walter still looks sleepy. "Are you going to cut me loose today?"

She ignores him and returns to Dante. She sits and watches him sleep.

Lisa and Dante go ranging again that day. They leave in midmorn-ing, and they take the jeep. They almost always range on foot—Abe wants to save gas, and before they found the jeep, his two pickups were the only vehicles they had—but today, Dante has a destination in mind that's too far to walk. It's a country club that lies ten miles south of the library. Dante had been there once before; in another lifetime, a couple of fellow Duke students had been in town and asked him to play golf with them. He went. He was terrible at it.

The country club lies at the end of a nondescript road that weaves through the woods. Dante thinks that it's possible that the Minutemen have overlooked it.

They haven't. The glass front doors of the country club have been smashed in, and snow is drifted across the lush blue carpet. There is nothing in the bar save a few empty liquor bottles. One bottle of vodka has a couple of shots left in it, and Dante stands behind the bar, pours it into shot glasses. He passes one to Lisa. "*Skol*," he says.

"*Skol*." Lisa takes the shot and feels the burn creep up into her sinuses.

Dante licks his lips. He reaches across the bar and touches her cheek, and then he kisses her. He doesn't wait. He doesn't pull back. He kisses her hard, gripping her head between his hands.

His lips are warm and his tongue is soft and strong and Lisa kisses him back, and the bar and the snow outside the windows recede as he pulls her onto the floor. She climbs on top of him, and his mouth is her world as his hands slide up the inside of her jacket, up under her shirt, and his fingertips glide across her skin. Down, down her back, squeezing past her belt and then his warm hands on her ass, and she's kissing him hard, biting him, tasting him, barely breathing as she undoes his belt.

And then he's inside of her, and it's a fullness and a warmth that she hasn't felt in months, and she feels complete, there as a part of a body made by two people. She moves with him, and she pulls back her mouth and looks into his eyes and no, he's not Guy; he is Dante, but that is fine. That is right. Maybe Guy is in his other universe with another Lisa, but the Guy here is as cold and dead as the withering core of the ember. Lisa and Dante are alive. They are alive and the world is cold but between them there is nothing but heat, skin and bones and sweat and heat.

❄ ❄ ❄

When they are done, she stays on top of him, her head on his chest. She looks out through the windows at the golf course. The snow is flawless; it's as if a bricklayer loaded up his trowel with white mortar and spread it across the green and rolling hills and left. He never came back with the bricks. "I feel warm," Lisa mumbles.

"Hmm?" He's twisting his fingers through her hair.

Lisa sits up and kisses him, softly this time. "I'm warm when I'm with you," she says.

"We'll keep each other warm," he says. "This is our family now. You and me and Virgil."

She touches his face. He's staring up through the ceiling, his eyes distant and troubled. "It's tough for him," Lisa says.

Dante nods. "It's tough for all of us. But him especially. If he was younger, he wouldn't understand, and he'd just go with it. If he was older, he could handle it like a man. But at his age, with Mama leaving and Dad dying, I don't know. It's going to screw him up." He rolls her off of him and rests his head on his elbow, looks into her eyes. "This world's not the place for a kid."

"We wanted a kid," Lisa says. "My husband and I." For months, she and Dante have avoided talking about the past. Something feels different now. Things have shifted; he opened up about Virgil, his parents. She feels herself opening to him.

"Why not? I bet you'd be a good mom. A badass mom."

She smiles, but her eyes are wet. "I wanted to. And Guy wanted to be a dad." She lies on her back and puts her hands on her stomach. "I lied to him for so long. And now he's dead. I should have told him. I fucked it all up."

Dante is running his fingers across her cheek, pushing her hair back behind her ear. "What do you mean?"

"In Africa," she says. "I ruined us."

Halfway through their community-based training in Malawi, Lisa and Guy got their weekend off and met up in Lilongwe. Lisa had talked to him on the phone every week—a short call through the static-clogged lines of the phone at the schoolhouse that doubled as her training facility. The phone calls were normal. She was worried that Chisulo would leak through during the conversation, that her betrayal would saturate her voice and tip Guy off, but he never seemed to know. She lied as though it was second nature. *Yeah, I've made some friends. No, not too lonely. I can't wait to see you.*

It was awkward when they found each other at the hotel in Lilongwe. Guy looked different: His skin was a deep tan, and his clothes hung looser. He had a bright, wild look in his eyes, as if he'd spent the previous six weeks living with a pack of hyenas.

They had sex on the tight-stretched white sheets of the hotel bed; it was one o'clock in the afternoon and the sun shone down on them brightly and the noises of the market were loud outside. Guy kissed her the way he always did, touched her where she liked to be touched, but it felt to Lisa like their bodies didn't fit. Where had they gone, the people that they once were? How did they spin outward into different worlds so quickly? How far could the tether that held them together stretch before it snapped and momentum carried them forever apart?

"I missed you," Guy said afterward. "I didn't know how much I missed you. We're busy, you know, but man. This. I miss this."

She lay with her head on his chest. He smelled different, a burnt, muddy smell like the sun-cracked earth of a dried-up lake. "Me too," she said.

She went back to Chisulo at the end of the weekend. It felt like she was coming home. He was waiting for her outside of her hut. He had a basket of mangos he'd picked from the orchard that other Peace Corps volunteers had planted years ago. Chisulo was sitting on the ground, his back against the wall, and Lisa sat down beside him and laid her head on his shoulder. He took out a pocketknife and peeled one of the mangos, cut a slice and held it up to her. Lisa ate it out of his fingers; she savored the fleshy sweetness of it.

"You had a good time?" Chisulo said.

"I don't want to talk about it."

They made love that night. She'd had Guy inside her that morning and Chisulo at night. She didn't want to want him, but something kept driving her to destruction, spiraling her straight down the rabbit hole. It was like a part of her was dead set on seeing just how deep it went.

Chisulo left for home while the moon was high and bright overhead, and Lisa walked down to the lake. She sat on the log where she and Chisulo watched the sunset many evenings. Lisa liked the way that the distant jets looked as they arced overhead just after the sun set. They sparked like stars, and their contrails were tongues of red fire strung out behind them. The sun had not set for the people on the plane. Hundreds of people in a metal tube, miles above her, and they were still in daylight while twilight swept across the savannah. Lisa felt like she was looking into the past; the jets were something from another world, something long forgotten, and the lake and the soil in Africa were reality.

The moon shimmered silver on the surface of the lake, and somewhere far away a crocodile croaked in its throaty voice. Lisa thought about swimming out there and seeing what would happen. Maybe the crocodiles would get her. Maybe she'd drown or get infested with some flesh-eating bacteria.

But no, she didn't want to die. She wanted the answer; she wanted to know why she was the way she was, why she destroyed everything she touched. She wanted to know how to change it.

She felt nauseated, and she staggered forward and vomited into the lake. Translucent minnows ate what she'd spit up. Her stomach lurched and cramped.

Of course she was pregnant; that's how these stories go, she figured. The world was throwing everything it had at her, and this was next on the list. She was still clinging to god—he was lowercase *G* at this point, something indescribable and vague, but at least *something*—and she was livid that he would do this to her. What did the world want? What kinds of trials was she supposed to survive?

She told herself it couldn't be Chisulo's. The condom broke one time—*one time*. Maybe the thing inside her was Guy's; not from the weekend in Malawi, but from early in the trip, or before they left America, anyway. When had she last bled? She couldn't remember. She had nightmares of the birth, of Guy holding a little brown baby. He looks at her with drowning eyes. He throws the baby against the wall.

And even if it was Guy's, what then? They raise it in Malawi? They abandon Africa and return to the States with nothing but a squirming kid?

She told Chisulo on one of those sunset nights by the lake. He leapt to his feet and stood in front of her. He leaned over, put his hands on her cheeks, and kissed her on the forehead, and then he jumped in the air and whooped and came down in the water, wetting his shoes. "I'm going to be a father!" he said.

"No," Lisa said. "It's not that easy. I can't—"

"I will marry you." He was on his knee in front of her now, her hand in his. "We will live together and raise him."

"But Guy—"

"Nothing ties you to Guy. We are tied by our baby."

"He's my husband."

"Do you love me?" His eyes were wet, and the huge African sun reflected orange in them.

Lisa looked away. "I don't know, Chisulo."

"I love you," he said. He stood and looked off at the sun. "You love me. I can feel it. God has blessed our love with this child. We're meant to be together." He looked like a child himself.

"I don't know what to do." But she did know.

Abortion was illegal in Malawi, and she had no way to get to a place where it was legal. So Lisa asked around, and eventually, someone told her about the medicine woman.

Lisa met her at night while the village slept. The woman was of uncountable age, with a face as shriveled as a shrunken head and lips that constantly moved, as though she was a cow chewing its cud. She didn't speak when Lisa entered her hut, a small, tin-roofed thing with a dirt floor and feathers strung up on the walls. A fire burned in an iron furnace in the center of the room.

The woman laid Lisa out on the ground and threw a blanket over her lower half. She gave her a bowl of something and gestured for Lisa to drink; she did, she drank it all—a murky, bitter tea with bits of leaves and dirt in it. The medicine woman built the fire higher and closed the flue, and smoke filled the hut. She began to talk, and she nodded her head at Lisa, wanting her to repeat the words. They chanted the nonsense verses together. The words were not like Chichewa or Chitonga or any of the other native languages; they were ancient and guttural, the voice of demons.

And then the woman put something inside of her. Lisa couldn't see her because of the blanket. She didn't want to see. She felt a sharpness, a pinch, a scraping. And then it was done.

She bled for a week, and then she felt normal again.

She told Chisulo a week before the training ended. He had spent the nights before planning out their life together. He was going to take over the ranch; they would raise this child and many others.

Now he looked at her with hate. "You killed my child," Chisulo said.

"It wasn't a child," Lisa said.

"You are a murderess." He had told her that his name meant *Strength of Steel*, and he looked it now: his face was rigid, his eyes sheets of black metal. His fists were clenched, the muscles in his arms trembling.

Lisa couldn't look at him. She stared at the ground. "This isn't my life, Chisulo. I'm sorry. I just couldn't do it. You knew I couldn't."

"I should kill you."

She looked at him. The rage burned hot inside of Chisulo, and he grit his teeth in an animal snarl. "Please don't," she said, but she felt feeble saying it. Right now, she didn't care if he did kill her.

Instead, he spread his hands between the two of them, creating an invisible wall. "You are dead. You died with my son." He stormed away from her.

"It could have been a girl!" she shouted after him, furious at him all of a sudden. The sexist bastard. But she couldn't sustain the anger. She collapsed and cried.

She saw Chisulo once more. The bus to Lilongwe was carrying her out of town, back to Guy, then off to their shared assignment. Chisulo was in the field with the cattle. He was beating a steer with a stick, trying to force it into a pen. He was yelling—she could hear his voice even in the bus. He was irritated to the point of madness; the steer wouldn't do what he wanted, wouldn't follow the path he'd set out for it. He beat it and beat it as the bus rolled through the dust.

Now she's crying, and Lisa turns from Dante, but he wraps her up from behind, squeezes her close to him.

"I'd have done the same thing," he says.

"I know." She looks out the window. Clouds are building in the west. They are dark gray, and they seem to swirl; they orbit north to south, sluggish and powerful as great rhinos in the sky. "I wasn't going to have that baby. But what I did to Guy. I let him keep trying to knock me up for a year, knowing damn well that I'm broken. I lied about what the doctor said. I let him think it was all his fault."

"What else could you do?" He's kissing the back of her head, wiping her tears with his fingertips.

She's brought back to that night years ago, the night after the doctor. Guy held her, just like Dante holds her now. "He thought I was crying for the baby," she says. "That's wasn't it. I was crying for us. That part of us that died in Africa."

"Lisa," he says.

She turns to him again. His eyes are wet and dark.

He kisses her forehead. "You do what you have to do. That's you. That's why you're still alive. You always find a way to move forward."

Lisa interlocks her fingers with his. She had kept the truth about what happened in Africa locked away for so long. It ate her up inside. It feels good to let it out now, like she's shed a worn-out skin. Guy is dead, and whatever lies she told him are meaningless now. Life is too fleeting to waste on worries about the dead. Better to move on. She kisses Dante. "Forward," she says.

He closes his eyes and kisses her again. When he opens them, they are full of trepidation, fixed on something behind her.

Lisa turns and looks at the clouds outside. As she watches, the ember plunges into them. It vanishes like an egg yolk dropped into a bowl of gray batter. "We should go," Lisa says.

They get back in the jeep, and Dante drives as Lisa looks up. The clouds are building above them; the arms of the storm reach out and snatch up all of the blue in the sky. Lisa is reminded of a spider she saw on TV once; it hides in a hole, and when its prey wanders close enough, it lurches, wraps its meal up in horrible hairy legs. The storm has arms made of cloud, and it's eating the world.

An eerie silence has settled across everything. Lisa waits for thunder or the sound of wind, but there is nothing. Only the low rumble of the jeep's engine and the crunching of snow beneath the tires.

They get on the main road and pass Margot's. The diner is barely visible beneath a hillock of snow.

"You hear it?" Dante says. He slows, and the engine quiets.

Behind them, there's a cracking sound. Then another, the echo of something distant snapping and splintering. "What is it?"

"I don't know," Dante says. He speeds up.

The sounds grow louder. The sky behind them turns from gray to white. From the clouds to the ground is nothing but a white sheet. As Lisa watches, the white spreads out. She can see Margot's, and then she can't. The white has become the horizon, and it's coming closer. There's a deafening screech, the rending sound of metal sliding across asphalt. "Go," Lisa says. "Go. Go."

Dante floors it, and the jeep careens down the hill and into the parking lot of the library.

Lisa leaps out and looks behind her. There are tall, scrawny pine trees at the edge of the parking lot, and the white horizon hits them, and they crack and tumble beneath its weight. "Inside!" Lisa yells, and they sprint to the doors.

Abe opens the doors before Lisa and Dante reach them, and he looks out on the parking lot, and his eyes go wide, his mouth falls open.

And then they're all inside, and Abe shuts the door behind them. They are running, running to the far side of the library, yelling for everyone else to run too, and then the horizon hits. It strikes the front wall of the library like an avalanche. The doors blow open and half of the windows blast inwards as though a bomb has gone off. The wind whips around the building, and snow flows in like water. It's a tsunami; the onslaught comes, and it keeps coming, and the snow piles up as the terrified survivors huddle in the far corner of the library. The storm scrapes across the roof above them, a monster dragging its claws. The walls themselves are shaken in the teeth of the beast.

And then it's gone. Silence sweeps in with the trailing edge of the storm.

Lisa looks at the people around her. Children are crying as parents hold them close. Men hold their guns at ready, as if they can fight off the weather. Dante has his arms wrapped tight around Virgil, and the boy sits with his eyes closed, his hands clasped over his ears.

She gets up and walks to the front of the library. The sky outside is already clearing, and the emberlight reflects blindingly on all the new snow. It's piled five feet high against the library. The snow is full of debris—garbage and sticks and the occasional dead animal— as if the storm has picked up everything it passed over and redistributed it in its wake. The jeep has been slammed against the side of the building, and only the tops of the seats stick out of the snow. Three of the library's windows are busted out, and the snow reaches into the building in fat strips. More comes through the doors; a mountain of the stuff is stretched down the middle of the entryway, and at the end of it is Walter. He's taped to the chair, and he sits upright, buried up to his waist.

"Get her out!" Walter says.

Lisa runs over to him. "Who? Get who out?"

"The old woman!" He jerks his head. "She's there!"

Margot. There is an enormous pile of snow where she sleeps; it covers half of her makeshift kitchen. "Here?" Lisa kneels in the snow, begins to dig, the cold burning her fingers.

"No, right!"

"Here?"

"Right!" Walter is struggling in his seat. "Cut me loose! We'll never find her in time. Jesus, she's going to die. Just cut me loose!"

Dante has made his way over, and he's watching Walter. He looks at Lisa.

She nods. "Cut him loose," she says.

Dante opens his pocketknife and saws through the tape around Walter's wrists. He drags the chair out of the snow and cuts loose the man's feet.

Walter jumps from the chair and plunges into the snow. He digs, tearing into the white like a dog, throwing it everywhere. After a moment, he stops. He's found a leg. "Help me," he says. "Help!"

Lisa and Dante grab the leg and pull. The snow weighs on Margot like an anchor, making it almost impossible to free her. Finally, they've got her out. They sit her up. Margot's face is blue and her eyes are open. Lisa shakes her. "Margot?" Her head bobs. Her muscles are loose, and her movements are lifeless as a doll's.

Walter sits back on his heels and folds his hands in front of him. "Too slow," he says. "Too slow."

One by one, the other survivors make their way to the front of the library. They stand back and watch as Lisa cleans the debris from

Margot's body. A hard cold creeps in through the broken windows. The ember begins to set, and the snow glimmers in the twilight.

After a while, they begin to dig.

METEOR

THEY WORK WELL INTO THE NIGHT. EVERYONE HELPS; they dig with empty tomato cans, with the covers torn off of large hardback books, with Abe's shovel. They dig with their hands. Lisa's fingers are numb and stinging by the time the moon begins to rise.

Abe passes out the ready-to-eat rations that Lisa and Dante found in the jeep, and the survivors take a break. They eat the cold food in silence.

It's been dark for hours before the doorway is cleared. Dante drags the doors shut, and Abe's sons rip the backs off of some bookcases and hammer them over the broken windows. Abe turns on the propane heaters, and the room begins to feel warm again.

Dante and Virgil spend two hours clearing the snow around the jeep. The moon is high overhead when Dante starts the engine and backs it away from the library.

The moon has crossed the sky when Lisa declares the job done. The doors open and close; the windows are secure. The tapered mounds of snow that flowed through the windows still sprawl across the floor, the tails of giant albino rats. They are melting slowly in the propane heat. They'll soak the floor, and it may never dry out entirely. *It doesn't matter*, Lisa thinks. Not at this point.

Margot's body has been lying in a corner of the library since they dug her out. Everyone has been trying not to look at her. Now, Abe, Dante, Virgil, and Walter each grab one of her limbs, and they carry her outside. No one speaks, but everyone follows. Men, women, and children follow the body through the parking lot and into the trees. The moonlight falls soft on the windswept snow, glossing it with silvers and blues. The skin of a whale as it passes beneath the midnight surface of the ocean. Beneath the bent and splintered pines, they lay the body down and stand a silent vigil.

Margot pulled them out of the cold. Fed them. Now, she is the first of them to be lost.

One by one, the survivors return to the library and sleep. At last it's only Lisa and Abe there in the snow as the moon slides silently across the stars. Abe touches Lisa's arm, and then he leaves her.

There will be loss, Lisa thinks. *For all of us, there will be loss.*

It's in the bluish darkness just before ember-rise that something wakes her. A sound, or something less than a sound—a sensation, a feeling of discord, a wrongness in the air. Dante is asleep beside her, his face set in a scowl. Virgil talks softly in his sleep. He says, "Not yet."

Lisa stands and puts her hand on the books. The books, the shelves, the floor beneath her; all seem to vibrate with quiet menace.

From the far side of the library, over near the office where Abe sleeps, near the store of supplies and food, comes a low groan. It's a long bass note that hovers in the bottom of the audible range. She feels it in her guts. The sound turns her stomach, and she wants to vomit. It fills her with unreasonable dread. It's the growl of a tiger hidden behind an emerald screen of jungle. It's a dragon waking in the back of a cave.

Dante has his eyes open. He looks up at her.

The groan comes again. This time, it's loud, and it shakes the shelves. Virgil starts awake and sits up, fear on his face. Lisa can see other survivors at either end of her row of bookcases. They are propped up on one elbow or crouched with a knee to the ground. They cock their heads, turn their ears to the noise.

A rumble. The groan again, this time a roar. Snapping sounds, things crashing, collapsing, and then *whump*. The muffled sound of a hundred tons of snow and ice and library coming down all at once. There is no time to move, no time to think.

A part of the library is there, and then it's not. The ceiling is rent, and the last stars are visible in the pre-dawn gray. Snowflakes swirl in the air and insulation drifts to the ground from the jagged edge of the ceiling that remains.

From Lisa's row over, everything is gone beneath the snow.

The books and the tables, the shelves full of food and water and clothes and guns, the offices and the storage rooms, and the people, the people, Abe and his sons in their office bedrooms, the other men, women, and children who shared that half of the building: all are gone.

Lisa blinks. She wants to yell commands. She wants to leap forward and dig.

In front of her is a frozen hell. The snow is piled fifteen feet high, and it's littered with parts of the building. Joists and two-by-fours stick out of it like pins in a pin cushion.

She thinks she can see a foot.

The snowflakes stirred up by the collapse dance before her eyes, and then they settle, and there is nothing but stillness around her. It's like the library has always been like this: a building half-destroyed. The demolition crew stopped for lunch and never came back.

Lisa does nothing. There is nothing to be done.

No one speaks. They climb around in the snow as the ember rises, trying to salvage what they can. A single water bottle. The grenades. A box of shotgun shells. It is treacherous; nails and broken glass are everywhere, and Virgil tears his ankle on the bent shard of a joist hanger. The nurse and her first-aid supplies are buried, so Dante simply ties a shirt tight around his brother's leg and keeps working.

One woman has lost her son. She digs until her hands are bleeding, and then she retreats to the corner and pulls her knees into her chest. She rocks quietly as the morning wears on.

By midday, it's clear that all is lost. There is too much: too much snow, too much ruin. They can't salvage anything worthwhile. She calls the survivors to the front of the library and counts the people who remain. She and Dante and Virgil, plus another nine people: four women, one man, three children, and Walter.

Lisa is standing on one of the piles of snow that came through the window. She looks down on what's left of the survivors, and she's overcome with guilt. They looked to her. She was the one who kept them safe. And now half of them are dead.

They're all looking to her now.

"We leave the library tomorrow," she says.

They spend the rest of the day gathering what supplies they can find. A few things scrapped from the ruin of the collapse, some food or water squirreled away in packs or forgotten corners of the part of the library that still stands. They dig out Abe's trucks and load everything into the beds. By dark, nothing remains in the library but the dead on one side and the living on the other.

Lisa doesn't sleep that night. She doubts that anyone does. They lie silently and stare into the endless sky overhead. The stars spill from horizon to horizon.

She lays her head on Dante's chest. She feels tears in her eyes, but she fights them back. "I did it wrong," she says.

"You didn't know." Dante's voice is barely a whisper, a murmur in her ear.

"The snow. So much of it. The roof couldn't hold it all. And then I heard it." She turns her head to look at him, but his eyes are closed. "I could have woken people up. I could have gotten them out."

"You didn't know."

She turns her head and looks into the stars. She wants to see something up there; some purpose, some plan, someone watching over the cold citizens of the black planet. Lisa looks into the deep of space and tries to connect the dots, the billion points of light.

It's too much, she thinks. No one can create this. *No one can control this.*

She feels flattened, obliterated by the emptiness and the beauty of the universe.

A flame appears in the sky to the west. It starts small, a brighter orange star amid the countless white ones around it, and it grows, burning, burning, until it's a miniature sun streaking across the heavens. It passes overhead, flying toward the southeast. It flashes blindingly for an instant, and then it comes apart, a dozen tongues of fire barreling through the night. Lisa can see the light on the books, the colors dancing on the snow.

Dante has his eyes open now. Lisa realizes that he's holding his breath.

"Is it a meteor?" Lisa says. For a moment, she imagines a rock the size of a mountain hurtling from the sky and slamming to Earth somewhere, annihilating the planet, ending this all in a single instant of heat. So easy. So warm.

The flames are spreading out, growing fainter.

Dante breathes out, a long, exhausted sigh. "It's the space station," he says.

They watch it burn. The sparks grow smaller, smaller, until they fizzle out completely near the horizon. There is nothing up there but black.

ASHEVILLE

THE SNOW SPARKLES IN THE MORNING EMBER. IT'S like a thousand diamonds are buried in the mound along with the rations and the water, the guns and ammo, the bodies of the dead.

Lisa watches the library as they drive away. She's leaving home, again. She feels an emptiness inside of her, like some part of her is buried back there, and whatever she carries forward is less than what she once was. Lisa felt it when she and Guy left the condo; she felt it when she and Heather drove out of Atlanta beneath that cold summer sky; she felt it when she and Dante and Virgil watched the trailer burn.

She is less, now, but she is more. She is tempered by the reality of life and the cold truth of death.

Dante drives the jeep, and Virgil sits in the passenger seat. Lisa sits in the bed, the M16 in her hands. She checks the magazine—full.

Abe had shown her how to load it; he'd guided the cartridges into the magazine with fingers that are now frozen solid.

In front of them are the two pickups, the remaining survivors in the cabs or hunkered down in the beds. They drive slowly, northeast along the densely-packed snow that coats the highway. They drive for Asheville.

Where else can they go? Lisa and Dante had talked about it the night before. Asheville is nestled in a dent in the lower Appalachian Mountains; to reach any other major city requires crossing passes, the vehicles scrambling up or down steep inclines buried in a winter's worth of snow. They'd have to pass through forests: the Chattahoochee to the southwest, the Pisgah to the north, the endless Great Smoky Mountains National Park between them and Knoxville. Gas? Food? Shelter? Who knows?

It is Asheville or nowhere.

They head for downtown, which lies a few miles north of the Biltmore stronghold. Far enough, they hope, to avoid the Minutemen.

Once, downtown Asheville was a thriving place. Cars lined the streets, and hip young locals knocked shoulders with aging tourists as they perused the trendy shops or ate at the overpriced restaurants. They watched local bands play at kitschy bars.

Now the streets stand like a memorial to the excess of the old world. The broad glass windows of the storefronts are shattered, and bits of broken glass sprout from the snow like the petals of translucent flowers. Beyond the busted windows is only darkness and silence. Here, the stillness of a bar that once overflowed with drunk people. The discolored spots on the wall of an art gallery where priceless things once hung. The tables at a gourmet café, snow glazing them like the icing of whatever expensive pastries sat beneath the glass of the display cases.

The only sound is the engines of the cars, and even that seems quiet here, the rumble swallowed up by the yawning mouths of stores.

"At least there's parking," Dante says.

They pass a store called *Doggy Delicacies*. There's a cartoon poodle on the sign, and it holds a cupcake between its paws. There are display cases in there like the ones at the café, and Lisa is both shocked and charmed by the excess of it; a few months ago, she lived in a world where an entire store could exist with no purpose but to sell doggie treats.

Lisa feels a rush of nostalgia, and for a moment, there is nothing she wants more in the world than to be standing in that store, florescent lights humming above her, heat flowing silently from vents near her feet. Jemi beside her, paws on the glass, drool slopping against the display case as she ogles the treats. Lisa buys her one, something delicate and pink, and she gives it to the dog, and she scratches her ears and the dog squints in pleasure and Lisa says, "Good girl! Good girl."

But the store is empty. Even the dog food has been looted.

They continue on, out of downtown, southeast on the interstate. Lisa's not sure where they're going. Forward, she thinks. On until they find something. Anything.

The interstate is like a white river that flows above the city, and they drive right down the middle of it. The road is elevated, and below it is the hushed ruin of the city. Houses are blanketed in snow, and some are collapsed, done in with by the weight of it all just like the library. The limbs of the trees hang heavy like the tired shoulders of an old man.

They cross a creek, and to their east is a clearing, a huge, snowy field. There's a building in the middle of it, and Lisa realizes it's not a field: it's a parking lot, and the building is a Walmart. She remembers the mad scramble at the Walmart the last time she went, when she made her final run before she and Guy left town. This one too, must have seen the same desperation, the same riotous dash for supplies. There can't be anything of use in there.

Still, she can't pass it by.

Dante honks the horn, and the three vehicles circle back to the exit. They cross the creek—it's almost completely frozen over, save a trickle that funnels through the middle of the icy banks—and cut through the center of the parking lot. The mountains rise stark and gray in the distance, the knuckles of a giant made of stone. The building itself looks exactly like it ought to, as if the cold and the storms were just minor inconveniences. The faux-brick walls stand strong, a deep crimson color against the washed-out landscape. The store's name is written in proud white lettering above the door. Walmart soldiers on.

They pull up to the doors and get out of the jeep. Metal shutters, heavy as garage doors, are lowered across them. Dante tries to lift one. It doesn't budge.

"How do we get in?" Virgil says.

Lisa looks at the doors and then at the jeep. "Back the trucks up," she says. When everyone is clear, she goes to the jeep and retrieves the box of grenades.

Virgil is grinning. "Can I throw it?" he says.

Lisa looks at him. It is the happiest the kid has looked since they left the trailer all those weeks ago. The grenade is heavy in her hand. She has no idea if it will blow through the door. She doesn't know how far she can throw it, anyway—probably not as far as Virgil can. What the hell. Let the kid blow some shit up.

She hands it to him, and Virgil bounces on his heels. "Okay," he says. "I'm going to count to three." Everyone else ducks behind the trucks. "One."

Lisa covers her ears.

"Two," Virgil says.

Dante is laughing beside her. Yes. They are boys, and this is fun.

Virgil looks back at them, his fingers on the pin. He opens his mouth to speak, and then there's a rattling sound, and the door slides open.

Behind the door are people. Too many to count. The crowd bristling with guns.

"Put it down!" someone in there yells.

Virgil sighs. His disappointment is palpable. He sets the grenade in the snow.

A young man walks out. He's tall and skinny, and he's got a beanie pulled down low on his forehead. He blinks in the ember-light, and he reaches into the pocket of his camo jacket and pulls out a pair of aviator shades. He puts them on. He's got a cigarette between his teeth, and he takes it between his thumb and forefinger and exhales slowly, the smoke clouding around his head. He looks at the survivors, still crouched behind the trucks. Then he looks past them, across the creek and off into the distance. "You with them?" he says after a moment.

"With who?" Lisa says.

"Minutemen."

"Hell no," Virgil says.

The man smiles and nods. He takes another drag. "Who's in charge?"

"I am," Lisa says.

He raises his eyebrows. "All right all right. You're going to want to talk to the council, then." He waves his hand, and a dozen armed people, men and women, appear from the doorway. "Got to take the guns for now," the man says. "Nice jeep, huh?"

A woman walks up to Lisa and holds out her hand. "Guns," she says. Lisa gives her the revolver, and she feels naked as soon as she does. Helpless and small. She watches as Dante and all the rest hand over the weapons.

They've disarmed us, Lisa thinks, *and now they're going to kill us all.*

But they don't. The man throws his cigarette on the ground and stomps it out. He turns to the door and beckons them onward. "Let's go. It's cold out here. Come along." They follow him inside. "Welcome, y'all," he says. "Welcome to Fort Walmart."

FORT WALMART

AFTER MONTHS IN THE LIBRARY, FORT WALMART IS
nothing short of amazing. For one thing, it's well lit. The library
was always varying shades of dark; the shadows clung to the back
walls even at midday. Fort Walmart is brightened by dozens of
electric lanterns. They hang strategically from the rafters, splashing
everything beneath them with a pleasant yellow glow. The store,
apparently, was not looted; there's still plenty of stuff on most of
the shelves, but space has been repurposed. The shelves have been
moved. They no longer form neat rows, but instead outline a series
of makeshift rooms with hallways in between. Lisa can see in them
as she walks by: a handful of people in each, tables and chairs and
bedding areas, personal items on the shelves. Larger rooms seem to
be community areas. There are long dining tables. Several couches
surrounding a TV that's connected to a generator.

The man in the camo jacket is named Terrence. He leads Lisa to the back of the store. The people in the shelf rooms look up as she passes. Some watch her warily, but some smile. Children wave.

Terrence leads her through a set of double doors in the back of the store and up a dark staircase. At the top, he opens the door to a small conference room with a round table in the middle. Big windows look down on the store, and from up here Lisa can see into every room, into every life. There must be over a hundred people down there, the citizens of Fort Walmart.

"You want some coffee?" Terrence says.

"I'd love some." Lisa can't remember the last time she had a cup of coffee.

Terrence is gone for a minute, and he comes back with a steaming cup. He brings a bowl of sugar and some individual packets of cream. "The council will be up in a few minutes," he says, and then he leaves her.

Lisa takes a sip of the coffee. It is dark and rich and intense, and the heat of it burns her lips and her tongue. But it is delicious. She drinks half of it, and then she mixes in the cream and sugar and begins to savor the rest.

She's almost done with the cup when the council comes in. There are three of them: two men and a woman. The men are about Lisa's age. One is wiry, and he wears some sort of military cap. He keeps his sunglasses on even though it's dark in the room. He has his hand on the shoulder of the other man, a tall, blond man with a handsome face and a yellow beard. He seems familiar to Lisa, as if she met him in some other life.

The woman is older than either of them, old enough to be Lisa's mother. She has gray hair cut level with her ears, and her green eyes glimmer with intelligence. She sits across from Lisa, and the blond man helps the other into the chair. That's when Lisa figures it out: the man with sunglasses is blind.

The woman sits in silence, watching Lisa. She has a searching look about her, as if by staring at Lisa for long enough she can uncover all of her secrets. After a while, she nods, apparently satisfied. She sits back in her chair and says, "I'm Malorie. And you're Lisa."

"I am." Lisa sets her coffee cup down and folds her hands in front of her.

225

"Why did you come here?" Malorie says.

Lisa shrugs. "We weren't coming *here*, specifically. We were just going away. And here is where we ended up."

"How did you know to come here?" This is the blond man. He speaks with an accent, the lilting tones of some far-off place.

Lisa cocks her head, looks at him. "I know you," she says.

He raises his eyebrows. "We've met?"

And then she remembers. "You're the scientist. Mathiasen, right?"

He smiles. "Call me Dagmar. But answer the question. How did you know about us?"

"We didn't. We just needed supplies. A place to stay." She tells them about the library, about the collapse. "We have nowhere else to go."

"More coffee?" Malorie says. Lisa shakes her head. "We have room," Malorie continues. "How many of you are there? Ten? Twelve? We have room."

Beside her, the man with sunglasses sighs.

"We *do*, Carter."

"We're low on food as it is," Carter says. He takes his sunglasses off and pushes his thumb and forefinger against his eyes. He keeps his eyes closed, and they have a weird, sunken blackness to them; it makes his whole face seem wasted and gaunt. His cheeks are lined with jagged red scars. "We can't take any more. We won't make it the winter."

"We take anyone who needs us, Carter. Those are our principles."

"But we can't—"

"Those are our principles." She turns back to Lisa. "We've been here since the beginning. I was on the city council here in Asheville. The mayor and the rest of the city council took off, but I couldn't go. I wasn't going to leave when my city needed me. So we came here. We came to Walmart before things got crazy. I and some of the National Guardsmen closed the store to business. We turned it into a shelter."

"The owner just let you take it over?" Lisa says.

"We didn't ask," Malorie says. "We did what needed to be done." She sighs. "Not that very many people came to take shelter. Everyone wanted to go south. There were only fifty of us at first, but we've grown with all the others who have shown up since the Big Aurora."

"And every one of them another mouth to feed," Carter says. His sunglasses are on again, and he's staring sightlessly across the table.

"Yes. We feed them. That is what we do," Malorie says. "You're the first in a long while. No one has come north since Atlanta burned." Her face turns serious. "All are welcome, but everyone has to carry her weight. Everyone contributes what they can. Carter is in charge of the weapons and the troops. Dagmar, well, Dagmar does what he does. He knows the ember. And I keep things organized." She smiles at Lisa. "What do you offer us?"

Lisa laughs. "I'm a librarian."

Carter scoffs. "A librarian. We're saved."

Malorie shushes him. "What else can you do?"

Carter stands up. "We don't need librarians!" he says. "And we don't need more people eating our food. We need guns. We need a plan. The Minutemen are going to come back at some point, and we won't be able to fight them off next time. We need people who can help us fight back."

"We have guns," Lisa says. "Grenades. The jeep."

"It's not enough. We need to take the fight to them." Carter sits, sighs. "Wherever they are."

Lisa leans back in her chair. "*That* is something we can help with."

They bring Walter up to the conference room, and the five of them spend an hour talking about the Minutemen. Walter tells them about the Biltmore House, the Minutemen, their leadership, their armament. A smile appears on Carter's face, and it grows as Walter talks.

By the time they're done, every member of the council is more than happy to welcome the survivors of the library.

They settle in. Malorie gives Lisa's people four rooms, and Dante sets up an area for Virgil and Lisa and himself. "Nice, huh?" he says.

Lisa takes his hands in hers, and she lifts her chin and closes her eyes as he kisses her. Later, she walks the hallways made of shelves, peering in on the people that she's lived with for so long. They look happy, safe. Lisa feels a warmth inside of her. *This is good*, she thinks. *I have done something good.*

The metal doors of the store are still open, and she steps outside into the snow. The ember is setting, and everything is glowing like a blade that's been held over a fire.

Dagmar stands at the far end of Fort Walmart. He's smoking a cigarette.

Lisa walks over to him. He nods and lights another cigarette, hands it to her. Lisa doesn't smoke, but she takes it anyway. She takes a long drag, and the hot ashy feeling is warm in her lungs. She doesn't care that it makes her cough. "What are you doing in Asheville?" Lisa says. "I thought you'd be in DC, or New York, or something."

"I was," Dagmar says. "But duty calls."

He tells her the story: he'd been sent to Atlanta just before the Big Aurora. They'd wanted him at the Centers for Disease Control; the doctors were worried that another cold winter could lead to unpredictability in the spread of viruses. They were anticipating a new flu, something horrible. They needed Dagmar's advice. They wanted to know how cold, how long. "And I hated to tell them," Dagmar says. "I really did."

"Tell them what?"

"That it would be very cold. And for very long."

Lisa smokes and looks off at the ember. It's nothing but a frail orange light hanging above the earth. "It didn't work, did it?"

"The Big Bang? Of course not." He stubs his cigarette out in a nearby snow bank and lights another one. "You can't restart the sun with missiles. It's ridiculous."

Now Lisa is angry. "Then why would you tell everyone it worked?" She shakes her head and stares at the glowing tip of her own cigarette. "Why have a Big Bang to begin with? Why lie? Do you know how many people you've fucked?"

"But can you imagine what would have happened if we told the truth? The panic it would cause?"

Lisa can feel his eyes on her, but she refuses to look.

"It was a necessary lie," Dagmar says. They are silent for a while as they watch the ember creep toward the horizon. "Look at it," he says. "It doesn't even burn your eyes anymore. You can stare and stare. It's just a spark. It's a coal in the campfire long after everyone has gone to sleep. It's, well, it's an ember."

Lisa tells herself that she knew. She always knew that the Big Bang had failed and the world was marching toward a cold death. But she always hoped she was wrong. Now, the confirmation of her fears is like a knife in her back: a subtle, sharp blade, slipped in quietly at midnight. "What's going to happen?" she says after a while.

Dagmar shrugs. "It will get cold. We'll have a few more summers, but then they will end. It will only be winter."

"How long do we have?"

"Who's to say?"

"So what do we do? We go south?"

Dagmar shakes his head. "South would only buy you a few years. It all goes cold eventually. Besides, where do you go? We have people in the fort who tried to go south and turned back. Once you get to Florida, there is nothing but gridlock. People starving to death in their cars. And after what happened in Miami," he pauses, "there is nothing for us there."

Her stomach turns. "What happened in Miami?"

"You have not heard?" He covers his mouth with his hand, and then he strokes his beard. "Miami," he says. "Miami is gone."

Her parents. Lisa throws the cigarette to the ground and watches as it burns out.

"Eventually, everyone realized that the power wasn't coming back on, so they went to Miami," Dagmar says. "There were a hundred million people there by the time the snow started to fall. It was ripe for attack, and that's exactly what happened."

She tries to imagine a hundred million people crammed into the tip of the Florida peninsula. In her head, the masses writhe and roil like maggots in a wound. "Minutemen?"

He shakes his head. "The Minutemen aren't the only terrorists. It could have been Marauders, Valkyries, Final Jihad, any of them. But whoever he was with, he had the bomb. A big one; they say it was snuck into Biscayne Bay on a freighter and loaded into a moving truck. After the power went out, there was no security. It may have come from Iran, maybe North Korea—it could have been stolen from Nevada for all we know. But they got it in." He closes his eyes, shakes his head. "Ground zero was downtown. There was nothing left for five miles in every direction. But you weren't much better off if you were six miles away."

Lisa's parents lived—already she finds herself thinking in past tense—in Coral Gables, five miles at best from downtown. She can see their house in her head. She sees them standing by the big windows that look out over the garden. There's a flash, and her father grabs her mother, wraps himself around her, puts his body between her and the light as if to protect her. Nothing can protect them. The house is aflame; their skin burns, and they scream in the instant before the shock wave obliterates them. "My parents lived in Miami," she says.

The ember touches the horizon and spills its molten light across the earth. "I'm sorry," Dagmar says.

Lisa nods. She wants to cry, but at this point, tears seem wasted. She's lost her parents, she's lost Guy. Heather and Jemi are as good as gone; all of her friends and loves are nothing but dust. She alone carries on. For what?

The ember disappears, and the sky above it begins to fade into night.

"This is how the world ends," Lisa says.

"No," Dagmar says. "Not yet." He tells her the story of the age of the ember. The star will get weaker each year, and the snow will stay on the ground longer. The snow deflects what heat reaches the planet, making it colder still, so less melts each year and more light is reflected—a self-perpetuating cycle. "It's called Snowball Earth," he says. "We think it happened once before, hundreds of millions of years ago. The entire planet freezes over."

Nothing can survive on that ball of ice, Dagmar says. It will orbit lifelessly until the ember dies completely, and then the solar system will be nothing but rock and ice, gas and dust.

The earth itself, though, is different. The earth is the key to survival.

Beneath the surface lies millions of tons of molten metal. Even buried beneath a mile of ice, the tectonic plates will slide against each other, bashing and clanking on their vast geological times-cales. The core of the planet will spin. Friction and pressure and heat, on and on inside the frozen ball of rock. The heat will still work its way to the surface. And the heat can be used.

"There are places you might survive," Dagmar says. They've retreated inside now; with the ember gone, the cold is so heavy that it's hard to breathe. "Places of great geothermal activity. The Ring of Fire around the Pacific, or in parts of South America. Out west in Yellowstone. Or volcanic islands: Hawaii, the Azores, Iceland." He smiles at this last one. "That is where I was supposed to go."

When the riots started in Atlanta and the city was set ablaze, he was put in a car headed north. They were evacuating the government and all other essential personnel to Iceland, they told him. The president, leaders of the military—they were already there. They needed minds like his to set up the new civilization, a city that could survive the cold that was coming. Supposedly there were plans to turn Reykjavik into a city cased in glass, kept warm by geothermal power. "We never made it, of course," Dagmar says. "Asheville is as far as we got." He shrugs. "The planes weren't flying anyway, and I doubt they'll get another boat out there until spring."

But that is his dream. They will survive the winter. They will travel north, find a boat. They'll sail to Iceland, and they'll live.

"Will it work?" Lisa says.

"It's the only plan we've got," Dagmar says. He rubs his hands together and looks up. All traces of the ember are gone by now, and night stretches from horizon to horizon. "So dark, the sunless sky," he says, and then he leaves her and retreats to the fort.

Lisa closes her eyes. She pictures herself in Reykjavik. She's surrounded by tropical plants beneath a glass dome while a blizzard whirls outside. Dante is beside her. They watch the storm from their bubble as the ember dies above them.

DOLLHOUSE

TERRENCE SCOWLS AT THE DOLLHOUSE. "BUT WHERE can we get in?" he says.

"That's what I'm saying," Walter says. "They've blocked off most of the entrances. The ones that are clear, they keep guarded. There is no easy way in."

There are a dozen of them in the room. All three council members: Dagmar and Malorie sit in chairs off to the side, observing quietly, and Carter stands beside Terrence. He looks down on the model as though he can see it. From time to time, Terrence speaks quietly into his ear, explaining the layout to him. There's also Lisa, Dante, and several former members of the National Guard. They form a ragged circle around a detailed model of the Biltmore estate that they've built in the center of the room. The house itself is a Barbie Dreamhouse. The gardens are represented by Lego trees. The greenhouses are overturned Tupperware containers. The woods, the roads, the fields—everything else that makes up the sprawling grounds—is carefully drawn onto the tile floor with sidewalk chalk. The book department had several tourist guides to Asheville, and each of these had write-ups on Biltmore. The pages are torn out and line the walls of the room: pictures, maps, architectural details.

They started planning the raid the day after Lisa and her people arrived. It's been nearly two months, and still, Carter isn't satisfied. "Can we draw them out?" he says.

Walter shakes his head. "They've got lookouts who'll see us coming, so we won't trick them into coming out. And why would they? They've got everything they need in there."

The council has decided that a raid is the only way to survive. Dagmar says that winter is ending. He spends long hours outside, looking up at the ember. He records the time of sunrise and sunset each day, and the days are getting longer. He has a thermometer he found in the lawn and garden department, and he marks the high and low temperatures. For three days now, the high has been above freezing. One day soon, he says, the snow will begin to melt. But not soon enough.

The food is running low. Carter has Guardsmen in charge of the rationing, and even with the great stores that lined the shelves of Fort Walmart, supplies are dwindling. Since they can't head north until the roads are clear, they're stuck in a race between melting snow and diminishing provisions, and right now, the food is winning. They eat too much too fast. Carter and Dagmar are in agreement: the food will not last the winter.

Malorie had the final word. She confirmed it. The raid will happen.

"We may outnumber them," Walter says.

"We have a hundred and fifteen," Carter says. "But twenty-eight of those are children. Only fifteen are trained soldiers."

The soldiers came in the early days of Fort Walmart. They had been with their different regiments, deployed to keep the peace, but the National Guard's organization fell apart rapidly and completely. The troops were rife with Minutemen, and they took off with weapons and other supplies. Some people went AWOL to be with their families or to try to make it south. Before long, the National Guard was just a few roving bands of soldiers, and these bands too, broke up, until they wandered in groups of two or three. Some showed up alone. They came to Fort Walmart, and Carter took charge, and now the former soldiers formed the backbone of the resistance.

"There's probably a hundred in Biltmore," Walter says. "But some are children. I'm not sure how many fighters. Fifty, maybe." He pauses, kneels beside the dollhouse. He points to the windows. "Look at this place, though. Look at how many places there are to hide. They have guns in the windows, guns on the roof. We'd never make it across the lawn, let alone inside. We'd have to take down a wall. We'd have to tear the place down."

Carter is nodding slowly. "All right. Get him out of here." A soldier leads Walter from the room. The council allows him in for logistics, but they sequester him when the planning gets detailed. Carter insisted. Once a Minuteman, always a Minuteman, he said. "He's gone?"

"Yes, sir," the soldier says.

"We don't have the weaponry to take down a wall."

"We have my grenades," Lisa says. She wants to contribute. She is happy to be in the safety of Fort Walmart, but part of her misses the command she had at the library. Despite the weight of the responsibility, she liked being in charge. It gave her purpose.

"Grenades won't do it," Carter says. "Not with walls like that. Maybe an RPG, but not just a hand grenade."

"This is going nowhere," Malorie says. She walks to the center of the room. She stands in front of the dollhouse and crosses her arms. "How long, Dagmar? How long until we can go north?"

He sighs. "A month would be pushing it. Two months is more realistic."

"And how much food do we have?"

"A few weeks," Carter says.

Malorie walks a slow circle around the mock Biltmore House. "I won't have a fort full of starving people. And I won't have another attack on our home."

"They'll come back," Carter says. "It's only a matter of time."

Carter had told Lisa about the attack. The Minutemen came a month after the first snowfall. They were going to loot the Walmart, apparently, and hadn't counted on it being full of soldiers. There had been a skirmish in the parking lot. Four Minutemen were killed, and Fort Walmart lost two of their own. A grenade went off ten feet from where Carter stood commanding his men. The shrapnel tore half his face off. He got drunk on cheap wine and lay on a cot as one of the residents of the fort, a former nurse, pulled the shredded ruins of his eyeballs from their sockets.

Malorie is back in front of the dollhouse. She looks at it for a long time. "We're going to tear it down," she says.

"And how do you propose we do that, Malorie?" Dagmar says.

She glares at him. "We'll find a way."

Two weeks later, Lisa and Dante are playing cards in their room when Virgil runs in, his face alight with excitement. "Come see," he says.

"What?" Dante says.

"Just come see!" He leads them outside and points.

Lisa follows the gesture to the eaves of Fort Walmart. Water is trickling from the roof and splashing to the asphalt. The snow feels squishy under her feet.

Virgil is doing a dance in the snow. "Spring," he sings. "Spring, spring, oh yeah, spring is on its way."

The residents of the fort begin to file outside. They stand in the snow, grins on their faces, watching the snowmelt flow. The ember beats down on them with something that could almost be called warmth.

Dagmar is the last to come out. He holds his thermometer in front of his face, reads it, nods at Malorie. She moves close to him, and Lisa follows. Terrence leads Carter over, and the five of them huddle and speak in low voices.

"We can go?" Malorie says.

"Not yet," Dagmar says. "It is melting here, yes, but we have to go north. We might find a boat in DC, but we may have to go to New York. Possibly as far as Boston. We can't go until the snow is melting there too."

Malorie sighs. "We raid, then."

"It won't work," Carter says. "Not yet."

"So what do you suggest we do? We starve?" She shakes her head. "I won't let it happen. The raid is on."

"It's a suicide mission. It's..." Carter puts his hand to his ear.

Lisa listens, and after a moment, she can hear it. A rumbling, a creaking mechanical sound. And then she sees it: something large on the other side of the trees, a great mechanical monster crushing its way through the melting snow. It turns, crosses the bridge, and there it is, huge in the parking lot: a tank. Tan like desert sand. Its black treads whirring through the slush.

People scream and retreat into the fort. The soldiers duck behind snowbanks, draw their guns.

"It's an Abrams, isn't it?" Carter says. He takes off his sunglasses and looks across the parking lot with his empty eyes. "Good god. We're all dead."

The tank rattles closer. There's a heavy machine gun mounted on the turret. The barrel of the main gun juts forward, thick as a young pine tree. There's something written on the side of it in dark green paint. When the tank is close enough, Lisa can read it: BIG BAD WOLF.

The tank stops fifty feet from the fort. Its engine powers down, and quiet settles back over the parking lot. Lisa can hear the drops of water plinking in the puddles.

The soldiers move behind the snow banks. They train their guns on the tank.

The hatch opens, and a man sticks his head out. He's black with a black beard and a beret on his head. "Oh, shit!" he says, and he ducks back into the tank.

The soldiers look at each other. Terrence whispers something to Carter.

A moment later, the man sticks his head back out. "Y'all ain't going to shoot me, are you? Shit, I thought you'd be happy to see me."

Carter stands up. "Berkley?"

"Carter? That you?" Berkley climbs down from the tank. He's short but stocky, built like a sparkplug. "No shit! I thought those sons of bitches got you."

Carter is smiling now, and Terrence leads him over to Berkley. The men hug and talk quietly for a moment. Lisa can hear them laughing.

People are trickling back out of Fort Walmart. Malorie stands beside Lisa.

A couple of other soldiers climb out of the tank. They shake hands with Carter. Then, the four of them come back to the fort.

"All right, Malorie," Carter says. "You've got your raid."

WHITE

THEY GATHER IN THE BATTLE ROOM THAT NIGHT. Someone found a miniature tank in the toy department, and it sits in front of the dollhouse along with dozens of plastic army men.

"They'll come out when they see the tank," Carter says.

Dagmar looks skeptical. "Why would they? Would you come out with that in your front yard?"

"Because we're taking the fight to them. They'll have to defend Biltmore."

"But they'll simply shoot from inside the house."

"Oh, their guns won't do nothing to the Wolf," Berkley says. Berkley had told everyone his story the night he arrived. He and Carter had been in the same battalion before the Big Aurora, and in the days afterward, Berkley's company moved south to root out Minutemen in Hendersonville while Carter moved toward

Asheville. They were supposed to meet back up two weeks later, but by then, the Guard was all but dissolved. Berkley and the few men he had left wintered in a middle school, and when the snow began to melt, they headed north, hoping to find troops in Asheville. He'd come to Walmart hoping to find supplies, just like everyone else.

Now, Berkley and his men sit in on the meetings along with the usual crowd. Berkley kneels and moves the tank to the far side of the yard and points the gun at a corner of the dollhouse. "We move over here, they can't get a good shot anyway. Not from those windows. And we stay out at the edge of the lawn, they can't get us with RPGs or nothing like that. They got RPGs?"

"We don't know," Carter says. "Walter wasn't sure."

"Even if they got them, they got to come closer to use them. We can stay back here and unload on them."

Some of the National Guardsmen squat in front of the dollhouse and reposition the army men. They've got gray ones all around Biltmore—the Minutemen—and green ones near the trees represent the soldiers of Fort Walmart. Carter gives commands as Terrence dictates the battlefield to him. The real soldiers move the fake ones around, and Lisa is struck by how much they look like children playing with toys. In a way, that's exactly what they are, exactly what they're doing.

Malorie approaches the dollhouse. "So we get them out," she says. "What then?"

Berkley smiles at her. He puts his foot on the tank, rolls it forward a few inches. "We're going to do what the Big Bad Wolf does best."

Berkley's men begin nodding, punching each other playfully.

"What we going to do?" Berkley says. "I'll tell you what we going to do. We going to huff."

"Huff," his men say quietly.

"I said we going to *huff*!"

"Huff!" They're on their feet, yelling along with their commander.

Berkley is pacing around the model of Biltmore now. His arms crossed, his eyebrows furrowed. He looks at the other soldiers in the room. He looks at Lisa. "What we going to do then?"

"Puff." More people are joining in, now. Lisa can feel tingles running down her back, the electricity of minds running in unison.

"We going to what?" Berkley is yelling.

"Puff!" Lisa yells now too, and Dante, and all the other soldiers.

Berkley nods. He turns to Malorie. "All right, Malorie. What we going to do then?"

Malorie looks at the people that surround her. Her eyes are aflame. The air in the room is taut with the intensity of the moment. She looks down at the dollhouse. "We're going to blow the motherfucking house in." And then she draws her leg back and kicks the dollhouse, and it flies through the air and crashes against the shelves and collapses in a heap on the tile.

The crowd roars.

They don't set a date for the raid—Dagmar wants to wait for more snow to melt, and he's not sure how long it will take—but they know it's coming soon. A week, two tops.

Before that, Carter wants eyes on the house. There are too many inconsistencies in the travel guides and in Walter's testimonials. Walter would look at the books, shaking his head. "I don't remember this," he said, or, "That's not what it looks like anymore." Carter refuses to start a mission based on out-of-date guidebooks and the messy recollections of one man. He organizes a reconnaissance mission. Four soldiers, including Terrence and one of Berkley's men, plus Walter. They're going to take the jeep and one of Abe's trucks.

There is something that has gnawed at Lisa since they laid out the plan. The Big Bad Wolf is going to blow the house in. She doesn't know who's on the other side of those walls. She doesn't know who is going to die.

Lisa can't stop thinking about Heather. Is she in Biltmore? Is she the one who Walter mentioned—Jefferson's girl? Lisa imagines the sound of the tank's gun echoing through the night, the shell whistling through the air, the terrible rumble of a wall coming down. She pictures bodies in the rubble, buried like her friends in the ruin of a building. She sees a broken arm jutting from the debris, a shock of red hair.

She has to know. Lisa has to know if Heather is in there. "I want to go with the scouts," she says to Carter as his men are preparing to leave.

"No way," he says.

"Okay. I'm not asking, then. I'm going."

"There's no reason for you to go." He speaks as though the argument exhausts him. "We've got enough men, and you'll just put them in danger."

"Carter."

He turns to her and takes off his glasses. He looks at her patiently through the dark holes in his head.

Lisa stares right back. "I brought you Walter," she says. "You'd have no plan if it wasn't for him. You wouldn't even know where the Minutemen are. And you're taking my jeep. And my truck. This is my mission as much as it is yours."

Carter blinks, and then he puts his sunglasses back on. He turns and listens to the sounds of guns being loaded, tires being inflated. Finally, he nods. "Take Dante with you," he says.

They leave in the midmorning beneath a clear sky. The ember seems warmer day by day, and Lisa drives the jeep with her hat off. She feels the light in her hair, warming her scalp. Dante sits beside her, his hand on her leg. Lisa shifts smoothly as they accelerate.

"Like a boss," Dante says.

She squeezes his hand. "I had a good teacher."

The road to Biltmore follows along the stream that runs near Fort Walmart; water flows freely down the center now, and the snow is pulling back, revealing the sandy edges of the banks.

They drive through the poor heart of Asheville. The stores downtown screamed of wealth and excess, but this part of town— an area of run-down auto-body shops and shabby taverns and convenience stores with bars on the window—seems forgotten. Snow falls in clumps from the roofs of abandoned houses.

And then, all at once, the poverty is gone. It's replaced by the garish sprawl of the Biltmore district. There are strip malls and condos everywhere, all of them built to resemble mountain cottages. It's the same fare that can be found anywhere: McDonald's and Starbucks and Jamba Juice, on and on. All of it done up to look rustic, to look special. Lisa is insulted by it. She pictures executives in a board room. It's before the Big Aurora, so the room is heated and fresh pastries sit in the middle of the table. The executives plan the new franchise. Someone suggests that the store should look quaint. It should look *mountainy*. That will get customers in the doors. That will make more money.

These stores, like everything else, are empty and dark, long-since looted. They too rot beneath the oblivious shine of the ember.

Walter is in the pickup in front of them. He waves, points, and they head east, avoiding the main entrance. "They might have guards there," Walter had said that morning. "We can take Vanderbilt Road and cut through the forest. No one goes that way."

They follow the road through the woods, passing a few empty houses before crossing into Biltmore property. Here, the road is narrow and the trees are dense. They press on through the snow, and it melts beneath the wheels; twin black trails of asphalt follow them. The ember is high overhead, and the needles of the pines sparkle as water beads, collects, falls to the ground. Birds flit from branch to branch. *How did they survive?* Lisa thinks. Birds, cowering in the nooks between branches, their wings over their heads as the snow falls and falls. How does life go on?

Far away, clouds are building, way off on the western horizon.

After a couple of miles, they turn off on a narrow dirt path. A bent, decorative sign reads OLD OVERLOOK ROAD. The road ramps up, and the wheels of the jeep spin, but they find purchase and the vehicle creeps forward.

Walter holds up his hand, and the truck comes to a stop. The driver shuts down the engine, and Lisa does the same in the jeep. They get out and walk the last fifty yards up that hill, and the trees thin out, and then there it is.

The mansion is a half mile below them, crouched like a lion in the middle of the snow. The forest rolls out for miles behind it, and in front of it is a broad lawn that was once well manicured. The ember casts everything in a bronze glow. The beige brick of the house is set alight and burns with an inner fire. The peaks of the roof glow blue like the swirling surface of Neptune. The thousand windows spark with every color imaginable.

The grounds are as Walter described them. Lisa can see the gardens, the greenhouse with the ember reflected on the glass. She imagines the tank, the people. She imagines war.

"Where is everybody?" Terrence says.

They watch from the overlook. No one is visible down there. The place is as still as the snow that surrounds it.

"What's on the other side?" Dante says. They're looking at the house from the front.

"More," Walter says. "More windows, more doors."

"More ways in," Terrence says. "We need to get closer. Carter doesn't want any surprises."

They spend half an hour climbing down the hill. They move slowly, pausing to listen to the forest. Birds twitter in the trees. A squirrel digs in the snow. Other than that, they are alone. The ember moves westward and disappears into the swift-moving clouds, and the world becomes damp, colder than before.

They stop in the trees a few yards shy of the front drive. They hide in the bushes and watch.

Now, they can see a few people. Two Minutemen stand beside the front door, and their flag—the hat and crossed muskets—flies above them. The men have guns over their shoulders. One of them laughs, and it carries across the snow. It's a high-pitched giggle, the laugh of a child. Another man is at the far end of the building. He's cleaning the gun that's mounted on the back of a Humvee.

"Did you know they had that Humvee?" Terrence whispers to Walter.

"I never saw it," Walter says.

Three more men come out of the house and head over to the Humvee. They are indistinct so far away, but one of them is huge, hulking over his friends. They get into the Humvee and the sound of its engine drifts across the lawn. "Can that stop the tank?" Lisa says.

"I don't think so," Terrence says. "But it's not good. You got to tell us this shit, Walter."

"I said I never saw it."

The Humvee pulls onto the road and heads in their direction. "Down! Down," Terrence says. They take a few steps farther into the woods and bury themselves in the undergrowth. The Humvee comes up the road, passes within a dozen yards of them, and drives on, disappearing down another road into the forest.

Lisa listens. She can't hear the birds. The squirrels. The sound of the Humvee recedes, and there is nothing but the deadness of the snow. She watches the Minutemen at the door. They have stopped laughing. They step away from the house and look past it, off toward the west. They say something to each other, and then they go inside. Lisa looks west to the horizon behind Biltmore.

The clouds are swirling, and great arms of gray are reaching out into the blue.

"We've got to go," Lisa says.

Terrence shakes his head. "We need to get around to the back."

"No. Look." She points to the hills beyond the house, where the storm is crawling across the sky like a predator lurking on the ocean's floor.

Terrence's face goes cold. "Again," he says. "Not again."

And then they are running. Dante and Lisa, Walter and Terrence, the other three soldiers; they scramble back up the hill, slipping in the wet snow, falling and rolling back downward, grabbing onto branches and tree trunks as they climb.

Lisa looks back, and the Biltmore house looks like it's a cutout on a blank sheet of paper: the snowy lawn stretches out in front of it, and the white horizon fills the space behind. Lisa keeps running.

Dante is behind her, pushing her. "Go," he's yelling. "Go!"

She looks down at him, and there's terror on his face, and then behind him, she sees white and white. Biltmore is gone.

The jeep and the truck are visible at the top of the hill. Terrence is almost there.

The lawn behind them is swallowed by the white horizon.

Walter is moving the slowest, and he's the first one gone. The wall hits him, and he vanishes from view. A tree bends and snaps; the sound ricochets like gunfire. Another soldier disappears, and then the horizon is almost upon them, and Dante leaps on her, pulls Lisa down in a low spot behind a tree, and then the storm hits.

The noise is deafening. A whirling, whining roar that blasts her eardrums. The wind tumbles Lisa and Dante uphill, slams them against a tree, pins them there. Lisa squeezes her eyes shut. She feels her face cover in snow. Dante grips her tight, and the tree behind them shudders from the force.

They are a piling sticking up in a river of flowing snow. A rock with an avalanche rushing around them.

The leading edge of the storm is the strongest. After it passes, they are half-buried in snow, but they can move again. They dig themselves out and stand.

Dante is saying something. Lisa can hear his voice, but she can't make out his words. She turns to him. He's two feet away, but she can barely see him through the snow. Beyond him, the world disappears into an endless cloud.

He keeps yelling, but she can't hear him, so Dante grabs her arm and drags her uphill. Then there's a sound like rocks banging together, and Dante staggers, slows.

Lisa looks upward. She can see a tree, the slope of the hill. "Let's go," she yells. "We're close!"

Dante stops. After a moment, he kneels, puts his hand in the snow.

"Dante!" Lisa says. "Come on!"

He looks up at her. His face is indistinct through the snow. His lips are moving.

She squats beside him and takes his face in her hands. "Come on!"

"Go," he's saying. "Just go." He tries to stand up, but he wobbles, loses his balance, and falls on his back.

Lisa bends to help him up, and then she sees it: red. Deep red-black flowing into the snow, melting it, steaming it into the snow-laced air. She puts her hand on Dante's stomach; her hand comes away coated in blood.

Terrence is beside her now, a ghost appearing out of the storm. "They're here!" he says. "We've got to move!" And then there's another *clack*, and he falls, slides a few feet down the hill. Blood pours from his head.

Lisa tries to help Dante up. He can't move. It's like he weighs a million pounds.

The blood is pooling around him. So much of it, cutting deep red holes into the snow.

"Lisa!" Dante says. "Go!"

She looks at him, dazed. *No*, she's thinking. *Not Dante. Not Dante too*. She grabs his arm and pulls, but he might as well be nailed to the ground.

"Go!"

And then she lets go. She touches his face, looks into his eyes, his eyes like night, the stars in them going out, galaxies unwinding, supernovae collapsing in on themselves. And then she runs. Up the hill, through the blinding snow, through the ceaseless whirling noise, until she finds the jeep. It's half-buried in snow. A soldier lies beside it, choking on his own blood.

She hears the sound again, and she recognizes it as gunfire this time. Close by. Someone screaming.

Lisa climbs into the back of the jeep and grabs the M16. She sweeps the barrel past the white that hangs between the trees. Something moves back there, and she fires. She gun rattles in her hands, the sound like fireworks going off inside of her skull. She follows the shadow, the gun spitting fire, bullets ripping the bark off the trees.

She stops. Her ears ring. The storm is quieting down now, the trees appearing out of the haze. Something moves behind her.

Lisa turns, and then there's a flash, an explosion of light on the backside of her eyes, and she falls from the jeep.

She lies on her back in the snow. The clouds are pulling back from the sky above her, and the blue of afternoon is beginning to show through. The pines are bent sideways, green feathers ruffled by the storm.

Lisa touches her head. Her fingers come away bloody.

Blackness closes in from the outer edges of her vision as the world disappears. She looks up, and a man comes into view. A huge man, a giant blocking out the ember. He wears binoculars that are attached to his head. Not binoculars. Goggles. Infrared? She is too confused to care.

Lisa's world is going, going. The tunnel closes in.

Above her, the man takes off his goggles. He grins down at her. His grin, his gleaming bald head; the terrible face of the Bull.

HEATHER

PRISONER

HER PALMS ARE PRESSED AGAINST THE CANVAS, AND she looks into the muddy paint of the dead president's eyes.

The living Jefferson is behind her. Heather feels his naked skin against hers. His stubble on her cheek, his breath in her ear. His hands on her hips, her breasts, the soft expanse of her pregnant belly.

He has told Heather that this is how he likes it best. He likes to take her from behind, up against that portrait, so that she can be surrounded by greatness: the old Father in front of her, the new one behind.

The portrait rocks beneath her hands as he thrusts. Heather winces, pierced by a bitter pleasure.

He pulls out of her and she turns around. She pushes him back onto the bed, a Victorian-styled monstrosity with an intricately-carved headboard and blue canopy suspended from the posts. She mounts him, and her knees sink into the old mattress. This is how she likes it. Heather likes looking down at Jefferson from above; he's not much taller than her when he's standing—he's a short, slight man, compact and toned—but when she's on top, she feels like she owns him. She puts her hands on his chest and rocks. She's tired of looking at the portrait; the dead Jefferson's face is like an old woman's, doughy and pale and too long, and his gray hair forms silly curlicues on his forehead. The new Jefferson—*her* Jefferson—is handsome, with a strong jaw and dark eyes and a few days' worth of beard darkening his cheeks. His hair is black and slicked with mousse, going gray above the ears.

Jefferson looks up at her, puts his hands on her. His eyes are wobbly and lost, like the pleasure is putting a haze between him and the real world.

His hands on her hips, guiding her, and Heather rocks faster, tilts her head back and bites her lip as she comes, and then she feels the twitching and the warmth of him finishing inside of her. She leans over him, kisses him hard. His eyelids are fluttering.

Heather rolls off of him and catches her breath. She closes her eyes and savors the tingles as he runs his fingertips over her skin.

Jefferson's hand comes to rest on her belly. "I know what we should call him," he says.

Heather looks down. Her stomach rises in a pink half moon that dominates her vision. She feels the baby moving often. A few times, she's seen it, tiny fingers and feet pressing against her skin. It's an experience that's both exhilarating and terrifying: that life writhing inside of her. "If it's a him," Heather says.

"Oh, it is. I've got a feeling." He's got a voice that could melt the ice outside. It makes Heather think of water flowing over smooth stones in a mountain creek.

"All right, then." She turns over and rests her head on his chest. "What's his name?"

"Marion."

Heather lifts her chin so that she can see his face. His eyes are closed, and he drags his fingernails across her scalp. "It sounds girly," Heather says.

"It's not girly. He'd be named after Francis Marion. He was one

of the heroes of the first Revolution. He was a guerilla, the first."
He opens his eyes. "They called him the Swamp Fox."

"We should call him Fox, then."

Jefferson nods. "I could see that. But Marion is more dignified."

Heather watches the candles flicker in the sconces that line the
walls. They light the room well enough, and there are furnaces burning that keep the mansion warm, but Heather still misses electricity.
There are generators somewhere that they turn on from time to
time, but for the most part, Biltmore is running the way it was when
it was first built. Some of the Minutemen talk optimistically about
the day when the power will be turned back on, but Heather knows
the truth. She's heard it in Jefferson's voice, the way he talks of the
days after the Big Aurora, the way he plans for the future. Whatever
they did to break the power grid is irreversible. Power plants across
the country are sitting empty and silent. They've flipped a switch
that cannot be unflipped.

There's a knock at the door. Heather pulls the covers up over
herself and Jefferson.

"Enter," Jefferson says.

It's one of the Minutemen, one of the dozens of interchangeable
ones who mill about Biltmore, doing chores, training and working and preparing, jumping at Jefferson's every command. Heather
has seen this one dozens of times—a middle-aged man who looks
like he could be a Sunday-school teacher—but she doesn't know his
name. "Big news, sir," the Minuteman says.

Jefferson stares at him. "Yes?"

"We caught one of the defectors. He was out there in the storm
with a few others. We think they might be some of those from the
Walmart."

Jefferson props himself up on his elbow. "How many?"

"We killed five, caught the defector plus one other. A woman."
The Minuteman is beaming, obviously pleased with himself. "Got
their pickup truck, and a jeep too."

"Well done," Jefferson says. "What did you do with them?"

"The dead ones are on the lawn. We're going to get rid of them
later. The live ones are in the servants' quarters. Here's a funny
thing." The Minuteman begins to step inside, but Jefferson stares

him down, and he takes a step back, leans in the doorway. "It's funny. Byron says he knows the woman. Seen her before."

"Where?"

"Back on the road. Months ago."

Lisa? Heather thinks, but she pushes the idea away. It couldn't be her—there are plenty of women, plenty of roads. It could be anyone. She's long since written Lisa off as dead. Lisa vanished into the woods so long ago, and who could survive out there in that icy hell? Still, part of Heather is stirred by the idea that Lisa is not just alive, but in this very house.

"Thank you, Francis," Jefferson says. "I'll see to them later." Francis closes the door, and Jefferson lies back down. "We could call him Francis, you know. Francis Marion."

Heather forces Lisa out of her head and smiles at him. "Francis is as girly as Marion. I still like Fox."

Jefferson rolls her onto her back. He turns his ear to her belly and listens. "I think I hear him in there," he says. He kisses the stretched skin. "How about this," he says, as much to her stomach as to Heather, "Marion Fox Jefferson. It has a good ring to it. Dignified and cool."

"I like it," Heather says. "And we call him Fox."

He glowers at her a moment, and then he laughs. "You always get your way, don't you?"

"Most of the time."

Jefferson climbs out of bed, and Heather watches him as he dresses in front of the portrait. Marion, Fox, Francis—it doesn't matter. In her mind, Heather has already named the baby. She long ago named him after his father.

She's going to call him Guy.

Heather stands on the lawn with Jefferson. She zips her jacket tight. The storm wrapped snow around the edges of the house; it's like a wave that froze while crashing around a sand castle. "Brr," Heather says.

Jefferson puts an arm around her waist. They look at the dead men.

The five of them are laid out side by side in the thinning snow. The first four are in military uniforms—National Guard, like some of the ones who were already at Biltmore when Heather arrived. She wonders why some joined the Minutemen and others didn't. What did the ones who stayed think of the deserters? What did the deserters—the new Minutemen—think of the ones who stayed?

The fourth is a tall man in a dark gray jacket. His face is handsome, his skin the light brown of Jefferson's leather boots. He grimaces at the sky above him.

"What were they doing?" Heather says.

"Trespassing," Jefferson says. "Bury them," he says to a couple of Minutemen who stand nearby. They nod, and set to work. Jefferson heads inside, and Heather follows.

"Are you going to check on the others?"

"Yes." He's walking briskly through the hallways. His heels clop on the patterned tiles like a horse's hooves.

Heather hurries to keep up as they pass through the conservatory, where the plants still grow fiercely, stretching their green arms against the glass, reaching ever for the ember. "Can I see them?" she says to Jefferson's back.

He stops, turns slowly. He looks at her for a long time, his head cocked. "You think it's your friend, don't you?"

Heather had told Jefferson about Lisa. Not everything—Jefferson doesn't know about Guy—but he knows that she wasn't alone when the Minutemen took her. "Maybe," Heather says. She has to find out. Heather isn't sure if she actually wants it to be Lisa—if she wants Lisa alive or dead—but the unknowing leaves her in a fog. Heather can't concentrate. The question demands an answer.

Jefferson smiles. "Even if it's her, it doesn't change a thing."

They pass through a long hallway with thick green and gold carpeting and gilded crown molding that sparkles in the flickering candlelight, and then they turn, head down two narrow flights of stairs, and come out in the servants' quarters. It's a dimly-lit hallway with doors to several bedrooms not much larger than closets. It reminds Heather of something out of a mental ward.

There are three Minutemen talking near the stairs. They come to attention when Jefferson enters. He looks them over, and then he says, "Where's the defector?" One of them points, and Jefferson disappears into the nearest room.

Heather stands with her hands in her jacket pockets. She smiles at the Minutemen, but they remain at attention, staring past her. "Which one is the woman in?" Heather says. They don't answer.

After a few minutes, Jefferson comes out. "Go get Crispin," he says, and one of the Minutemen salutes and hustles up the stairs. Jefferson looks at the other two. "The woman," he says.

"She's unconscious, Father," the taller one says.

"Why? What did you do to her?"

"Byron shot her."

"She going to die?" Jefferson says this in the same sort of voice he would use to say *Is she coming to dinner tonight?*

The Minuteman shakes his head. "Don't think so, Father. The bullet grazed her. She's out, though."

Jefferson nods, and the Minutemen lead them to the other end of the hall. Jefferson opens the door and sticks his head in.

Heather holds her breath.

He looks back at her. "You want to see?" She nods, and Jefferson moves out of the way. Heather steps into the room.

It is Lisa. She lies on her side on the narrow bed. Her hair is long and dirty-looking; it was blond before, but now it seems like tarnished bronze. On the left side of her head, the hair is thick and matted with brownish blood. Lisa's eyes are scrunched tight, and she frowns; her face looks less like she's been shot and more like she's *waiting* to get shot. Lisa breathes shallowly, and Heather moves to the bed and pulls the sheet over her.

"It's her," Heather says.

"It's not going to happen, Heather," Guy said.

They were in his car on the south side of town. A creek ran through the center of town, and Guy liked to park beside it here, where the water spilled over a dam and scuttled between boulders in a whitewater gush. It was the same creek that ran behind his condo, and he said he liked the thought of it: that water moved by him while he slept and ended up here hours later, here where he could see it again. He said it was like going back in time.

Heather thought this was stupid. The dam was boring.

They'd had sex in the back of Guy's Toyota and he was sitting naked beside her, looking at the water through the fogged-up windows. She'd just asked him to leave Lisa again—for the millionth time, it seemed.

Guy drew a heart on the foggy glass. "I love her. I've told you that."

It killed Heather every time he said that, a quiet murder, a little death. She looked at her own naked thighs. They were fatter than they used to be. She could see patches of cellulite. She tried to adjust her legs so that the dimples disappeared. "But you tell me that you love me," she said.

"I do."

"But it's not fair! You can't love me and her. I'm sick of it, Guy."

Guy sighed. "I don't know why you can't understand it. You love both of your parents, right?"

No, she thought. They both left her. But Guy didn't know that. "Yes," she said.

"So there's enough love for everyone. I love you. I love Lisa. And I won't leave her." He leaned over and kissed her leg. "But we can have this. We can have this for as long as you want."

She put her hand on his head and looked out the window. The water kept rushing by. Going and going.

Things with Guy had not gone according to plan. Not the way they had with other men, men who—through a little flirting, a little sex—she could bend into anything she wanted. Heather had never forgotten what her mother told her the day she left her, when she took off for Tuscaloosa with her latest boyfriend. "Men will use you if you let them," her mother said. "You've got to use them first."

Heather had tried, but Guy wouldn't let himself be used. Now, she was tired of waiting. She would have this man.

She stopped taking her birth control that day. It took much longer than she thought; for a while, she worried that she too was barren. Guy had told her about Lisa's useless womb, and Heather thought this was the key: this was something she could give him that Lisa could not. Lisa was prettier than her, smarter than her. Not that Guy let her know. This was something Heather loved about him, maybe the reason she fell in love with him to begin with:

he lied to her fantastically. He made her feel beautiful even as she got older and softer. He made her feel like a genius, even when she knew nothing compared to his librarian wife. The books Lisa must have read. All those things she knew.

But Lisa couldn't have a baby. And when Heather got pregnant the following summer, only weeks before the Big Bang, she knew that she had finally won. She had the trump card, the one thing that could pull Guy away from his wife.

And then he had to go and die.

Crispin appears at the end of the hall. He has always terrified Heather. He's old, thin, with eyes that seem buried too far in his skull. He wears his baldness as though he's never had a hair on his head. He looks at Jefferson with a sort of bored indifference. "What do you need to know?" he says.

"Everything," Jefferson says. "Where he's been. Who he was with. What they're planning."

Crispin has a small metal briefcase in his hand. Heather has never seen it opened, but she knows what's in there.

"Okie-dokie," Crispin says, and he goes into the defector's room. After a few moments, the screaming begins.

Jefferson touches Heather on the shoulder. "You don't have to listen to this, you know," he says.

She hates hearing it, but she puts on a blank face. She stands on her toes and kisses him. Behind the door, the volume increases. "He betrayed us," Heather says. "He deserves everything that's coming to him."

"Good girl."

"Not her, though," Heather says, pointing down the hallway. She puts her hand on Jefferson's chest and runs it slowly downward. She bites her lip and gives him a half smile. "You leave her to me."

JEFFERSON

HEATHER HADN'T MADE IT FAR THAT NIGHT ON THE road. She watched Lisa sprint into the woods, her dog trailing after her, its bark sharp in the night. Heather opened the door, and someone was on her immediately. She didn't know where he came from; maybe he was one of the Minutemen from the truck at the tail end of the caravan, or maybe he came out of the woods. It didn't matter. His hands were on her, pulling her to the ground, and she screamed.

Gunshots. With Byron chasing Lisa, a couple of people had tried to rush the remaining Minuteman at the lead truck. He fired his gun into the air, pointed it at them. They stopped, hands raised.

Heather was dragged to her feet. She struggled, but the Minuteman's grip was strong.

At the end of the road, an old man climbed from his car. He ran—it could hardly be called a run, really; he lurched—toward the woods, and a Minuteman from the tail truck shot him, left him on the shoulder of the road.

The Minuteman who held onto Heather drug her to the front of the caravan. A shot rang out in the woods where Lisa had run. Heather wanted to cry out, to run to her—why, she didn't know. A few days ago, she'd hated Lisa. Now, Heather couldn't help but feel herself twist inside out at the thought of her among the branches and the dead leaves, bleeding out into the dirt.

Someone caught Lisa's dog. It struggled at the end of a metal pole, yelping, a wire around its neck.

Heather's Minuteman whistled an idle tune.

More gunshots in the woods. Closer, from a different gun, multiple guns. The firing went on, and Minutemen dropped what they were doing and ran to the edge of the woods, peered in with guns drawn. Heather's Minuteman held her with one arm, lifted his pistol with the other.

Some of the men fired, the bullets and the noise vanishing into the dark woods.

After a while, Byron came out. He was cussing and gripping his arm. When he got closer, Heather saw that his sleeve and his fingers were red with blood. "Bitch shot me," he said, leaning against the truck.

Heather's Minuteman laughed. "Let a girl show you up?"

Byron's face was like granite. "Let go of her," he said. The Minuteman released Heather, and Byron punched him in the face. The Minuteman fell hard, unconscious. Byron turned to Heather. "Get in the truck," he said.

Heather looked at him. He was breathing heavy, clouds of vapor snaking out of his nose and up into the night. She nodded and climbed into the truck.

Heather goes back upstairs and winds her way through the labyrinthine hallways of Biltmore's main floor. The first time she walked through, she was amazed by the place—dining rooms with crystal chandeliers and tables that sat a hundred, the foyer with its grand columns and sweeping staircases, the huge fireplace and the lingering cigar smell of the cave-like library—but now, she's bored by it.

She wants a TV. She wants a phone that works. She wants to order a pizza and eat it on a piece of furniture that's younger than her while listening to music, new music she's never heard. But no. That will never happen again.

She is furious that she only lived twenty-four years before they turned the world off.

Heather heads into one of the sitting rooms. This one has been repurposed; now, it's one of the classrooms. Twenty girls sit on the floor in there, and the teacher stands in front of them, a piece of chalk in her hand. She's drawing on a portable chalkboard. She's pointing at some sort of graph: a line starts high and gradually falls and falls before suddenly rocketing to the top of the board.

"Our country started in greatness," the teacher says. "The Founding Fathers were brilliant men, and their plan for our country was perfect. We were to be a nation like no other, founded on freedom and truth." She traces her finger along the line. "The country was steered wrong, though. For years, our freedoms were taken away, and the truth gave way to lies. Just a few months ago, we were at an all-time low."

The girls boo, and the boos break into a chorus of giggles.

The teacher smiles. Her finger passes the bottom of the curve and shoots skyward. "And what happened then, Daughters?"

"The Refounding!" The girls cheer.

The teacher sees Heather at the door and approaches her. "Hey!" she says.

Heather doesn't particularly like this woman. She's a few years older than Heather, and pretty, and Heather has seen her flirting with Jefferson. It has never gone further than flirting, though. Heather is sure of that. Pretty sure. "I need to borrow a Daughter," Heather says.

"No problem. We're about done, anyway." She turns to the girls. "Daughter?"

One girl looks up. She's about thirteen, small and frail with black hair and pale blue eyes. Heather has no idea how she, specifically, knew to look up. "Ma'am?" Daughter says.

"Ms. Heather needs your help. Would you like to help Ms. Heather?"

Daughter looks down for a moment and closes her eyes. Then

she looks at Heather, smiles. "I'm happy to help. Anything for the Refounding."

Heather knew that they must have taken more people from the caravan than just her, but she never saw the others. What they did with them, she never knew.

They brought her back to Biltmore and put her in a small room on the second floor, locked the door behind her. The room was comfortable: a canopied bed, a dresser, a closet-sized bathroom with a mirror and a jug of fresh water. When the ember rose the next morning, Heather could see out the window. The view was magnificent. A dense forest rolled away from her across an undulating landscape. The trees were the washed-out green of a grasshopper's wings, and a few of them were beginning to burn red and orange and yellow at the edges. The mountains marched along the horizon in the far distance, blue and hazy in the morning light, and above them, the sky was turning from the pink and purple shades of ember-rise to a deep azure. A few fat clouds drifted lazily among the mountaintops.

It was much better than the parking lot in Atlanta.

Various Daughters came and went, bringing her food, clothes, toiletries. Once, they let her shower, and she stood beneath the stream of hot water that flowed from a barrel and savored it like it was the greatest delicacy on Earth.

Jefferson came on the fifth day. He strolled into the room and filled it with his bravado. He looked out the window without speaking for a long time as Heather sat on the bed, her legs crossed, her hands folded in her lap. Then he turned around, folded his arms. A smirk spread across his face. "What do you do?" he said.

Heather blinked. "What do you mean?"

"We have to put you somewhere. You're not staying for free. What do you do?"

"I'm a secretary."

"We don't need secretaries." Jefferson walked slowly toward her, his footsteps soft on the thick Persian rug. He stopped at arm's length away, looming over her. He was handsome and trim, and he smelled like the woods. Heat seemed to drift off of him. He gripped the bedpost in his fist, and his tendons moved beneath his skin.

"What else can you do?" he said.

Heather smiled, uncrossed her legs.

It was too easy with Jefferson.

When Guy died, a clock started ticking inside of Heather's head. She'd been pregnant at least a few weeks, maybe over a month. It would only be a few more months before she began to show. At that point, she'd be damaged goods. Who, in this new world, would want to take on a woman carrying some other man's child? No one.

Heather didn't remember much about biology, but she did remember the cuckoo bird. The cuckoos laid their eggs in the nests of other birds, and those stupid mothers raised the cuckoo babies. They'd feed them and feed them, letting their own babies die.

No one would do that deliberately. They'd have to be tricked.

Heather needed to be the cuckoo, and she needed someone to be the idiot bird who took care of her egg. Jefferson was all too happy to make himself that idiot.

Heather leads Daughter down to the servants' quarters, and they stand outside of Lisa's door. At the other end of the hall, the defector's screams have turned to sobs, pleas. Heather tries to ignore the noise. She opens the door to Lisa's room.

Lisa has rolled over, and her face is obscured. There's a blotchy red stain on her pillow.

"I need you to tend to her wound," Heather says. "Can you do that?"

"Yes, ma'am," Daughter says. She's staring at the floor.

"Daughter. Look at me."

The girl looks up. Her eyes are like faded hydrangea petals.

"I need you to take good care of this woman." She glances at Lisa. When Lisa was lost, a part of Heather—a part of herself that she detested—mourned her. Heather is ashamed to admit that she doesn't want to lose her again. "Do you have a best friend, Daughter?"

Daughter shrugs. "Some of the other Daughters, I guess."

"This woman is my best friend." Heather intends this to be a lie, but she realizes that it might actually be the truth. How could this possibly be true? "Her name is Lisa. Will you take good care of Lisa?"

"Yes, ma'am."

"Good, I know you will. Let me know if she wakes up." She leaves Daughter at the door. As Heather heads back upstairs, the defector's screaming begins again.

Being Jefferson's woman came with other benefits.

Jefferson kept Biltmore running like a machine. Everyone who joined them had a role to play in the Refounding, he said, and he put them all to work. Many of the Minutemen became soldiers, but some were better suited elsewhere; women and men, doctors and nurses, farmers and teachers. Builders and mechanics and cooks. All were put where they could serve best.

Some contributed to day-to-day life in the house. Their job, according to Jefferson, was to help the Minutemen make it through the period he called Valley Forge. Like Washington's troops so long ago, if they could survive the winter, weather it in the valley, they'd have a clear path to victory.

Others were working toward the future. This was vaguer to Heather, but she knew this much: Biltmore was not permanent. Once the snow melted, the Minutemen were moving on. So a lot of the work was preparation for whatever was coming next. Education, mostly. People were preparing to take on their new lives in New America.

These were the jobs of the Minutemen themselves. The people they captured became slaves.

Heather should have been scrubbing floors or washing clothes. She saw other women working dusk till dawn. The children too— some of the Daughters and Sons were the children of captives, and when they weren't in school, they were working.

Jefferson found another job for Heather. "You're my eyes and ears," he told her. "I can't be everywhere, every day. You're going to do that for me."

So this was her job: each day, Heather was to walk the grounds, checking in with every department. She'd report back to Jefferson in the evenings, and he'd nod quietly as she spoke, looking out the window or staring at the portrait of President Jefferson.

There was something that stunned her when she began her job:

the determination of the Minutemen. No matter what job the people had, they did it with passion and fervor. Like Genevieve: she truly believed what she was teaching the children. She was readying them for a future that she thought, she *knew*, would be better than anything that had come before. The same went for the rest of them. In the infirmary, the doctors and nurses looked after the wounded and trained recruits in first aid and emergency care. You will need this, they said. You can save a patriot's life. And the farmers. They were growing the food that would feed New America, the children of the future. To them, the New Founding Fathers were modern-day prophets, and the Refounding was history's most noble cause. New America was the City Upon a Hill that they had waited so long for. They glowed with exuberance and life. They felt it; they felt the dream, the love.

After a while, Heather began to feel it too.

Heather zips her jacket up and walks through the gardens toward the greenhouses. She moves slowly, her hands on her belly. She finds that she tires more easily now. The baby can't weigh that much, but it feels like she's carrying a boulder with her everywhere she goes. It puts her off-balance, makes her feel like she's some sort of babushka hauling a basket full of fruit.

Some of the greenhouses are empty, and some are used for storage. She goes to the second one, where the agriculture class is meeting. Inside, it's warm. It's warmer than the mansion itself, warmer than anywhere Heather has been since the power went out. This is her favorite part of the day. She breathes in the damp air and lets it warm her lungs. She takes off her jacket and sits down on a bench.

The head gardener is on his knees next to a long planter filled with tomato plants. The Sons are gathered around him, a dozen or so. He pinches a young tomato in his fingers. It's the size of a cherry and pale green. The plants are studded with them. The emberlight is filtering weakly through the glass, putting everything into a kind of emerald haze. The UV lights are off right now; every night, the gardener fires up the generators and runs the lights for a few hours. He says it's the only way the fruit will grow.

The gardener sees Heather. He smiles, waves to her.

She relaxes for a while, listening to the gardener as he teaches the boys. Finally, Heather gets up and puts on her jacket and steps back into the cold. She stomps through the melting snow to the house and stands in the foyer a moment, trying to decide what to do. She's supposed to check the dogs next. Heather doesn't want to check the dogs. She doesn't like seeing them; it scares her, those animals that were once pets now foaming, mad-eyed killing machines.

She'll put it off. Right now, Heather's thinking of Lisa. It's like Lisa is back from the dead, and part of Heather is excited, anxious for her to wake up. Another part of her is afraid. What will Lisa say to her? What will she think of Heather's job, her warm clothes and her clean skin and hair?

Heather follows another staircase to the basement level. She walks through the natatorium and its empty pool, her footsteps echoing on the white tile and the empty metal cages that sit poolside. It's clean now, but the smell of blood seems to linger in the air.

Heather hates this room. The things she's seen in here.

Beyond the pool is a series of storage rooms. The Minutemen have crammed them with the things they've looted: items from local houses and stores, and from the people they captured. It is dark down here; the only light is what sneaks in through the barred, ground-level window slats. Heather finds a flashlight and turns it on, and then she moves slowly from room to room, examining the various piles. After a while, she finds a familiar-looking bag. She opens it up, and inside is all of Lisa's stuff. She roots around, touching the clothes, turning them over in her hands. Heather finds a photo of Lisa and Guy, and she shoves it back under the clothes.

At the bottom are several small sculptures. A giraffe, a lion, an ebony elephant. Heather holds them; they are elegant things that hold the weight of the world. She hefts a colorful hippo in her palm, runs her finger down its smooth back.

"Miss?"

Heather slips the hippo into her pocket and turns. It's Daughter. "Hey, Daughter," Heather says. "What's up?"

"It's Lisa," Daughter says. "She's awake."

WAKE

HEATHER STANDS OUTSIDE OF THE DOOR IN THE servants' quarters. A single Minuteman stands at the end of the hall, and Daughter lingers at the bottom of the stairs. Beyond them, Heather is alone. Crispin has left, and there are no sounds in the hall other than the quiet crying of the defector.

She adjusts her jacket and looks down at her own stomach. The bump is nearly hidden beneath the down and cloth. *Lisa won't notice,* Heather thinks, *and if she does notice, she'll just think I've gained weight.* There's no way she can know. She won't know.

Will she know?

Heather takes a deep breath and opens the door.

Lisa is standing with her back to Heather. There's a single small window in the room and it sits at ground level, looking out at the melting snow and the spindly blades of grass that are beginning to poke through. The ember is setting out there, and the light lingers in bloody pools in the snow. Lisa's on her toes, peering outside. She turns when she hears Heather come in. Lisa looks confused, a little wobbly; the bandage that Daughter wrapped around Lisa's head is already beginning to spot with blood. Lisa blinks a couple of times, and then her eyes brighten, her mouth turns up into a weak smile. "Heather," she says.

"Hey," Heather says. She's unreasonably excited, giddy to see Lisa. She doesn't know why. For years, Lisa was the one person on Earth she hated more than any other. She'd have done anything to see her disappear. Now, it's like she's greeting an old friend.

Lisa takes a step forward, but she loses her balance, grabs the bedpost for support.

"No, sit," Heather says, rushing toward her. She helps Lisa onto the bed then sits down beside her.

Lisa touches her wound, looks at her fingers. "I'm sorry. I'm just, I'm a little dizzy," she says. "I thought I was dead. The Bull. I thought he killed me."

"Byron? He almost did."

"Byron," Lisa says, the word slipping from her mouth like a curse.

Heather puts her hands on her own stomach, and then she moves them aside. She's been absently touching her belly for a month now, its size and shape a mystery of her body. *How can this be me?* she asks herself. Now, she tries to put her hands anywhere else. She feels like the life inside of her is so obvious, like it's screaming at Lisa to notice it. But Lisa seems oblivious.

"We're in Biltmore?" Lisa says after a while.

"Yes."

Lisa nods. Then she looks at Heather, and her eyes are deep and desperate. "The others who were with me," Lisa says. "Where are they?"

Heather looks at her hands. "Most of them are dead. One is in another room on this hall. The defector."

"Walter?"

That sounds familiar. Heather remembers a Walter—an older man with glasses. She hasn't seen him in a while. It must be him. "Yes."

Lisa's lip trembles. "And others? Others you brought back?"

Heather shakes her head.

Lisa licks her lips, and then she nods. She looks up at the window.

The look on Lisa's face—it was that same stony expression, that stoic coldness, that she wore after Guy died. Who was it this time? One of the soldiers? The good-looking black guy? Heather decides not to ask. She stays quiet, and she begins to feel awkward. She tries to think of something to say, and then she remembers the hippo. She takes it from her pocket. "I found something for you," she says, handing Lisa the sculpture.

Lisa takes it with two hands. She holds it in her lap. Squeezes a leg between two fingers. She presses the smooth stone against her cheek, and then she looks at Heather. "I got this in Lilongwe. The first week we were in Malawi." She laughs. "I had to carry the stupid thing around with me for two years, but it was just too beautiful. I couldn't pass it up." Now her eyes are wet. She's grinning and trying to blink back the tears. "I never thought I'd see it again. I never thought I'd see any of this stuff."

Heather squeezes Lisa's hand in her own. Lisa has dirt smeared on her cheeks and her forehead. Her hair is tousled as though she slept in a pile of leaves. But her eyes are the color of the green foam on the ocean, and her skin is like cream. She is beautiful, so beautiful; it's no wonder Guy was hers and hers alone.

"Thank you, Heather," Lisa says, and she hugs her.

Heather hugs her back, careful to turn her belly away. Lisa is crying into Heather's shoulder, and then Heather is crying too, and she's taken back to their nighttime drive toward Asheville, when there among the mountains she realized that somewhere beneath her hate for Lisa was a sort of weird love. That's what she feels now. Heather hates her, and she loves her, and she hates herself for loving her.

Lisa lets her go. "I feel sick, Heather," she says. "Like I'm going to throw up. And like I can't stay awake."

"You've probably got a concussion or something," Heather says. "He shot you. You got shot in the head!"

"Crazy," Lisa whispers. She smiles, her eyelids fluttering.

Heather wonders what she's supposed to do. What do you do for a concussion? Daughter might know. "I should let you rest," Heather says.

Lisa looks worried. "You're leaving?"

"Just for now."

"You'll come back?"

"Tomorrow. Tomorrow, you'll feel better, and we'll talk."

"Okay," Lisa says, her voice distant and wobbly. Her head bobs a little, like she's fallen asleep and caught herself. She lies down on the bed, her hippo pressed against her chest. "Thank you for the hippo. Thank you, Heather."

"It's nothing." Heather gets up to go.

"Heather," Lisa says. "I'm happy to see you."

Heather touches her leg. "I'm happy to see you too." Then she leaves her and goes outside to where Daughter is waiting. "She needs to get better, Daughter. You need to help her."

"Yes, ma'am."

"And it needs to be fast. She needs to be well. In case."

Heather sits on a stool at the bar, the empty café behind her shadowy in the lantern light. Jefferson is cooking risotto. He splashes a ladle of hot broth into the pot and whips the spoon round and round, turning the pot deftly over the flame.

He cooks all of their meals here, in the café attached to the side of the mansion. It used to serve the thousands of tourists who visited daily. Now, it serves only the two of them. While the rest of the Minutemen eat stew or casserole or sandwiches prepared in the Biltmore kitchens, Jefferson cooks a delicacy every night. He made sure the gas lines to the café remained open, so the appliances in here still work; they are sleek stainless steel, perfect machines. He works them like he's known them all his life.

Heather holds a glass with one sip of wine in it as she gives Jefferson the daily report. "We'll have tomatoes soon," she says. "They're getting big. The Sons were tending to them this afternoon."

He nods, adds another ladle of broth. "I could have used some tomatoes tonight."

"It looks delicious as it is."

Jefferson looks up at her, smiles faintly. "Have you tasted the wine?" He picks up the bottle and tops off his own glass. Biltmore has a winery on the grounds. In addition to the thousands of bottles of Biltmore wine, the cellars are stocked with priceless bottles from around the world. Jefferson brings a different one to dinner every night. "This is a 1961 Chateau Palmer Margaux. From France, I believe." He takes a sip. "I think it's exquisite. So delicate. So complex. Do you like it?"

Heather thinks that with the baby, she should drink nothing at all, but Jefferson insists. One sip a day won't hurt little Marion, he says, and there may never be wine again—not in their lifetimes, at least. After the Refounding, there will be crops, but the land and the effort needed to grow thousands upon thousands of grapes simply to smush them up and let them ferment—that is wasteful. As wasteful as so much of the nation's former ways. Jefferson's New America will be humble. It will be a place of simple pleasures, not a place of excess and greed.

Heather swallows her dose. The wine has a flowery taste and smells vaguely of potpourri. She doesn't like it. "It's amazing," she says.

"For three thousand dollars a bottle, it ought to be." Jefferson throws the rest of his wine back in one long swallow and sets the glass down on the counter. He contemplates the rice for a moment, and picks up a lemon and a paring knife. "Your friend," he says.

"Lisa."

"Yes. How is Lisa?"

"She's—she's sort of out of it right now." Heather tells him about their meeting.

Jefferson nods as he listens, all the while running the knife around the skin of the lemon. The zest comes off in bright yellow curls, leaving the bitter white pith behind. "Is she going to cooperate with us?"

Heather runs her finger around the rim of her glass. It makes a low humming sound. "What do you mean, cooperate?"

"There are things we need to know." Jefferson tosses the lemon aside and returns to the pot. More broth, more stirring. "The people we killed, the ones we captured. They're with the people we fought before. The ones from Walmart. They're planning a raid."

"On us? When?"

"We don't know. Crispin got a lot out of Walter, but Walter didn't know everything. They didn't let him in on all of the planning." He picks up a chef's knife and goes to work on the lemon zest.

Heather stands slowly, her hand on her belly. She goes behind the bar and wraps her arms around Jefferson's waist, looks over his shoulder. The knife is practically a blur as he chops, turning the zest into a bright yellow powder. "Did you cook like this for your wife?" she says. "Before?"

He turns and wags the knife as if he's scolding her. "Uh-uh-uh. You know what came before means nothing here." He lets the knife linger between them a moment longer, and then he sets it down, opens the oven.

Heather has tried to pry clues out of him about his family, but Jefferson is unreadable. He could have been a bachelor; he could have been a father of ten. He'll never let her know. Of what he did before, however, she's certain. The way he moves through the kitchen, the way he carefully selects the best vegetables from the greenhouse, the way he holds the knife—he must have been a chef.

Jefferson sets a steaming pan of diced squash and red peppers on the counter and returns to the pot. He tosses in a fat spoonful of butter and a handful of grated cheese.

Heather returns to her seat at the bar. She looks at the knife and remembers Walter's screams, the way they echoed through the empty halls of the servants' quarters. "Did we get everything we could out of Walter?"

Jefferson nods. "He would have talked if he knew more. Anyone would have." He takes the pot off of the stove and spoons the risotto onto two clear glass plates. "They have a tank."

"Like, a *tank* tank?" The idea scares her. "Do we need to be worried?"

"We have the mines..." Jefferson trails off. "But we need to know their plan. That's why we need Lisa. I need you to get it out of her." He shakes the vegetables from the pan onto the risotto and puts more fresh cheese on top. "If you can't, I'm sure Crispin can."

She imagines the screams, a woman's this time, filling up the bowels of the house. "We shouldn't do that to her," she says. "It would be a waste."

"How so?"

"Lisa's smart. We could use her. She's a librarian—we don't have any librarians, do we?"

"Not to my knowledge."

"But we'll need one." This feels desperate at first, but the more Heather talks, the more reasonable it becomes. "We're making history. Won't we want a record of it?" She wants to sell Jefferson on this. Lisa is essential to the cause. She shouldn't be tortured; she shouldn't be killed. She can be one of us. Jefferson is nodding. Heather is convincing him. She's convincing herself. She's certain she can convince Lisa. "And if she's with us, she'll tell us about the raid," Heather says. "To save herself, to save her friends. It will work."

Jefferson grabs a pinch of the lemon zest and sprinkles it delicately over the plates. Then he sets a plate in front of Heather and sits down across from her. He stares at her, waiting.

She takes a bite. It is fluffy and savory, like a cloud raining flavor inside her mouth. "Amazing," she says.

He nods and begins to eat. "You think you can make this work. With your friend."

"I can do this," she says.

"Then do it, but don't waste time." He eats quickly. He spent an hour preparing their dinner, but his plate will be empty in five minutes. "You know I don't like to waste time," he says. "Tomorrow. Get it done tomorrow."

LISA

DAUGHTER IS LEAVING LISA'S ROOM WHEN HEATHER arrives the next morning. She's holding a tray with empty dishes on it. "I brought her breakfast," Daughter says.

"That's nice of you, Daughter," Heather says. "Is she feeling better?"

"I think so." Daughter smiles. "Lisa is really nice. We talked for a long time. She showed me her hippo and told me about Africa. Can you believe she went to Africa?"

"Pretty cool," Heather says. This makes her jealous. She never wanted to go to Africa—she couldn't give a shit about the whole continent—but the fact that it was something that Lisa shared with Guy that Heather never could drives her insane.

"She told me about the hippos and the crocodiles. And we talked about my parents."

Heather has never seen Daughter's parents. They may be here, somewhere in the house, but if Heather hasn't seen them, it's more likely that Jefferson long since got rid of them. This is something that Daughter shouldn't know. Part of the goal for the Daughters is to start them new, erasing the children they were before. "You know you shouldn't talk about your parents, Daughter," Heather says.

"I know." The girl looks at her feet and twists the toe of her shoe on the tile. "She asked, though, and she was so nice."

"Don't talk to her about your parents. She doesn't need to know that."

"Yes, ma'am."

Heather is tired of her now. "Go put those dishes away," she says, and Daughter scurries off. Heather opens the door.

Today, Lisa is sitting cross-legged on the bed, her hands folded in her lap. She wears fresh bandages on her head, and they're free of blood. She looks at Heather as she enters. Lisa smiles, but her eyes are unchanged—serious, cold.

Heather can feel Lisa's eyes moving up and down her body, scrutinizing her. She tries to suck her stomach in. "Hey, Lisa!" she says.

"Hi, Heather." Lisa speaks quietly. She's different today. Yesterday, she was happy to see Heather, but today, she seems wary.

Heather sits on the bed, a few feet of sheet separating her from Lisa. "How are you feeling?"

"Better."

Heather waits for her to go on, but that's it. Lisa is watching her patiently. Heather says, "Daughter took good care of you?"

"She did," Lisa says. "Nice girl."

Heather tries to smile, but Lisa is staring into her. The tension is like smoke in the room. Whatever peace was there yesterday is gone. Heather wonders what she did wrong. Weren't they friends, of some sort, at least?

"Why am I here, Heather?"

"At Biltmore?"

"In this room." Lisa waves her arm. "This cell. This is a prison."

"It's not."

"It is. You've got me locked down here. There are guards out there. I can hear them talking. And don't think I didn't hear Walter screaming." Her eyes are narrow and fiery now. "Is that what you're planning for me?"

"No, Lisa! No way that's happening to you." She scoots toward her, but Lisa leans away. Heather moves back to where she was. "I have good news for you," she says.

"Ha," Lisa says.

At first Heather was taken aback by Lisa's mood, but now she's feeling annoyed, angry even. She's here to help, and Lisa is just being a bitch. Heather smiles anyway. "We've got you a good job."

Lisa arches her eyebrows. "We?"

Heather sighs. "A good job is available for you. Something you'd be good at, since you were a librarian. I mean, you liked your job before, right? Before…before everything?" Lisa doesn't answer, and Heather continues. "The Refounding needs a historian. You can keep track of everything. All the letters and journals and all that. You'll be keeping the record of the early days of New America!"

Now Lisa is shaking her head. "So now you're all gung-ho about the Refounding?"

"I mean, if you really think about it—"

"It's crazy."

"It's not that crazy, Lisa." She scoots back down the bed, and this time, Lisa doesn't move. "Think about it. The country was in bad shape. The government was spying on us. It was starting wars in places where it had no business being. Sending people off to die." Heather realizes that she's just repeating things that Jefferson has said to her, but it feels right. She sees the truth in the words as she speaks them. "We were being taxed so much, and all that tax money was being spent on entitlements while the country's infrastructure fell apart. It couldn't go on. There had to be a change. And the New Fathers are bringing us that change."

An incredulous look spreads across Lisa's face. "You sound exactly like them," she says.

"But don't you see that that's not a bad thing?" Heather says. "They're reshaping the country for good. We're going to come out of this better than ever. And you can be part of it, Lisa! We want you to be part of it!"

Lisa stands up. She's taller than Heather anyway, and now, with Heather sitting on the bed, she seems to loom. "You're insane, Heather."

Heather gets up, and she's unconsciously standing on her toes, trying to come to Lisa's eye level. That tall, beautiful bitch. "So what do you want to do, then? You want to go back to the way it was? The old government's gone. They abandoned us. America's not coming back." She's struggling to keep her voice level. All Heather wants to do is scream. "You want to go live in Walmart? You can't live in Walmart! You want to go south, get blown up like Miami? It won't work! This is the way, Lisa! This is the future! Can't you see it?"

"It's not a future I want to be a part of."

Heather feels exhausted all of a sudden, wrung out by the emotion. Heather sits back down on the bed. "I'm sorry, Lisa," she says. "I wanted to help you. I was trying to help."

Lisa sighs. "I know, Heather." She sits down beside her.

"Life can be really good, you know? If you'll just let it. You don't have to fight all the time."

"Yes, you do, Heather," Lisa says. "You can't ever stop fighting."

"But you can fight with us." Heather can tell that Lisa's about to say something else, but she cuts her off. "Just think about it, okay? The job is here for you. We can get you out of the servants' quarters. We can get you clean clothes, a shower, good food. It can all be so good. Will you just think about it?"

Lisa is quiet for a long time. Finally, she nods. "I'll think about it."

In the afternoon, Heather checks on the dogs.

They keep them penned up in the darkest reaches of the basement. Even with the dogs locked away down there, Heather can still hear them sometimes as she walks the halls of the estate, as she lies in Jefferson's bed at night. When she enters the room itself, the sound curdles her blood. Yowling, barking, whining. The smell of piss and shit and blood. The dogs themselves, dark ghosts barely visible in the candlelight. They snarl and gnash their teeth.

In the middle of the room, a few Minutemen stand around a golden retriever. The dog is crouched low, growling and baring its teeth. The men jab it with long sticks. It lunges at them, and they beat it back. Again and again, the dog worked up into a furious lather.

Heather turns her head, steps back into the hallway, catches her breath.

Jefferson is there. He is a sleek figure in the dark. "Hey, Red," he says. He takes her by the waist and pulls her to him, kisses her deep.

His tongue is heavy in her mouth, an organ pulled from someone else's body and jammed inside of her. Down there with the dogs, Heather has no interest in romance.

Jefferson lets her go. "You spoke to your friend?"

"She needs more time," Heather says. "But I think she'll come around."

"I figured as much." He walks to the end of the hallway and stands watching the men and the dog. He's silhouetted against the horror in front of him. "We need something from that woman. What we got from Walter isn't enough. A lot of people are going to die. Do you understand?"

Heather looks past him to the dog. It's crying now, cowering in a corner. The men continue to prod it with the sticks.

Jefferson turns back to her, grabs her arm, presses her against the wall. "I asked you a question," he says. "Do we understand each other?"

"Yes! Yes." Heather struggles under his grip. "I'll get her talking."

Jefferson lets her go. He runs his fingers tenderly over her arm where he grabbed her. "I'm sorry," he says. "I didn't mean to be so rough with you. I'm just frustrated." He leans back against the wall. "A courier came today with a letter from Washington."

Heather waits for him to go on. He rarely tells her much about his work with the other Fathers.

"He and Franklin are done. Franklin doesn't like the way he's doing things. He doesn't like the violence." Jefferson shakes his head in disbelief. "Father Franklin is leaving us. He doesn't want to be part of the Refounding."

Heather steps forward and kisses him, and he takes her in his arms.

"This isn't the way it was supposed to go," Jefferson says. "Franklin is the smartest of us, but he's the weakest. And Washington's the strongest. We need them both. I don't know that New America can work without one or the other."

She leans her head on his chest. At the end of the hall, the dog has gone quiet. "New America has you," Heather says. "And you're strong. You're smart."

He nuzzles his nose into her hair. "The New Fathers are fighting. The Minutemen will fall apart if we can't lead."

"But *we're* not falling apart," Heather says. "You're the leader in this house, and we follow you. You're doing your job. You're doing it well." She looks up at him. His face is all angles and shadows in the candlelight. "We'll follow you anywhere," she says.

When Heather opens the door to Lisa's room that evening, Daughter is there. She's sitting on the bed, the hippo in her hands. She's laughing, and Lisa is smiling, and they both look up at Heather when she comes in. Daughter's smile vanishes. Lisa's becomes a smirk.

"Get out," Heather says, pointing at the door.

"Yes, ma'am." Daughter hurries past her and vanishes down the hall.

Heather shuts the door. There is a small chair in the corner of the room, and she pulls it over to the bed, sits down in front of Lisa. "Did you think about the job?" she says.

"Yes."

"And?"

"What do you think?"

Heather bites her lip. She looks up through the window. A gray sliver of moon is hanging up there among the stars. "You need to be reasonable," she says. "You don't have to take the job. But you have to give me something. You don't know the things they'll do to you."

Lisa shrugs. "There's nothing to give."

"We know about the raid, Lisa." Heather feels a sense of pride as Lisa tenses and the smirk slides from her face. "Walter told us everything."

"He doesn't know everything."

"He knows enough." Heather drags the chair closer to the bed. The legs screech across the tiles. "A lot of people are going to die. Your friends are going to die. Is that what you want?"

Lisa doesn't speak. She looks at the ground.

"They can't get in here. Even with the tank."

"I can't tell you anything," Lisa says. She's twisting the bed sheet in her hand. "I don't know anything."

"Please, Lisa. Please."

Lisa's eyes are softer now. Her lips are trembling.

"We can stop it before it happens. If we know when the raid is, where they'll be, we can just capture them. In time, they can work with us." Heather touches Lisa's knee. "More important than anything, though, is they'll survive. Isn't that what we all want? Isn't that what everyone's trying to do? To survive?"

Lisa jerks her knees away, and her eyes turn to fierce slits in her face. "What do you know about survival?"

Who does she think she is? Everyone struggles. The ember is a dying speck above them and the winter stretches on without end. Every day is survival. "We went through it together," Heather says. "We were both doing what we had to do."

"And what you had to do was cozy up with the Minutemen." There are tears on Lisa's face, but her eyes are full of anger. "Do you know what I've done? The people I've lost? The people I've killed? Do you know what that's like, Heather?"

Heather shies away from her. "I don't. But it's still hard. Jefferson…"

"What, Jefferson's the one? You're fucking *Jefferson*?"

"You know him?"

"I know enough. From Walter."

"I don't know what Walter said," Heather says, "but Jefferson's not a bad man. He's a visionary. A leader. I—I love him." Is this true? She doesn't know. It doesn't matter.

"Like you loved Guy?"

"That's not fair." Heather stands up and moves to the window. It's so dark out there, still so cold.

"Heather, can't you see that you've joined up with the bad guys! These people you're with. They're the ones that killed Guy, remember? And Jefferson's the leader." Lisa's on her feet now, in the middle of the room. Her voice bounces off the walls and makes the place feel claustrophobic. "You don't care. You don't care who they are or what they do. You just fuck your way into whatever situation suits you best. You do it with Jefferson. You did it with Richard. And you did it with Guy."

"I loved Guy." Heather is boiling with emotion now, anger and sadness and resentment roiling inside of her.

"You don't know what love is, Heather. I was with him for fifteen years. Fifteen years."

"It doesn't take fifteen years to love someone," she says. She's crying, but she doesn't care. Those tears say as much as her words, so let Lisa see them. "I loved him. He loved me."

"He didn't love you," Lisa says. She takes a step toward Heather, and Heather feels small, so small in front of her. "He fucked you. That's it. You were his fuck buddy."

"He loved me...."

"You had nothing. Guy was mine. There was nothing between you. Nothing."

Heather sucks in her breath. She wipes her eyes with the back of her hand, and she stands up straight, raises her chin, looks Lisa in her cold gray eyes. "Not nothing," she says, and she raises her shirt.

LISA

CHILD

TO SEE IT IS TOO MUCH. ANOTHER WOMAN'S BELLY, bulging, the skin stretched taut over the life inside. Life that belongs to *Lisa's* husband. And Lisa's own womb scraped barren in that hut in Africa.

She won't accept it. Lisa tries to bend reality into something else. "Heather," she says. She can barely hear her own voice. "Whose baby is that?"

Heather shakes her head. Sighs. She lowers her shirt.

Lisa can hear her own heart pounding in her chest. She's trembling, her fists clenched so tight that her nails are digging into her palms. Anger and disbelief are burning inside of her like lava, and she opens her mouth and the words explode out of her, shattering the quiet of the room, echoing like gunfire off the walls and the ceiling and the hard tile floor: *"Whose fucking baby is that?"*

"You know whose it is, Lisa."

And at this, Lisa screams. It's a high-pitched shriek that comes from somewhere deep within her and fills the room like the wailing of a banshee. She could take the cheating; she could take the lying and her empty womb; Guy's death and Dante's death and her capture and imprisonment. She could take it all, but not this. She lunges at Heather, grabs her by the throat, pins her against the wall. Lisa is cursing and raving, and her own words sound foreign in her ears, and Heather is pushing at her, clawing at her, and Heather's face is turning red, the veins going bright inside her eyes. Lisa squeezes. Tighter. Tighter.

And then there are hands on her. Two Minutemen. They throw her down on the bed. One of them holds her there; the other returns to Heather. "You okay?" he says to her.

Heather has her hands on her own throat. She's crying and massaging her neck with her fingertips. She coughs. "Yeah," she says. "Yes. I'm okay. Thank you. Both of you."

The Minuteman's hands press Lisa's arms into the mattress. Every muscle in her body is tensed. "Let go of me," she says.

"Can you sit still?" the Minuteman says.

Lisa breathes deep. She forces her muscles to relax. "Yes." He lets her go, and she glares at Heather. "He was never yours," Lisa says.

Heather has regained her composure. She's standing tall now, flanked by the Minutemen. "Maybe not," she says. "But his baby is mine. *Mine*." She turns to the Minutemen. "She's no use to us. I'm done with her." And she leaves. The Minutemen follow her out, shutting the door behind them.

Lisa curls up on her side on the bed. She's still shaking as the adrenaline works its way out of her system. She stares at the wall across from her. White walls in this room, white ceiling and floor. A small painting of a potted plant hanging above a tiny desk. Her one window, the moon floating silently beyond the glass.

How much? How much is she supposed to take? How many times is the world going to fuck her before it's satisfied?

Since the Big Aurora, life has been nothing but a series of tragedies. Guy. Richard and the ambush on the road and Jemi disappearing into the forest. Dante's trailer, billowing smoke. A bullet in Tom's throat, Lisa's finger on the trigger. Abe and half of the library buried in snow. And then Dante—Dante bleeding into the snow, painting that white canvas with the crimson color of life. It's like Lisa is a wrecking ball, swinging wildly through the universe, turning everything she touches to ruin.

Things might be better if she wasn't there at all.

Daughter comes in later that evening. She has brought a simple meal: soup and stale bread. She sets it on the table and turns to leave.

"Wait," Lisa says.

Daughter pauses. "I'm not supposed to talk to you anymore," she says.

Visits from the girl have been the highlights of Lisa's days. Daughter seems to enjoy talking with Lisa; she lingers in the room when she brings food. She giggles and gossips. She's a bright spot in this dim room, and Lisa doesn't want her to go. "Why can't you talk to me?"

"Miss Heather says."

Lisa smiles at her. "You don't have to do everything Miss Heather says, you know. We can talk."

Daughter sits down in the chair, but she doesn't look at Lisa. She keeps looking at the door as if someone is about to come through and drag her away.

Lisa's not sure how to act around the girl. She likes Daughter, wants her to like her back. But it's been so long since Lisa was a child. She can hardly remember what it was like. She wonders what it's like now, to be a child in this cold world. "I won't tell on you," Lisa says.

"She won't let me come back if I don't follow the rules," Daughter says. "She'll just send one of the other Daughters."

"You're all called Daughter?"

"Daughters of the Revolution," she says. "And Sons of Liberty."

Now Daughter is looking at her. Lisa pats the bed, and Daughter moves beside her. "What was your name before?"

The girl tenses. "We're all called Daughter."

"I know. But we're friends, right?" She nods, and Lisa continues. "I just want to know my friend's name."

Daughter looks at the door. "You promise you'll still call me Daughter? I don't want to get in trouble."

"I promise."

She leans in to Lisa's ear and whispers. "It's Abigail." She smiles, and there's a light behind her eyes that Lisa has never seen before.

"Thanks, Abigail." The girl's eyes go wide and she puts her finger to her lips. Lisa covers her own mouth playfully. "I mean Daughter," she says, smiling.

Daughter laughs. "I'll see you tomorrow," she says.

But she doesn't come back the next day. Another girl shows up with Lisa's breakfast. She's a sour-looking girl with frizzy blond hair and eyes that are too far apart. She doesn't speak. She sets an uncooked Pop-Tart on the table and leaves.

For four days, Lisa sees no one but this new girl. The girl never speaks; she brings food and water, changes out Lisa's chamber pot. When she's gone, Lisa listens at the door. Occasionally, she can hear the muffled voices of the guards as they talk. The distant sobbing of Walter in his room at the other end of the hall. Footsteps that approach her door, pause, and draw away.

The snow is melting. Squirrels hop through the yard, digging into the white and coming up with seeds. Tight-wrapped, velvety buds have appeared on the bare branches of the tulip tree outside her window. The ember seems brighter than before. Its light falls in a rectangle on the floor of her prison, and Lisa lies in it like a dog; like Jemi, the way she used to curl up on the carpet beside the sliding glass doors. Here in the emberlight, Lisa almost feels warm.

She sets her hippo on the floor in front of her and watches its flimsy shadow pan across the floor while the ember moves overhead. She waits.

The sour-faced girl undid Lisa's bandages once. They came away clean, and she replaced them with a large Band-Aid. Lisa's head feels much better. That first day was a haze. It comes back to her like a dream: the afterimage of the Bull's face blacking out the morning sky, and then waking in this room, so small and close. Daughter wrapping her wounds. And Heather's visit. That first day, Heather was an angel. Lisa had wondered if Heather was alive, struggling to survive in Biltmore among the cruel soldiers of the Minutemen. And then there she was: not just alive, but comfortable, happy. Maybe the Minutemen weren't so bad after all, if they treated their prisoners so well. It was everything Lisa had hoped for her.

And then her head cleared. The next day, she woke up thinking about it. *Why* was Heather so comfortable, so happy? Why had they sent Heather to talk to her? *Who* had sent her?

It didn't take long for Lisa to put it together. They weren't treating Heather nice because they were nice people. They were treating her nice because she wasn't a prisoner. She was one of them. And that was something that Lisa could not abide.

On the night of the fifth day, Lisa goes to bed with the ember. She has no candles, and the moonlight through the window is scarcely enough to see by. There is nothing to do but sleep.

She's been out for a while when the door swings wide open. It is a man, his small frame a black outline against the lights of the hallway. He speaks with a voice like pooled mercury. "Rise and shine," he says. He lights a candle, and the light curls over his face. "You know who I am?" he says.

She knows. Lisa can't say how, but she knows it's him. "Jefferson."

"*Father* Jefferson," he says. He remains standing in the doorway as he looks her up and down. "We tried to be good to you, you know. Heather wanted nothing but the best for you. You really hurt her feelings."

Lisa sits up. "Well boo-fucking-hoo," she says.

"Get up."

She stands.

Jefferson steps forward. He's shorter than her by an inch or so, but he has a confidence about him that makes it seem like he fills the room. "Heather wanted to do things the nice way. I told her it wouldn't work, but she did it anyway. And look what you've done. So mean, and she's just a sweet girl. Pregnant at that."

He's looking into her eyes as if he can see her soul. *Let him look*, Lisa thinks. There's nothing in there but hate.

"No one treats the mother of my child that way," Jefferson says.

Lisa tries to fight it, but she feels the grin spreading across her face, and then she's laughing. He's standing there staring daggers, but she laughs and laughs in the dark.

"What?" he says.

She shakes her head. "You think that's *your* baby?"

Jefferson blinks. He opens his mouth as if he's about to speak, and then he closes it, bites down on his cheek. He blows out the candle and goes to the doorway. "You got anything else to say to us?" he says. "It's your last chance. If you can't help us, you're of no use to us."

Lisa stands in the middle of the room and smirks. "I have nothing to say to you."

"All right then," he says. "Tonight's your night." He beckons to someone down the hallway, and a moment later, Heather is beside him.

HELLHOUND

THEY LEAD HER OUT OF THE SERVANTS' QUARTERS and down. Lisa can hear the sounds before she sees anything: shouting, laughing, cheering. Dogs barking.

A narrow staircase with stone steps and curved, tile walls. There is no light in the stairway itself, so as the light recedes behind them, it gives the impression of passing through a tunnel. It's like they're being born; they're sliding from the warm pink glow of the womb to the harsh reality of the world.

The noises are loud in Lisa's ears. Barks and screams reverberate in the stone chamber.

They exit the stairs and step into a huge room with a white-tiled ceiling and walls. At least a hundred people are in there, yelling and jeering. Most of them are men—Minutemen, their heads as bald and white as the tile—but there are women too; a few children even

289

scurry among the legs of the adults. Everyone is standing in rows around the edges of the room, shoulder to shoulder.

"This way," Heather says, her voice barely audible over the noise. The crowd is deafening and it seems a thousand different dogs are barking. Heather grabs Lisa's wrist and drags her to the far end of the room, where there is a bit of space between people. They wedge their way to where they can see.

A Minuteman stalks past them, a dead English Pointer over his shoulder. He's followed shortly thereafter by a small, limping Asian man. The man grips his forearm; he's trying to cover a bite that's bleeding freely onto the floor. He looks at Lisa, and his eyes are confused and hollow.

Lisa looks down into an empty pool, floored and walled with that same white tile. The pool slopes downward from where they stand; the shallow end is a couple of feet deep, and the deep end is like a pit, the bottom of it ten feet below the roiling crowd that leans over the thick wooden railing. Blood is spattered on the walls and pooled on the floor down there.

The cheers go on until Jefferson raises his hand, and they stop all at once. The barking continues, and now Lisa sees the source: there are a dozen cages lining the wall beside the pool, and each cage contains a raving, angry-looking dog.

All eyes in the room are on Jefferson. He steps to the edge of the pool and rests his hands on the railing. He looks out over the crowd. "My fellow New Americans," he says. When he speaks, his voice is amplified and sharpened by the acoustics of the room; it's like he's speaking through a loudspeaker. "I'm so pleased to see your *passion!*" The crowd cheers, and Jefferson closes his eyes and basks in the sound.

Lisa scans the room: there's the Bull, sneering from near the cages. Brett is there, his head shaven now. He still won't look at her.

And there's Daughter. She stands at the shallow end of the pool, near the end of the row of cages. A Minuteman is behind her, his hands on the girl's shoulders.

"You're making her watch?" Lisa says to Heather.

Heather shrugs. "It will be good for her."

Jefferson silences the crowd. "It is because of our passion that we gather here. Our passion for the Refounding. Each and every one of us must share this passion if we want New America, our dream, to succeed. And I see it in this room tonight." He pauses, lets the words sink in. "There are some, though, who do not share our passion. There are those who seek to undermine our plans. The defectors. The traitors."

Now the room resounds with boos.

"These traitors have no place in our midst," Jefferson says. "And they must be punished accordingly." He points to a door at the shallow end of the pool. "Bring him in."

The door opens and Walter is led inside by two Minutemen. He isn't wearing his glasses, and he looks confused, lost. The crowd jeers at him, throws things: food, empty bottles that crash against the tile. The Minutemen toss him into the shallow end of the pool. He slips in the blood and slides downward.

"Walter," Jefferson says.

Walter looks up at him, blinking, struggling to focus.

"Why'd you go and leave us, Walter? We liked you. We thought you liked us."

He struggles to talk. "I said I was sorry," Walter says.

Lisa looks closely. Walter has no fingernails. There are cuts up and down his arms, long thin slices in his face.

"Sorry just doesn't cut it, now, does it?" Jefferson says. "You've cost us, Walter. You've cost us a hell of a lot. We may never know the full price." Jefferson looks at Lisa, smiling slightly, and then he turns back to Walter. "You have anything to say for yourself?"

It's like Walter is out of breath. His voice is a low quaver. "No. Except. Fuck this. Fuck all of this. And fuck you."

Jefferson nods. He looks across the pool at Byron the Bull. "Give him the black dog," he says.

The Bull nods, and he signals to a Minuteman who stands at a panel at the end of the row of cages. There are a bunch of small levers on the panel, as well as one large lever with a red handle. Lisa realizes that the cages are all connected—one big containment unit—and the Minuteman at the end controls them. He pulls a small lever and the cage door nearest to the Bull swings open. The Bull stands back from it, tense, as if he's about to let a dragon loose. The result is not much different. A huge Dobermann leaps forth and turns on the Bull, who curses and prods at it with a long, heavy stick. It grabs the stick in its teeth and shakes, and the other Minuteman comes up behind and kicks it into the pool. Then he and the Bull position themselves at the shallow end, where there is no railing, and they stand guard with their sticks. The Dobermann leaps to its feet and snarls up at the Bull. It scrambles up the slick tile slope, snapping at him furiously, but the Bull beats the dog back down with the stick. At last, the Dobermann gives up. It turns, and this is when it spots Walter.

Walter is crouched down in the corner of the deep end of the pool. He's got his knees pulled into his chest, his arms over his head. "Keep it away from me!" he yells.

The Dobermann charges him. Walter puts his arms up to block it. He's lucky with his first attempt: he misses the dog's open mouth and grabs ahold of its throat. He holds the dog at arm's length as it lunges, its jaws coming inches from Walter's face. Walter shoves it hard and jumps to his feet. The dog attacks again, and Walter holds out his leg, tries to keep it away from him with his foot. The Dobermann clamps down on Walter's shoe and pulls, and Walter falls. The Dobermann drags him across the pool like he's a chew toy. It's wagging its nubby tail. Laughter knocks against the tile walls.

"Help me!" Walter yells. He's panicked, terrified. He's trying to shake the dog loose, but the thing is huge and doesn't seem to care. Walter kicks at it with his other foot, but the Dobermann barely notices.

"This is pathetic," Jefferson says. "Help him out."

The Bull tosses his stick into the pool, and Walter crawls across the ground—the dog dragging behind him, its feet scratching the floor as it tugs the opposite direction—and grabs it. He brings it around and cracks the Dobermann hard in the side of the head. The dog yelps and lets go of his foot, and Walter stands up.

They circle each other. Walter prods at the Dobermann, keeping the dog a stick-length away. It bites at the stick, but Walter brings the heavy end of it down on the dog's nose, keeping it at bay. In this manner, Walter manages to back the dog into a corner, and he seems to sense that he has the upper hand. He raises the stick high above him and brings it down like a club. He connects with the Dobermann's back near its hind legs, and it yowls and leaps out of the corner.

The dog's back is to Lisa now, and Walter has turned to face it. He's smiling; he's got the dog where he wants it, and now he's enjoying it. He raises the stick again. And the dog leaps at him.

The Dobermann's body slams into the center of Walter's chest, and Walter falls backward, the dog on top of him. For a moment, it's unclear what's going on. There's nothing but a confusing flurry of fur and teeth and fists and blood. Then, Walter flings the dog off of him and begins crawling toward the shallow end. He has one hand on his throat, and the blood is flowing freely, leaving a red trail behind him. He's crying, and his eyes are filled with horror.

The dog rights itself and prances back over to Walter. It sniffs the streak of blood behind him. It licks some of it off the floor. Then it steps delicately onto Walter's back and sinks its teeth into his neck.

Walter collapses. The crowd explodes. The dog lifts its head, chewing placidly, and looks around the room. Then it lowers its jaws to the body again.

Lisa turns away. She looks at Heather, who stands beside her. Lisa says, "This? This is what you want to be a part of?"

Heather's eyes are wet, but her jaw is set, a determined look on her face. "This is just part of it," she says. "A society needs order. And order requires consequences."

"You're completely brainwashed."

The crowd has quieted down, and an uneasy mood has settled in the air. Lisa can hear the crunching of bones down there. Someone climbs into the pool, pulls the dog off of the body.

"Just don't be so stubborn, Lisa," Heather says. She has a weird look about her now. Part of it is that same anger and resentment that she showed the other night in the servants' quarters, that smug look on her face when she raised her shirt. But there's something else too: worry, pity, desperation. "You're going to die here. You're going to die right now. And you don't have to. Don't do this to yourself."

And there's part of Lisa that wants to give in. It would be so easy now, to say a few words to Jefferson, give away the secrets of the raid, live out her life as a librarian in the comfort of New America.

But she can't. She is hardened by emberlight and ice. "Bring the dog," she says.

The pool is clear; the Dobermann's back in its cage, and Walter's body has been taken to wherever it is they take them. A Minuteman leads Lisa into the pool, and then he prods Lisa with the end of a stick, and she walks to the deep end. She looks up, and Jefferson is leaning over the railing, smiling down at her.

"You could have been a part of this," Jefferson says.

"This is your revolution," Lisa says. "Not mine."

"We live in a new world, and it requires a new nation." He slaps his palm on the railing. "It requires new leaders, new citizens. Everyone has to do his part."

"It's not up to you to decide what my part is," Lisa says. Someone spits at her, thick, black tobacco spit that splats on the tile near her feet. Lisa steps away. "The world's different, but it's still ours. We decide how we live our lives."

"I see." Jefferson looks over at the Bull. "The dog, if you please," he says.

"Wait." Heather is beside him. She looks at the cages and whispers in his ear. Jefferson looks over at the row of dogs, smiles, nods. He signals to Byron.

The barking of the dogs is loud in her ears, but still she can hear the metallic sound of the lever being thrown, and from the corner of her eye, she sees a cage door swing open. A growl, more barking, and then a dog is in the pool with her. A syrup-colored boxer, its teeth bared in a ferocious snarl. Its tail held low and bristling.

That tail that Lisa couldn't bear to have docked.

"Jemi," Lisa says, her heart in her throat. "Hey, pup. Hey, girl."

Her dog's eyes are dark and wild. The pupils are dilated crazily; the normal amber color is hidden behind an evil pool of black. What have they done to her?

"Good girl," Lisa says, getting to her feet. "You know me."

Jemi growls and takes a step backward. She is crouched low to the ground, and the hair on her back is standing up. She barks menacingly at Lisa, pounces forward and jumps back. There is no recognition on the dog's face. She is feral, cruel, terrifying. They have stripped her of everything that made her Jemi; the creature that stands before Lisa is some horrible hellhound, a tortured beast red of tooth and claw.

"Come on, pup." Lisa takes a step forward. "Come here—"

And that's too much. With a rasping, high-pitched yap, Jemi jumps at Lisa's throat. Lisa moves instinctively; she lifts her hands and ducks to the side, deflecting the dog with her arms. Jemi lands hard on the tile and her nails click as she scrambles around to face Lisa again. She charges forward, baying viciously. Lisa runs for the shallow end, but the Bull and another Minuteman are waiting for her with their sticks. The Bull presses her back down. Jemi is at her heels, and Lisa kicks the dog hard in the side of the head. Jemi yelps and staggers away; she looks surprised and annoyed.

"It's me, Jemi," Lisa says. She looks back at the Minuteman, who waves his stick at her. Off to his side is Daughter, her eyes clenched shut. Lisa turns back to her dog. She reaches out her hand, advances slowly. "Good girl. Who's a good girl?"

Jemi backs away, growling. She looks confused. She keeps looking up at the crowd around her, then focusing back on Lisa and barking at her.

"Come here, pup. Come here and I'll pet you."

Jemi rushes her again, leaps, and Lisa ducks and rolls forward. The dog flies over her and smacks against the wall of the pool. She stands up, shakes her head, and stumbles, dazed.

"Don't hurt yourself, Jemi. You don't have to." Lisa realizes that the crowd is silent. They ought to be howling and going wild, but they're listening; they're listening to Lisa as she talks to her dog. "Come on, girl. Be a good girl."

And now Jemi is rushing at her again, and Lisa can't jump in time. She gets her hands up and catches the dog by the throat, and they fall together and tumble into the deep end. They land with Jemi on top, and she barks and her breath is hot on Lisa's face. Drool splats on her cheek as the sharp teeth gnash inches from her face. Lisa tries to push her away, but the dog is big and powerful, and Jemi forces herself lower. Lisa's arms give, and Jemi's teeth gash her cheek, and she feels the blood warm on her skin.

Now the crowd's composure breaks, and they explode all at once. Their voices shake the hall, and the movement of the churning bodies fills the corners of Lisa's vision. A man shoves the Bull out of the way as he fights for a better view.

Jemi is startled by the sudden noise, and she stops attacking Lisa and looks up. Lisa takes the chance to hurl the dog off of her, and she scuttles to the corner of the deep end and crouches in a protective position. Jemi remains in the middle of the pool, looking up at the crowd in a mix of surprise and confusion. She gets as close to the ground as she can, her tail between her legs. She whines, looks at Lisa, back up at them. Then she's running from one edge of the pool to the next, yelping up at the crowd, leaping and scrambling up the walls. Minutemen beat her down with sticks, and she growls at them. She clambers to the shallow end, where she jumps up, grabs a stick, and wrenches it from the Minuteman's hand. It clatters hollowly on the tile.

"Good girl," Lisa says, and Jemi looks at her, and for an instant, the dog's eyes focus, and a softness, a kind of recognition, comes over them. Lisa smiles at her. "Who's a good pup?"

Then the lone Minuteman at the shallow end jabs Jemi with his stick, and she turns and lets out a terrible yowl that silences the room. In the stillness of the next instant, Jemi sprints up the ramping shallow end of the pool, dodges the Minuteman's stick, and springs at him. It's like she's flying; she clears the edge of the pool and collides with the Minuteman's chest, and her jaws are at his throat, and he's yelling and gurgling and the crowd begins to scream.

Lisa is a calm fire burning in the midst of the bedlam. She gets up from her corner and strides to the center of the pool. At the shallow end, Jemi has finished with the Minuteman, and she's barking and tearing at the ankles of the other spectators, who are rushing and shoving their way backward. Above the clamor, there is something else: frantic voices from the staircase, from the hallways. A low rumbling sound, a whistling, a distant thud.

A Minuteman on the far side of the pool shoots at Jemi, but the bullet misses, ricochets off the tile, and lodges in a woman's thigh. She screams and collapses, and then the mad instinct of the mob takes over. The loosed hound and the gunfire are more they can handle, and the crowd becomes a mindless mass of bodies, pressing against each other, throwing elbows, trampling the fallen in an effort to escape.

Another thud, closer. A sound like firecrackers.

From behind her, Lisa can hear Jefferson's voice. He's shouting orders. "Weapons!" he yells. "Go! Go!"

Lisa picks up the stick that Jemi tore from the Minuteman. She throws it over her shoulder and walks up to the shallow end.

Jemi is a whirlwind of teeth and muscle; she has pulled another man down, and he's trying feebly but to no avail to push her off of him.

"Good girl," Lisa says, and she climbs out of the pool.

The Minuteman lets go of Daughter, and the girl ducks away. "You stay put," he says to Lisa, but Lisa brings the stick around in a sweeping arc, and it connects with the side of the Minuteman's head with a resounding *crack*. He falls hard on the tile floor.

Lisa looks for Jemi. A couple of Minutemen have got ahold of her, and one of them is trying to hold her mouth shut. The dog is thrashing and giving them everything she's got, but the men are strong, and they pin her down. The initial shock of the loose dog is wearing off. Jefferson is still shouting commands, and the crowd is gradually coming to order. More Minutemen are advancing on Lisa. She raises the stick, turns slowly in a circle.

And spots Daughter. The girl is standing at the end of the cages. The panel with the levers is right beside her. Daughter looks at the levers, then at Lisa.

"Do it, Abigail," Lisa says to her.

Daughter grabs the red-handled lever and pulls. The doors swing open all at once, and a thousand pounds of dog is unleashed on the room. They carry with them the fury of their wolf ancestors; two Labrador retrievers and a Rottweiler and a St. Bernard, a springer spaniel and some sort of bulldog mix, the Dobermann, a basset hound, a carefully-groomed poodle, and a schnauzer surge through the room, bringing people down left and right.

Above the riot of the dogs comes a louder sound: another whistle, a wraith screaming through the night, and a deafening crash. The room shakes. Mortar trickles from the ceiling.

The raid. The Big Bad Wolf.

They're going to blow the house in.

Lisa swings the stick again and drops a Minuteman who stands between her and the rear exit, and immediately the bulldog is upon him. Lisa looks for her own dog, and she catches a glimpse of Jemi, running full out, a brown blur in the hallway in pursuit of the panicked horde. Lisa turns back to the other side of the pool, where she can see Jefferson and Heather escaping up the narrow stairway. Then she steps over the fallen Minuteman and walks out.

She's filled with adrenaline and a kind of euphoria as she leaves the turmoil behind and heads up the stairs. People are everywhere. Some are running in a panic as the dogs pursue them through the house like demons. Others are carrying machine guns, rocket launchers; they head toward the sounds of battle.

No one pays any attention to Lisa.

She reaches the main floor of the house and speeds up; she jogs toward the front door. It's like she's on some sort of drug; endorphins or something are flowing through her and making it feel like she's floating.

Lisa drags the door open and steps into a war.

In front of her is the expansive lawn of the Biltmore estate, stretching out a hundred yards to the woods, and at the edge of it, barely visible in the half-light of the rising moon, is the army of Fort Walmart. They are shadows among the trees. Guns are blazing back in there, and the muzzle flashes light something larger: there's the Big Bad Wolf, illuminated in flickering white and orange, a celebrity behind the flashbulbs, a dancer lit by strobe lights. It looms, a massive darkness blocking the darkness around it. The soldiers fire from behind its heavy metal flanks.

The ground seems to shake as the tank rolls forward.

Minutemen are pouring from the house. They run past Lisa, ignoring her. They take positions behind columns, in corners, sheltered by heavy potted plants. Windows are opening above her. Minutemen are taking positions on the roof of the mansion. They shout to each other. They fire back.

Lisa is transfixed. One of the Minutemen on the roof has a huge gun that fires bullets with tracers. They streak across the sky like lasers. They smash into the *Wolf* with the sound of pots banging together.

The fire of battle lights the night.

The St. Bernard runs past her. It sprints across the melting snow, vanishes into the trees.

The Big Bad Wolf rolls onto the lawn, and the turret turns slowly, the huge barrel of the main gun swinging, panning up. Lisa can hear Berkley's voice, shouting some sort of orders. A silent fireball spews from the cannon, and the sound flies across the lawn; an instant later, it hits Lisa's ears. It's like trains colliding. Buildings imploding. And then that scream as the shell tears through the sky, and another explosion as it hits the corner of the house. Fire and smoke and rubble; a Minuteman's scream as he falls from the roof.

Lisa wants to run to the tank. To her comrades. But there are Minutemen between her and the army, and the lawn in front of them is being ripped apart by gunfire. She looks the other way, toward the gardens. It's clear. She can go that way, circle back around.

And then the night turns bright orange. Lisa turns in time to see the *Wolf* enveloped in smoke and fire. She feels the explosion's shockwave in her teeth.

The tank makes a weird sound, a grating, clanging racket like an engine running with no oil. It begins to back up, and from the rear tread comes another huge explosion. The soldiers of Fort Walmart are running from the tank. Some of them are on the ground, screaming. Some are on the ground, not screaming.

With the second explosion, the Minutemen cheer. There's the sound of a roaring engine, and the Humvee comes around a corner of the house. It throws dirt and grass and snow into the air behind it as it tears through the lawn. Three Minutemen are in it; one stands behind the machine gun, cackling as the gun dances in his hands. The concussion of the gunfire rattles Lisa's bones. The Humvee stops, and two of the Minutemen jump out. One holds a rocket launcher. The other loads it, slaps his friend on the back. The rocket blasts through the air and hits the tank, and the explosion flowers out like a firework. The tank's engine struggles, and then it winds down and stops. The Big Bad Wolf is a lifeless hunk of metal. The Minuteman loads another shell as the machine gun blarcs.

Lisa blinks. It's been thirty seconds. Thirty seconds, and the tank was destroyed; the attack went from perfect to useless. They are screaming out there, her people. Burning. Dying. The Minutemen advance on the remnants of the army.

Help them, she thinks, but another part of her thinks, *Leave them. It's too late.*

Lisa is frozen in indecision.

"Hey!" A voice from behind her, low, angry. It snaps Lisa from her trance. She turns. The Bull stands in the foyer, ready to charge. He's bleeding from a wound on his thigh. "You're not leaving," he says. "You're never getting out of this house."

Lisa begins to run.

GREENHOUSE

NOW LISA CAN THINK. SHE CAN FEEL. SHE FEELS THE cold: not the numbing cold of the ember winters, but the crisp and enlivening cold of spring. It wraps around her and electrifies her as she runs. *Not me*, she thinks. *They are dead, but not me. Not tonight.*

The Bull is behind her, but the need for survival makes her invincible. Lisa's feet seem to glide across the paving stones; she's light as the ether, fast as a cheetah.

She runs away from the battle. She leaves the walkway and rockets between two rows of tall evergreens. The grass is soft under her feet; much of the snow is melted, and that which remains crunches delicately beneath her. She sprints, and there's no end to her speed, to her endurance. She can hear the Bull far behind her, cursing and breathing hard, and beyond him, the rattling voices of the guns and the screams of dying men and women.

Lisa veers from the row of trees and weaves her way through a garden of shrubs. They were once carefully maintained, but now they grow wild and full. Azaleas reach skyward with scraggly, uneven branches. Boxwoods are swollen like blown-up balloons. She hops over a small pond that's still ringed with ice, runs on. She can no longer hear the Bull. Lisa leaps a low wall and finds herself in another garden, this one twice as big as the one before. Once there were rows of meticulously-tended flowers here; she remembers them vaguely from her visit so long ago. Now there is line after line of bare, withered earth. She wonders if the flowers will ever bloom again.

Ahead of her is a series of greenhouses, their glass walls murky with dirt and mold. She makes for them at full speed, reaches the first one as the Bull heaves himself over the distant wall. She ducks inside and looks around. Nothing there but empty pots and planters. She sprints to the other end and leaves. The second greenhouse is glowing with blue-white light; it shines like a firefly in the darkness that surrounds it. Too bright. She runs past the second greenhouse and dips inside the third.

This greenhouse has been completely repurposed. Instead of plants, there sit three rows of pickup trucks that stretch to the other end of the building. There must be sixty in all. She runs halfway down and climbs into the bed of one of them. The bed is half-full of cans of gas. There are also various boxes and bags full of stuff. Lisa buries herself under some of the bags. She realizes that she's breathing loudly; she closes her eyes and takes several deep breaths, brings herself under control.

A few minutes later, she hears the sound of the door opening and closing. There is no other sound, but Lisa can feel that the Bull is in the greenhouse with her. His presence hangs over the room like smog.

She lies still and waits, listening to the distant sounds of battle, now so faint, like a war movie playing in the condo next door. After a while, she hears footsteps. The Bull is at the truck beside her, and he shuffles through the bags, curses, moves on. He's out of earshot for a moment, and then the footsteps again, and he's right above her. Lisa can hear his heavy breathing. From between the bags, she sees the shadowy outline of his body against the dark glass ceiling of the greenhouse. He looks in the bed where she lies. He picks up a bag near her foot, tosses it aside. Lisa wants to scream, to leap and run, but she forces herself to stay still. The Bull shoves a box aside, curses again, and moves on.

Lisa listens as he searches the other trucks, and after what feels like an eternity, she hears the door at the other end of the greenhouse open and close.

She waits another five minutes to be safe, and then she moves the bags off of her and sits up in the bed. She's alone in the greenhouse. She sighs and closes her eyes and collects herself, and then she keeps moving. She opens the boxes around her: food, cooking supplies, bottled water. The bags are full of clothes.

She climbs out of the truck and looks into the bed of the truck next to her. It's outfitted identically: cans of gas, boxes of food, bags of clothes. A third truck is the same; every one of them is stocked with supplies.

Lisa goes back to the end of the greenhouse where she entered. Against the wall is a series of corkboards with papers pinned all over them. Most of it is random lists and memos, but in the center of it all is a map of the United States. Several pushpins are stuck in it at various places across the country. There's one in Asheville, but there's also one in Tallahassee, one in western Texas, one in Sacramento. There's one up north in Buffalo and another in Fargo, one right in the middle in Topeka. Each of them has a red line reaching out from it, a series of roads carefully traced with red marker. The lines all lead to the northwest corner of Wyoming, to Yellowstone National Park.

She looks back at the pickups. They're preparing for their exodus.

There's a desk beneath the corkboards. She opens the drawers and goes through them rapid fire. The third drawer is full of keys. Car keys.

She reaches into the drawer and pulls out a fistful of keys; it feels like she's just opened up a pirate's treasure chest and is wrist-deep in gold bullion. She spills keys on the floor as she holds the wad of them against her chest. Lisa goes to the first truck in the row nearest to her and pulls on the door handle—locked. She sets the keys on the ground and begins trying them. The first one doesn't work; she tosses it aside. Same with the second, the third. She goes through her handful and returns to the drawer for another.

As she's trying to force the next key into the lock, she hears the door at the far end of the greenhouse open. She looks up and, across the rows of trucks, makes eye contact with the Bull. "Bitch," he says, and he runs.

She drops the key and tries another. No luck. "Come on," she says. She tries the next one. No good. "Seriously?" Another key, another failure.

The Bull is almost on her. He's yelling something at her, something about what he's going to do to her. She tries to tune him out.

Another key. It slides into the lock like a hot knife into butter. She turns the key, pulls the door open, and jumps inside, slamming the door and the lock closed behind her. The Bull is there a moment later, pounding on the window, his face contorted with a furious madness. His knuckles bleed, leaving bloody streaks. The glass crackles like ice on a frozen lake.

Lisa puts the key in the ignition, mashes the clutch, and starts the truck.

"You're not leaving," the Bull says. He runs in front of the truck, stands with his palms on the hood. "You'll never get out of here, you bitch."

"Go fuck yourself," Lisa says, and she throws the truck into first gear and slams her foot on the gas. The engine roars and the tires squeal and she's thrown back in her seat under the force of the acceleration. The Bull bends forward where the truck hits him, and he's the first thing that strikes the glass wall of the greenhouse. The wall shatters into a million pieces, and shards of it are everywhere, puncturing the Bull's body and raining down on the windshield. Lisa keeps her foot mashed down, and the Bull's mouth opens and closes and his fingers claw at the hood, and then he slips and disappears below the truck. The wheels spin in the snow and the soft grass as she climbs the hill behind the greenhouse, and Lisa looks in the rearview mirror to where the Bull lies crumpled in the ruin of her wake.

At the top of the hill is a road, and she spins the wheel and rockets up it, away from the greenhouses, away from Biltmore, away from her prison. For a moment, she thinks of the soldiers of Fort Walmart, dying there on the mansion's well-manicured lawn. *It's too late*, she tells herself. They were dead before the battle began.

And she thinks of Jemi, disappearing down that hallway. Did the Minutemen catch her? And Daughter—what will happen to her? Do they know what she's done? Will she be punished?

But she can't go back, and right now, though it makes her feel horrible inside, she's too excited to care. She howls with triumph as the truck flies past the guardhouse that marks the edge of the property. Lisa turns north onto the highway and laughs like a maniac as the horned moon rises in the east.

HEATHER

SHADOW

IT'S LIKE HE'S CUT OUT OF BLACK CONSTRUCTION paper and pasted against the dawn. His shoulders back, his hands on his hips, his head down in frustration as the purple leeches up from the east into the black of night. The horizon is tinged in gold dust, and Jefferson casts a fearsome shadow.

It seems to Heather that he's always a shadow. He's always lit by what's behind him.

Jefferson stands in front of the mansion as Heather watches him from the doorway. Beyond him are the ruins of the battle. The Minutemen are dark shapes moving in the last minutes of night. They tread carefully, avoiding the remaining unexploded mines near the lifeless tank. Occasionally, the quiet of dawn is punctuated by a gunshot—another wounded rebel put out of his misery.

Two men with a stretcher approach from the gardens. They are carrying Byron. Even in the shadowy morning light, Heather can see the extent of his injuries: his leg is bent sideways at the knee, and a shattered bone protrudes from his wrist. His face is torn apart, and shards of glass jut out like diamonds. He's coated head to toe in blood, and he looks dead, except for his eyes. His eyes burn with a ferocious life, a fury that spills out of him and heats up the air.

"Wait," Jefferson says. The men stop, and Jefferson approaches them.

Heather steps out onto the front drive. She wants to hear. She wants to be part of this.

"I take it, then, that you didn't catch her?" Jefferson says.

Byron tries to talk, and it sounds like he's gargling mouthwash. He turns his head and spits, and the blood splats on the brick near Jefferson's boots. "Bitch will get hers," Byron says.

Jefferson sighs. "But not today, apparently."

This fills Heather with a weird sense of pride, of admiration. Everything about Lisa makes Heather feel mixed up inside. She wants to hate her, but deep down, Heather wants to see her free. That's why she rigged the dogfight: she told Jefferson to pick Jemi because, after all Lisa had been through, she deserved a chance. And Heather loved seeing Lisa talk that dog down, bring its madness into check. She knows it could have been Lisa on the stretcher, but now she's elated to see Byron crushed and shredded by the librarian.

Heather took the easy road. Lisa has chosen the hard way every single time, and she's still alive, still free. Heather can't help but root for her.

"Take him..." Jefferson pauses, and then he waves dismissively, "take him somewhere else." The men carry Byron away, and Jefferson turns to another Minuteman who's lingering nearby. "Did we get the dogs at least?"

"A couple of them. One of the Labs, and the poodle, I think."

"And the rest?"

"I don't know. They ran off."

His eyes narrow, and he turns away. The horizon is glowing now, the earth spinning, spinning, ever onward, and in moments now, the land will roll eastward until the ember appears, the first light of a new day, the bulging orange arc shimmering against the edge of the world. The snow on the lawn seems to glow. The buds on the trees glisten, the melting snow becomes pearls of light.

The aftermath of the fight can be seen plainly now. There are dead Minutemen near the house. Twenty at least, maybe more. The dead at the other side of the lawn are too numerous to count. Smoke drifts lazily from the ruin of the tank.

Jefferson shakes his head. "This was a disaster."

Heather approaches him from behind. She puts her hands on his hips, and then she runs her palms across his flat stomach, up to his chest, and she crosses her hands on top of one another and presses her body against his. He smells of gunpowder and sweat. "It wasn't," Heather says. "We wiped them out. Look at them. It was a massacre."

"But look at ours." He points to a dead Minuteman who lies fifty feet away. He's on his stomach, a neat hole in the back of his bald head. "We lost too many," Jefferson says. "We had a plan. That plan called for soldiers. A place for everyone in the Refounding. In New America."

"We can recruit more."

"There's no time." He steps away from her and out into the lawn. The snow is stained red with blood, and it crunches beneath his boots. "We're supposed to leave in a month."

She knew they were leaving at some point. He's never told her where. Heather holds her breath.

"I suppose there's no need for secrets at this point," he says. He turns to her, his eyes narrow. He looks at her belly. "Is there?"

Heather tenses. She touches her stomach. *Does he know?* "No need for secrets," she says.

Jefferson stares at her for a moment, and then he nods. "We're going to Yellowstone. That's the new capital. That's the heart of New America." He points westward, as if Yellowstone is just beyond the trees at the end of the lawn. "Washington was supposed to get there first, a few weeks from now, and set up camp. Then Franklin. Then us. But now, who knows. Washington and Franklin fighting. It's a clusterfuck."

Heather steps into the snow. She's wearing tennis shoes, and she can feel the cold on her toes. "They're a thousand miles away," she says. "Why are you waiting for them?"

He cocks his head. "What do you mean?"

She takes Jefferson by the elbows and pulls him close to her. "Look around you," she says.

The ember appears on the horizon, and it grows, a burning orange ball, still so bright even in its death throes. It spreads and stretches, growing, pregnant with possibility. The Minutemen stop in their duties and turn to the east. They watch the ember rise.

One has climbed onto the tank. He shimmies out on the gun and plants the flag of New America in the barrel. It flutters on the morning breeze, the muskets and tri-corner hat bathed in light.

The Minuteman stands up on the turret. "The Refounding!" he yells, and his voice echoes against the cold stone of the Biltmore House.

The others on the lawn cheer. They turn to Jefferson, raise their hands in silent salute.

Heather waits as Jefferson nods to his soldiers, and then she takes his chin in her hand, turns his face to hers. "*You're* their leader," she says. "You don't need Washington. You don't need Franklin. It can all be yours." She kisses him, and he grabs her, lifts her off her feet.

Jefferson sets her down, a grin on his face. "What do you propose, then?"

"We leave now," Heather says. "We take Yellowstone. We build New America the way we want it. If the other Fathers want to come, they come on our terms." She can feel an energy inside of her, a power. This man is hers. Maybe Lisa was right, and what she had with Guy was something ephemeral, something false. But Guy is dead. Jefferson is alive, and he has an army at his command. The future of the country rests on his shoulders, but Heather holds him in the palm of her hand. She kisses him again. "You'll be the king," she says.

The light chases the shadows away from Jefferson's face, and he's afire with the promise of the future. "And you," he says, his hand on Heather's belly. "You'll be my queen."

LISA

LIGHT

THEY STAND JUST INSIDE THE DOORS OF FORT WALMART and look out on the dawn. The trees cast spindly shadows across the parking lot, spider's legs stretching across the half-melted snow.

Dagmar raises his gun. "There," he says, pointing to the bridge over the creek.

A figure, moving quickly. Running. Its shadow runs beside it.

"Ready," Malorie says.

Lisa had made it back to Fort Walmart as the first light of dawn stretched into the sky. Dagmar met her outside, hugged her, brought her in. The place was nearly empty. Other than Dagmar and Malorie, there was no one left except for a few of the smallest children and their mothers. Everyone who could carry a gun took part in the raid. It was the only way it would work, Carter had said. Battle stations. All hands on deck.

They'd left Malorie behind to lead in case things didn't go as planned. And Malorie insisted that Dagmar stay: his brain was too valuable to end up with a bullet in it.

They'd waited by the doors all night. Occasionally, the distant sound of explosions drifted across the frozen city. Other than that, there was nothing but silence from the raid. Lisa was the first person they'd seen.

"You saw the raid?" Malorie said.

Lisa still felt breathless from her flight. "Yes."

"And?"

She shook her head.

Now they watch the figure coming across the parking lot. Lisa doesn't know if it's the last survivor of the raid or the first soldier in a Minuteman counterattack. She holds a twelve-gauge shotgun against her shoulder. It's like the one that Guy had, the one he kept in the back of the closet, the one he used to kill the Minutemen who invaded their house. She pumps the gun and trains it on the approaching person.

The ember comes out from behind the trees, and now they can see him. Virgil.

Dagmar opens the door and Virgil sprints inside. He puts his hands on his knees and catches his breath. Malorie touches his shoulder, but he shrugs her off. He stands up and tosses his rifle away from him, and it clatters and slides along the tile. Then he sees Lisa. He blinks at her in disbelief, and then he steps forward, hugs her tight. "I thought you were dead," he says.

"Me too," Lisa say.

He looks up at her. Those dark eyes, so much like his brother's. "Dante," he says.

"No."

Virgil nods. He lets go of her and sits down on the tile.

"Virgil," Malorie says.

He looks up at her. His eyes are wet, but his face is strong. He seems a decade older than he was the last time Lisa saw him.

"Is there anyone else?" Malorie says.

"I don't think so," Virgil says. He looks at the backs of his hands. "I barely got out. They blew up the tank. And there were so many of them. It—it didn't go right."

Malorie looks at Dagmar, and he nods. "Are you sure, Virgil? We can't wait much longer, but we don't want to leave anyone behind."

Virgil stands and retrieves his gun. "We're all that's left."

"They'll come for us," Lisa says. She knows it's true. They won't let this go. They will come, and they'll come soon, and they'll burn Fort Walmart to the ground, along with anyone who's inside. "We should go."

"Where?" Malorie says.

Dagmar looks out toward the gray mountains. "North," he says.

They drive. Lisa drives the truck she took from the Minutemen. Dagmar sits beside her, and Virgil and Malorie sit in the back. The rest of the survivors follow in Abe's other pickup.

The highway heads back in the direction of the Biltmore House before turning northward. They keep their guns close, but there is no sign of life.

Above them, the ember continues its silent journey through the heavens. Beyond it, against the dim blue of day, are a few pinpricks of light. Lisa can barely make them out; they're like the afterimages that dance on the backs of her eyelids after a camera's flash.

Dagmar sees her looking up. "They're stars," he says.

And now Lisa can tell. There they are: the brightest stars of the night sky, dimmer now, but still plainly visible in the light of day. She wonders about those stars. So far away, but burning so bright. Points of white fire in the sky that her own dying star cannot extinguish. What planets are making their slow revolutions about those distant suns? What people are looking back on her from light years away, wondering about the ember, that fleck of yellow in their sky that gets dimmer night by night?

But then she remembers. They can't see it yet. They won't see it for a thousand years, and by then, what will be left?

Something, she tells herself. The Minutemen are going to Yellowstone. She and her small band of survivors are heading north. Dagmar still thinks that there are people alive up there. He believes in Iceland: there is a civilization there; a city encased in glass. They'll find survivors. They'll find a boat, cross the ocean. They'll find a home.

The road in front of them is nearly clear of snow. The trees move in the breeze.

They crest a hill, and far ahead, in the center of the road, is a shape. Small, low to the ground. "Slow," Malorie says.

Lisa slows. The shape is moving. Something alive, walking—limping, slowly, painfully northward.

There are drops of blood in the center of the road. A thin trail flanked by paw prints.

Virgil is leaning between the seats. "It's a dog," he says.

It is a dog, and it takes shape as they approach it.

"It's hurt," Virgil says.

A syrup-colored dog. A boxer.

"It won't survive," Dagmar says. "Not injured. Not out here." He adjusts the gun in his lap. "We should put it down."

Lisa stops the car and gets out. The ember shines on the back of her neck. Somehow, even after its quicksilver journey through the vacuum of space, the light finds a way to warm her. Behind her is Asheville and Biltmore, Heather and the Minutemen, Atlanta and South Carolina and Dante and Guy. Ahead of her is the north, the future.

And the dog.

It turns to her, wags its tail, a tail that by all rights a boxer shouldn't have. "Not this dog," Lisa says. "She's going to survive."

*   *   *

HUB CITY PRESS

HUB CITY PRESS is a non-profit independent press in Spartanburg, SC that publishes well-crafted, high-quality works by new and established authors, with an emphasis on the Southern experience. We are committed to high-caliber novels, short stories, poetry, plays, memoir, and works emphasizing regional culture and history. We are particularly interested in books with a strong sense of place.

Hub City Press is an imprint of the non-profit Hub City Writers Project, founded in 1995 to foster a sense of community through the literary arts. Our metaphor of organization purposely looks backward to the nineteenth century when Spartanburg was known as the "hub city," a place where railroads converged and departed.

RECENT HUB CITY PRESS TITLES

Strangers to Temptation • Scott Gould

Over the Plain Houses • Julia Franks

Minnow • James E. McTeer II

Pasture Art • Marlin Barton

The Whiskey Baron • Jon Sealy

In the Garden of Stone • Susan Tekulve

The Iguana Tree • Michel Stone